Karyn's Memory Box

STEPHANIE GRACE WHITSON

THOMAS NELSON PUBLISHERS
Nashville

To Bob,
my leader, my example,
my beloved, my friend.

In loving memory of B. Celest Higgins (1947–1996).
Her faithful friendship, loving care, caring love,
encouraging words, sweet wisdom,
pure heart, perfect visits,
understanding spirit,
knowing thoughts made
her all it means to have a friend
of like mind, and her departure left a void
in my life that will remain until we meet again.

Copyright © 1999 by Stephanie Grace Whitson

All rights reserved. Written permission must be secured from the publisher to use or reproduce any part of this book, except for brief quotations in critical reviews or articles.

Published in Nashville, Tennessee, by Thomas Nelson, Inc., Publishers.

Scripture quotations are from the Holy Bible, KING JAMES VERSION.

2 in 1 ISBN: 0-7394-0698-1

Printed in the United States of America

Prologue

1997

I hope this is worth it," Reagan muttered to herself as she sipped the last of her lukewarm coffee. She had been on the road since before dawn that morning, determined to be one of the first antique dealers to arrive at what had been billed as one of the largest estate auctions held in Custer County in years.

Pulling off the interstate, Reagan headed northwest on Route 2, but not before stopping to fill both of the pickup's gas tanks. Leaning against the truck while the gas pump clicked off gallon after gallon of gas, Reagan reached into the cab and pulled the auction announcement from where she had tucked it between the sun visor and the roof of the cab. As she read through the long list of items to be sold, she thought, *Daddy and Mother would surely have loved this one.*

Reagan smiled to herself, remembering the moment she became "hooked" on auctions. She had been only fourteen, and she and her father had driven the light blue Volkswagen "Beetle" to an auction. When a beautiful antique love seat and matching chair came up for sale, Daddy raised his hand. "Just starting the bid for George, Reagan," he whispered when Reagan looked at him in surprise. But "just starting the bid" for their auctioneer friend George backfired that day. No one else bid on the furniture.

Daddy had looked down at Reagan with his easy grin. "Well, now. Your mother's been wanting some new furniture. Guess the Lord just gave her some." They strapped the furniture to the roof of the little car, and drove home not sure which was more fun—the looks from other motorists or the look on Mother's face when they drove up the driveway at home.

Well, it was a good buy, anyway, Reagan reasoned. She still had the love seat and the chair, and no amount of money in the world would make her part with them. Recovered and refinished more times than Reagan could count, those two pieces of furniture and the story of their acquisition were now a permanent part of the Bishop family legacy.

The chair and love seat had been only the beginning. Nearly every Saturday after that, when the weather was good—and some Saturdays when the weather was abominable—the little blue Volkswagen took Reagan and her dad to some estate sale or country auction, "just to look things over." Reagan developed an interest in Depression glass. She began collecting a pink pattern called "Mayfair." Her mother soon followed suit, although she preferred the green "Rose of Sharon" pattern. With Mother along, the adventure was even more sweet. The two women chided Daddy for buying rusted tools and broken chairs, and he complained about hauling boxes of glassware to the car. Soon, they had to stop driving the Volkswagen in favor of "the big car."

By the time her mother and dad passed away, Reagan had begun to dabble in buying and selling antiques. She rented small booths in two antique malls. Neither booth made much money, but being a dealer justified Reagan's attendance at auctions.

She discovered that she had an uncanny knack for buying things just before they "caught on." Once everyone else wanted something and the bidding at auctions became frenzied, Reagan's strict budget usually made her stop buying. However, even when other dealers began to show interest, Reagan's passionate fascination with antique textiles never waned. She had been known to stand in the hot sun for hours, just to procure one small set of quilt blocks stashed in the bottom of a box of towels. She had paid five dollars for a pile of oil-stained rags out of a rickety garage just to retrieve a used-up gold-and-green quilt that had been thrown out with the rags.

Once a casual boyfriend had asked, "What are you going to do with that?" when she excitedly showed him a hand-pieced quilt top.

"Well," Reagan said laughingly, "I'm going to *have* it."

"But what exactly is it *for*?" the young man wanted to know. "I mean, it isn't even finished."

Reagan had looked at him with pity. Their relationship didn't last long.

Over the years, she had driven thousands of miles to auctions that advertised patch quilts or quilt tops. More often than not, the patch quilts were tied comforters, and the quilt tops were stained beyond repair. Still, something drew Reagan to the old fabrics. She didn't bother to philosophize about why she felt such a link to other women in other times. She simply enjoyed the wondering as she held their handwork and asked herself why it had never been finished, or what the woman was like who made it.

And so, as the sun peeked over the horizon in the rearview mirror of Reagan Bishop's pickup, she fingered the auction announcement that promised a "large amount of quilts, linens, etc." and thanked God aloud for the clear blue sky and the cool spring air. Added to the verbalized prayer was an unspoken hope that Helen Stapleman would not drive this far just to check out a few quilts.

Reagan was only a few miles northwest of Grand Island when she began to wonder if she had taken a wrong turn. She had seen only two other pickups—and they had been headed in the opposite direction. Just when she was thinking she might need to turn around and retrace her route, she saw the small sign at the side of the road. "Auction" it proclaimed, with an arrow pointing to the northeast and a gravel road that was barely more than two tracks through a pasture.

Reagan followed the road for over half a mile until, at the top of the next ridge, she could see a weathered white frame house surrounded by ancient cottonwood trees. A few vehicles were already parked in the pasture. Reagan swung in next to them. Stuffing her long red hair up into her "auction hat" and grabbing her driver's license, she hurried across the pasture to a small trailer with a sign that read "Bidding Numbers Here."

A few minutes later she pinned her bidding number to her hat and set off on the quest for treasure. Looking up toward the house, she saw that this would, indeed, be a huge sale. Row upon row of folding tables in the front yard groaned beneath piles of glassware, cookware, and tools.

It was going to be a wonderfully long day. It would likely be long after midnight before she made it home. She recognized another dealer, nodded hello, and feigned interest in a blue granite roaster on the table before her. As soon as the dealer turned his back, she made her way around the side of the house, wondering if the "large amount" of quilts and linens that had been promised in the auction ad would turn out to be a half dozen rotten comforters pulled out of the barn loft.

Well. I guess not. Hanging on the clotheslines on the east side of the house were some of the most glorious quilts Reagan had ever seen. Her hand almost trembled as she reached out to touch a blue-and-white Ocean Waves quilt. She walked between the clotheslines, inspecting quilt after quilt, bemoaning her limited budget and praying that Helen Stapleman had either not seen the ad or, if she had, was too busy or too sick to come. *Not really sick, Lord,* Reagan thought guiltily. *Maybe just a mild headache.*

Of course God in His wisdom often responds to prayers with a resounding NO. And thus did He answer Reagan Bishop. Helen Stapleman, the woman with the silver hair and the bottomless wallet, the woman who held her bidding number high and never, ever gave up on something she really wanted, was just now striding confidently across the lawn toward the quilts.

All right, Helen, Reagan thought even as she nodded hello and flashed a friendly smile, *but you can't have them all. I'm going to have that Ocean Waves; I don't care what you bid on it. It's mine. It's going home in my truck to live at my house.*

But hours later, when the auctioneer walked along the

clothesline, selling quilt after quilt, the Ocean Waves went to Helen Stapleman. Reagan fought back tears of frustration when the quilt was taken off the line, folded, and passed across the crowd and into Helen's waiting arms. How could she have known that Helen would give nearly a thousand dollars for it? In spite of her disappointment, Reagan also felt a glimmer of relief. She had bid over eight hundred dollars that she really could not afford. Reluctantly, Reagan had to admit that it was a good thing that God had saved her from her own stupidity.

As the last quilt sold, Reagan turned away. *I ought to go.* But she had stood for an entire day and dropped out of bid after bid in order to save her money for that quilt. Now she faced the antique dealer's ultimate defeat: a drive home in an empty truck. She followed the auctioneer down a slope to where a kind of shed jutted directly out of a ridge that ran along the back of the house. A few crocks and half-rotten barrels and about a dozen orange crates had been dragged out in the sun. For some reason, one of the crocks drew Reagan's attention. It had been a watercooler, but both the spigot and the lid were missing. Someone had used it to hold empty burlap bags. When no one bid on it, Reagan raised her number and paid fifty cents for the crock and fifteen orange crates.

"But I don't want the orange crates," she protested.

"Sorry," the auctioneer insisted. "That's the lot that sold. You want me to resell it?"

Reagan shook her head. "No. It's all right. I've got room in the back of the pickup. Maybe I can find a use for them."

Someone stepped forward who had missed the sale of the orange crates. "If you don't want the crates, I'll give you a buck for them."

Reagan nodded. "Great. Take them all." She pocketed the dollar, congratulating herself on having earned a free cup of coffee on the deal.

The auction ended. By the time Reagan had paid her bill and retrieved the crock, the auctioneer's own truck was the only vehicle still parked in the pasture. As Reagan lifted the crock into the bed of her pickup, he teased, "You sure must have wanted that crock bad. You got a stash of old spigots and lids at home? It's probably worth nearly two hundred dollars complete."

Reagan grinned, talking as she lifted the tailgate and walked around to the driver's side of the cab. "Actually, I wanted the burlap bags. Couldn't care less about the crock. I heard yesterday that they're making curtains out of burlap bags on the coast. It's as big a craze as the fifties' look was last year. Why, they're willing to pay five dollars a piece for seed bags if they've still got farm dirt on 'em to prove their authenticity." She opened the door, got in, and rolled down the window, laughing as she concluded, "And if you believe that . . ." She began to sing a familiar country-western song, "I've got some oceanfront property in Arizona . . ."

They both laughed again. Reagan waved, started the truck, and headed across the pasture, down the gravel road and out onto the paved highway, completely unaware that, had Irene Peale's grandmother been present at that sale, she would have paid more than the entire farm was worth to have retrieved what lay in the bottom of the broken crock in the back of Reagan Bishop's pickup.

Reagan left the broken crock in the back of her truck for several days before even bothering to unload it. When she did, she just set it by the back door of her bungalow and ignored it. Then, one day when she was planting geraniums along the front walk, she thought of a use for the old crock. *I always buy too many flowers for that little bed out front,* she scolded herself. Walking around the back of the house, she pulled the burlap bags out of the crock, intending to shovel in some dirt and use it for a planter. But the crock held more than just bags.

With a little "Oh" of surprise, Reagan lifted a box out of the crock. In the light, the box elicited an admiring "Ohhhhhh." It was covered with dark fabric, which at one time had been sculpted green velvet. Even with the velvet pile nearly worn off, the box was beautiful. There was an oval beveled mirror set in the lid. The corners were protected by ornate brass protectors, and an exquisite hinge held closed what proved to be a photo album. Carefully lifting the lid, Reagan was delighted to hear the tinkling of a music box. A tiny latch was attached to the hinge, so that whenever the photo album was opened, music played. Reagan sat and listened, trying to identify the tune. When she could not, she carefully pushed in the latch to silence the music and began to study the top two photos. From the left smiled a young, dark-eyed woman with a beautiful lace kerchief knotted about her throat. Her dark hair was almost entirely hidden by a crushed velvet hat. On the right was a full-length portrait of a very handsome, dark-haired man. He was standing beside a chair, and as Reagan peered at the photo she realized he must have been very, very tall. He had the largest hands she had ever seen, and startlingly pale eyes. *Hello, gorgeous.*

There were other photos as well: a golden-haired woman, with curled hair, sparkling eyes, and a mischievous smile, and an older couple, obviously husband and wife. There were two young men with drooping mustaches seated at a table with a bottle of beer or wine between them. Reagan chuckled, thinking they must have caused some trouble in their day.

The last photo in the album was of a farmstead. Looking closely, Reagan recognized the farm where the auction had been held. Written in pencil across the bottom of the photo was "Mikal Ritter, 1914." Reagan recognized the gigantic windmill in the center of the farmyard and the huge barn with two cupolas that had housed the refreshment stand on the day of the auction. But the photo showed at least half a dozen other outbuildings of varying sizes that must have been torn down since the photo was taken.

The box was more than a photo album. A second compartment beneath the section of photos held an odd assortment of items: a pressed flower, a Belgian lace handkerchief with the monogram "C," knitting needles, a lock of someone's hair, and what Reagan guessed was a rattlesnake's tail.

Reagan took the items out one by one and spread them on her picnic table. Intending to wipe the years of grime away from the bottom of the box, she found the greatest treasure of all. The box had a false bottom, and in the hidden compartment was a leather-bound book. Reagan opened it with trembling hands, revealing line upon line of beautiful handwriting . . . in German.

Her heart pounding, Reagan laid the book aside. Once again opening the photo album, she peered at the photos, wondering, *Who are you?* Turning to look over the things spread across the top of her picnic table, she wondered who had kept such an odd array of things . . . and how they had come to be in the bottom of a broken crock in an old shed.

Reagan went inside and rummaged through the pile of papers on her desk until she found the auction bill. She dialed the auctioneer's phone number. "Tom, this is Reagan Bishop. You remember that old crock I bought at the end of the Ritter sale? Yes, that's the one. The huge sale out in Custer County. Well, I've found something the family might want to know about. There was something in the bottom of the crock. It's really unusual—a photo album with a music box, and then a compartment below it. And there's what appears to be a diary. I've never seen a combination of a photo album and a music box like this before. It's probably fairly valuable, but I'm more concerned about what's inside it. The family really should have it back if they want it . . . Yes, well, just let them know." Reagan provided her phone number and went back outside to gather up the treasures and return them to the box.

Nearly ten days after her phone call to the auctioneer, Reagan answered her doorbell and ushered a tiny, white-haired woman named Irene Peale into her living room. The box was sitting on the cobbler's bench Reagan used as a coffee table. At the sight of it, the little woman clasped her hands before her. "I can't believe it! After all this time. I can't believe it." The woman reached for the box with trembling hands. At Reagan's invitation she sat down.

Ever so carefully, she opened the top section. "Oh, it still works!" she exclaimed softly as the music began to play. Then, with tears in her eyes, she studied the first two photos. Finally, she looked up at Reagan. "I cannot begin to tell you how very grateful I am that you called about this."

Smiling softly she tapped her index finger next to the photograph of the man. "This is the only known photograph ever taken of my grandfather, Mikal Ritter. We have others of my grandmother," Irene explained, "but there was only the one of Opa Mikal." Irene looked up at Reagan. "Do you speak any German, dear?" When Reagan shook her head, Irene explained, "*Oma* is the endearing term for Grandmother. And *Opa* means—"

"Grandpa?" Reagan offered.

Irene nodded. "Oma Karyn* told me about when she insisted Opa have that picture taken. He was quite put out with her, but he did it." Irene's eyes clouded with tears. "We always intended to have copies made, but Oma wouldn't part with it for even a day. We thought we could do it after she was gone . . . but then the box was lost." She looked up at Reagan. "Thank you so much for getting in touch with me."

"I wouldn't have dreamed of keeping it until I was certain no one was interested." Reagan hesitated before asking, "Would you like a cup of coffee?"

"Oh, you don't need to do that," Irene said, starting to get up. "I've already been enough of a bother to you. I should be going."

Reagan shook her head. "Really, it's no bother. If you have time, I'd love to hear about the box—and your grandparents. Do you have any idea why such a beautiful thing would have been in an old crock?"

Irene thought for a moment before asking, "Where did you say the crock was at the auction?"

"Just outside a caved-in shack of some sort. I suppose the auctioneer dragged it out along with the orange crates and barrels."

"The dugout!" Irene exclaimed. She smiled. "Things are falling into place at last." She looked about the room. "You seem to like antiques."

Reagan chuckled. "I can't afford real antiques. But I sure do love 'old stuff.' " She explained, "Neither of my parents knew very much about their family history. They grew up very poor in

* A note to the reader: Karyn is pronounced Kah'-rin, not the American Karen.

a rural setting and were kicked out to fend for themselves early in life. We didn't have any family heirlooms, so I've begun collecting my own." She nodded toward the end table by Irene's chair. An array of sepia-toned photographs seemed to deny her lack of family history. "My friends think I'm crazy, but I frame some of my favorite auction finds."

She reached for one of two barefoot, very cross-eyed children. "Doesn't your heart just go out to these poor kids? Imagine how they must have been teased." She shrugged, slightly embarrassed. "My friends joke about my 'ancestors for hire,' but I don't care."

Suddenly Irene changed her mind about staying to visit. "I believe I would like some coffee, if it's not too much trouble."

Irene followed Reagan through the dining room and to the kitchen door. While Reagan made coffee, Irene stood in the doorway. Reagan told the story of the acquisition of the love seat and chair. She told the story of the day her father had bought her a sterling silver thimble with an elegant border of birds. "It was in a half-rotten sewing basket. He bought it for only a dollar. The sewing basket is in a corner by the front window. That's it with the gangly philodendron growing out of it."

Reagan handed Irene a cup of coffee. As they walked through the dining area and back toward the living room, Reagan pointed out the window to a backyard flower bed. "Recycling broken things is fun. Just look at what a beautiful planter that old watercooler from your grandparents' homestead made."

Irene looked outside. The cooler was filled with blooming geraniums and asparagus fern. "Well, you picked the perfect flower. Geraniums were Oma's favorite." The two women settled in the living room as Irene continued, "She said she was welcomed to America with a small geranium. The pressed flower in the box is from a geranium, although it's hardly recognizable after all these years. Oma used to talk about how they bloomed on the ledge of her sod house window all winter long."

"She lived in a sod house?" Reagan said, amazed.

Irene smiled. "Yes. She and Opa lived in a sod house for

nearly twenty years before building the house you saw at the auction."

"There was a sod house on that land?"

Irene laughed. "Not at first. Actually, Opa lived in the dugout you thought was just a caved-in shed before there was a real house. It's bigger on the inside than you might think. Over the years he dug far back under the ridge to enlarge it. But he had built the sod house before marrying my grandmother. When the time came to build the farmhouse, Oma insisted it be exactly on the same site as the soddy, so they both moved back into the dugout while Opa razed the soddy and built the frame house."

"I didn't realize history was so—so near," Reagan murmured.

"My own mother was born the year before the new house was built. In the soddy," Irene said. She set her coffee cup down on the cobbler's bench and took up the treasure box. Sitting down, she opened the lower compartment and inspected the contents. "After Opa Mikal died, Oma used to sit in her rocking chair in her room with this box on her lap. She would lay her hand on the lid and gaze out the window with the most contented smile on her face."

Irene reached into the box and withdrew a small wooden cylinder, pulled it apart, and smiled as she withdrew a rusty needle. "These things each had some special significance for Oma Karyn. When I was a child and I visited her, she used to let me select one thing from the box, and she would tell me a story about it." Irene put the lid back on the needle case and returned it to the memory box. She sipped her coffee absentmindedly.

The two women sat quietly for a moment. Reagan finally broke the comfortable silence between them, murmuring, "What a wonderful legacy."

Irene nodded. "Yes, Oma was a dear, dear woman. She was quite a character for her day. Independent, strong-willed. Even so, I don't remember ever hearing her say an unkind word either about or to another person. I don't think I ever saw her really, really angry. Except once."

Irene chuckled. "One day after Opa died, my parents tried to persuade her to come and live with us. I was supposed to be playing in the orchard, but I sneaked up under the kitchen window and peeked in. There Oma stood, her dark eyes flashing with anger. She had her hands on her hips and her feet planted."

Irene explained, "Oma spoke fluent English, and she always prided herself on the fact that she had almost no discernible accent. But that day her German resurfaced. She shook her finger at Mother and Father and came the closest I ever heard to shouting when she said, 'Never I live so long that I am told by my own *kinder* what I can and cannot do. If I die all alone on this place, what is so bad? Hundreds of times I could have died alone on this place when your father was away. Is not bad, to die at home. Don't you worry. God knows when I will die, and God knows how I will die. As long as God knows where to find Karyn Ritter when she is dead, you don't worry.' "

Irene sighed. "As it happened, Oma had a stroke not long after that confrontation. She managed to get to the telephone and call for help, but before anyone got to her, she had slipped into unconsciousness. She never woke up." Irene reached out to touch the box. "This was the first thing we all thought of when we had to plan her funeral. We wanted to make a little display of what was important to Oma. But we couldn't find it. Mother and Dad thought perhaps she had lost it on one of her long walks. I was hoping it would turn up when we sorted things for the auction, but my brother supervised everything." She sighed. "He isn't as attached to the place as I am. When I tried to sort through things he became angry. In the end we just tossed items into boxes."

Irene sat back. "Oma must have gone down to the dugout to reminisce just before her stroke. When she wasn't feeling well, I'll bet she secreted the box in the crock where it would be safe. Maybe she was a little confused . . . maybe she thought she was back living in the dugout those weeks when Opa was building the new house. Then, she headed for the big house . . . and the treasure box was lost."

"It's an interesting collection of items," Reagan offered, not wanting Irene's visit to end. "Do you know the names of the other people in the pictures?"

Irene nodded. She opened the lid. "The couple are the

Delhommes.* They were older homesteaders who befriended my grandparents as soon as they arrived in Custer County. And the two young men are their sons. Evidently they were real characters." Irene went on to point out Sophie, Karyn's younger sister, and a young girl named Tilda Stoddard, who had taught Karyn to speak English. "The sour-faced old woman is Amalia Kruger. Oma had a lot to say about Amalia. She's the woman whose biscuit recipe is in the box, although Oma always suspected that Amalia left out one ingredient when she copied it. Oma said she never managed to make biscuits quite as good as Amalia's."

Reagan listened, fascinated. When it appeared that Irene was thinking of leaving, she asked, "Is that really a rattlesnake's tail in the box?"

Irene hesitated. Then, with a wry smile, she asked, "Young lady, are you asking me to tell you a story?"

Reagan blushed, gave a short laugh and admitted, "Yes, I suppose I am."

Irene picked up the diary and opened it. "I always wondered how much of the stories Oma told me were true. She never wanted to give that away. At least not while she was living."

"Well, now perhaps you can discover the answer to that mystery," Reagan said. "Do you read German?"

Irene shook her head. "No, I'm afraid not. I was around Oma enough to learn a few everyday words, but that's all. Oma was well-educated. This is probably beautifully written. Do you know anyone who might translate it?"

Reagan nodded. "Yes. I think so. When you didn't call right away, I hoped it meant I'd get to keep the box. I made a few calls to the university. There's a professor there who seemed very interested. He said he has two graduate assistants who need a new project." Reagan stood up. "I've got the information on my desk. I'll get it for you."

When Reagan came back into the living room, Irene was standing by the front window looking out at the blooming geraniums. She held one of Reagan's "purchased ancestors" photos

---

* Pronounced De-lum with the accent on the second syllable.

in her hand. She set the photo down. "I should be going," she said, taking the piece of paper that Reagan offered and bending to tuck it in her purse. She picked up the box and turned to go. "It's very refreshing to meet someone young who still cares about the past."

When Irene had climbed into her car and started the engine, she rolled down the window and called out, "I'll be in touch, Miss Bishop."

Reagan watched as Mrs. Peale backed out onto the street and drove away.

A few days after their first encounter, Reagan returned home to a message on her answering machine from Irene Peale. Irene wanted to go to lunch. It was only their second meeting, but in an odd way, Reagan felt that they had known one another for years. She found herself telling Irene about her own family, her varied employment experience, her love of history. As they rose to go, Reagan said, "I hope you'll call again soon. This was really fun."

Irene grinned. "Do you like Cary Grant?"

"I've seen *Charade* twenty-seven times," Reagan said. "And I still laugh at the shower scene."

"Then, how about joining me for your twenty-eighth viewing Friday evening?" Irene asked. "Unless, of course, you have a date."

Reagan shook her head. "No dates. No prospects. *Charade* sounds wonderful. I'll bring the popcorn."

"Twenty-one thirty-five B Street," Irene said. "Seven-thirty."

"You live in the *Dressbach Mansion*?" Reagan exclaimed.

Irene laughed. "Tell me how it is that you recognize the street number of my musty old relic of a house."

"My first apartment was over the carriage house just across the street. I used to lie in bed and absolutely lust after that house!"

"Well, now you'll get to see the inside. You probably won't be quite so enamored when you see the old albatross close up."

"I'll adore it," Reagan insisted.

Reagan not only adored Irene Peale's "old albatross," she grew to adore Irene Peale. The two women were, indeed, kindred spirits. They agreed to forgive one another's "brash youth" and "doddering old age." They watched old movies, haunted antique malls, and made an incredible mess in the kitchen one rainy afternoon trying to make authentic rye bread from one of Oma Ritter's handwritten recipes. Occasionally, Irene shared a story about her grandmother, but rarely did the stories seem connected to anything in the box.

All the while Irene Peale and Reagan Bishop were growing closer, Karyn Ritter's diary was being translated. Finally, nearly a year after her discovery, Reagan received a phone call from Irene about the diary. The translation was complete. Irene was offering to share it with Reagan.

"I think you have a singular gift that will enable you to cherish what it says almost as much as I do," Irene said over the phone. She paused and added, "There have been a few surprises for me. Things I thought that Oma was just making up to entertain me have turned out to be true. It's really quite a story. You won't believe why that rattlesnake's tail is in the box. And I never knew the reason for the piece of rose-colored silk. Now I do. I understand so much more." Irene's voice trembled. "I don't have any children, Reagan, and no one else in my immediate family really cares about the past. If you have the time, I'd like for you to know the story."

But entering into the lives of Karyn and Mikal Ritter was to be much more for Reagan than just a way to enjoy a good story. The finding of Karyn Ritter's diary was to change Reagan Bishop's life.

> *I've not been called to tell the tale*
> *of prophets, priests, or kings,*
> *But oh, the things that I have learned*
> *observing simple things.*

CHAPTER 1

1880
A Pressed Geranium

----

*How shall we sing the LORD's song
in a strange land?*
Psalm 137:4

Dirt. He expected her to look at dirt and call it home. Disgust flickered in Karyn Ensinger Ritter's great, dark eyes as she stood before the miserable hovel he expected her to inhabit.

Home meant crisp white curtains flapping in the summer breeze and bright flowers growing in window boxes. This house of dirt had one very small, very bare window. There were no curtains, no flowers—nothing but huge slabs of earth piled up like bricks, with dead grass sticking out between the layers.

Home meant a door that opened just off a cobblestone street to welcome visitors onto spotless wood floors that were scrubbed daily. In place of a door, this soddy had a tattered quilt. Stepping toward the doorway, Karyn pushed the rag aside. The corners of her mouth turned down. She pressed her lips firmly together and swallowed hard, barely succeeding in smothering her favorite German swearword. *Wer hatte es geglaubt! Not even a floor to sweep. And he expects me to call this home?*

Home meant a nightly climb upstairs to a tiny room to laugh and giggle with her sister Sophie until Mama shouted, "Karyn! Sophie! *Ruhig!*" Stepping farther inside the sod house, Karyn

1

saw that it was only one cavernous room. At the center of the room, a lifeless tree trunk stretched upward from the earth to help support the roof. Karyn looked up. There was no upstairs, not even a loft to escape to. She wondered how much rain would seep through when a storm flung itself at the pathetic shack.

Her vivid imagination created a dripping roof and a sea of mud inside the house, mud dripping onto everything about her, staining the hem of her soft green calico skirt, ruining the lace tablecloth Mama had worked so hard to finish.

It seemed that the walls were closing in on her already, and she had only been inside for a few moments. What would it be like to actually try to live in such a place?

She had to get outside—to breathe. She turned to go, but the expanse of sky and grass stretching away as far as she could see from the doorway of the tiny hut offered no relief to the sick feeling in her midsection. *Oh . . . why did I ever leave Brandenburg?*

At the age of twenty-one, Karyn Ensinger had been eager to leave Germany. Just over a year ago she had lost her beloved Hans. His enthusiasm fueled by his older brother's tales of victory in the Franco-Prussian War a few years before, Hans had volunteered for the army in spite of his wealthy father's protests. He had died of pneumonia during his first winter of duty. Karyn had shown no interest in marrying anyone else, beginning her own sewing business in a back corner of her father's store. Telling herself that she would be an old maid now, that love was not for her, Karyn had waged war daily with her emotions until she believed that she had won.

But then Hans's father, Anton, began to patronize the store. Karyn welcomed him politely. He spoke of Hans in reverent, loving tones, brushing away tears of grief. Karyn listened willingly, finding solace in the memories that she could share with Hans's father. As his visits became more and more frequent, the subject of his ramblings broadened. He spoke less of Hans and more of his own loneliness. He began to ask Karyn's advice, complaining of the difficulties of running an estate alone.

While her father looked on Herr Gilhoff's visits with approving nods, Karyn grew increasingly uncomfortable. Ever so subtly, she began to change her appearance. She took less care with her hair, appearing not to care when dark strands of it fell out of her formerly neat coiffure. She didn't look up when Herr Gilhoff first arrived. But her efforts to offend only served to attract. Herr Gilhoff dreamed of the dark strands of hair that framed Karyn's face. He interpreted Karyn's ignoring him as maidenly shyness.

Karyn had been trying to avoid Herr Gilhoff for over a year when, one afternoon, he reached out to touch her dark hair with a tobacco-stained finger. Revulsion washed over her, and Karyn reached up to push his hand away. But he grabbed her hand and squeezed it. Karyn looked up at him, furious. She pulled her hand away forcefully, stood up, and turned away. But Herr Gilhoff misinterpreted the passion that flickered in Karyn's eyes, the color that flushed her ivory cheeks. Karyn was furious. Herr Gilhoff was in love.

The next day, Ida Gerstenschlager brought news into the store of the invitation from single German farmers in America to German women who would come and build a future. The rules had been laid carefully. The girls would be escorted across the United States by a bilingual guide. They would meet their prospective husbands at a church. There would be a meal and conversation, and if couples so desired, they could be married right away. They would have to remain in Grand Island for twenty-four hours, after which any marriage could be annulled. Ida said that she was going.

That evening at home, Karyn announced that she was going to America. Mama said she was terribly impulsive. But Papa had five other daughters to feed. He made it clear that he thought it time for his eldest daughter to make her own way. If she would not marry Herr Gilhoff, if she wanted to go to America, so be it. Perhaps they would all go to America if Karyn wrote that things were good. Perhaps then little Sophie's health would return.

And so Karyn had come to America. Surrounded by other German girls, Karyn found the trip to Nebraska exhilarating—a grand adventure. The escort who met them in New York was bilingual. She lectured them often about the new customs and the new land to which they had come, painting a charming picture of life in America. It was March when they arrived, and unseasonably warm weather made the journey comfortable. Newborn lambs skipped in the fields they viewed as their train lurched across the country. Other than to tell the girls that there were no forests in Nebraska, the escort had been somewhat vague about the countryside where they would live, but Karyn didn't mind. Gentle breezes blew, and she breathed deeply of her new freedom, rejoicing that she was far, far away from Herr Anton Gilhoff.

Grand Island itself was a disappointment. There were no gentle breezes on the day the young women arrived. The dust kicked up from the street by wagons seemed to hang in the air, and Karyn had her first premonition that things in America might not be as she had imagined them. But she buried her fears beneath a veneer of confidence. She ate a hearty supper and then organized the girls into teams to help with the ironing of dresses and the curling of hair in preparation for the next morning. The evening ended with a rollicking pillow fight that very nearly got them all thrown out of the hotel. Long after the girls finally tumbled into bed, Karyn lay staring out the window at the Nebraska moon, wondering what the morrow would bring. She glanced toward the opposite side of the narrow bed where Ida Gerstenschlager lay curled up like a kitten and shivered with the realization that the very next time moonlight shone through her window, it would probably not be Ida's form lying next to her.

During the first few awkward moments of the awful next morning, the young women had stood in a tight group, whispering and smiling as men filed into the church. When a very tall man with startlingly pale blue eyes came in, the girls tittered and whispered admiring comments about him. In spite of his beauty, Karyn had thought him rather frightening. He came in alone, spoke to no one, and leaned against the back wall of the room, openly inspecting the girls. When he finally removed his hat, revealing a thick mane of unfashionably long, black hair, Karyn thought he looked like some wild animal, only recently tamed and brought to town to be tested in civilization.

4

Karyn found herself wishing that she could shrink back and not be noticeable. *Why couldn't I have been petite, like Sophie?* Sophie could have slipped into the middle of the little group and disappeared. But Karyn was tall, with square shoulders and an almost-regal bearing that precluded her from ever "shrinking back" in any setting. Long ago she had learned to hide her fears behind a thin veneer that looked like self-assurance.

Much to her dismay, Karyn's ruse attracted the wild-looking giant. After a brief look at the other girls, he had bent to set his hat on a chair at the back of the room and walked straight to where Karyn stood next to Ida. Without a glance at Ida, he extended his hand and said in a surprisingly gentle voice, *"Mein name ist Mikal Ritter."*

Even Karyn's large hand was swallowed up in Mikal Ritter's grasp. Taking a deep breath, Karyn returned his firm grip, lifting her chin so she could meet his gaze. "Karyn Ensinger."

Herr Ritter offered his arm. "Would you sit with me, Fräulein Ensinger?" He spent the morning describing a good farm with a promising future. They dined together, parted for the evening, and were married the following morning. Karyn was relieved the first night when Herr Ritter left her alone in the hotel room and went to sleep in the livery. In the thirty-six hours since they had met, he had proved himself a complete gentleman. Karyn began to feel positive about her decision to come to America.

But that had been before the interminable ride over increasingly barren land, seated alongside a stranger she must now call her husband. Standing in the doorway of the one-room house made of dirt, Karyn wanted to cry.

While Karyn was inspecting the interior of the soddy, Herr Ritter lifted her trunk from the back of the wagon and to the ground. He waited outside, growing more and more nervous. When she finally reappeared at the doorway, her face revealed what he had most dreaded.

He took his hat off and shook his head. His long hair fell about his shoulders. His voice shook a little as he said, "I visited Brandenburg once. I remember a beautiful little village in a forest that came right up to the banks of a river." He hesitated, clearing his throat before continuing. "This must seem like a horrible place to which you have come." He paused. "I knew you wouldn't like it at first. Still, I hoped you might—" He stopped abruptly and bent to hoist her trunk back up into the wagon. Then, he seemed to think of something. He straightened up, towering over Karyn. Before speaking again he leaned against the wagon as if to make himself smaller.

"Even though it is not at all like Brandenburg, it is a good land, this Nebraska in the United States of America. I have a timber claim, a preemption, and a homestead. That's 480 *morgen*—'acres' they say in English. And unlike those who are coming now into this land, all three of my claims are together." He nodded toward a line of scrub trees a few hundred feet away. "The creek provides water for the fields and the livestock, and I have dug a good well just behind the house." He smiled faintly. "I—we—have neighbors." He nodded toward the southeast. "A little over twelve kilometers that way. You won't be so lonely as some of the wives." He stood away from the wagon. "I need to water the team and feed my livestock." He led the team away, disappearing around the edge of a rise of land that jutted up directly behind the soddy.

Livestock? Karyn wondered. There was no sign of a corral or a barn. *How could he have much livestock?* Curious, she walked in the direction he had gone, surprised to find a good-size corral tucked just around the edge of the bluff not a hundred feet from the house. An obviously pregnant cow stood next to the corral fence, which was made of strips of earth piled up to create a four-foot-high wall. On the opposite side of the corral there was a small pen containing a very large sow. It, too, was "fenced" with sod. Herr Ritter didn't see Karyn. He had unhitched the team and was leading them to the creek.

Karyn turned to head back for the house but was brought up short at the sight of a crude porch. She went under the porch to the opening of a cave cut perpendicularly into the side of the low bluff. Stepping inside, Karyn waited for her eyes to adjust to the dark. Gradually, the room came into focus. On the left there was a single sleeping bunk, then a rough board table and a small stove. On the opposite side of the cave were two stalls. Evidently this room had been kitchen, dining room, parlor, and barn. Karyn wondered for how long.

Herr Ritter's voice sounding from the doorway made her jump. "This is where I started. Two winters I spent here. Alone." He bent down and stepped inside. The space seemed to grow smaller with his giant frame blocking the doorway. He nodded toward the stalls. "Last winter was the worst. Early in the winter there was rain. Just when everything was completely wet, the cold set in. Everything froze into a solid mat of ice. Then came the first snow. Two meters of it. Next there was more rain followed by two meters of snow. The temperature stayed below zero for weeks at a time. Ordinarily the winds blow the snow off of the hills, exposing the grass. The grass here is called buffalo grass, and everyone tells me that livestock wintered on buffalo grass are in better spring condition than cattle fed on the best wheat. But last winter the wind had no effect at all on the thick layers of ice and snow. It covered the whole country in a thick, solid blanket of white. Thank God I had no cattle that winter and only two horses to feed. Breaking through the snow bruised and cut their legs so badly I ended up tying them in the dugout and hacking through the snow with my ax to get grass for them."

He smiled. "And with such talk I have now given you another reason to think that coming here was a mistake."

"You saved your team," Karyn said with admiration.

He nodded. "Yes. We formed a partnership. I saved them from starving to death, and they saved me from freezing to death." At Karyn's questioning look Mikal explained, "I had not spent nearly enough time collecting fuel that fall. When I ran out, I hung my comforters around the stalls to try to trap a little warmth."

Karyn tried to picture the huge man before her huddled in this cave while a blizzard raged outside. She felt the cold, imagined the walls closing in as the wind howled outside. She clutched her arms to herself and shivered. "How did you stand it?"

With a wry smile he answered, "I vowed not to clear one more *morgen* for planting until I had built a house." He leaned against the opening of the cave. "In my head I paced off the

7

dimensions, cut the sod, arranged windows, built furniture." His blue eyes looked at Karyn intently. "Then I realized that no matter the size of the house, it would still be just me through the next winter of storms."

He stepped back outside, under the porch where he could straighten up. He explained, "The ranchers farther west lost thousands of cattle. Many of them gave up and moved away. Cay Miller—he is another German who just started his own town about fourteen kilometers southwest—says it is a good change. He thinks that more settlers will come now. That there will be fewer problems with the ranchers."

Herr Ritter nodded toward the cow in the corral. "I am hoping that Cay is right. Her calf is to be the beginning of a respectable herd for the Ritters."

After a brief silence, Herr Ritter continued. "This is a good start, Fräulein Ensinger. The land here is rich, and in a few years I will have a good farm." He broke off and looked down at the hat in his hands. "But when I look at it now, through the eyes of someone just arriving from Brandenburg—well, I can see that it must be a terrible place."

When Karyn did not disagree, he took a deep breath and plunged ahead. "I made it through the worst winter in a dozen years. I am strong and healthy. I work hard. We could make a home here."

You cannot make dirt into a home. Karyn wanted to say it, but kindness prevented it.

He looked at her earnestly. "I have been saving money for a new team. The Irvine brothers have imported some English shires. I had a pair of bay mares reserved, but the money could just as well be used for passage back to Germany." He managed a faint smile as he said, "Stay for one month. See about it. See about me." His face turned crimson as he added softly, "I promise you that we will be husband and wife in name only. After one month, if you want to go back, I will take you to Grand Island. The marriage can be annulled, and I will buy tickets for your return to Brandenburg."

Karyn took her eyes from the cave and its contents and put them on the man who stood before her, his hat in his hands. She focused on his hands. They were the largest hands she had ever seen, prematurely aged by hard labor. It seemed impossible that such hands could belong to the young, handsome face that was Mikal Ritter. Studying those hands, Karyn was struck by the likelihood that they would indeed succeed in wrenching a good future from the land. Karyn reminded herself how unlike her darling Hans this Mr. Ritter really was. Hans had had fine, delicate features, gentle brown eyes, the beautiful hands of a musician. But Hans was gone. If she went back to Brandenburg, to what would she be going? Papa would take her in, but then he would marry her off to old Anton Gilhoff, with his perpetually stained shirtfront and his nasty habit of spitting tobacco at the can on the floor beside his chair.

"I still have to feed the animals," Herr Ritter said. Nodding toward the cow he added, "She will calve soon. Then there will be milk." He ducked from under the porch and walked toward the well.

Karyn forced the picture of refined Hans Gilhoff and his father from her mind. She made her way back to the front of the soddy. She sat on her trunk, contemplating the dirt house that Mikal Ritter had labored alone to build. It seemed to challenge her: *You can't do it. You can't make dirt into a home.*

In her mind, Karyn hung starched white curtains at the window. She took down the tattered quilt that hung in the doorway and washed and patched it. That would do, until Herr Ritter could be convinced to haul in lumber to make a proper door. Karyn spun about on the trunk to contemplate the treeless sea of grass rolling into the distance as far as she could see. And how far would he have to go to get the lumber for a door?

She spun back around and looked inside the doorway at the dirt floor. It mocked her: *You can't do it. You can't make dirt into a home.* Suddenly, Karyn remembered. Papa had once told her of mixing straw and clay to make a surface that hardened like a brick when it dried. She looked about her. *If there is one thing that there is plenty of in this land, it is grass. I wonder if grass would work as well. I wonder if there is any clay. I wonder if Mr. Ritter could be convinced to delay his farming long enough to help me make a floor I can sweep.*

9

Getting up, Karyn stepped inside the house. Outside the sun was blazing, the seemingly ever-present wind blowing. Inside, it was surprisingly cool and still. Karyn looked up. Herr Ritter had spent some money on that roof. She remembered him describing how he had cut sod for a neighbor to earn the money to buy planks, then tar paper to serve as an underlayment before he put on the layer of sod that would insulate the house so well. He had looked at her matter-of-factly and said, "I could not expect a woman to come to live in a house where the roof drops huge clods of mud on everything inside whenever it rains." Hearing Herr Ritter speak of lumber, Karyn had imagined a frame house, perhaps with green shutters at the windows. She smiled at her own naïveté.

Karyn heard footsteps outside. Herr Ritter ducked under the doorway and came in. He was carrying something half hidden in one hand. He held it out to Karyn. "From our neighbors." He nodded toward the east. "Celest Delhomme grows them. Her window ledge is full of them. When I said I was going for a wife, she said I should take this as a welcome gift from her." He set a small pot with a sprig of green peeking just above its rim onto the twelve-inch-wide window ledge. When Karyn said nothing, he laid one huge hand along the wood that framed the opening in the sod wall, explaining, "I cut it away at an angle like this so it would let in more light. You can grow flowers right through the winter. Celest's geraniums bloom into February."

When Karyn still didn't say anything, he sat down on the window ledge, the tiny potted geranium at his side. Finally, he shrugged his shoulders and stood up. He did not hide his disappointment as he said, "I'll get the team. We can leave right away."

He had bent to go back outside when Karyn surprised even herself by saying, "That will not be necessary, Herr Ritter. Perhaps I was impulsive in coming here, but to return to Brandenburg so soon would be just as foolish. A month does not seem so much to ask."

Turning around, Mikal Ritter displayed the first wholehearted smile Karyn had seen. It revealed fine, straight white teeth. Anton Gilhoff's tobacco-stained teeth flashed in Karyn's mind, giving her at least one reason to be glad she was not going back to Brandenburg right away.

Herr Ritter walked over to the bed and collected his bedding. "There is not much furniture yet, but if you want anything changed, I will do it as soon as I come back."

Karyn nodded. She followed him to the doorway. He seemed happy to be returning to the dugout where he had been so lonely. He was halfway down the slope when he turned and called out, "Fräulein Ensinger . . . Would you call me Mikal?" Karyn nodded, and he smiled his beautiful smile again.

Karyn opened the lid of her trunk. Even Mikal Ritter's beautiful smile could not prevent homesickness from flooding in at the sight of the trunk's contents. Karyn shook her head, wondering what Mama would think if she saw the lace tablecloth that she had crocheted gracing the stack of empty fruit boxes that served as a table in the soddy. Karyn draped the tablecloth over the side of the trunk. She pushed her hands into the folds of a feather tick and withdrew Oma's fine porcelain teapot. It, too, was set aside.

In the end, it took only a few moments for Karyn to unpack. She hung two cotton dresses and three crisp white aprons on hooks that protruded from the tree trunk positioned in the center of the room. She put on a fourth apron and prepared to make up her bed, which was little more than a shallow box laid atop two long poles stuck into adjacent walls of the soddy. The corner of the box, which stood out into the room, was supported by a stump.

Retrieving a bunch of broomcorn suspended from the ceiling near the door, Karyn did her best to sweep out the bed-box before unrolling her feather bed and pushing it into place. She covered the feather bed with two woven coverlets and stood back to survey her work, blushing at the mental image of Mikal Ritter's massive frame crowded into the bed alongside—*husband-in-name-only. He had promised.*

Karyn had gone outside and was repacking her best things into the trunk when Mikal strode up. He bent down and handed the lace tablecloth to Karyn. "You have fine things, Fräulein Ensinger," he offered.

"Thank you, Herr—" She corrected herself. "Thank you, Mikal. And you must please call me Karyn." She reached out to take the lace tablecloth from him. Something in his expression made her want to comfort him. "I fear I was foolish in bringing such things. They are not very practical." She laid the tablecloth in the trunk and closed the lid.

"If God had intended life to be filled with only practical things," Mikal said, "He would not bother to paint the colors in a sunset." He bent to pick up her trunk, saying over his shoulder, "I will build a beautiful home someday, where a woman's lace tablecloth and a china teapot are needed."

Karyn followed Mikal inside the soddy. He set her trunk down beside the bed.

"Are you hungry?" Karyn asked, crossing the few feet to where several wooden crates had been stacked on their sides to form a cupboard. "If you will kindly show me where you keep your rolling pin and cake cutter—oh, and the eggs, please—I see the flour here—I can—"

Mikal cleared his throat. "I have no eggs. As for a rolling pin and cake cutter—" He smiled sheepishly.

"Oh," Karyn said. "Well, then. Sausage. I can just fry some sausage."

Mikal shook his head. "I have no sausage. Would you like me to show you how I make pancakes?"

Karyn arched one eyebrow. "I do not think that I need cooking lessons, Herr Ritter. What I need is a proper kitchen." She turned toward the stove. "If you would bring in some firewood, I will manage something for supper."

"There is no wood, Karyn."

Of course there is no wood, idiot. Karyn chastised herself. *Did you see some huge forest on the ride to this miserable sod house?*

Karyn stood a little taller. "Then what do I burn in the stove?" Her face was hot with embarrassment.

"Hay and corncobs after harvest. Now I am using chips."

"Chips?" Karyn asked.

Mikal nodded. "Come outside. I will show you."

She followed him outside and to the opposite side of the

house where a small mountain of "chips" lay drying in the sun. Mikal explained, "The buffalo are gone now, but they left enough fuel for many winters to come, free for anyone who picks it up. Fortunately, one of their old trails leads right along the edge of my tree claim, so we have chips in abundance."

Dear Sophie . . . America is a wonderful land, where the settlers live in dirt houses and burn buffalo droppings for fuel. There are no eggs just yet, and trees have yet to be invented. My husband is Mikal Ritter. He is tall with black hair and blue eyes and he sleeps in a cave.

Looking at the disgusting pile of dried manure she was supposed to use to cook a supper without eggs, Karyn gave in to homesickness. The emotions of the day rushed in. Abruptly, she turned away. She blinked and tried to will her emotions back under control, but she could not stop the flow of tears.

Seeing the tears streaming down Karyn's cheeks, Mikal contemplated all the toil of the last two years of his life and counted it meaningless. *Mein Gott,* he asked heaven, *for what have I been striving if a woman looks upon my labor and weeps?* He started to walk away.

At the sound of his footsteps, Karyn rubbed her cheeks briskly and called him back. "Oh, please, Mikal," she said through her tears. "Forgive me. I do not mean to be unkind. I was just—" She bent down, hiding her disgust as she put some chips in her apron. "I am so very ignorant of your ways here in America." She looked up at Mikal, forcing herself to smile. "I am afraid that you are going to be very disappointed in me. I know nothing about cooking without milk or eggs—or of using chips for fuel."

Mikal was quick to answer. "I can show you how I have been cooking." He added, "I am certain you will be able to improve on my methods, but it is a place to start. We will visit the neighbors tomorrow. Emile and Celest Delhomme have been here the longest of any other settlers. Celest is Belgian, but she speaks fluent German. Her cooking is a little different, but you will like her."

As if angels had borne a summons to the Delhomme homestead, a voice called out, "Mikal! Mikal Ritter!"

Mikal smiled and looked down at Karyn. Relief sounded in his voice as he exclaimed, "Emile and Celest!"

Karyn dropped the vile chips from her apron and followed Mikal around the side of the house to see Emile and Celest Delhomme riding up on matching gray horses. Karyn hid her amazement that Celest did not ride side-saddle. She wore a calf-length black divided skirt and knee-high riding boots. Her thick gray hair was tied back loosely with a scarlet ribbon. As slim as a young girl, she dismounted quickly, removed her hat, pulled off her riding gloves, and tossed them into the crown of the hat.

Unaware that her own cheeks were streaked with the trails of homesick tears, Karyn extended her hand to greet Celest. *"Es freut mich, Sie Angenehm.* Thank you for the kind gift of the geranium, Frau Delhomme."

But Celest would have nothing of such formality. Looking severely at Mikal, she shoved her hat into his hands. Holding Karyn momentarily at arm's length, she inspected her new neighbor with cool gray-green eyes. Then, she abruptly engulfed Karyn in a hug, kissed both her cheeks, and wiped away the traces of Karyn's tears with her hand.

"So this is the young woman Mikal chose in Grand Island." She spoke flawless German. "Such a lovely girl." Barely pausing to take a breath, she began to shake her finger at Mikal, scolding him. "I suppose you have no eggs, little flour, and no firewood and yet you are expecting your supper soon, *ja?"*

Mikal grinned sheepishly.

Celest opened her saddlebags and pulled out a sack. Taking Karyn's arm, she headed inside the soddy, calling over her shoulder, "Emile, bring in some chips. And see that they are good and dry. Then you men go busy yourselves somewhere. Karyn and I will call you when supper is ready."

Inside the soddy, Celest took charge. From her sack she produced two small jars, one of cream and one of butter. "God has blessed us with a cow that gives enough milk for us to have butter and cream all we want. And enough to share. My boys could not locate a single egg from my worthless hens, or I would have brought eggs. But I can show you a trick for pancakes—"

Rolling up her sleeves, Celest went to work, talking all the while. "Stoke the stove. Now, nearly a teacup of sugar . . . about half so much of cream, and then another half of water. You are so blessed that Mikal found water so close to the house. Now a lump of butter and a little soda." Celest paused. "Stoke the stove again, Karyn. Chips burn quickly. Now, add just enough cornmeal to make the batter stiff." She looked up. "You are probably accustomed to always having flour, but here cornmeal is more common. You may not like it at first, but really it is not too bad." She stirred the mixture. "See how stiff it is? That will make the best pancakes. Now, you see you do not need eggs after all. We stoke the stove again, and then we can cook. I brought you some molasses and my last jar of chokecherry jelly."

Celest smiled. "I can show you chokecherry bushes later this week. There is a good stand just halfway between our homestead and yours. And there are plum trees. It is only April, of course, so things are just beginning to bloom, but we have wild fruit in abundance. At night, when all is quiet and the breeze blows, you can sometimes catch the sweet scent of plum blossoms." She smiled. "We can pick fruit together and make jam. Oh, it will be wonderful to have another woman so close by!" She rummaged for a spoon and offered some jelly to Karyn. "Taste. I wonder if Mikal has any coffee."

From the doorway Mikal called out, "In the tin on the top shelf." He carried a bucket full of fresh water in and poured it into the waiting coffeepot. He picked up both of the wooden chairs from the kitchen and headed back outside, explaining, "There is shade on the side of the house. We can eat there."

Karyn took a coffee grinder and Mikal's tin down from the shelf, happy to at last have a task assigned that she could perform. After grinding nearly a cup of coffee beans, she added them to the pot of already warm water on the stove. Returning the grinder and the tin of coffee beans to their shelf, she made a mental note—tomorrow the shelves would need to be scrubbed.

While Karyn made coffee, Celest filled a basket with tin plates and cups, the jelly and molasses, talking while she worked. "You will want to live outside as much as possible, Karyn. Mikal has bought a very good stove, but when summer arrives, using it will transform this entire house into an oven." She explained, "Three-foot-thick walls hold in whatever air is inside. If you do not cook in here, it will be blessedly cool even on the hottest day. And in winter, just as wonderfully warm. Last winter even in the worst blizzard, water in a bucket did not freeze inside our house."

Emile appeared in the doorway. He growled at Celest in mock anger, "Have you no supper cooked yet, woman? The men are about to starve."

Celest shoved the plate of cakes at him. "Tell the men to be polite or they just might find themselves without a cook!" She kissed her husband just above the line of his gray beard.

Emile chuckled and headed outside, followed by Karyn and Celest. The men had erected a makeshift table at the side of the soddy with a plank and two low sawhorses, and now stood waiting by two upended orange crates. They made quite a ceremony of drawing out the two kitchen chairs and seating the women.

As soon as everyone was seated, Emile said, "Let us join hands," and spoke a simple blessing,

Komm herr Jesu, sei Du unser Gast, Segne uns, un alles was Du uns bescheret hast. Amen.

Reaching for a pancake, Emile smiled kindly at Karyn and explained, "I had a German nurse. It has been over forty years, but I have never forgotten the simple blessing she taught us to say before every meal. Welcome to America, Karyn Ritter."

Thus began the friendship of Karyn Ensinger Ritter and Celest and Emile Delhomme, a friendship founded upon the cornerstone of loneliness, joined with the mortar of chokecherry jelly, and sealed with a simple German blessing.

The Diary
April 1, 1880
  My name is Karyn Ensinger Ritter. I am twenty-one, and I have just come to Custer County, Nebraska, from Brandenburg, Germany. I begin this diary as a way of sharing

my heart when I cannot speak it. My husband is Mikal Ritter, and he seems to be a kind man. He is handsome in a wild way that is sometimes almost frightening. The "house" is a pile of earth, and the "farm" is nothing but a few scratches in the earth made with something called a "breaking plow." But I have determined to do something with the house, and although I may be only a woman, I have no less resolve than Herr Ritter displays in his struggle to transform a barren land into a farm. Today I met Celest and Emile Delhomme, our Belgian neighbors. Thanks be to God, they speak German. What they must think of me, coming so far to marry a stranger! Indeed, I am asking myself what I was thinking to do such a thing. But I am here, and I will not flee before the adventure has begun. If only Herr Ritter will keep his promises regarding our marriage, and if only God grants me courage, I will manage. I have agreed to stay one month. Then we will see.

CHAPTER 2

A Silk Ribbon Nosegay

Behold, how great a matter a little fire kindleth!
And the tongue is a fire, a world of iniquity.
James 3:5–6

Only seven days after her arrival in Custer County, Karyn lay in her bed one night listening to coyotes howl, reviewing things as she had imagined them and things as they were.

Of course the labor was tiring, but Karyn's good health and inborn physical strength met the challenge of hard work willingly.

Of course the absence of trees was disturbing. But in the absence of trees Karyn looked more closely at the grass and found an ocean of variety. Besides, trees could be planted.

Of course the eternally blowing wind was sometimes annoying. But Karyn watched the way the wind tossed the grass and decided it created a wild kind of beauty. Besides, she could always retreat inside the thick-walled soddy.

Yes, things in Custer County of Nebraska in America were different from Germany. There were no forests, no great, deep rivers, no picturesque villages.

Yes, Mikal Ritter was different from Hans Gilhoff. He was not musical, not refined, not genteel.

Still, as Karyn lay beneath her thin coverlet listening to the coyotes howl, she consciously resolved to like both Custer

18

County and Mikal Ritter. She felt her cheeks grow warm as she admitted that liking Mikal Ritter would probably require minimal effort.

But then, at the end of the second week, in spite of all the reviewing and resolving; in spite of Mikal Ritter's kindness and blue eyes; in spite of Celest Delhomme's friendship; in spite of the dread of Anton Gilhoff, Karyn was struck with a desperate longing for home. Like thousands before her in thousands of different times and places, she considered her choice and called herself a fool. But unlike thousands before her, Karyn's homesickness had little to do with her physical surroundings. Her homesickness was caused by neither the wind nor the heat nor the loneliness, but by the words of Frau Amalia Kruger.

It was the fourteenth day of Karyn and Mikal Ritter's residence together when Mikal said at breakfast, "I need to have the plow sharpened. Perhaps you would like to see Millersburg." He smiled. "The post office is in Cay Miller's store. You can send your letter home." Seeing the delight that shone in Karyn's dark eyes, Mikal added, "We can go on from Millersburg to visit the Delhommes. I promised Emile to help plow a firebreak around his homestead."

Karyn thanked him, trying to control the trembling excitement in her voice. Millersburg! Finally, she would get to see the little village to the southwest. The Delhommes! She had suppressed her loneliness these past two weeks, but the prospect of communion with Celest Delhomme was sweet.

Karyn hurried through her morning chores, drawing water, feeding livestock, washing dishes, working on mending the tattered quilt that served as a door to the soddy. When Mikal drove up the slope from the barn, she was waiting, her first letter home secreted in the pocket of her fresh apron.

Karyn fairly leaped onto the wagon seat, reaching behind her to settle the basket that held their lunch into the corner of the wagon box. When Mikal climbed up beside her and reached for the reins, their shoulders touched. He did not move away. Karyn blushed. Telling herself that it would be rude to offend her husband, she did not move away.

They headed southwest. The wagon had covered nearly two kilometers before Mikal said, "It is not far to Millersburg. Only about fourteen kilometers. We should get there yet this morning." He paused. "Cay Miller has great plans for the town he has named for himself. But at present it is only his store and a few other sod buildings."

Karyn's vision of a nice excursion to a little village where she would go from shop to shop while Mikal attended to the sharpening of the plow died. As she had done dozens of times in the past two weeks, Karyn resolved to make the best of the difference between her expectations and reality.

"Do you know Herr Miller well?"

Mikal nodded his head. "As it happens, I do. Cay rescued me from myself one night when I had had far too much to drink." He hastened to explain, "I do not drink anymore. But when I first came to Custer County . . ." He paused, choosing his words carefully. "I was in a dangerous frame of mind one night. I stumbled into Cay's store hoping to buy more beer. Cay convinced me to talk instead of drink." He paused again. "Some people laugh at Cay behind his back and call him a foolish dreamer. But he is a good man."

As the wagon made its way across the open prairie, Mikal began to tell the story of Cay Miller. Karyn willed herself to listen, all the while wishing that Mikal would return to the night when he had been drinking too much.

Cay Miller had begun his adult life as a bank clerk. Small of stature, unremarkable in appearance, Cay was not the kind of man whom people took very seriously. But then he lost an eye in what the Americans called their "War of the Rebellion." Aware that he was very average in appearance, Cay had always taken special care to be well groomed, to wear the latest fashion. Looking in the mirror one morning after his release from the hospital, Cay Miller made a decision that changed his life. He decided that an eye patch was much more stylish than the ill-fitting glass eye provided by his government. Around that eye patch Cay Miller created a persona. Not long after he began wearing his eye patch, he succeeded in turning a small savings account into a small fortune. Suddenly, everyone began to take

Cay Miller very seriously. They sought his advice. They even imitated his taste in clothing. The eye patch became a badge of honor, a symbol of sacrifice, a tangible reminder that here was a man who had *experience,* a man to be listened to, a man who knew whereof he spoke.

And then Cay did something that amazed even the closest of his friends. Having won the respect of his fellow townspeople, having been invited to be on the board of the First National Bank, Cay Miller headed west. He rode the Union Pacific Railroad to Grand Island, Nebraska, where he disembarked and headed northwest into Custer County. He looked the county over before returning to Omaha where he spent a considerable amount of money fraternizing with railroad officials and surveyors. What he learned from the railroad men, he applied at the land office.

And so Cay Miller, a second-generation immigrant from Ohio, purchased a homestead on Lillian Creek, built a sod house, and raised a red flag declaring the presence of a "store."

"Now he waits," Mikal concluded.

"Waits? For what?" Karyn wanted to know.

"For the railroad. He says it will come, and when it does he is perfectly positioned to make a fortune."

Karyn had been quiet for so long, that Mikal finally apologized. "I am sorry, Karyn. I did not mean to bore you."

She answered quickly, "But I am not bored, Mikal. I was just thinking that now I know more about a man I have yet to meet than I know about Mikal Ritter." She asked boldly, "Just why is it that you were drinking so much? More important, what made you stop?"

Mikal turned to look her full in the face.

Something in his expression made her wish she could take her questions back. She looked away. "Please forgive me, I have been too bold."

He leaned forward, resting his foot on the edge of the wagon. "I was eighteen when I took part in the Franco-Prussian War. Then, I was witness to the civil war in Paris." He paused, seeming to grope for words. "I was dissatisfied and restless. Sick at heart. There seemed to be no hope of a good life for me anywhere. I began to doubt that I would ever accomplish anything at all in life. It was a dark time for me. Then I met someone." And then Mikal made a grievous error. Months before he had decided that he would not tell whomever he met in Grand Island about Marie-Louise. Not right away. After the trial period he had planned, if it appeared that things were going to work out, then he would mention her. That would put things in proper perspective. God had healed his grief, and raising the specter of a dead wife was no way to welcome a new one. And so, when it would have been only natural to speak of Marie-Louise, Mikal spoke instead of her brother. "I met someone who had traveled in America. He made it sound so wonderful, so promising, that I came. That was in 1872."

"Just so?" Karyn inquired. "You heard of it and you came?"

He nodded. "Not so unlike one Karyn Ensinger. I was far to the south of Nebraska in Kansas at first, but"—he stopped again, hesitating before continuing his story—"well, Kansas was no good for me. I had some difficulties and I grew to regret having settled there. Sometimes I am a slow learner. It was five years before I finally admitted that I could never be happy there."

"But why not?" Karyn wanted to know. "Is Kansas so different from Nebraska?"

Once again, Mikal avoided speaking of Marie-Louise. "Well, for one thing, I did not come to America to build another Germany. In Kansas everything was German—Volga Germans, Black Sea Germans, Catholic Germans, Mennonite Germans. Many of the Germans there did not even want to learn to speak English. I am not like that. My homeland is precious to me, but America is my home now. I have worked hard to learn English." He glanced sideways at Karyn. "I think in English now, not German." He paused before adding, "And I want my children to grow up speaking English."

"How long did it take you to learn?" Karyn asked. "Of all the languages I heard on the ship and on the way here, English seemed the most difficult."

Mikal nodded and smiled. "Yes, I know. But it will not take you so long as it did me. I was surrounded by Germans for so long, there was no need to learn right away. Here there are settlers from many different countries. Learning English together has drawn us all closer." He teased, "Perhaps I should speak only English from now on. Then you would learn more quickly."

Karyn felt a sudden flash of panic. Would he really do it? After bringing her so far out into a wilderness, would he now remove even her ability to communicate?

Mikal looked down at her. "I was only joking, Karyn. I would never do such a thing to you." He hesitated, then said, "I know loneliness. When first I came to Nebraska, I was miles away from the closest human being for nearly two years. Eventually I discovered that God was here. Now I believe He brought me here, to a lonely place where I would be forced to settle things between God and Mikal."

He lowered his voice and continued, "There was much bitterness in my heart when I came to Nebraska, but" he gestured toward the horizon—"there is a strange sort of power in all that. Power to remind a man that he is very, very, small." He smiled. "I began to realize that Mikal Ritter and his problems were not quite so monumental, after all."

Suddenly, he turned to look at Karyn. "You are too polite, Karyn. Your gracious listening encourages me, and I talk too much."

Karyn protested, "Not too much. At home I had voices about me all day long." She hesitated before adding, "It is one of the things I miss."

Mikal frowned, wondering how he could have been so stupid as to not realize how lonely she must be. Having been alone for so long, Mikal had had some difficulty adapting to the constant presence of another human being in his life. Even though he and Karyn actually spent little time together other than at meals, he was continually aware of her presence. At the slightest sound from "up at the house," he would look up sharply from whatever he was doing and then laugh at himself for forgetting that he was no longer alone, that the sound was not some errant wildlife wreaking havoc in the doorless soddy. It was only his wife.

23

Just last evening some sound had made him glance up toward the house to see Karyn bending far down to immerse the entire length of her hair in a bucket of water balanced on the seat of one of the kitchen chairs just outside the soddy door. He had watched as she reached up to scrub her hair and rinse it. When she stood up water streamed off her hair in a silver sheet until she reached out to wring it like a towel. She had continued to bend over while she rubbed the long tresses nearly dry. Then, with one motion she had tossed her hair back over her shoulder and stood up straight. Her back was to Mikal, and he caught his breath at his first sight of her luxuriant hair spilling down her back past her waist. He was struck anew by her regal bearing. She was not in the least delicate, and yet her broad shoulders tapered in a very pleasing way to her waistline.

Remembering, Mikal realized that he had enjoyed getting used to hearing the sounds of another human being. But he had been so busy adapting to her presence that he had given no thought whatsoever to the monumental adjustments Karyn was making—adapting to the absence of rather than the presence of other humans.

He apologized, "I should have driven you to Millersburg days ago, Karyn. And I should have taken you to visit the Delhommes. I am sorry. I should have thought." He grinned. "I hope that letter in your pocket does not tell of how your husband ignores you. Your father will be coming to rescue you."

Karyn laughed. "Have no fear, Herr Ritter. My father is more likely to send two or three more of his daughters to Nebraska than to come to take one back!"

Just as Mikal prepared to ask Karyn more questions about her own home, the wagon reached the crest of the hill that had hidden Millersburg from view. Karyn looked down at it, barely hiding her disappointment. There was one small building with a sign above it. They were too far away for Karyn to read the sign, but she noted wryly that it appeared to be almost bigger than the store itself. Next to the store there was a sod hut, and then a larger, more substantial building. As they approached the fledgling town, Karyn noticed that what appeared to be a private residence across from the store boasted not one but two glass windows. A stack of antlers adorned the roof. A few other nondescript buildings had risen up along what was meant to be the street. Perhaps someday it would be a street, but on this April morning in 1880, it was no more than a path through virgin prairie that had yet to be trodden into a dust trail.

Watching Karyn inspect Millersburg, Mikal did not ask her to voice an opinion. Instead, he drove straight to Cay Miller's.

Cay emerged from his store to meet Karyn, presenting her with a tiny nosegay of silk ribbon roses. "Welcome to Millersburg, Frau Ritter." Cay turned his patched eye away from her and stared openly with his one good eye. "Well, Mikal, I would say you filled the shopping list quite well."

"Be quiet, Cay. You will embarrass Karyn."

"What list?" Karyn wanted to know.

From his pocket Cay produced what appeared to be a page torn from some sort of pamphlet. "This Emigrant Guide was written in English, but for Frau Ritter, I will translate . . ." Clearing his throat dramatically, Cay said in German:

> *The Emigrant Adviser here lists the qualities necessary for a woman to be successful in the American West. Men planning to be married and homestead are advised to select their partner with particular attention to the list which appears below.*
> *—a strong, resilient body*
> *—robust health*
> *—a resilient soul*
> *—strong nerves*
> *—a great lack of consideration for herself*
> *—friendly obligingness to others*

Karyn teased, "But, Herr Miller, it is not possible for you to know if a woman meets those requirements when you have just met."

Cay joked back, "Ah, but I know you must have them all, or you would never have agreed to let this brute bring you into the wilderness."

Mikal turned to Karyn and said, "Herr Miller suggests that

one shop for a wife as one would for a piece of livestock. Which is why Herr Miller remains unmarried."

He looked toward Cay. "I would suggest that you add one qualification for your wife, Cay. She should be very, very short."

In mock anger, Cay Miller blustered back, "Listen, my dear friend. One giant in this community is quite enough." He tapped his temple. "The size of the brain is what matters, Mikal, the size of the brain." He looked at Karyn and then back at Mikal. "And now that I have had the pleasure of meeting the new Frau Ritter, I have hope for you yet, Mikal. Perhaps there is a brain beneath all that shaggy hair, after all."

Mikal was finished with joking. He hoisted his plow out of the back of the wagon and lifted it to his shoulder, then turned to Karyn. "The third building down there." He pointed at an unimpressive soddy. "I will not be long."

Cay led Karyn inside the store. While the room wasn't large, it was surprisingly well-stocked. To the left, a counter stretched down the length of the room. Except for a small space near a cash register, the counter was stacked high with bolts of cloth. Karyn's eyes took in at least a dozen calicoes as well as bolts of heavier cloth and something with an open weave she was to learn to use for making carpets. Below the counter a glass case displayed lace and gloves, earrings and silver rings.

Behind the counter, shelves were cluttered with jars of candy, tins of biscuits and coffee, rolls of ribbon, and countless other "necessities." Opposite the dry goods department, various farm tools and garden seeds were displayed along with boxes of nails and balls of string. An attractive display of pipes and tobacco dominated what appeared to be the "men's department" of Miller's store.

Cay said, "It has been very quiet this morning, Frau Ritter. Feel free to rummage about. There is coffee and a few biscuits on a table in the back corner. I keep the Wards Catalog back there. I can order anything you want." He bowed low. "Now, if you will excuse me, I am going to follow your husband down to the blacksmith shop and try to convince him to join me in a business venture. I will be back shortly."

But both Mikal and Cay were gone too long. As Cay headed up the street after Mikal, old Amalia Kruger watched from the window of her home across the street. She waited until Cay was out of sight and then hurried across the grassy street and into Miller's Dry Goods Store.

Karyn was admiring Cay Miller's bolts of calico when she heard Amalia grunting her way up the stairs. She turned about with a smile, but something about the bent old woman standing by the door made Karyn feel self-conscious. The woman shuffled across to where Karyn stood. She made no effort to hide the fact that she was inspecting the newcomer. Pursing her thin lips, she squinted her watery gray eyes as she looked Karyn up and down. She made an odd clicking sound with her tongue before finally saying, "So. This is the girl from Germany that Mikal Ritter brings to Millersburg." She tapped her cane on the board floor and shook her head. Making her way to the back corner of the store, she pulled out a chair and sat down heavily.

Karyn followed her and graciously held out her hand. "My name is Karyn. Mikal didn't tell me there were other women living in Millersburg."

Amalia smiled briefly, revealing two spaces in her upper row of teeth. She motioned toward the stove. "Let us have a cup of coffee and visit, Frau Ritter." While Karyn looked for clean coffee cups and stirred the fire in the stove, the old woman introduced herself. "My name is Amalia Kruger."

Soon the women were seated opposite one another with steaming cups of coffee before them. Amalia hunched over her coffee, noisily sucking it down while she inspected Karyn. Finally she asked, "Tell me, Mrs. Ritter, what do you think of Nebraska after two weeks?"

Karyn answered honestly. "It's very different from Brandenburg. But I think I can make adjustments."

"Do you have family in America?"

Karyn shook her head. "No. Only I came to America. My sisters remain at home with Mama and Papa."

"Sisters." Amalia repeated the word with a satisfied air. So that was it. Too many girls and not enough husbands.

"Will your sisters be coming to join you?"

Karyn relaxed a little. "Oh no," she said, laughing. "They are good, obedient daughters. They will stay at home and do as Papa tells them." She sighed dramatically and tried to include Frau Kruger in a joke. "I am the only evil child who must have her own way. I hope you won't tell Herr Ritter what a bad choice he has made."

But Amalia Kruger had no patience with chatter and joking. She set her coffee cup down with a thud. And then, with one sentence, she colored what Mikal had intended as kindness in an ominous light that would threaten to build a wall of distrust between Mikal and his new wife for weeks to come. "I hope Mikal has had sense enough to pick someone more suited to the situation this time."

This time? Karyn wondered.

At the surprise on Karyn's face, Amalia smiled. Karyn thought the smile looked triumphant.

"So," Amalia said. "You didn't know." She snorted softly. "Just as I thought. It has been five years, and still he cannot speak of her." She thrust her thin, wrinkled face forward, peering at Karyn as she continued, "But whether Mikal Ritter thinks so or not, you should know." Amalia scooted her chair back from the table and took a deep breath. "You should know so that you can make—what did you call them?—'adjustments.' "

Getting up to pour herself another cup of coffee, Amalia waited until she was again seated before she continued. "I knew Mikal Ritter when he first came to America. He had been in France, with the army of occupation. And there, in Paris, he met Marie-Louise Jacquot. Marie-Louise's father was a baker. She herself told me that her parents were horrified at the thought of their own daughter consorting with Germans at the very moment the Germans were occupying the French countryside. Still, she ran off with Mikal, and against all laws of nature they married outside their own people."

Amalia's eyes narrowed as she looked at Karyn. "It is quite a romantic story, is it not? Like a fairy tale." She frowned. "But it does not end like a fairy tale. On the ship Mikal and his little French wife met other Germans—Mennonites from Russia—a peace-loving people with no difficulty welcoming Mikal and Marie-Louise into their circle. They crossed the country together and settled in Kansas. Mikal built a dugout. Marie-Louise used to stand at the doorway of that dugout and stare off to the south across the creek, across the valley, and beyond. She tried to adapt, but she lived in constant fear. Fear of wolves, fear of snakes, fear of Indians."

Amalia paused and shook her head. "I knew the minute I met her that there was sadness in her future." She sighed. "Poor Marie-Louise. She was like a jewel. A beautiful, sparkling jewel." She snorted. "Young people are such fools, thinking love can overcome everything against them. Well, it can't. Marie-Louise Ritter tried with all her might, but she was never meant to live a hard life. Love is not enough. *Das ist es ja eben!*"

Karyn wished someone would come in and stop this wretched woman's talk. *She is making it all very dramatic, but you do not know her and you do know Mikal—a little. Do not overreact before you know the facts. Do not allow her to make you suspicious of Mikal. He probably had a good reason for not mentioning all of this.*

Amalia pointed her finger and shook it at Karyn. "Some things need to be known. I know this is a shock. But you need to know the truth."

Karyn didn't want to hear any more, but her pride would not let her betray how she felt. *You can ask Mikal about this later. Do not give this horrid old woman the satisfaction of seeing she has upset you.*

"My own daughter was a good friend to Marie-Louise. The last winter was mild, and we saw her often. She was trying, poor thing, but we could see that she was slipping away from us. She seemed to have taken up residence somewhere far away. When Mikal was present, she managed to find her old self. But more and more often, even Mikal could not bring her back.

"On Easter Sunday, Marie-Louise seemed better than she had been in weeks. Mikal mentioned a trip to Lawrence to buy flour, and she seemed content. She assured him she would be fine staying behind. She promised to come spend the night with us. But at four o'clock in the afternoon, the wind changed from the south to the northwest. Clouds flew in and the air was filled with dust. It turned cold and began to mist and rain. Then sleet and snow filled the air, driven along by a furious wind. Mikal turned around to come back home. Facing the driving wind, he was almost frozen. But he persevered. By God's grace he located the fence of woven willows that he had put around his wife's garden. He followed the fence to the door, but to his horror he found that the ridgepole of the dugout had broken from the heavy load of dirt and snow. Marie-Louise was nowhere to be found."

Amalia's hand trembled slightly as she raised it to her lips and pressed against them, shaking her head from side to side. "Even though it was nearly dark, Mikal rode to our home, beating on the door, shouting for Marie-Louise." Amalia's eyes filled with tears and she continued. "He was half wild with fear and grief. He would hardly believe us when we told him that she was not there. We all hoped that perhaps she had gone to Koukle's. We convinced Mikal that to go searching in the night would mean certain death for us all. Surely, we thought, she was at that very moment huddled next to the fire at Koukle's."

Amalia's voice lowered and she half whispered, "But it was not to be. The next morning Mikal and my Jacob found her about a mile south and east of the dugout. She was on the open prairie, barefoot, dressed only in a thin nightgown." Amalia paused dramatically. "If she had only stayed in the dugout, protected under the fallen roof, she would have survived the storm."

Her cold gray eyes met Karyn's as she concluded the tragic story. "I can still remember that day. Mikal carried Marie-Louise's body to our home in his own arms. He made a coffin from the boards of an old wagon. There was no cemetery, no minister to hold a proper service. He buried his little wife only a few feet from the door of the caved-in dugout. He stood by the grave as a dead man while my Jacob read the Shepherd's Psalm. The moment Jacob concluded the reading of the Scripture, Mikal climbed into his wagon and drove away. Two weeks later he returned with a tombstone. He must have gone all the way to Independence for it. He came to tell us after he had set it in place. It was the last we thought we would ever hear from Mikal Ritter.

"That spring we were so disheartened, and the news from the north was so promising, that Jacob decided we would come and cast our lot with the settlers of Custer County." Amalia took a deep breath. "My Jacob died before we reached our destination. I had no choice but to continue on with my family." She snorted. "Of course, they did not really want me, but they could not just leave me sitting alongside the road, could they?"

She sighed and then returned to the topic at hand. "Imagine our amazement when we arrived here in Millersburg and recognized Mikal Ritter. Cay Miller told us he was living like a wild man, dug into the side of the bluff on his new claim, that he rarely came to town, that he stayed to himself. That was two years ago. Then, suddenly, he built a sod house and left again. And, just like that, he returns with a new wife. Well," Amalia said, her eyes narrowing, "it's a wonder, that's all I can say. Anyone who had seen Mikal Ritter stagger into our log cabin with Marie-Louise's body in his arms would never have expected him to go for another wife."

Amalia stood up stiffly and tapped her cane twice before concluding, "He must have finally realized. *Wo Keine Frau ist, da fehlt's am besten hausrat.*" (Where there is no wife, the best household utensil is missing.) She looked Karyn over critically. "I will hope for your sake—and Mikal's—that you have the good sense to dispense with the romantic notions that destroyed Marie-Louise." With a final tap of her cane on the rough board floor, Amalia turned to go. "Good day, Frau Ritter. I have told you what you need to know to adapt to this God-forsaken place. I hope you can do it."

Amalia left, grunting her way across to the door and outside. For several minutes after she had gone Karyn sat motionless, trying to absorb what she had just been told, fighting the temptation to accuse Mikal of lying—or in the very least, of purposely misleading her. Oh, why had he not spoken of Marie-Louise? Her hands shook as she mechanically lifted the coffee cup to her lips. She put the cup down and rubbed her hands together, wondering if it was anger or hurt that made her tremble so. Or, was it fear . . . fear that she had come thousands of miles to be nothing more than a convenient replacement for a dead loved one?

Karyn had no time to settle her thoughts before Mikal and Cay came back from the blacksmith's. She could see them through the door as Mikal set the newly sharpened plow in the back of the wagon. When he turned to come inside the store Karyn hurried to the door and stepped outside. Forcing herself to smile, she called out to Cay, "Thank you for the coffee, Herr Miller."

Cay smiled up at her. "You are welcome to my coffee any time, Frau Ritter. Is there anything you needed help with?"

Karyn shook her head and made her way around the wagon. "No, thank you."

Mikal looked across the wagon box with surprise. "What about mailing the letter?"

"Oh, yes." Karyn took it out of her pocket absentmindedly and handed it to Cay.

Then, without a word, she climbed up to the wagon seat.

Mikal looked at her carefully. His gaze went to the little soddy across the street from Cay's store.

"Are the Krugers at home, Cay? I should introduce Karyn to them."

Karyn reached up to adjust her bonnet as Cay replied, "I saw the wagon head out this morning. Isaac said he was going to Kearney to get a shipment of lumber."

"Well, then." Mikal climbed up next to Karyn and with a parting nod to Cay, urged his team forward. As they rode along, he explained, "We can be at Emile's in time for a late lunch. My homestead is almost directly to the north of town. The Delhommes are north and east." Mikal stole a glance at Karyn. It was clear that something had happened to upset her.

"Are you certain there wasn't something you needed? We could have given Cay an order. It sometimes takes a few weeks, but Cay is very resourceful."

Karyn shook her head. "No. You were right about his store. It is very well-supplied."

Mikal pulled his hat down over his eyes and clucked to the

team. As the wagon jolted away from the store and toward the northeast, he said, "Isaac Kruger's announcement that he is hauling in some lumber spurred Cay to want to enlarge his store. I think it bothers him to think of someone else progressing faster than he is. He plans two stories—a larger store below with rooms above. He wanted my help with the building."

Mikal cleared his throat. "To haul the lumber from Kearney is more than a week. Then there would be the time to do the building." He paused uncertainly before concluding, "I told him I did not want to leave you alone for so long."

Angered by what she perceived to be Mikal's lack of confidence in her, Karyn swallowed hard and said coldly, "You do not have to worry over me, Herr Ritter. Just because I said that I miss the chatter and noise of my family does not mean that I will be in despair if left alone." She paused before adding, "If you must go away to take advantage of this opportunity, then go. I assure you that I can make the necessary adjustments."

After an uncomfortable silence, Mikal said, "Well, then. I will go. It will pay for all the seed for spring planting and more." Out of the corner of his eye he watched Karyn. They had seemed to be getting along so well this morning. They had had a pleasant drive together. And she had been so good-natured about Cay's joking. Mikal frowned. Her sudden change of mood troubled him. Marie-Louise had begun to act like that not long after they came to the wilderness in the heart of America. Days of contentment would be suddenly interrupted by fits of tears and temper. At first Mikal was angered by what he interpreted as a willful refusal to accept the challenges of their new life together. But as time went on and the cycle repeated itself over and over again, Mikal had begun to wonder if Marie-Louise was truly unable to cope with the life to which she had come. Finally, something happened that convinced him that his beautiful little wife was slipping away from reality, that he could not stop the tide of her insanity.

It was after a rare week of normalcy when Marie-Louise had risen each morning and made Mikal's breakfast. On the sixth day of happiness, Marie-Louise went outside after breakfast to weed the garden. Mikal was lingering over a cup of coffee when

33

he heard her shrieks—an unearthly sound that sent chills down his spine. He bolted out the door and found her crouched in horror, white-faced, staring at a fat bull snake curled up around a cabbage. The snake had raised its great head and was hissing at Marie-Louise. She seemed to be in a trance of horror.

Mikal had reached out to touch her shoulder. "It is only a bull snake, Marie-Louise. Remember? They are harmless." He reached around her and grabbed the snake, hoisting it up and tossing it away from her.

She covered her hands and began to moan. "Kill it. Kill it. Kill it."

"But it is harmless, Marie-Louise. And they eat rats. We should be glad such a huge fellow stays near the dugout. He will keep more harmful creatures away."

"Kill it! Kill it! Kill it!" She stood up, clenching her fists, screeching at him.

Mikal wrapped his arms around her, trying to comfort her in French. "Come now, *mon petit chou . . . ce n'est rien . . .*" He tried to comfort her, but she began to laugh, pushing away from him, dancing in the garden, shouting and singing in a mad, horrible display that immobilized Mikal. She danced, bending to pick up a clod of mud, smearing herself with it as if it were rouge. When she finally stopped, she walked up to Mikal and said sweetly, "Would you rock me now, Papa? . . . I am very tired."

Mikal had led her inside and sat down in the rocking chair recently purchased in hopes that rocking would somehow calm her nerves. Marie-Louise slid into his lap, laid her head on his shoulder, and fell asleep. When she woke, she seemed to have no recollection of the incident. She didn't mention the snake and was horrified by the dirt smeared on her face. For a few days, she was better . . . and then, another downward spiral began. Mikal came to be haunted by the specter of his own future caring for a woman who would no longer be any kind of wife, but rather a child requiring his constant care.

Mikal's thoughts were interrupted by Karyn's abrupt demand, "If you will slow down a little, please, I would like to walk alongside the wagon for a while."

Surprised, Mikal pulled the team up. Karyn slid to the earth almost before the wagon came to a stop. She began to walk along briskly, and Mikal pulled back on the reins, holding the team to a slow walk. He let Karyn get a little ahead of the wagon seat and watched as she trudged along, newly aware of the pleasing line of her figure.

While Mikal was watching, Karyn was thinking back over the two weeks since her arrival in Nebraska. It had been quite a shock when she saw where she was expected to live. But she had risen above the disappointment. She was rather proud of herself. She had to admit that she was also rather proud of the fact that a handsome man wanted her. Of course, he had shown no sign of *wanting* her, but the habit of replacing the memory of Hans with the very real Mikal Ritter had borne the smallest hope that someday—her mind whirled. Still, try as she might she could not argue away Amalia Kruger's wrinkled face telling her firmly that while she might have come hoping for love, she would do well to adjust her expectations.

Karyn glanced back at Mikal. *My, but he is a handsome man.*

The Diary
April 15, 1880
My first trip to Millersburg. There are six buildings. Cay Miller is the founder of the town and proprietor of the store. I met Amalia Kruger, a rather unpleasant woman.

35

CHAPTER 3

A Monogrammed Lace Handkerchief

A friend loveth at all times, and
a brother is born for adversity.
Proverbs 17:17

Karyn walked nearly two miles before finally tiring and agreeing to ride in the wagon again. The walk settled her emotions, and she was glad that Mikal appeared willing to allow whatever it was that lay between them to remain dormant. As they drove along, Mikal explained, "Now we are going north and east to the Delhommes'. Between here and the route we came this morning is the Tappan Valley. There are no settlers between Millersburg and the Delhommes yet. You cannot tell, but we are slowly going uphill. The Delhommes live up on a great tableland called the French Table." He continued to describe the land for her, helping her to see in her mind that from Millersburg, north to his homestead, and then southeast to the Delhommes', then southwest back to Millersburg, formed a great triangle. The distance between each point of the triangle was almost equal. "Only twelve or fourteen kilometers." Karyn smiled, thinking that within the space of such a triangle in Germany, there were several villages nestled in the forest.

At last the team descended a low hill toward what Mikal called Clear Creek. As the wagon forded the creek, birds flitted in and about the thick undergrowth.

Mikal nodded toward the bushes. "A lot of wild fruit grows along the creeks here. Gooseberries, currants, chokecherries, buckberries, wild grapes, and plums."

"Celest said we could harvest them all together. She promised to show me how to use them all," Karyn offered. She wondered if Mikal had caught the hint that she might decide to stay longer. "Which do you like best, Mikal—jam, jelly, syrup for pancakes, or pie?"

"Ja!" Mikal answered. When Karyn laughed, he joined her, glad that the tension between them was finally gone.

Karyn asked, "Do you think any of the seedling trees would transplant? We could try some around the house."

"I want to do that, but I have been so busy tending and replanting trees on the timber claim that I have not managed it." He explained, "To finally get title to my tree claim, I must plant ten acres of timber, with trees no more than thirty-five meters apart, and keep them in growing condition for ten years. If I lived on that section, the requirements would be less, but then I would have had to give up on the homestead. So I just keep replanting trees there." He added, "Now that you are here"— then corrected himself—"if you decide to stay, we can certainly put some around the house. Perhaps even some fruit trees. Emile and Celest have an entire orchard of seedlings."

As the wagon pulled up a long, steady hill on the opposite side of the creek, Mikal said, "Already you have seen that Emile Delhomme is a very gracious man. He is also ambitious. Of his five sons, two already have their own homesteads on the opposite end of French Table from Emile's. Each one has taken a preemption, a homestead, and a timber claim. That means that between the three men, the Delhommes own over a thousand acres of America."

Karyn thought for a moment. "Can women get a preemption?"

Mikal looked at her, surprised.

"Don't seem so amazed," she shot back. "Since you have no sons, perhaps your wife could add to your holdings. Is it possible?"

Mikal shook his head. "Part of filing for the land is promising to live on it for five years."

The team was pulling them up a steep incline. At the top, they gave such a mighty heave that the wagon lurched and nearly threw Karyn off the seat. Mikal grabbed her, teasing, "One of the most basic skills of homesteading, Karyn, is not breaking your neck falling out of your wagon."

Karyn smoothed her apron and laughed with him. But the talk of preemptions and timber claims was interrupted as they drove up onto the plateau known as French Table. When Karyn said something about the unbroken distance, Mikal took the opportunity to mention a common phenomenon. "You might think you see a vast sea or a great city. Once I could have sworn there was a river with huge trees along its banks. It was only a mirage."

Shielding her eyes, Karyn pointed into the distance. "Is that what you meant? Is that castle a mirage?"

Mikal laughed. "No. That's very real. That is Emile and Celest Delhomme's home." While Karyn exclaimed over the size of the house, Mikal told her, "Cay handled the materials orders. He said Emile spent five hundred dollars on that house."

Karyn was speechless, contemplating the incredible expenditure of five hundred American dollars on a home. The closer she got to the house, the more she began to envy Celest Delhomme. Of course, it was made of sod, but such a mansion! Two stories tall, it had a wood, shingled roof from which protruded a brick chimney. The front boasted no less than six windows, a beautifully carved front door, and rounded turrets at each corner. It did, indeed, resemble a small castle.

"Karyn! Mikal!" Celest's voice called out through one of the windows. Turning to look for her, Karyn noted that Celest not only had six windows, she had windows with screen coverings.

Celest came hurrying out the door just as Emile and two of his sons rounded the corner of a huge barn nearby. Celest introduced her sons. Sunburned almost the color of his auburn hair, Remi bowed low, kissing the back of Karyn's hand. Celest rolled her eyes and laughed. "My son, the actor." She put her hand on Serge's shoulder as she introduced him. Not to be outdone by his brother, Serge clicked his heels and bowed low. He whispered something into Mikal's ear, and Mikal shoved him playfully.

"Boys, boys!" Celest intervened, scolding in French. Then, she turned to Karyn, switching almost in midsentence to German. "Who would believe they are all in their twenties! They behave like such children!" She appealed to Emile, "Get these young thugs to work, husband. There is hardly time before supper to get half the firebreak plowed."

Karyn and Celest headed for the house just as a huge black dog came tearing around the edge of the barn in hot pursuit of a yellow cat. "Frona! *Platz!*" Celest ordered. The dog dropped to the ground as if someone had shot her. Her chin in the dust, she looked up apologetically at Celest, stirring up clouds of dust as she beat the earth with her tail.

"All right, Frona. You are forgiven." Then Celest said to Karyn, "Do you like dogs? When Frona has puppies, you must have one. She protects the livestock as if they were her very own, but for some reason she has decided the house is her holy habitation. She won't let the cats set foot inside. She kills mice and rats herself—and I have no worry of rattlesnakes when Frona is here."

"Are rattlesnakes a problem?" Karyn asked.

"Not to frighten you unduly, but yes, you must always be watchful." Celest shook her head. "They wreak havoc among our sheep." The women paused just outside the front door of the house while Celest explained, "The first few warm days every year, the snakes come up out of the prairie-dog burrows where they have spent the winter. They bask in the warm sunshine for hours before slithering off. The men all congregate and have contests to see who can kill the most. This year they had their contest while Mikal was in Grand Island. Over one hundred rattlesnakes were killed." Celest nodded toward Frona. "That wonderful dog killed several on her own."

She pulled Karyn across the threshold and into the house. "Come in, come in. I chatter on and on. I am just getting ready to bake bread. You can help me knead it. Wait until you see what a huge mound of dough I have made up."

Celest glanced back at Frona, who had remained in her *platz* by the door. She didn't move, but she did continue to watch Celest hopefully. "*Komm,* Frona," Celest ordered. The dog rose and followed the women into the house. Celest led Karyn into the large kitchen, promising a tour of the other rooms as soon as the bread was kneaded and shaped.

Karyn removed her bonnet and sat down at a small table beside the kitchen window to catch her breath. Frona walked up slowly and laid her massive black head in Karyn's lap.

Celest nodded with approval. "Not everyone receives such a welcome. Obviously she approves of our neighbor's choice for a wife." Celest made her way toward the opposite wall of the kitchen where she checked the fire in the largest stove Karyn had ever seen. As the stove lid clattered back into place, Celest pulled a huge crock down from a shelf and scooped flour from one of three large barrels positioned underneath a row of shelves lining another wall. She set the crock beside a huge mound of dough on the table.

Frona had not moved. She waited patiently while Karyn scratched her ears. Without warning, Karyn began to cry. When she leaned over to hide her tears, Frona licked her. Karyn laughed, crying all the more in spite of herself.

Celest frowned. "What is this, dear Karyn? You must tell me." She crossed the kitchen to Karyn's side. Patting Frona on the head she pushed the dog gently away. "Frona. *Geh Weiter.*" The dog padded away, curling up in the corner of the kitchen from where she watched the two women carefully.

"It's nothing. Just homesickness, I guess." Karyn wiped the tears away and tried to get up. "Your bread. We must get to the kneading."

Celest pulled a wooden chair up beside Karyn. Handing her a beautiful lace handkerchief, she sat down and put one hand around Karyn's shoulders. "Not until I know the reason for these tears. What has suddenly made you so homesick?"

After studying the kitchen's spotless plank floor for a few moments, Karyn said softly, "Did you know that Mikal was married before?"

Celest didn't hesitate. "What of it? You should be happy that he is so open to tell you." She patted Karyn's hands. "Why worry over the distant past when the future holds such promise?"

"Because," Karyn choked out, "because Mikal is not the one who told me of another wife. I learned it in Millersburg today."

"Amalia Kruger!" Celest nearly spat the name out. "Oh, I should have warned you about that woman!"

Karyn shook her head. "Don't be angry with her, Celest. I think she had good intentions." She sighed. "You know, when I first saw the house Mikal expected me to live in, I wanted to get right back in the wagon and demand that he take me back to Grand Island. But he seemed so lonely." Karyn blushed. "He convinced me to stay for one month. He promised he would send me home if I did not want to stay after a month." She paused, moistening her lips before continuing. "Only—"

Celest interrupted. "—only now you see that Mikal has a good beginning on an excellent piece of land. You see that he will be a successful farmer some day." Celest added with a little laugh, "And I suspect that two weeks of living with that mane of black hair and those blue eyes have tempted you to do a little romantic dreaming."

Karyn looked down at her hands. "I am no fool, Celest. I do not expect that a man would fall in love with me in only two weeks." She blushed. "But I will admit that I have been doing some 'romantic dreaming,' as you call it." She swallowed hard. "I want to believe that he did not speak of Marie-Louise out of consideration for me. But after hearing what Mrs. Kruger had to say, I wonder if Mikal offered only partnership because he cannot offer more—because he will never be able to offer more." She took a deep breath and said, "I have been disappointed once in romance. I do not want to put myself in a situation to be hurt again."

Celest grasped both Karyn's hands and shook them as she said firmly, "Mikal offered partnership and demands nothing more because he is a man of integrity, Karyn. That kind of man does not take unless a woman offers with her whole heart." She released Karyn's hands and said, "Why did he not tell you about Marie-Louise? I do not know. Even after twenty-five years of marriage to Emile Delhomme, I would not presume to say that I understand the way a man thinks." She looked out the window to where the men were plowing. Then, her eyes overflowing with kindness, she said, "From what I know of Mikal, I do not think you should read anything sinister into this. I suspect that he wanted to avoid the possibility that you might feel threatened by his past with another woman—which is exactly how you have reacted. And he probably wanted to see how things go with the two of you. Why should he open old wounds and speak of the past if you decide not to stay?"

"Mrs. Kruger said that Mikal will never belong to me. She said that he belongs to the past."

Celest leaned forward. "Amalia Kruger is a very unhappy old woman who must live with a son and daughter-in-law who are not very kind. She is the one who belongs to the past. Listen to me, Karyn. She clings to the old ways as if they were holy. She was very happy living in Kansas in a little Germany where nothing American was forced upon her.

"Before Cay Miller came to begin his city, the post office was here in this house. I thought Amalia would choke the first time she was forced to actually come into my home and try to speak English to a Belgian regarding the American mail system. I know that she only spoke to me because there was no other way. She said as much to her son one day in my presence. I must confess that her attitude had already galled me so that I gave no hint of speaking German. I am sinful enough that I enjoyed making her struggle to speak English—and understanding her comments to her son without her knowledge.

"I could see her shake the dust from my yard off her heels—literally—every time she left. Of course after the post office was moved and she discovered that I speak German—" Celest broke off. "Well, that is another story. Let us just say that Amalia and I do not have tea together on a regular basis."

Taking a deep breath, Celest continued, "The Krugers came here after terrible disappointments in Kansas. Their only daughter, Ida, ran away to marry a man of whom they did not approve. Then Amalia's husband died on the way north. She is a bitter old woman who seems to take special delight in squelching other people's happiness. But you must not allow Amalia Kruger's gossip to ruin what you have begun with Mikal Ritter. And you must not assume the worst of Mikal. He deserves better. Give him time to tell you about Marie-Louise in his own way. Keep your heart open. You just might be rewarded with a friendship that blossoms into love."

Celest stood up. "Now. To work."

The two women began to punch and knead Celest's mound of dough. They shaped a half dozen round loaves and six dozen rolls and left them to rise in the kitchen while Celest showed Karyn the rest of the impressive house. They went upstairs first, where a central hall stretched the length of the house. Off the hallway to the left was Emile and Celest's room and a bedroom converted into an office for Emile. Along the other side of the hallway were three more bedrooms, each one furnished with sturdy, handmade furniture, each bed adorned by a lovely woven spread or quilt.

Celest was almost apologetic about the size of the rooms. "I told Emile we didn't need anything nearly so fine, but once he began building, he seemed to get such joy out of the process, I could not refuse him."

Celest told Karyn about each of her sons. Thierry and Pascal were both married and had their own homesteads. "You met Serge and Remi." Love for her boys shone in her eyes. "They are incorrigible, but they are good boys. Their younger brother Luc is staying with Thierry for a few weeks. He is my baby. Only nineteen. Very quiet. Completely unlike his older brothers."

Having inspected the upstairs bedrooms, the women made their way downstairs. The dining room boasted beautiful rag rugs over polished wood floors. When Karyn commented on the rugs, Celest explained, "Cay Miller carries the warp. Keep all your worn-out clothing. You tear it into strips so wide"—Celest held her fingers apart to show the proper width of the strip—"sew those strips together, and then roll them into balls." She bent to pick up a ball of strips from a basket in the corner. "Then, the strips are woven through the carpet warp. This makes sections about a meter wide. Once the sections are sewn together, you have a beautiful rug created out of worthless old clothes! That is the American way. Everything is used, and used up, and used again."

"It will be some time before we have enough worn-out clothing for a rug," Karyn said. "But of all the things about that house I dislike, the floor is the worst. I have been wondering . . . do you know if anyone has tried mixing clay with straw to make a hard floor? My father once described some process like that, but I have forgotten exactly how he said it was done."

"I don't know anyone who has done that," Celest said thoughtfully. "But the clay we used for plastering these walls would surely work as well for a floor." She was suddenly enthusiastic. "I can help you. When Luc comes back from Thierry's, he and I will come over. The boys can get a load of clay from the buffalo wallow."

"Oh, no," Karyn protested. "I didn't mean—"

Celest interrupted her. "Now you listen, Karyn. You must get used to how we do things here. We help one another. You help me with bread-baking; I help you with a new floor. You help me with harvesting and drying wild fruit; I help you with sewing. Do you need any wool?" They were near the back door of the house, and Celest led the way outside and into a lean-to attached to the house. Karyn wrinkled her nose at the strong odors emanating from the room. In the corner stood two gigantic spinning wheels.

Celest grinned, picking up a thick wool pelt. "The shearing this spring yielded a wonderful supply. I have managed to wash only a part of it. There is wool to be washed, wool to be carded, spun, dyed." She held out a wad of wool to Karyn. "Perhaps you can help me experiment with some of the local plants for dyes. Do you need wool for knitting? You can have as much as you want if you will knit a pair of socks for the boys once in a while." She leaned toward Karyn and whispered, "Don't tell Emile, but I despise knitting. And since he brought home a sewing machine, I really cannot seem to make myself knit."

Celest led the way out of the lean-to and back into the house. In the parlor, a sewing machine stood just inside the largest window at the front of the house. But Karyn gave the sewing machine only a cursory glance, staring instead at a walnut reed organ that stood against the opposite wall from the doorway. "I never expected to see an organ so far away from—"

"—civilization?" Celest chuckled as she finished Karyn's sentence. "Well, our son Luc seemed to have music inside him from the day he was born. Emile thought an organ would be a nice addition to the community. He was right. The boys often haul the organ into the wagon and take it to dances. Emile plays the violin, and he is finally beginning to learn the American music so that he can play the dances. He and Luc play very well together."

Through the window Karyn caught a glimpse of green. Celest said, "Would you like to see the garden?"

The two women went through the kitchen, out the back door, and around the lean-to where Celest had planted a huge garden inside a wall of sod. She explained, "It isn't a very attractive fence, but it keeps the tiny shoots safe from marauding wildlife and the relentless wind. Has anyone told you what they say about the wind here?" Celest chuckled. "Hang a log chain outside your window. If it stands out at a forty-five-degree angle, there's a mild breeze. If the chain is horizontal to the earth, the wind is blowing."

Leaning on the top of the fence, Celest reminisced. "One of the most difficult things for me when we first came here—besides the wind—was simply dealing with the space just outside my door. As far as I could see there was grass and more grass, sky and more sky. Some days, I thought I would get crushed between them. I felt that there was no place for me to simply *be*. After a while, I began to notice that there were ways to divide the space in my mind. A buffalo trail divides the north of the tableland from the south. Clear Creek divides the table from the valley. My fence divides the prairie from my garden. And," she said, pointing to the horizon where the men were working, "the firebreak divides the yard from the prairie."

"Have you seen a prairie fire?" Karyn asked.

Celest nodded. "It's terrifying. The flames race along, destroying everything in their path. But then out of the ruins comes lush, new growth." Celest smiled. "Another one of God's lessons. Sometimes what seems ruinous to our human eyes is only God burning away the weeds so that new life can begin."

She touched Karyn's arm and nodded toward the barn. "Let me show you the rest of the homestead." She led Karyn toward the barn and a small chicken house. As the two women stood outside the wire enclosure where a fine flock of hens was kept safe from coyotes, Celest shared, "Emile and I have been here only three years, Karyn. It will not be that long before you have your own flock, your own herds, your own garden. Even your own sewing machine. Did I hear Mikal say that his cow is due to calve soon?" When Karyn nodded, Celest suggested, "Cay Miller will buy all the butter and cheese you can take him. I think he pays almost fifteen cents for every pound of butter and as much for a dozen eggs."

Karyn said, "At home I earned extra money by sewing for women who frequented Papa's store."

Celest finished Karyn's thought. "You can be as busy as you like sewing for other women. Cay can order you a very good machine from Montgomery Ward for less than twenty dollars. He has the catalog in his store. And you are welcome to use my machine until you have your own."

Karyn looked back toward where the men were plowing. It looked as though they were making very slow progress. "Is it really necessary to have such wide furrows?"

"In the fall, when things are dry, lightning, an ember from a campfire, sparks from a train—anything can start a fire. They can burn for days. And believe me, when twelve-foot-high flames come roaring toward you faster than a running horse, you thank God—and the men who plowed—for those furrows with burned earth between them."

Karyn was horrified. Celest encouraged her. "No prairie fire can burn through three-foot-thick walls of sod." She smiled wisely.

"But Mikal's roof is wood, as is yours."

Celest laughed. "Well, then, I suppose we would have to hide in the cistern!" She hastened to reassure. "Don't worry, Karyn. We always get a warning. From your house high on the ridge, you could see a big fire coming for three nights before it reached you. The flames light up the night sky in a wonderful, terrible golden light." She added, "A very wide and deep creek separates Mikal's home from any potential fire. With the creek and a firebreak, you have no cause to worry." She changed the subject abruptly, nodding toward the men. "Mikal seems to be enjoying our new team."

"They are magnificent," Karyn agreed.

"English shires. The Irvine brothers have just begun importing them." Celest laughed softly. "I was afraid to ask Emile what he paid for them." She sighed. "Let's get the fire going for supper. I'll bake some potatoes."

As night fell, Karyn lay on her back atop the beautiful quilts that adorned Celest's guest room bed, staring at the ceiling. She was trying her best to relax the knot in her stomach, but it would not go. At the sound of footsteps coming down the hall, she clutched her hands nervously. When the footsteps stopped outside the bedroom door, Karyn leaped to her feet.

Mikal ducked and entered the room. He tossed his hat on the chair just behind the door and closed the door before saying, "Thank you."

"Thank you? For what?" Karyn asked.

As he talked, Mikal was spreading a quilt he usually carried in the back of his wagon on the floor beside the bed. "Thank you for giving no hint of our agreement in the presence of Remi and Serge. They would never have let me hear the end of it." He stretched out on the quilt and put his hands behind his head. "Remi and Serge fancy themselves Romeos, and they were quite vocal about their opinion of my signing that letter to Brandenburg. Of course"—he lifted his head enough to see her over the edge of the mattress and smiled—"now that they have met you, they are probably wishing they had joined me in the adventure." He settled back on the floor. "Thank you. And good night."

Karyn lay back down on the bed. Presently, she moved toward the center of the mattress and peered down where Mikal lay. He had turned on his side and tucked one arm beneath his head. "For heaven's sake, Mikal. Take a pillow." She dropped a pillow on top of him. Then she got up and pulled the top quilt off the bed. Walking around the foot of the bed she spread the quilt over him. "And a quilt."

"Quiet, you two newlyweds!" someone shouted as they pounded loudly on the door.

There was uproarious laughter and then Celest's voice could be heard whispering intensely in French. Serge answered in an apologetic tone, but Celest repeated herself angrily and then closed her door. The boys' footsteps retreated down the hall, but not before there was a good deal more snickering and whispering just outside Mikal and Karyn's door.

As soon as the boys' voices quieted down, someone knocked softly on the door. It was Celest, with another blanket. She whispered, "Use this on the floor, Mikal. I am sorry I do not have another feather bed," and then crept back across the hall.

Mikal settled on the floor while Karyn lay back on the mattress, unable to relax, horrified by the realization that she was going to have to sneak out of the room and "out back" before the night was over. She waited for a long time, until Mikal's breathing grew even. Then, she picked her way around the end of the bed and made for the door. She prayed that the floorboards would not creak and awaken Mikal. The floorboards didn't creak, but Mikal was awakened anyway when Karyn tripped over his feet and nearly fell on top of him.

"What?!" Mikal started up. "What is it? What's wrong?"

Karyn could barely control her embarrassed laughter. "It's nothing. Except that I forgot you are so tall and I failed to allow for your feet sticking out at the end of the bed. I just need to—" She couldn't say it.

Mikal understood immediately. He bent his legs at the knees. "My feet are out of the way now. Go along."

Completely mortified, Karyn made her way downstairs and "out back." When she returned, Mikal had turned over in a vain attempt to get comfortable.

"Mikal," Karyn whispered as she closed the door. "This is ridiculous. I am used to sharing a bed with three of my sisters. I can certainly share it with you. Please. Come up off the floor."

Mikal hefted his frame up and onto the very edge of the bed.

He turned his back so that Karyn would have as much privacy as possible.

"You must be very tired. I am sorry I insisted on walking alongside the wagon today. We could have arrived here earlier and perhaps the plowing could have been completed. You could have slept in your own bed tonight."

"Do you mind telling me what happened in Millersburg to make you so angry with me?"

"It was nothing important," she lied. "Things are very different from what I expected. Very different from the railroad booklet I saw at home. Different from the letters sent to Brandenburg about America."

Mikal asked, "Tell me more about Brandenburg. I only marched through it on the way to France. And tell me more about your family."

Lying on her back in the dark, Karyn told Mikal about her life in Germany. "We live on a small farm just outside of town. But the farming is really only something Papa does for amusement. He is a merchant with a store in Brandenburg. I am the oldest daughter. Then comes Sophie. When she is well she is lively and fun, but unfortunately she is often sick and unable to work in the store. She sews beautifully, and together we used to make garments for the women who shopped in Papa's store. After Sophie is Jette, then Vroni. Jette is engaged to be married. Vroni says she is coming to America as soon as she can, but not to get married. Vroni wants to teach music." Then, Karyn surprised herself by describing Anton Gilhoff.

"So you came to America to escape one husband and ended up trapped in a dark room with another."

Karyn wasn't certain, but she thought Mikal's tone was teasing. She bantered back through the darkness. "With one little exception. This husband agrees to let me have some say in my future. Anton Gilhoff would never be so considerate."

"Which brings me to the matter of my working for Cay Miller. Our agreement was that you would stay one month. If I go to work for Cay, I must leave in a few days to get the lumber in Kearney. Then there is the time to help Cay with the building. It

49

is hardly a way for us to get to know one another. And I will probably still be away when our agreement expires."

"I am not afraid to be alone, Mikal," Karyn said, hoping she sounded more certain than she felt.

He sounded relieved. "Cay Miller has offered to buy as many cedar posts as I can cut. That requires a trip to the cedar canyons west of here. But once I have the money from Cay for the building and for the cedar posts, then I will need to go to Kearney—or perhaps even Grand Island—to get provisions for the spring and summer."

"Does the wife always stay behind?" she asked.

"Someone must care for the livestock."

"I will be fine, Mikal. There is no need for you to worry over me."

"Does that mean you have already decided to stay past a month?" Mikal asked abruptly.

Even in the dark, Karyn could feel her cheeks growing red. "It means that I see no reason for me to abandon you when I can be of help."

Mikal mumbled, "Good." Presently his even breathing indicated he had fallen asleep. Karyn turned on her side. Mikal had drawn his knees up to keep his feet from sticking off the end of the bed. Moonlight coming in the window made his long black hair shine. Karyn watched him for a long time before finally closing her eyes and falling asleep.

The Diary
April 15, 1880

Mikal is to be gone. I have agreed to stay past the month. It will be strange to be alone in my own home. I do not ever remember that happening before. It appears that women here are often alone. I will adapt. I must learn to speak English as soon as possible. Celest promises me one of Frona's puppies. Already she is a good and wise friend. There are poisonous snakes in this area. I pray to God that I never see one.

CHAPTER 4

Knitting Needles

She looketh well to the ways of her household,
and eateth not the bread of idleness.
Proverbs 31:27

Eager to show her self-reliance and to banish any possible comparison between herself and Marie-Louise, Karyn sounded almost angry when, on the ride home from the Delhommes', Mikal expressed renewed doubts about working for Cay Miller. Impatience sounded in her voice when she insisted, "I can certainly feed and water a cow and a pig, Mikal."

Mikal looked at her soberly. "I know that. But being alone here—you don't know what it's like."

"Planning the garden will take some time. Then I can walk to the creek and dig up some seedlings and plant them around the house. I have promised to do some knitting for Celest. I will be so busy I will hardly miss you—except to be grateful that I do not have to cook so much." Mikal seemed to be weakening, so she continued, "And besides that, I will not be alone. I will have Ella and the sow." She teased, "I shall give the sow a name, and if I get desperate I can walk to Celest's."

Mikal expressed doubt about her visiting without him. "You are too new to the country. It is very easy to get lost."

Karyn tossed her head. "From our doorstep it is not so difficult to follow the valley for the first few kilometers. Then there

51

is that huge ridge of boulders sticking up out of the earth. After that, there is a clump of trees right on the edge of a canyon. Then down to cross Clear Creek, and up the long grade onto the tableland. From the tableland, you can see the house—like a mirage—in the distance. And if I make a mistake so that I cannot see the house, I will wait until sundown and look for the lantern shining from the top of the cedar pole right in Celest's front yard."

Mikal was impressed. "You paid attention."

Karyn forced herself to sound much more confident than she felt. "You said that you could earn enough from Cay to make a good down payment on a pair of horses like Emile's. I will not be carried about like an uncooked egg in danger of cracking. If my presence here is a hindrance to your doing what needs to be done, then you should send me home." Hearing herself express such an independent attitude encouraged her. She finished her speech with bravado, "Go do the work for Cay Miller, cut your fence posts—and I expect to see a beautiful team of shires pulling this wagon when you come back."

Finally, Mikal was convinced, although he made an unspoken promise to himself to have Emile check in on Karyn from time to time.

When the day came for him to leave, Mikal spent the morning repeating instructions he had already given several times before. He reminded Karyn about the lantern. "Be certain you light it and leave it in the window. Someone lost on the prairie will know where to get help." Then he handed her a rifle. "And keep this beside you. Any strangers needing help are welcome to sleep down in the dugout. Just make certain they see the rifle. And make them think you know how to use it."

Karyn reached for the rifle, checking to make certain it was loaded. When Mikal looked surprised, she said simply, "We do have guns in Brandenburg, Mikal. Papa liked to hunt."

So it was that Karyn Ritter (in name only) stood one morning barely two weeks after her arrival in Nebraska, watching as the distance swallowed up the last trace of Mikal and his team. In only a few moments she washed the dishes from their simple breakfast and made her way outside to the spot just northeast of the house where Mikal had said they would have a garden. Karyn leaned against the side of the house, inspecting the area. She made a mental list, imagining rows of beets, tomatoes, potatoes, melons, cabbage, cucumbers, carrots, muskmelon, turnips, and beans. She imagined sod walls like those around Celest's garden, and stepped off the space where she would ask Mikal to build them. Rummaging about in the dugout, she found a pile of stakes. She marked the fence line by forcing a sharp spade through the sod and inserting a stake in each slit.

Standing up to survey her efforts, Karyn smiled to herself. *Only two weeks ago you agreed to stay no longer than one month. Now your husband is to be gone for at least two weeks, and you are planning a garden.* She made her way back down the slope and to the corral, where Ella the Jersey cow stood patiently chewing her cud. At Karyn's approach, Ella thrust her head through the fence, waiting to have her ears scratched. When Karyn lingered near the dugout barn, Ella protested. Karyn laughed. "All right, Ella. I come." She scratched the heifer behind the ears. Next, she hauled a few buckets full of fresh water from the well behind the house.

For the remainder of the morning, Karyn wandered aimlessly about the homestead, from the soddy to the dugout barn, into the barn to contemplate living there, and back to the soddy. She took up a rag and dusted the rough-hewn furniture inside the soddy. Looking out the window, she was inspired to open her trunk and withdraw what was supposed to be another feather tick. She had packed it, imagining that geese would be plentiful in the countryside. Chuckling at her ignorance, she measured the little window where the tiny geranium from Celest sat. It had new sprouts along both stems, and Karyn found herself looking forward to the day when her own window would be filled with blooming plants. The afternoon was taken up with the transformation of part of the empty feather tick into curtains for the window.

Evening came on. As the sun slipped below the horizon and twilight sent shadows across the landscape, Karyn became newly aware of her aloneness. She slipped down the slope to the corral, fed and watered Ella and the sow, and hurried back up the slope to the soddy. She lit the lamp and placed it in the window. She didn't feel hungry, but she wasn't tired either, and it was too early to go to bed. Far off to the northwest, wolves were howling. A breeze made the quilt hanging over the door swing to and fro. Karyn dismantled part of her cupboard and weighted the bottom of the quilt down with two crates. For added security, she braced a chair against the crates. She looked nervously about her.

Finally, she settled by the lamp in the window and took up her knitting. Celest had given her a basketful of yarn with the promise of more to come. Once she started knitting, Karyn relaxed. She began to hum. Having added several rows to the knitted sock in her lap, she looked about her, thinking with longing of the organ in the Delhommes' parlor. Her fingers moved soundlessly over an imaginary keyboard for a few measures. Then, she returned to her knitting.

Karyn spent the morning of her first full day alone on her homestead transplanting seedlings from the creek bed to the yard around the house. With a basket in one hand and a shovel in the other, she headed for the creek. Extracting even twelve-inch-high seedlings from the sod required a surprising amount of effort. Time and again, she failed to get enough roots to ensure successful transplanting. But finally she had about two dozen promising seedlings in the basket. She spent the afternoon planting: two cottonwoods a few feet from the front door of the soddy; a row of what she hoped were elms along the path down the slope toward the corral; and hackberry trees for the opposite side of the corral.

In the corral, Ella had been moving about restlessly for quite some time. "What is wrong, Ella?" Karyn worried. She drew fresh water, offered more grain, but Ella could not be appeased. She continued to pace about the corral until suddenly, she went down on one side. Karyn was nearly frantic, until she realized what was happening.

Totally ignorant of what to do, Karyn looked about her for a reason to stay nearby. She found it in the dugout barn. She hauled Mikal's bedding out into the sunshine, draping the blankets and a quilt over the fence to air. Pumping more water, she hauled a bucketful into the barn and began to scrub every square inch of wood inside. She emptied ashes from the small stove and polished it until it shone. She spent the rest of the morning pretending to work, when in reality she was continually poking her head out the door to check on Ella. Finally, after what seemed like an eternity, Karyn watched as a perfectly formed calf slid into the world.

Instantly, Ella was on her feet, mooing contentedly, licking her calf. Karyn laughed with relief. "Good work, Ella. You can be very proud of yourself." At the sound of Karyn's voice, Ella looked over her shoulder and flicked an ear as if to agree with her. Then, she turned back to nuzzle her calf.

Karyn watched happily as mother and calf got acquainted and was delighted when the calf rose on spindly legs, searched and found her target, and nursed greedily. Karyn went back to work in Mikal's dugout, with visions of milk and butter and cheese dancing in her head. As soon as she finished her cleaning, she walked up the slope to the soddy, intending to drag the churn out into the yard and ready it for use. But she had just wrestled the churn to the door when a wagon drove up. Celest sat beside the driver, a young man about Karyn's age.

As Celest introduced her son Luc, Karyn nodded and reached up to shake his hand even as she announced the birth of Ella's calf. "Can you make certain everything is all right?" She started down the slope, followed by Luc and Celest. With a few quiet words to Ella, Luc stepped into the corral, checked things over, and assured Karyn that all was well. "That's a good-size calf," he offered in German. "You will have some good steaks from him."

"You have been planting trees," Celest observed, nodding toward the seedlings around the corral.

"Mikal said he meant to plant some last year, but he was too busy on the tree claim to have the time to water them. I thought I would try." Karyn was uncomfortably aware that Luc had noticed the bedding airing along the corral fence. She said vaguely, "I found these old things in the dugout. I can put them back now."

"Come and see what we have brought you today," Celest said, walking back up the hill toward the house.

Karyn hastily folded Mikal's bedding and restored it to its place inside the dugout. When she came out, Luc was pouring water into a gigantic wooden tub just outside the door. Smiling at Karyn, he climbed up into the wagon box and began to shovel gray clay into the tub.

Celest explained, "We've brought your plaster. This clay and the sand toward the back of the wagon, mixed with water, will make a good plaster for the walls. With all three of us working, it shouldn't take long. Then we can try your mixture on the floor. Emile and the boys will meet us at the buffalo wallow again in the morning to shovel more clay. If we work hard, we might be finished by tomorrow night."

"I cannot ask you to spend so much time away from your own home," Karyn protested.

"You didn't ask. I offered to help you. Emile and the boys are perfectly willing to have me gone. They are grown men. I left plenty of fresh bread. They can have scrambled eggs for breakfast and whatever game they can shoot for supper. They will be fine."

Luc reassured Karyn, "We grew up learning to fend for ourselves, Mrs. Ritter. Mama is often called to tend to a sick neighbor." He smiled affectionately at his mother. "She has been the only doctor in this part of the county since we arrived."

Luc ducked inside the soddy and emerged with the crates Karyn had used to block her doorway the preceding night. "Mikal already smoothed the walls," he said to his mother, "which saves us a lot of time." He set to work without giving Karyn any further opportunity to protest.

Together Celest, Karyn, and Luc hauled the few pieces of furniture out of the soddy. Luc mixed sand, clay, and water to just the right consistency. Then, he hauled bucketfuls of the mixture inside for Celest and Karyn to smear on the walls. As the walls were gradually covered with plaster, Karyn began to feel excited about the improvement. *What a difference this makes!*

When it came time for Karyn to feed the animals, Luc insisted she and Celest rest. He handed them both a cup of water and made his way down the hill.

"What a fine boy," Karyn said. *"Er kann gut Deutsch."*

Celest nodded. "Yes. He does speak good German. Luc is unlike his brothers in every way. He has applied himself well as a student." She smiled. "I poured all of my schooling into Luc. Latin, German, the classics . . . and he eagerly absorbed everything I could give him. Now he is counting the days until he can leave and learn even more. He hopes to study music. After this year's crop, the money should be there," Celest explained. "His father offered to help, but Luc insists he will pay his own way. He is raising his own beef and hiring out to his married brothers and anyone else who needs help. If all goes well, he will be at a conservatory in Philadelphia this time next year. He hopes to teach."

As Luc headed back up the hill and began to mix more clay, Karyn asked Celest to accompany her around the back of the house where she had dug a little opening in the hillside. Inside, she had started a fire and now only glowing coals remained. With an iron poker, she raked the coals out of the space. "I want to see if this will work like an oven." She placed a pan of corn bread into the hole, then put a piece of tin over the opening and raked the coals over the improvised oven door. In an hour, Celest and Luc and Karyn were feasting on fresh bread.

"And soon," Karyn mused, "there will be fresh milk! Life is good."

As the sky changed from orange to dark violet, Luc spread a blanket under the wagon. Celest and Karyn headed for the dugout.

Early the next morning, Luc drove off in the direction of the buffalo wallow. While he was gone the two women mixed up the last of the clay and began plastering. They were hard at work, when Luc returned with the wagon full of fresh clay. Celest rushed outside while Karyn continued smoothing plaster around the corner where the bed-box jutted out from the walls of the soddy.

At noon, when Karyn headed down the slope with a pail of

fresh water, she was amazed to see a bay pony trotting around the corral. Luc and Celest came up behind her.

"She's a gentle little thing," Luc explained. "She won't give you any trouble."

Celest added, "She is worth about ten dollars, Karyn. I hope you will accept her in payment for the knitting you agreed to do for my men."

Karyn looked from the pony to Luc to Celest and back again.

Luc spoke up. "Perhaps we should have asked if you know how to ride."

"Not very well," Karyn admitted.

"Then she is the perfect pony for you," Luc said. "She has not one evil bone in her little body. Thierry broke her himself for his children to ride. He mentioned trading her for something a little more lively. The timing was perfect."

Celest asked, "You did say you don't mind knitting for the men?" When Karyn nodded, she offered, "Cay Miller charges a dollar for a pair of good German socks and fifty cents for mittens. What do you say we agree that you will knit a pair of socks and a pair of mittens for each of my men?"

Karyn nodded, swallowing hard. "Thank you." She was embarrassed by the tears that sprung to her eyes. "You are so kind, I hardly know what to say."

Luc grinned at her and said, "The truth is, Mrs. Ritter, our motive is not completely unselfish. We are having a dance next Friday, and you must come. If you ride Sugar, that saves us from having to pick you up, which means more time for dancing!"

Karyn smiled back at him. She asked Celest, "What is *danke* in English, please?"

" 'Thank you,' " Celest answered.

With a thick German accent, Karyn said to Luc, "Thank you." Her cheeks blushed crimson with embarrassment. Luc nodded and smiled.

The Delhomme men made two more trips to the buffalo wallow, and Celest, Karyn, and Luc worked a day longer than they had anticipated, but at the end of Karyn's first week without

Mikal, she stood at the doorway of the soddy and surveyed the plastered walls with pride.

Serge and Remi had arrived one day to teach Karyn how to saddle Sugar. They demonstrated her gentle nature by crawling under the little mare several times, pulling her tail, and lifting her feet. Karyn was reminded of a circus horse she had seen at home that patiently allowed a trained monkey to scamper over the entire surface of its body without budging. When the Delhommes finally headed for home, Karyn kissed each one on both cheeks, using her new English vocabulary to thank each one personally. She watched as their wagon disappeared into the distance, her heart filled with gratitude.

It was nearly dawn before Karyn managed to get to sleep. She blamed her insomnia on the insistent howling of coyotes. As soon as the morning light illuminated the interior of the soddy well enough for Karyn to see, she opened her trunk. Pulling out the lace tablecloth and the china, she set them aside. Then, ever so carefully, she brought out the object of her night's musings. She held it to her, wishing for a mirror like the one in Mama's room at home, a mirror before which she could stand and pose. She had had no thought of wearing it until Luc had mentioned that Mikal might surprise them all by returning in time for the dance. Anticipating Mikal's homecoming, Karyn had spent the greater part of the night imagining the look in his blue eyes when he saw her in her rose-colored silk ball gown.

The Diary
April 21, 1880
   What a blessing good friends are! The walls of my house
are plastered, and I have a floor I can sweep. I have
planted trees. Cottonwood (I think) by the house, elm and
hackberry (I hope) by the corral. Ella has a new calf. I have
begun to learn English. There is to be a dance at the
Delhommes' next Friday. I will wear the rose ball gown,
hoping to see M. The week ahead looms before me as vast
and empty as the prairie around my little house.

CHAPTER 5

Rose-Colored Silk

For jealousy is the rage of a man.
Proverbs 6:34

"Ouch—that was my ear!" Celest giggled like a girl as she reached up to touch the red spot on her ear. She and Karyn were in the kitchen of the Delhomme home, alternately heating a slate pencil and then using it to curl their hair.

Karyn already had a fringe of curls about her face. "I apologize. I am so nervous my hands are shaking."

"There is nothing to be nervous about. It's a party. You will have a wonderful time."

"So many new faces, so many new languages." Karyn asked, "Will everyone speak English?"

"Well," Celest responded, "everyone—except of course Amalia Kruger—will try. Really, Karyn, you have no reason to be so worried. There will be a few other Germans. And everyone, but Cay Miller and Emile and I, is fairly new to Custer County. Many are still learning English just like you. Everyone will be anxious to visit and get to know one another—to get to know you." She reassured Karyn, "Good food and dancing do much to cross language barriers."

Dancing! Karyn had not contemplated that. Here was a new

reason to be nervous. She began to reheat the slate pencil in her hand before asking, "Will they do any German dances?"

Celest nodded. "Of course. German, English—at least one Danish trekant. But if Fred Smith is there, we will have a caller, and that means many, many good American square dances. You will love it. It's very lively."

"A 'caller'?" Karyn asked dubiously as she wrapped another bunch of Celest's gray hair around the pencil.

"Oh, you will see," Celest answered. She stood up and took Karyn's hand. "Come now. It's time to get dressed, and I want to see my foolish old self in a mirror."

The two women ascended to Celest's bedroom, where what the mirror revealed of her new hairstyle made Celest blush with pleasure. She reached up to touch her curled bangs. Peering into the mirror, she squinted and turned her head from side to side. "I wonder if Emile will even notice."

The women turned their backs to one another as they donned an array of petticoats and undergarments. Then, there was the rustle of black and rose silk as they pulled their best dresses on. Reaching for a cameo that lay atop her dresser, Celest turned toward the mirror. "Oh, Karyn," she exclaimed softly. "How lovely you look! That color makes your skin glow."

Standing before Celest Delhomme's full-length mirror, Karyn smoothed the bodice of her rose-colored silk gown. "Do you really think so? I hope it is not overdoing to wear it. When you said that Cay Miller would certainly leave a note for him, I hoped that Mikal might come, after all." She smiled softly. "I wanted to surprise him."

Celest raised her eyebrows. "Has he never seen you in this gown?"

Karyn shook her head. "No. I had planned to wear my other gown the day we met, but then—" She told how she had given the dress to Ida. "And then there was no time to press this one. So I met Mikal wearing a plain green calico."

"Well, it obviously made no difference to Mikal. And it will make this evening more special if he does, indeed, arrive." Celest smiled warmly. "Every young husband should see his

61

bride in such a beautiful gown, with the glow of anticipation on her face. It is a vision he would cherish."

Karyn smiled hopefully. "Do you really think he would come all this way for a dance after such a long journey?"

"Look in the mirror again, Karyn," Celest insisted. "And tell me which you think Mikal would choose—unloading lumber or seeing you."

Karyn inspected herself again in the mirror. She turned sideways, admiring the way the gown draped softly down the back with a fullness that served to accentuate the cinched-in waistline. Her eyes met Celest's in the mirror, and she smiled. "But he probably won't be back in time."

"In that event, my three boys will keep you busy dancing." She motioned to Karyn. "Come. I want to make certain Serge and Remi made enough lemonade."

As Celest and Karyn emerged from the house and headed toward where the men had erected a bowery over the dance "floor" in the front yard, Emile stopped tuning his violin and gave full attention to his wife. Early in the Delhomme marriage, after only a few unhappy drives home, Emile wisely realized that telling his wife she was already beautiful, that insisting she needed no improvements, was totally unsatisfying in light of her careful preparations for dances and literaries. In the interest of marital harmony, he decided it would be worthwhile to make a study of his wife. Thus, the moment Celest arrived at his side, Emile kissed her on the cheek and said, "I have always loved the natural waves in your hair, dear, but these new curls are most attractive. I shall have to watch that old bachelor Fred Smith very closely, or he will be stealing you away from me."

Blushing with pleasure, Celest pushed him away. "Don't be silly, Emile. It's nothing. Karyn insisted I let her try to give me a few curls. I feel rather foolish." She reached up to touch the curls. "Do you really like it? You don't think I'm too old?"

"You, my dear," Emile said softly, putting his arm about her, "will never be old."

Celest patted his hand on her waist and held it there for a moment before turning her attention back to the party. Wagons were beginning to come into view from several directions. Just as Celest said, "The boys had better get the organ out here," Remi and Serge heaved the instrument through the doorway. With Luc's help, they positioned it near the bowery. Luc sat down at the organ, and Emile finished tuning his violin.

Karyn stood next to Celest, surprised at how excited she was as she peered at a wagon approaching from the direction of Millersburg. *It's only Cay,* she told herself. *Mikal told you the drive to Kearney and back would take at least a week. There is very little chance he will be back. And even if he is, he will be too tired to drive so many miles just to see you.*

Even as Karyn Ritter was peering toward Millersburg, Mikal was making his way to his homestead. Unaware of the social at the Delhommes', anxious to know how Karyn had fared for an entire week alone, he had decided to bypass Millersburg completely in favor of a brief stop at his homestead. He drove his team only a half mile to the east of Millersburg, but he missed meeting Cay Miller's buggy heading toward the Delhommes', and he missed reading Cay Miller's notice regarding the dance. Mikal arrived at his homestead near sunset.

When Karyn did not come outside to greet him, a lump rose in his throat. Thinking of Marie-Louise, he called Karyn's name and jumped from the wagon seat. Hurrying down the slope to the corral, he took notice of Ella's calf with a flicker of satisfaction. He stood with his hands on his hips and called for Karyn again and again. Ella walked across the corral and poked her head through the fence. Mikal ignored her, hurrying back up the hill. Finally, he noticed the row of hackberry seedlings by the corral and the cottonwoods near the house. The knot in his stomach relaxed even more when he saw Karyn's new "oven" and the results of her garden plans. *She wants a sod wall like Celest has,* he reasoned, walking along the row of stakes toward the front of the house.

At the doorway of his house, Mikal stopped short. *Plastered, whitewashed walls.* He stepped inside and stopped again. Bending down, he felt the textured surface of the floor. *She mixed clay with straw.* Where had that idea come from? And how had she accomplished so much in such a short time? Examining the

63

walls carefully, he realized that Karyn's inexperienced hands could never have accomplished such an excellent result. A flash of color made him turn his head, and he looked toward the window, smiling at the windowsill now crowded with potted geraniums. Obviously Emile Delhomme had done significantly more than just "look in on" Karyn. The Delhommes had hauled clay in from the buffalo wallow and stayed long enough to plaster the interior walls.

It would be like Celest to insist that Karyn come home with them for a visit. What better time for the two women to get to know one another? What better time for Celest to teach Karyn more about frontier living? Perhaps she would even help with Karyn's English. Heaven knows he had had little opportunity for that. Looking down at the floor, Mikal smiled at yet another example of Karyn's ingenuity. *She may not realize it yet, but she is exactly the kind of woman this county needs.*

As Mikal considered that Karyn was also proving to be exactly the kind of woman that he needed, disappointment set in. He really had been looking forward to seeing her. He stepped outside the sod house and looked toward where Ella lay in the corral, contentedly chewing her cud. Walking to the well, he drew a bucket of water for the team. Then he noticed an extra rope tied to the windlass, running over the edge of the curbing and down into the well. He drew up a bucket containing two well-wrapped rounds of butter. His stomach rumbled, and he took one round out, lowered the bucket back into the well, and headed for the grub box in the wagon. There was still half a loaf of stale bread in the box. Mikal slathered it with butter and ate with relish.

After he had eaten, he watered the newly planted seedlings. Wandering into the dugout barn, he was met with another surprise when he realized that the crude furnishings had been scrubbed. Even the bedding seemed fresh.

His disappointment at Karyn's absence growing, Mikal considered driving to the Delhommes' even as he realized the lunacy of having the team haul a load of lumber such a distance when they had already come many miles farther than necessary. He considered unhitching the team and leaving them overnight while he went to see Karyn. Cay Miller could certainly wait an extra day for the lumber. But his sense of responsibility to Cay finally won out. Going back inside the soddy, he pulled the packets of garden seed he had bought in Kearney out of his pocket and laid them on the table where Karyn would see them. Then, he went back outside and climbed up onto the wagon seat. With a last glance of regret at the empty soddy, he headed back toward Millersburg.

Luc Delhomme claimed the right to the first dance with Karyn. She shook her head. "But I know nothing of these American dances."

"Half the people here will get confused in the middle of Fred's calling and then all will be chaos. But we get better at every dance. I won't let you get too far off." He grabbed her hand and pulled her onto the dance floor. "Come, Karyn. I have to play the organ most of the night. Just one dance."

There was no time to escape. Fred Smith called out, "S'lute ye pardners," and the dance began, with Emile fiddling and Fred stomping and clapping out a rhythm while, with his head thrown back and his eyes closed, he sang in a droning monotone, "J'ine hands and circle to th' left."

Karyn relaxed a little. She understood nothing of what the caller was saying, but by studying the movements of the other dancers she thought she might be able to keep up.

But then Fred called out, "Right hand to yer pardner an' gran' right and left." Luc held out his right hand and pulled Karyn around, where another man took her hand, and thus she and the other women dancers were "passed" around the circle.

Another woman went first when Fred called out, "Lady in the center an' three hands 'round; min' yer feet, fellers, don't tromp on her gown."

Karyn was all set to imitate the first woman, when Fred changed the call to something about "hoe it down" and "caper 'round." She was hopelessly lost, but by then so was everyone else, and the dancers collapsed with laughter.

Fred finally opened his eyes. Surveying the chaos he never missed a beat, but concluded the call of the first dance with,

"Ringtailed coons in the trees at play; grab yer pardners and all run away."

Karyn followed Luc's lead and tromped off the dance floor, laughing and gasping for breath.

When Luc went to join the musicians, Karyn rejoined Celest. That was when the trouble began. In spite of the fun of the first couples' dance, the beginning of the Delhommes' social saw Karyn Ritter perched on the very brink of a chasm of feminine rejection.

Frederica G'Schwind and Anna Ohelsberg greeted her cordially in high German, but had to excuse themselves to check on their children. During the first dance, they had both agreed on one thing: Celest Delhomme was expected to have a silk dress. She was, after all, the wife of one of the leading citizens. Karyn Ritter, on the other hand, had no right to flaunt a rose-colored silk gown in the presence of women who did well to manage a clean, unpatched calico.

Neither Julia Ross nor Lizzie Spooner spoke German. But they both spoke "fashion." After Celest translated a few pleasantries, both Julia and Lizzie remembered that they had promised Serge and Remi a dance. As they walked away, Karyn saw them whispering to one another and assumed that she was the subject of some none-too-friendly remarks. She was correct. In spite of the fact that Julia and Lizzie had never been close, they were agreeing on one thing: There were Germans and there were Germans, and apparently that nice Mikal Ritter had chosen an "uppity" German in the vein of Amalia Kruger. Poor Mikal.

Time after time throughout the next few minutes women nodded introductions and then excused themselves. Karyn despaired of her minuscule English vocabulary and grew increasingly frustrated by her dependence on Celest to translate. She took notice when Amalia Kruger looked her up and down and leaned over to whisper something to another elderly woman seated beside her.

When Emile took a break from fiddling to dance with Celest, Karyn escaped and went inside the house and back upstairs. She was struggling to undo the tiny buttons at the back of her gown when Celest found her. "I should never have worn this gown. They think I am a snob." She paused, blinking back tears of frustration.

"Give them time," Celest said, putting a hand on Karyn's shoulder. "I apologize, Karyn. I knew there would be a stir. But, like you, I was hoping that Mikal would come."

Sitting on the edge of the bed, Celest motioned for Karyn to sit down beside her. She took Karyn's hand. "The pleasure of your new husband is much more important than the opinion of other women. You will win the women over. When you can speak better English, they will see for themselves how charming you are. And, in time, they will get over their jealousy. Right now, it is more important to win your husband."

Celest stood up, pulled Karyn up beside her, and began to refasten the myriad tiny glass buttons that ran down the back of Karyn's gown. "Our socials last until dawn. He may yet come." As she fastened the last button, Celest said, "I think God has some very special plans for you and your Mikal, Karyn. Just let Him work." She added, "You have a real man, Karyn. A man after the heart of God. Thank God for him. Cherish him. And win his heart. It will be worth the effort . . . and well worth putting up with a little jealousy from the Julia Rosses and Lizzie Spooners of Custer County."

As the two women got to the bottom of the stairs, people began pouring into the parlor, piling their plates high with generous helpings of potatoes, fried fish, roasted prairie chicken, bread and jam. When two women next to her crowded in and conversed pointedly in English, Karyn filled a plate and slipped out the back door of the house to sit down alone on a bench just outside the door of the lean-to.

"There you are," Luc said from the back door. "Remi and Serge have been looking for you. They want you to try another dance after supper." When Karyn didn't answer, he asked, "Do you mind if I join you?"

Karyn slid over, making room for Luc.

He plopped down beside her. Instead of attacking the plate of food before him, he said quietly, "You may not believe me right now, but most of the people here really are good and kind at heart."

Karyn looked up, surprised, and Luc smiled gently. "I heard Julia and Lizzie talking about you. It seems they cannot see past their jealousy over a silk ball gown." When Karyn didn't say anything, he added, "I do not mean to excuse their behavior, but it probably is difficult to be reminded of all the lovely things they no longer have."

"But I never intended to—" Karyn protested.

"Of course you didn't," Luc said. "And when they have the chance to know you, they will understand that."

"I was hoping Mikal would come."

"And he may yet," Luc said, attacking the chicken leg that lay atop the mound of food on his plate with relish.

For a few moments, Karyn and Luc sat together without speaking. Luc ate heartily. When Karyn feared that he would get up and leave her alone, she asked abruptly, "Did you teach yourself to play the organ?"

When he nodded, she said, "One would never know. Your fingering and sense of timing are excellent. I wish I had had such talent all those years when Mama and Papa insisted I play."

"You didn't tell us you play the organ!" Luc exclaimed.

Karyn shook her head. "I don't. Not as well as you. I took lessons for years and years, but I never sounded half as good as you." She offered shyly, "I had more aspirations with singing."

"You must sing something for us tonight," he insisted. Standing up he said, "I am going for cake. You should get a piece of Mother's beroggie before they are gone. It's the best dessert on the table." He leaned down and whispered, "Russian. It is a family mystery where she learned to make them." He headed for the house. At the door, he turned around to suggest, "Sing a German hymn. That should warm even old Amalia Kruger's cold heart."

It was nearly midnight before Mikal arrived at Cay Miller's. He unhitched his team and led them into the sod stable behind Cay's store, where he found a note tacked to the harness rack:

Dance at Delhommes'. Karyn is there. Ride Buddy. Two new extra-large shirts on bottom shelf behind counter. Choose one.

It took Mikal about twenty minutes to restock his grub box, scrub himself clean, don the new shirt, and saddle Buddy. If he galloped most of the way, he could get to the Delhommes' shortly after 1:00 A.M. Grateful for the pioneer custom of dancing all night and returning home at dawn, Mikal urged Buddy forward. He envisioned the bowery, the dance floor, the tables laden with food. Supper would already have been served. Mikal didn't really care. He was hungry for only one thing, and that was the sight of Karyn Ritter smiling with pleasure at his surprise appearance. He would commend her work on the homestead, and then—well, he would stop imagining anything beyond that. After all, it had only been a month. But she had agreed to stay longer than a month . . . and she had plastered the walls . . . and planted trees . . . and planned a garden. That could mean anything.

With tremendous effort, Mikal refused to let himself presume the meaning of plastered walls and planted trees. Instead, he made himself think about the next two weeks of work awaiting him in Millersburg. He spent the rest of the ride to the Delhommes' thinking through each step of building Cay Miller's new store.

The supper hour had extended a little past an hour when Emile strode to the bowery, picked up his violin, and began to tune it. When people began to filter back to the dance floor, he played a few measures and then stopped. "Before we begin to dance again, we have the privilege of hearing from our newest citizen, Karyn Ritter."

From where Karyn stood by the door of the house, she could see several women exchange glances.

From behind her, Celest whispered, "Luc has trapped you, Karyn, and it is a good idea." She gave her a little shove. "Go. Sing."

Her heart pounding, Karyn went to stand by the organ. Luc sat down and played an introduction.

Her midsection so tight with terror that she could scarcely

breathe, Karyn warbled out a few notes. But then, she closed her eyes, envisioning herself standing among the choir members in the old church at home. She relaxed. The beauty of the music took over. She could breathe, and with the renewed breath, her voice took on its usual richness. She sang out in such a beautiful, clear soprano that even old Amalia Kruger wiped away homesick tears.

Mikal had pulled Buddy to a walk as he approached the Delhommes' house. It was quiet, and he realized that supper must be going on longer than usual. As he dismounted behind the barn, he heard a beautiful female voice singing. Sneaking around to the back of the house and up the stairs, he stood in the shadows of a bedroom peering down at the circle of people gathered about the organ.

As he listened to his wife sing, the excitement he had felt at surprising her came rushing back. Suddenly the organ accompaniment stopped, and there was only Karyn's hauntingly beautiful voice. Mikal looked toward Luc. He was sitting on the little organ stool, his hands on his knees, his eyes on Karyn, drinking in every note. His eyes never left her face. Mikal frowned.

Whatever it was that Mikal saw on Luc's face sent him out of the room, down the stairs, and out the door of the house. He intended to hurry across the yard and make his presence known, but before he could get to the bowery, Karyn had finished singing. People seemed to have decided that "that new German woman" was all right, after all. And who were they to begrudge a pretty girl an evening of dancing in a lovely gown?

Luc pulled Karyn onto the dance floor, fiddles began playing . . . and then Mikal appeared. At the sight of him, Karyn's face flushed with pleasure. But then Mikal grabbed her hand, pulled her away from Luc, and strode off the dance floor, half dragging her behind him. Luc Delhomme shrugged his shoulders and cut in on Serge, finishing the dance with Julia Ross.

The moment they had rounded the edge of the house and reached the backyard, Karyn jerked her hand away from Mikal. "What do you think you are doing?" she demanded, her dark eyes flashing.

"I am your husband, and I will not be humiliated in public while you flirt with Luc Delhomme!"

He's jealous! Hoping it was true, Karyn suppressed her own anger. "I wasn't flirting. Luc encouraged me to sing because he thought it might be a way for me to make amends for wearing this." She rustled her skirt.

Mikal frowned. "What?"

"I wore a silk dress. It made the women jealous."

"The women?" Mikal said stupidly.

"Yes, Mikal, the women." *Good. Now we can both calm down a little.* She tried to explain. "Women compare themselves to one another constantly, and nothing good ever comes of it. Either we end up feeling hopelessly inferior, or we conclude that we are better than others and become prideful."

"What does that have to do with you and Luc?"

"Everyone thought I was trying to show off by wearing a fancy dress. They were not very friendly. Luc and Celest thought that if I sang, it might soften their hearts a little."

"Did it?"

"How could I know? You stormed the dance floor like a jealous schoolboy and dragged me out here before I had a chance to find out."

"I am not a jealous schoolboy! I am your husband!" He gestured angrily, defending his childish behavior. "I think you might be lonely. So I ride for hours to check on you at the homestead. But you are gone. I return to Millersburg, and find the note about the dance. I think you might be happy to see me, so even though I am tired from a long journey, I come. I think you might like to be surprised. But it is I who am surprised. Instead of a wife who misses her husband, I find a woman having a wonderful time with another man."

Karyn stuck her chin out stubbornly. She abandoned her plan to humor him. She began to tremble with emotion. "Apparently you expected to find me at home, pining away for loneliness. If that is your expectation of your wife, Mikal Ritter, you married the wrong woman." She lifted her chin proudly. "Did you see Ella's calf? I can make butter and cheese and sell it. Did you see that I staked out the garden? Did you see your clean bedding?

71

The plastered walls in the house? The new trees? I worked hard for you while you were gone, Mikal." She took a deep breath. "We had an agreement, and I have more than kept it. I thought you would be pleased."

Karyn threw her shoulders back. She stared fearlessly up into Mikal's cold blue eyes and said firmly, "You do not ever have to love me, Mikal Ritter. But you do have to respect me. Never, ever treat me like that again."

She strode away. At the back door of the house, she whirled around and said, "And, for your information, your friend Luc Delhomme gave many hours to the plastering of your home, when he could have been earning money for himself."

Karyn's resolve to not show any more emotion broke down. Hurt tears flooded down her cheeks, and she blurted out, "Also for your information, Herr Ritter, the only reason that I wore this gown was so that I would look nice for you." In a flash of rose-colored silk, she was gone.

Mikal took a deep breath. He called her name, but Karyn had already fled into the house. She didn't come back.

Mikal sat on the bench by the lean-to shed for a long time, impervious to the joyous sounds of music and dancing wafting through and around the huge sod house. Weariness settled over him. He knew that he should find Karyn and apologize. With a sigh he went inside the house and upstairs. From the window of the bedroom he surveyed the dancers below. Nowhere was there a rose-colored dress. Dawn was beginning to light the sky. A few wagons were heading across the prairie.

"She left a little while ago," Celest said, when Mikal finally went outside and asked her. "She didn't want the calf to get all of Ella's milk."

Mikal frowned. "I don't like her being out alone."

"Oh, she didn't go alone," Remi said, walking up behind Mikal. "I thought you went with her, but I guess it must have been Luc." He looked soberly at Mikal and his mother and walked away.

Totally dejected, Mikal saddled Cay's horse and rode southwest toward Millersburg where he would build Cay's new store. He needed time to think. He had to find a way to convince

72

Karyn to stay longer. It wouldn't do to have her leave when things were in such a muddle. He laughed at his own naïveté. He had expected that sharing the workload of homesteading would simplify his life. But there was nothing simple about being husband to a woman he barely knew.

The Diary
April 30, 1880
The disappointment I felt upon my arrival here has been replaced by a determination to succeed. Every day there are improvements. The plastered walls look so clean, and now the inside of the soddy is not so dark. I have a window filled with geraniums. And I have planted a garden. All is work and more work, but I do not mind. I am beginning to understand why those who have come wish to stay. It is very satisfying to know that your days are meaningful. If only accepting disappointment regarding certain people were as easy as adapting to a new house.

CHAPTER 6

Sewing Machine Needles

---

*Let all bitterness, and wrath, and anger, and
clamour, and evil speaking, be put away from
you, with all malice: And be ye kind one to
another, tenderhearted, forgiving one another,
even as God for Christ's sake hath forgiven you.*
Ephesians 4:31–32

During the two weeks following Karyn and Mikal's disagreement at the Delhommes', Karyn began each day by talking herself out of riding to Millersburg to "settle things with Mikal." She told herself she was not really avoiding him, but that she was simply too busy planting the seeds he had left on her kitchen table to even consider a ride to town. If Mikal took the initiative and came home to talk, she would be glad to discuss things.

Her resolve usually weakened early in the afternoon, but by then she was too tired to ride nine miles. Stabbing hundreds of holes in the virgin sod had left her with aching arms. Kneading dough and failing again and again to create acceptable bread often reduced her to tears. Milking and churning, and making butter and cheese kept her so busy that by early afternoon she hoped sincerely that Mikal didn't come home, because she was too weary to think.

It was several days before Karyn tried to think through the situation. One evening she settled in her chair beside the kitchen window to knit. As her hands mechanically added row after row to the sock in her lap, she tried to sort things out. While she liked to imagine herself an independent woman, she knew that, in reality, coming to America had not been evidence of an independent nature. Rather, it had been a way for her to run away—from the memory of Hans, from the reality of Anton Gilhoff, from her father's hints about marriage, and from nursing Sophie's varied ailments. *If I were really independent, I would have begun my own business. Instead, I took the first road to America that opened to me.* She laughed at herself. *You wanted to escape the memory of one man and the attentions of another . . . and how do you go about it? By binding yourself in marriage to another man—and a complete stranger, at that!*

Karyn sighed, thinking back to the day when she had first caught the attention of Hans, the youngest son of a wealthy landowner. She and Sophie had been sent on an errand. They were to deliver a precious package of imported spices to a nearby village. They were just outside their own little village when Sophie began to complain.

"Stop, Karyn," she gasped, staggering slightly and slumping to the ground. "I have to—to rest."

Karyn frowned impatiently. "If you didn't want to come, Sophie, why didn't you just tell Papa you didn't feel well back at home?"

Sophie looked up at her with a puzzled expression. "But I wanted to come. I like being with you. And so many interesting people come by on the road—"

At that moment, an exquisite carriage approached from the north. It was drawn by two perfectly matched black horses. Karyn noticed that the horses lifted their snow-white socks in perfect harmony. As the carriage came near, its driver pulled up. He tipped his hat and then removed it before saying, "Could I be of help?" His blue eyes smiled warmly.

Sophie blushed. "Thank you, yes . . . perhaps if you could take us—"

But Karyn interrupted her. "Thank you, sir. Sophie often has these little spells. After she rests for a moment, all will be well. I can walk her home and then complete my errand."

The young man protested, "But you were headed up the

mountain, and it will soon be growing dark. Please, let me help you."

Sophie jumped up with surprising energy. "Thank you, sir. You are very kind. If you could perhaps assist me to my home—I am Sophie, Gottlieb Ensinger's daughter. Do you know his shop?" When the young man nodded yes, Sophie blushed prettily and ducked her head. "Well then, if you could perhaps see me home, my sister could complete her errand."

Karyn was horrified by Sophie's boldness and not a little angry at her once again succeeding in simultaneously escaping work and inspiring sympathy. The young stranger jumped down to help Sophie. He took charge of the situation, smiling brilliantly at Karyn while he introduced himself, helped Sophie into his carriage, and headed off toward the village, but not before learning where Karyn's errand would take her.

Karyn smiled, remembering that Hans had delivered Sophie home, refused her invitation to tea, and made his way back up the road to retrieve Karyn and insist that he help her finish her errand before night fell. Arriving at home, Karyn had alighted from Hans's carriage and gone inside, dreading her father's wrath for her brazen acceptance of the attentions of a young man without proper introduction. But to her amazement, her father had seemed pleased when she told him of Hans Gilhoff's kindness. He had silenced his wife's timid protests. "She is nearly a woman, Anna. We must allow her to grow up. To make decisions."

Remembering her father's words, Karyn wondered what he would think of her decision to come to America if he could see the tiny sod hut in Custer County to which she had come. And what would he think of Mikal Ritter in comparison to Hans Gilhoff? Karyn found herself defending Mikal against her father's imagined criticism. Mikal Ritter might seem little more than a rough peasant in comparison to Hans Gilhoff. Still, many good things had resulted from her marrying him.

Karyn stopped answering her father's imagined criticisms and began a mental list of the things she liked about America. There was her friendship with Celest Delhomme. And there was a new sense of accomplishment. At home, she had worked hard executing her mother's plans, meeting her mother's goals. In her own home, she could make decisions and improve things to please herself.

Mikal had given her free rein to do as she pleased about the house and garden, and she liked it. Hans Gilhoff would have expected her to play a preordained role. He would never have let her make so many decisions on her own. Even changing the flowers in one of the many gardens on his estate would have required approval from Anton and the cooperation of the gardener.

Karyn's mind wandered to Celest's comment that God had special plans for her and Mikal. In spite of regular church attendance and confirmation classes, she had spent very little time thinking about God's part in day-to-day life. Still, she liked the idea that God had followed her to Nebraska and was interested in what happened to her.

All the while that Karyn was thinking, she was knitting. Her hands worked mechanically, adding row upon row of stitches while she contemplated her new life. She convinced herself that any difficulties she and Mikal faced could be talked out. Once he came home, she would have calmly assessed the situation, and they could discuss their disagreement and live peaceably.

Karyn sighed and paused in her knitting. The altercation with Mikal at the Delhommes' was probably just because he was tired from his long drive. Yes, they would discuss their disagreement reasonably. And they would live peaceably.

Karyn continued to knit for a few moments when an unwanted memory raised itself to challenge her peaceful view of the future. Looking out into the darkness she remembered a night long, long ago, when Hans Gilhoff had caught her hand and drawn her back toward the carriage. He had given her the sweetest, gentlest kiss. The memory of that kiss created a new knot in Karyn's stomach as she assessed her situation with Mikal Ritter. He seemed to be having no difficulty at all keeping the "husband-in-name-only" part of their agreement. And yet, Karyn knew that Mikal Ritter could not possibly be expected to spend the rest of his life living in the dugout. And she also knew that she could not possibly spend the rest of her life sleeping beside a man who loved someone else. Karyn laid aside her knitting and went to bed.

While Karyn was justifying not riding to Millersburg, Mikal was justifying not driving to his homestead. He told himself that he was too busy. He convinced himself that he owed Cay Miller his every waking moment. But while he was hauling boards and hammering, planing doorways and installing floors, Mikal was thinking and praying about the situation with Karyn.

His motive for going to Grand Island had been to find a suitable partner, a sensible girl with a physique that would hold up to hard work and, if God so willed it, to child-bearing. He congratulated himself on having found a resourceful woman with both the will and the strength to work hard. Karyn had plastered the walls, even thinking of a way to rid herself of the despised dirt floor—and without asking him to spend any money. There were curtains at his window and geraniums blooming in his house. There was fresh butter for his bread, and he had no doubt that Karyn would raise abundant produce in the garden.

He had given little attention to the idea of romance. After all, he reasoned, was it not romance overcoming reason that had resulted in the tragedy of Marie-Louise? Marie-Louise's passion had swept him into a seven-year odyssey of extremes. After days of bliss, something would unexpectedly plunge her into emotional darkness. God forbid that that ever happen again.

But at the Delhommes' social, Karyn had looked so incredibly beautiful. And she sang like an angel. Thinking about it, Mikal forced himself to remember Marie-Louise. He must pray for more self-control in the matter of romance. A steady friendship was a much more sure foundation for a meaningful life.

After days of both mental and physical hard work, Mikal grew eager to get back to his homestead and clarify things with Karyn. They could have a good life together, if she wanted it. And he, Mikal Ritter, was going to make her want it. He owed her an apology for his behavior at the Delhommes'. He would convince her to stay longer. And it was time he told her about Marie-Louise. It might help her understand.

Mikal had the building framed out and was nailing the last floorboard into place when Luc Delhomme rode up.

Luc grinned. "I thought I'd let you calm down before I showed up for work. Cay hired me at the dance. The sooner I can earn money and get to school in Philadelphia, the better I'll like it. Remi and Serge will join us tomorrow. You'll be back with your wife in no time."

Mikal looked at him soberly and thrust out his hand. "Shake my hand and tell me you forgive my stupidity, Luc."

Luc shrugged. "There is nothing to forgive, Mikal. Perhaps I was flirting a little. Can you blame me?" He grinned again. "And by the way, I don't think you have anything to worry about. I only rode back to the homestead with Karyn because I thought I could calm her down. She let me come, but she had absolutely nothing to say, other than to ask a thousand questions about you." He picked up a hammer and a bag of nails as he teased, "I assured her you only experience brief moments of insanity. I think if you show up with a significant peace offering, she may just let you in the door."

Looking up at the sun, Mikal said, "Let's get to work. With you here, maybe I can get home a couple of days early."

When Mikal finally drove into the yard at home, Karyn was inside the soddy wiping down the insides of the crates she used as a pantry. She heard him call her name, but she didn't go to the door. After all her reasoning and logic, she had been ready to begin again—after she asked about Marie-Louise. But then, Mikal had been delayed for another week, and he hadn't even cared enough to come and check on her. He had sent Luc Delhomme to tell her. Luc had been on his way home to visit his mother. But Mikal could not spare a few hours to check on his own wife.

Mikal called her name again. She rattled pans to let him know that she was there and that she was angry. She heard him jump down, heard the sound of something scooting across the bed of the wagon. She rattled her pans more loudly, pretending not to hear. It made her even angrier when she thought she heard him

79

chuckle. She heard him walk to the back of the house. Peeking out the window, she watched him water the team. His broad back was toward her. The veins stood out along his muscular forearms as he lifted a full bucket of water from the well.

She went back to her scrubbing, expecting to hear the wagon headed down to the corral. But the wagon was still standing just outside the doorway. What was he waiting for? Try as she might, Karyn could find nothing else to do inside the little soddy. She went to the door, planning to scoot along the front of the house and disappear from sight. He could look for her if he cared to know where she was. And why should he care? Had he cared that they had parted angry with one another? Had he cared to do something about that?

Karyn stood in the doorway blinking in disbelief at the back of the wagon. Tears stung her eyes. From where he stood at the head of the team, Mikal saw her. He finished watering the horses and took the bucket back to set it on the curb of the well. Then he returned to the wagon, pausing to run his hands across the broad neck of a beautiful bay shire mare. He played with the mare's mane, pulling at imaginary tangles while he waited for Karyn to speak.

It seemed like hours, and Karyn said nothing. Mikal frowned and asked gently, "Is it not a good model, Karyn? Cay Miller said that Celest's machine was a Singer. He thought it was the right one to order." He cleared his throat before explaining, "I sent Luc out here to tell you we had to work a few more days, hoping you wouldn't suspect. The machine didn't come until this morning. Luc offered to come by with an excuse. Then he rode home to check with Celest to make certain Cay had ordered the right one. Luc didn't give away my surprise, did he?"

When Karyn still didn't speak, he worried aloud. "I should have asked you if a Singer would be all right. I thought it would be a good surprise." He walked to the bed of the wagon and began to cover the sewing machine with a tarp. "I can take it back. Cay said that Amalia Kruger was very angry when he told her that I had already bought this one for you. We can let Amalia have it. You can order what you want."

Karyn raised both her hands to her face and burst into tears.

"*Ach,* Mikal. *Danke.* It is wonderful." Mikal left off covering up the machine and turned toward her as she said, "I was so angry with you, Mikal. So very angry."

Mikal nodded. "Yes, I know. First I make a fool of myself at your first social here, and then I seem to ignore you for three weeks. I don't wonder that you are angry." He climbed up into the wagon bed. "Let's get the machine unloaded. Then I think we must talk."

"You got your new team," Karyn said, nodding toward the horses. "They are magnificent."

"Yes." He pointed to the mare on the right. "That is Lena. The other beautiful lady is Grace. With their help, I hope to plant double the corn crop I did last year. We can plant melons and pumpkins in with the corn. Emile said it would help keep the deer and antelope out of the fields." He nodded in the direction of the garden. "But first, I will build your sod wall about the garden."

He hoisted the machine to the ground. Karyn opened the lid, running her hand lovingly over the graceful curved arm of the little black machine that popped up into place. "Now I can sew for others. Already Celest has asked that I make her a dress. She was going to have me usc her machine, but now that won't be necessary. And knowing Celest, she will let it be known if I do well. Celest said that on your Fourth of July, there is quite a celebration. She thinks I can be very busy making new dresses."

Mikal laughed. "And with all that money you will buy—?"

"Hens. Cay pays almost fifteen cents for each dozen of eggs."

"And with the egg money you will buy?"

"Geese. Then I can make you a fine feather bed." She blushed at her reference to Mikal's bed, which was not also hers, hastening to repeat a German proverb. "*Eine sorgliche Frau fullt das Haus bis unters Dach.*" (A thrifty wife fills the house up to the roof.)

After he had unhitched his new team and turned them into the corral, Mikal positioned the wondrous new sewing machine just outside the front door of the house. When they parted to do their evening chores, Karyn baked bread in her improvised oven and made potato soup. After supper, Mikal went to bed down the team in the dugout. Karyn had just carried a chair outside and positioned it where she could watch the sun set while she knitted when Mikal walked up the hill, his hands in his pockets.

"*Was darf es sein, bitte?*" Karyn asked, starting to get up. "What can I get you?"

"*Bitte setzen Sie sich!*" He waved her back into her chair. "Sit. I thought I would have another cup of coffee. Would you like some?"

"I can get it."

"No. Keep to your knitting. I can make coffee." He made the coffee, then carried another chair outside. Instead of sitting, he put one foot up on the chair and rested his coffee cup on his knee. He sipped coffee for quite a long time before finally saying quietly, "I want to make things right between you and me."

Karyn spoke up. "Thank you again for the wonderful gift. And for the surprise of the garden seeds. It was very thoughtful of you to include some flower seeds. Celest suggested I throw those up onto the roof. She said they would grow and bloom there. Is that true?"

"What?" Mikal asked stupidly. "Oh, the flower seeds. Yes, now that you mention that, I have seen flowers blooming on other roofs." He took a sip of coffee then took a deep breath. "I think it is time that I tell you about something. I could have done so before now, but I didn't want to make more of it than necessary." After another moment of silence, Mikal said quietly, "I told you that I had difficulties in Kansas. Everything I told you was true. What I did not tell you was that I was married when I lived in Kansas."

Karyn didn't look up from her knitting as she said quietly, "Yes. I know. Amalia Kruger told me about it."

Mikal was dumbfounded. "Amalia Kruger? When?"

"The first time you took me to Millersburg."

"Cay said the Krugers were gone."

"Well, Amalia wasn't. She came into the store while you and Cay were at the blacksmith's and told me all about Marie-Louise."

Mikal sat down. He set his coffee cup in the dirt beside his chair and leaned forward, his elbows on his knees. "But why didn't you say something?"

Karyn shrugged. She didn't look at him, but concentrated on her knitting as she said carefully, "As you said, why make more of it than is necessary? You don't owe me an explanation of your past life."

Mikal leaned back in his chair. "I can imagine what you heard from Amalia Kruger." He tapped his foot. "You deserve to know the truth." After a brief pause, he began, "I met Marie-Louise Jacquot in Paris when I was serving in the army of occupation. Against the will of her parents and the advice of my fellow German officers, we were married in secret and fled together to America. On the ship, we fell in with a wonderful group of people called Mennonites. Even though my family was not religious and Marie-Louise was a devout Catholic, we were both drawn into their circle of love. When we landed in America, it was only natural that we stay with them."

Karyn gave up all pretense of knitting as Mikal spoke. He told her exactly the same story that Amalia Kruger had whispered—without emphasizing his emotional despair. She detected no emotion at all in his voice when he recounted the details of Marie-Louise's death. Only once did he pause in the telling, and that was to refill their coffee cups.

"After Marie-Louise died, I fled north into Custer County and filed on my three claims, never intending to be anything but a hermit for the rest of my days. I lived very much like a wild animal for the first year. The second year, I ventured into Millersburg more often. Cay Miller took great pains to be kind to me. Eventually, I grew to think of him as my friend. One day, he introduced me to Emile Delhomme."

Mikal chuckled and rubbed the back of his neck. "My hair was past my shoulders, and I hadn't bothered to wash or comb it in weeks. I don't imagine I smelled very pleasant. But Emile put his hand on my shoulder and looked into my eyes with such kindness—" Mikal's voice wavered. He cleared his throat. "Two days after I met him, Emile came riding up to my little dugout with Luc. I was, to say the very least, not a very good host. But they didn't seem to notice. They brought me a pie

83

from Celest. Then they lured me to their house for dinner with the promise of more pie." He laughed softly. "Even an animal can be lured with food. They didn't ask me to talk. They just fed me and sent me home. After that, I slowly came back to life. Then came the long winter I have told you about. It was at once the most difficult and the best winter of my life."

Karyn had been trying to avoid looking at him, but when he paused she finally gathered courage to look up at him. He was staring toward the horizon, and the golden light of dusk reflected in his blue eyes, giving them an unusual warmth. Karyn looked away just as he glanced at her. She bent to set her own coffee cup on the earth and took up her knitting as Mikal continued.

"Right before the first blizzard I had been to the Delhommes'. Celest succeeded in getting me to let her cut my hair. When I left, I had a German Bible tucked under my arm. When the blizzard hit, I had nothing to do for days on end but sit out the storm. Tending the fire in the stove was a constant job. And as I tended the stove, I began to read. It changed me." He pointed to his heart. "In here. I began to feel alive in a new way. I read that God loved me. I began to make a mental list of questions to ask Celest and Emile as soon as I could get to their house." He laughed. "Of course, it was weeks at a time between visits with them. But they answered many questions. Many they could not. Still, I found a new peace. I began to feel human again and to want something to end the desperate loneliness." He paused and looked at Karyn. The sun had set. She was listening attentively, her knitting needles lying in her lap.

Mikal stepped toward her and put his hand on the back of her chair. "You can't see to knit. Let's go inside."

"No," Karyn said softly. "Let's just stay out here. The stars are so beautiful."

From where he stood behind her chair, he apologized. "I'm sorry you had to hear about Marie-Louise from Amalia Kruger. I didn't tell you sooner because it is part of a past I have put to rest." His voice was sincere as he half whispered, "I can imagine that Amalia spoke of Marie-Louise in very glowing terms. Amalia was very fond of her." He paused before saying, "But life with Marie-Louise was not always the symphony of joy that Amalia probably described. Living with someone who is mentally unbalanced is its own kind of hell. In some ways, it was a blessing that Marie-Louise was taken when she was. I think she would have gone completely mad if she had not died that day."

"Mikal," Karyn said quietly, turning to look up at him, "I have been angry with you about something of which I myself am guilty. I was not married before. But there was—someone. His name was Hans Gilhoff. He died in the army."

"I see." That was all Mikal said. He took his hand from her chair and sat down again opposite her. It was dark now, and Karyn found herself wishing that she could see his blue eyes more clearly as she explained. "I didn't tell you any lies. There really is an Anton Gilhoff, and my father really did want me to marry him. And that really is why I came to America."

"This Hans Gilhoff," Mikal asked softly. "He is still in your heart?"

Karyn answered firmly. "*Nicht im geringsten.* I have a new life here in America."

"Then I don't need to wonder about Hans Gilhoff, and you no longer need to wonder about Marie-Louise. Now, about my behavior at the Delhommes'—"

Karyn interrupted him. "I'm sorry if I appeared to be flirting, Mikal. Regardless of whether or not we continue as husband and wife, I would never do anything to dishonor you before your friends. It won't happen again."

Mikal put his hands on his knees and pushed himself up. His voice was almost playful as he said, "I know. I made it clear to Luc that unless he knows how to play the organ with broken fingers, he will remember that your last name is Ritter." He said good night and stepped away from her. Karyn could hear him whistling softly as he walked down the hill to the dugout.

The next morning, Karyn was awakened by an unfamiliar sound just outside the soddy. She got up and dressed quickly. Going to the doorway, she saw Mikal drive a posthole digger into the earth. He explained, "The wind I cannot stop, but the sun—that I can manage a little." He spent the next two days erecting a large porch to cover both the doorway and the spot where Karyn had said she would like her sewing machine.

The weather was unusually cool the evening that Mikal laid the last piece of sod on the porch roof. Karyn said they would eat inside. When Mikal finally came in for supper, the rough-hewn table had been covered with a fine lace tablecloth on which sat two china plates with matching cups and saucers. The small tabletop was crowded with two platters, one piled high with blina pancakes, the other with sausage. There was even a pie. Karyn had donned her best apron. She stood waiting to pour his coffee from the fine china pot that had been repacked into her trunk the day of her arrival.

Mikal paused at the doorway. He looked down at his filthy overalls and back at Karyn. Without a word, he hurried off to the dugout. Karyn waited for only a few moments before he reappeared, his face scrubbed, his muscular frame crowded into a rumpled suit.

As they sat down at the table to eat, Karyn sighed happily. It already seemed that she had lived a lifetime on this treeless prairie where even the smallest things, like a nice dinner, required exhausting effort. Looking across the table at Mikal Ritter, she thought to herself, *This is my husband . . . mein mann.* And she decided that the exhausting effort that brought Mikal to her table looking so handsome was quite worth it.

Her new sewing machine expanded Karyn's world far beyond Emile and Celest Delhomme into the varied ethnic groups who conducted their business in the growing settlement of Millersburg. As soon as Cay Miller let it be known that a seamstress resided only nine miles away, women began making the drive out to the Ritters' to visit. Karyn soon learned that visiting and socializing were quite common, even when "dropping in" required a few hours' drive across the prairie.

Most of her visitors wanted Karyn to sew for them. If they didn't speak German, Karyn communicated with smiles and gestures. She nodded and sketched, and the women smiled back at her, refusing to allow such a little thing as a language barrier stand between themselves and a new dress.

Karyn was paid with everything conceivable except actual money. In addition to many new phrases in English, she acquired two cats, several yards of shirting, more flower seeds, some blood sausages and cheeses, and an extra feather tick. By mid-June Karyn had learned to measure in miles and inches instead of kilometers and centimeters. She had acquired a basic understanding of simple English and orders for eleven dresses to be made before the Fourth of July celebration in Millersburg.

Cay Miller delivered a letter from home (they had celebrated her birthday and hoped that she had had some chocolate) and expressed interest in having her make shirts for him to sell in his store. Karyn insisted that he stay and eat supper with her and Mikal. After Cay left and Mikal went down the hill to the dugout, she took time to sit down and answer the letter from home. She took a kerosene lamp outside and used her sewing machine as a desk.

I did not have chocolate. In fact, I did not tell Mikal it was my birthday, so the day passed unnoticed. But save your pity. If we had everything all the time, we would not know how good things were. Really, I am having the best time in the world. I have progressed with my English. If my customers speak slowly and use simple words, I understand. But I must learn more. It is so annoying to be in Millersburg and to stand like a clockhead and be unable to answer when the women try to include me in their chatter. I think I may ask Mikal and Celest to speak only English so that I am forced to learn more quickly.

I can earn $1.50 in American funds in only one day with my sewing machine, all of which Mikal insists that I keep for the needs of the house as I see them. When we get a fine house and one hundred acres under cultivation, I would not trade with anyone. Mikal is kind. He is very tall, with black hair and blue eyes.

Karyn looked up from her letter and stared off toward the horizon. Pondering Mikal's blue eyes reminded her of the thing she was learning to suppress. It had been raising its head more and more often of late, and Karyn was growing impatient with herself. It was obvious that Mikal Ritter had selected a wife to be his partner in achieving a successful homestead. He had not chosen for love, and he had promised that they would be husband and wife in name only. He appeared to be having no difficulty keeping that promise.

Karyn scolded herself for lapsing once again into a state of contemplating Mikal Ritter's considerable physical attractions. She finished her letter home, reporting on Nebraska with glowing terms, stating that, if only Sophie had had the strength to accompany her sister to the new land, she would undoubtedly find herself enjoying vastly improved health.

The Diary
June 5, 1880
  Mikal has come home now and things will be better between us. We have had a good talk. Oma would be pleased to know that I have used her teapot. And Mama's tablecloth as well. Even in a soddy, one can enjoy nice things.

CHAPTER 7

A Methodist Prayer Book

----

*She stretcheth out her hand to the poor; yea, she
reacheth forth her hands to the needy.*
Proverbs 31:20

Karyn was inside the soddy one afternoon when she heard the
now-familiar cadence of Sugar galloping up to the house. Mikal
had made a hurried trip into Millersburg to have the blacksmith
repair a harness ring.

"Do you want to ride along?" he had asked pleasantly.

Karyn had declined. "No, if I have time I must get Frau
Zoerb's dress finished. I still have seven to make before the
celebration. But you can bring me two spools of thread. And
there are four pounds of butter in the well for Cay."

Later in the day, Mikal came galloping back. He reined in
Sugar and slid down, speaking hurriedly, "Karyn, I have
brought you some sewing. But this customer is very proud, and
we must be unusually creative in finding a way for him to pay.
He has nothing. His wife is gone, and he has two children. They
are dressed in rags, and there is no money. Cay Miller made one
of his mathematical errors when he prepared the bill. This resulted in him owing the customer the price of a bolt of cloth,
but—" Karyn smiled as Mikal described yet one more example
of Cay Miller's generosity.

Mikal had no more time for explanations, for just outside the soddy, Karyn could see a thin young man climbing down wearily from a wagon. As Mikal introduced her, Karyn stared at the wagon, wondering how it had possibly held together for the nine-mile drive from Millersburg. The wonder of the wagon was exceeded only by the wonder that the two nags pulling it had not collapsed. But it was the sight of two pairs of eyes peering at her over the wagon box that almost made Karyn cry. When their father called to them, the children slithered over the edge of the wagon box and stood barefoot, looking shyly at Karyn.

As the young man introduced himself, he put his hands affectionately on each child's shoulder, "Sten, Tilda. Greet Mrs. Ritter." Sten and Tilda nodded at Karyn and mumbled something she took for a greeting.

Karyn smiled back at them as their father explained, "Their Ma died last winter. We're headed back east. Can't seem to make a go of it on my place, not without Anna. You can see the children are kinda' poorly. I traded in my tools at Miller's. Got a couple sacks of flour, some coffee, a bolt of calico. Miller said you might be able to make a new dress for Tilda. A shirt or two for Sten. Something fittin' for the trip back east." He swallowed hard. "I got to get them better fixed up before I take 'em to see their ma's folks. They didn't like her marryin' out of the clan." He smiled bitterly. "I thought they was just bein' proud Swedes thinkin' they was better than a boy born and raised in good old Kentucky." He looked at the dirt as he mumbled, "Maybe they was right." He swallowed again, then looked up at Karyn, his eyes pleading. "Their Anna died having their third grandchild."

Karyn understood almost nothing of the stranger's words, but seeing his hand placed gently on the shoulders of the too-thin children, hearing the brave desperation in his voice, she understood all that was necessary.

Without waiting for Mikal to translate the details of the stranger's speech, Karyn took the bolt of cloth from the man's hands and nodded. "*Ja.* I sew. For Tilda. For Sten." She smiled down at the children. "My name is Karyn." She urged the stranger, "Come. Eat. Sleep. Tomorrow I sew."

The stranger spoke up. "I can't pay money for—"

Karyn shook her head. "No pay."

The man turned to Mikal. "You got any work I can do?"

Mikal looked perplexed. Certainly there was no lack of work on the homestead, but the stranger's team was in no condition to be plowing. Indeed, the stranger himself appeared near the end of his own strength. Mikal hesitated.

Inspiration struck. Karyn knelt down before the girl. "Tilda?" The girl nodded, managing a shy smile. Karyn asked, "You speak English, *ja?*"

Tilda giggled. "Of course I speak English. My ma was a schoolteacher. She grew up speaking Swedish, but she knew English better than most Americans."

Tilda's father said proudly, "I never had time for learnin', but my Anna was a real scholar. She taught the young'un's real good."

Karyn looked up at him. "You have English. I want English." She pointed to the girl. "You teach." She pointed to herself. "I sew." She looked up at Tilda's father. "Is good trade. *Ja?*"

Tilda pulled at her father's sleeve. "We still have Ma's Bible, Pa. I could use it to teach Mrs. Ritter, just like Ma did when she taught Sten and me. I remember how she did it."

Sten spoke up. "Me, too. I'll help."

Tilda's father looked from Karyn to Mikal, who nodded and winked at the stranger. He accepted the arrangement. "That's fair. Sten and Tilda will teach you as much as they can."

Karyn stood up and laid the bolt of cloth on her sewing machine. She held out her hands toward Tilda and Sten. With a glance toward their father, the children took Karyn's outstretched hands and followed her inside the soddy where they overwhelmed Karyn with their willingness to help and their eagerness to impart fluency in English before the evening meal was fully prepared.

The sun had barely sunk below the horizon when a well-fed and well-scrubbed Tilda and Sten Stoddard slithered between two thin blankets that had been spread over a thick layer of hay, which their father laughingly called "prairie feathers."

Through Mikal, Karyn tried in vain to convince Doane Stoddard to move the sleeping children into her bed. He insisted they were already accommodated in a far better fashion than they expected. Karyn relented until the men bid her good night, Mikal to the dugout and Doane to his own bed of "prairie feathers" in the dilapidated wagon bed. She watched the men disappear into the darkness. Then, she went inside and folded back the two quilts that covered her feather tick. She was amazed at how light Tilda and Sten were. It took little effort to lift them into her bed. She took great satisfaction in watching as, fast asleep, they snuggled into the depths of the feather tick.

The first morning of the Stoddards' stay on the Ritter homestead, Mikal took Karyn aside. Nodding toward Sten and Tilda, he whispered, "They are too thin. They need rest and good food. Their father and I are going hunting. There is no hurry with the sewing." The two men departed on a hunting excursion that day.

That first day, Karyn washed Sten's and Tilda's hair. It took the greater part of the morning to gently untangle and de-mat Tilda's waist-length, thick brown hair. When it was finally done, Karyn presented a wide-eyed Tilda with two lovely ribbons for each of her long braids. The child was speechless with delight.

After lunch, it was Sten's turn. He shuddered when the cold well water was poured over his head, but sat patiently while Karyn washed and cut his shaggy hair. What emerged from the session were two quite attractive children.

By their second day on the homestead, the children were accompanying Karyn everywhere. When she weeded her garden, Tilda and Sten each took a row. When Karyn fed the livestock, Tilda and Sten shoveled manure out of the corral. Karyn learned words like *garden, hoe, horse,* and *cow.* But even with the children's help at chores, Karyn found no time for sewing their new clothing that day. Patting the bolt of cloth, she shook her head and sighed with mock regret. "Maybe tomorrow."

That evening, Tilda produced her mother's Bible, opened it to Genesis 1:1, and began to instruct Karyn in the reading of the English language. With the dust in the yard as a blackboard and a stick for chalk, Karyn learned to read and write, "In the beginning, God created the heaven and the earth." Long after Sten and Tilda were asleep that night, Karyn sat by the lamp turning the pages of the Bible and searching for words she could recognize.

Mikal and Doane were gone for several days. By the time they returned, Doane's horses had begun to regain their strength. He was thrilled to see them trotting about the corral, neighing loudly as he and Mikal rode up. The trip had also had its effects on Doane. He climbed down from Mikal's horse, laughing with delight as Sten and Tilda ran up and embraced him.

Karyn watched the children greet their father, her face wreathed in smiles. She called out in English, "You have good children, Mr. Stoddard. They teach me to talk like real American." Having spoken the two sentences she had practiced over and over again, Karyn found herself once again fumbling for words.

Karyn greeted Mikal in German. She blushed with the realization that she had almost followed the children's example. She had almost run to Mikal, almost thrown her arms about him. She reached up to swipe her flushed cheeks with her open palms and turned to go inside and begin preparations for a feast of wild game.

Mikal and Doane worked most of the next day oiling and repairing harnesses. Karyn unrolled Cay Miller's donated bolt of cloth and began to plan her sewing for Tilda and Sten. Lessons in English continued throughout each day. Karyn added words like *sewing machine, calico, scissors,* and *dress* to her ever-expanding English vocabulary.

At the end of the week, Mikal announced that he and Doane would be going on another trip, this time in search of fence posts to replace the sod wall around the corral. While they were gone, Karyn took apart one of her own skirts, which she insisted was worn beyond repair, thereby managing to create a brown calico dress with pink trim and a pink calico dress with brown trim for Tilda. She teased Sten, threatening to sew pink cuffs onto one of his shirts.

When Mikal and Doane returned ten days later with their load of lumber, they dug postholes and fenced the corral. They moved the sod from the corral and built the wall around Karyn's garden.

The men drove into Millersburg. On their trip they had used deer meat to lure and poison three wolves. Mikal insisted that since Doane was the one who devised the successful scheme, he was the rightful recipient of the bounty, which amounted to $2.50 for each pelt. The money provided lumber to repair Doane's wagon and supplies for the drive east.

Karyn grew less shy about speaking English. She was fanatical about pronunciation, wanting to rid herself as much as possible of any accent.

Finally, Doane Stoddard announced that they must leave. "Do you think you can have Sten's shirts finished soon?"

At mention of the sewing, Karyn admitted, "Oh, except for a few buttons, the sewing has been finished for a while." She looked at Mikal for support. "Can you not stay for the Fourth of July celebration? I want everyone to meet my English teacher." She grinned at Tilda and tugged at one of her long braids.

Doane was resolute in his insistence that they leave.

Karyn smoothed her apron and said softly, "I can do the buttons tomorrow morning." She fought back tears as she looked at Tilda and Sten. "We will miss you."

Doane stood up. "And we won't never forget you." He cleared his throat awkwardly. "We stayed on longer than we planned. And now we're mended." He held out his hand to Mikal. "You done us all a heap of good and we thank you."

The next day came too soon. Tilda climbed up beside her father on the newly constructed seat of their repaired wagon. Their meager supplies had been added to by Mikal, who insisted that Karyn's sewing was not ample pay for all the work that both Doane and the children had done during their stay.

Finally, Doane clucked to his team and the wagon pulled out of the yard. Karyn, who had determined not to cry at their departure, complained to Mikal about the dust in her eyes and headed for the well to rinse them out. She turned her back as the Stoddard wagon faded into the distance, only to hear Tilda calling her name. When she turned about, Tilda was running toward her, something clutched in her hand.

"We—all of us—we want you to have this. Please. It will help with your English." She lowered her voice before adding, "And it will help you to remember us." Impulsively, Tilda kissed Karyn on the cheek, thrusting something into her hand. She was gone in a flash of brown-and-pink calico. As the Stoddard wagon disappeared into the distance, Karyn stood in the yard of her dirt house, crying softly and clutching a prayer book, the inside cover of which identified it as the property of "Anna C. Stoddard."

The Diary
June 30, 1880
   I am speaking English like a good American now, although I will continue my diary in German. It feels more comfortable. Two dear children who stayed with us for a few weeks taught me. They left this morning, and how I miss them. They gave me their mother's prayer book, my first book in English. My garden is fenced. How odd that I have been here now for weeks and weeks, and yet I know my husband no better. We see one another in passing from one chore to the next, but there is little time to talk. Perhaps now that the Stoddards have left us, things will be different.

CHAPTER 8

A Photograph of Four Girls

Withhold not good from them to whom it is due,
when it is in the power of thine hand to do it.
Proverbs 3:27

Sophie. Karyn could not believe it. The very morning that Doane Stoddard headed his wagon off toward the southeast, Cay Miller drove in from the southwest bearing fragile cargo in the form of Karyn's younger sister Sophie. Even as Cay jumped down to help Sophie, Karyn blinked in disbelief. Even with Sophie sitting at the breakfast table, delighting Cay and Mikal with her spirited account of the long trip from Brandenburg to America and across America by train to Kearney, Karyn could scarcely believe it.

"So there I was in Kearney," Sophie was saying in nearly flawless English, "alone and feeling completely lost. No train. I think, *What shall I do?*" She smiled brightly. "But then along came Mr. Hawks."

Cay nodded and looked at Mikal. "And can you believe it? She actually convinced Judson Hawks to bring her, even though he didn't have a full load of freight yet."

Sophie winked at Mikal. "We women have our ways of getting what we want." Sophie's soft accent changed the *w*'s to *v*'s as she spoke. Still, Karyn was amazed at her seeming ease with English.

Karyn rose from the table and slipped outside. She drew water for coffee and set the pot on the fire. It was a good way to get the time to collect herself, for Karyn was less than delighted by Sophie's sudden appearance. Sophie was petite and fragile-looking. Men had always been attracted to her golden hair and sparkling blue eyes. She had a way of affecting childish innocence that made them want to protect her. And now, her soft accent made her seem even more vulnerable. Sophie had flawless skin. Karyn regretted having forgotten to wear a bonnet the day before. She was sunburned, and freckles had begun to break out on the backs of her hands. Sophie had a dimpled smile and charming self-assurance that made it easy for her to talk with anyone. Why, already her storytelling had so fascinated Cay and Mikal, they had taken no notice at all that Karyn was outside alone.

As she stood over the fire in the front yard, listening to the sound of Mikal's laughter, Karyn admitted to herself that she had always resented that dimple in Sophie's cheek. Oh, just a little bit, to be sure. But resent it she did.

"Karyn." Sophie stood in the doorway of the house, coffee cup in hand, looking very stern.

"Yes, Sophie. What is it?"

"You are doing the work, and you have not asked for help." She stepped outside, followed by Mikal and Cay.

Karyn ignored Sophie, nodding instead toward Cay. "Thank you for bringing Sophie to me, Mr. Miller. America has held many surprises for me, but to have my little sister arrive in such a way—that is the greatest of all surprises." Wiping sweat from her brow with the back of her hand, she drew the coffeepot off the fire. "Your coffee is ready now."

Cay looked honestly regretful as he said, "Thank you, but I must be getting back and open my store, or the people of Millersburg will be gossiping. Amalia Kruger saw me driving out of town with this lovely girl at my side." He chuckled. "I can imagine the rumors she has begun already."

Sophie thanked Cay, offering her pale, tiny hand even as she looked up at Mikal and said, "I must apologize to you, brother-in-law, for arriving unannounced." She looked behind her at the

97

soddy, barely hiding her disdain as she added, "I will only require a tiny corner of space for a very short time. I hope to begin a dressmaking business in Millersburg."

"Nonsense, Sophie," Mikal insisted. "You and Karyn will share the house. I have plenty of room in the dugout."

When Mikal pronounced *dugout,* Sophie glanced toward Karyn with a questioning look. It was not a word that her language instructor at home had included in her lessons.

Cay snorted. "You'd better get busy building onto the house, Mikal. I remember how you were the spring after that second winter of blizzards." He looked toward Karyn, smiling wisely. "If you want a sane husband, Mrs. Ritter, you will talk him out of taking up residence in that dugout." He turned toward Mikal. "I will provide a window and lumber for the roof on credit—as a welcome gift to our newest citizen." He helped Mikal haul Sophie's massive flat-topped trunk into the house and then, with a flourish, kissed Sophie's hand and left.

The moment Cay drove off, Mikal headed toward the corral.

"Where is he going?" Sophie whispered, slipping back into German.

"When did you learn English, Sophie?" Karyn asked.

Sophie smiled. "You must know that I could never go for long without my dear sister in my life, Karyn. As soon as you left for America, I badgered Papa until he agreed to hire an English tutor. I knew I would be coming to America soon, and I worked hard to learn as quickly as possible."

Karyn nodded. "You always were a good student, Sophie. And now that we are in America, we will speak English."

With a slight frown, Sophie nodded and answered in English, "All right. As long as you are here to explain new words. This word *dugout.* What is that?"

"I'll show you in a little while," Karyn explained. "Look down the hill and you can see the edge of the corral. Just around the edge of the bluff there is a barn—well, a dugout, actually. In the side of the hill." She led Sophie inside the soddy. "We don't have a word for it in German. You will see. But first, you must unpack."

Sitting on the wooden edge of the box-type bed, Sophie surveyed the inside of the house with mournful eyes. "Oh, Karyn, it isn't at all like you wrote. I should never have come. Do you think Mikal will build another room soon?"

Karyn was defensive. "It is different from Brandenburg, but we have a good start. I would never think of asking Mikal to leave off his work right now. We manage just fine, and you will, too. Why, in ten years—"

"In ten years you will be a dried-up old woman. Just look at your hands, Karyn. Why, they used to be as white as mine, and now—"

Karyn retorted, "Mikal says that in ten years he will have the finest farm in Custer County." Karyn's brown eyes flashed. "He has faith in God, faith in himself, and faith in his Nebraska soil. And so do I. I'm not afraid of hard work."

Sophie's beautiful blue eyes narrowed a little. "You know, Karyn, you were not really truthful about things in your letter. Your house is not at all what I imagined. You said it was small . . . but I never imagined this—this house of—"

"Sod, Sophie. The house is called a soddy. The men use something called a breaking plow. They slice up the top layer of earth and then lay the slices atop one another. Just like a brick house, only better for Nebraska."

Sophie pronounced the word *soddy*. Lifting her eyes to the rafters above she shook her head gently. Then, her expression changed as she teased, "Your house is not at all what I imagined. Nor is your husband." She smiled slyly. "Although that part of your little deception is better in reality than in your letters. You wrote that he is tall, and you mentioned black hair and blue eyes. But you said nothing of how handsome he is." She turned around to smooth the bed pillows. "I can see exactly how it is that you have managed to bear it here. And I do not think it is because of the hope of a nice home in ten or so years."

Karyn shook her head. "Mikal and I are friends, Sophie. Partners." She looked away, feeling her cheeks turn crimson as she said, "He would never take advantage."

Sophie pondered for a moment. Her eyes widened. "I see," she half whispered. "Then you haven't . . . you don't . . ."

Karyn turned away and opened Sophie's trunk, surveying the

contents with disapproval. "Didn't you read any of the immigrant guides, Sophie?"

"Of course I read them." Sophie added, "But I also read your letters about the wonders of America and your homestead. I read about the dances and your good neighbors, the Delhommes, and about the beauty of the spring flowers."

"I also mentioned gardening and soap-making, Sophie. Did you expect to do those things wearing these?" Karyn asked, lifting the third silk dress from the trunk.

Sophie drew her bow-shaped lips into a pout. "Of course I know you can't wear silk every day. But I thought there would be a department store here for everyday things. I thought they might not have nice silk, so I brought that and planned on buying whatever else I needed. Papa sent a generous amount of money to get me started. I thought you would be pleased." She whined. "I even brought you a new silk dress. The blue one is for you."

Karyn thanked her. "It's lovely, Sophie. But, really, didn't you bring any practical clothing besides your traveling suit?"

"I brought my best apron," Sophie offered hopefully. "And a shawl, and felt boots for when it gets cold. And Mama sent two fur mitts for winter."

Winter, Karyn thought. *She speaks of winter when Mikal has not even asked me to stay through winter.* Karyn shook her head in dismay. "Well, perhaps we can cut down my plaid dress enough to fit you."

"But that's too much work for you, Karyn. And besides, plaid doesn't suit me. That golden stripe will make my skin look green. Tomorrow we can go to Mr. Miller's store and buy some dress fabric." Sophie hesitated. "I realize he has no finished goods for women, but surely he has fabric."

Karyn shook her head. "Calico is thirty-five American cents a yard, Sophie. It would cost nearly four dollars to buy buttons and cloth for a new dress. We don't have means to go to Miller's and buy dress fabric."

"But I do," Sophie argued. "I told you Papa was very generous."

"You also said that you are hoping to start a business. How much do you have?"

"After I paid Mr. Hawks for bringing me to Millersburg, I still have nearly twenty dollars."

"To rent a room in Millersburg—if you can find one—to buy a sewing machine and a few sewing supplies—this will take more than twenty dollars, Sophie."

Sophie looked up, enthusiasm shining in her eyes. "Oh, that won't matter. Cay Miller offered a window and lumber on credit for an addition to this miserable hut." She raised her blue eyes to meet Karyn's gaze. "Surely he would extend credit to pay for one new dress." Her mouth was set. It was a familiar expression. Sophie Ensinger was going to get her way, and that was that.

Karyn shook her head, determined to be just as stubborn as Sophie. "No. We do not buy things we don't need, Sophie. Cay Miller's generosity allows credit sometimes. But Mikal is determined to reserve credit for emergencies. He would feel responsible for your debt, too. He is my husband, and I will obey him. We are not going into debt to buy you a dress."

Sophie's lower lip protruded in the severe pout that had always succeeded in bringing matters her way. But instead of giving in and finding a way to grant Sophie's wish, Karyn was rankled by the attempt to manipulate. She said firmly, "In another week or so, I will have enough butter and eggs to afford fabric for a dress. Until then, you can wear the plaid dress. If we work together, I think we can finish the alterations tomorrow."

Sophie wheedled, "But you only have three dresses, Karyn. I can't ask you to make such a sacrifice for me." She reached for her little bag, and withdrew a small roll of bills. "Please. Just this once. Can't we go into Millersburg—"

"I have been in America for three months, Sophie. I have been to Millersburg twice. Once when I arrived, and once with Mikal. We do not go to town on a whim. Besides, I am making dresses for several of the women for the Fourth of July celebration. I have too much work to do to take an entire day to go to Millersburg."

"The Fourth of July?" Sophie asked.

Karyn explained, "The day when the Americans celebrate the beginning of their country. Mikal says it is the biggest party of the year. Even bigger than Christmas."

Somewhat mollified by the prospect of a party so soon after her arrival, Sophie calmed down.

Karyn had continued to unpack the trunk as they talked. With the exception of Sophie's hair combs and apron, a feather tick and a few books, her possessions were, like Karyn's, not suited to life in a soddy. Karyn ran her hands lovingly over one of the books. "I'm glad you brought this," she said softly. "I will enjoy reading it again."

Sophie teased, "I remember you sitting on the front step pretending to read that book. What you were really doing was waiting for Hans Gilhoff to drive by."

Karyn sighed. "Yes, poor Hans." She surveyed the pile of things on the bed. "We must repack these things. Then you can see the dugout where Mikal spent his first two winters." Karyn smiled. "And you will realize that our little sod house is an improvement."

When the trunk was once again nearly filled with Sophie's treasures from Germany, Karyn asked, "Could we use your trunk for a table over by the stove?"

Sophie was hesitant. "What if the wooden slats across the top make things tip? Something might seep inside and ruin my things."

"I'll make a flat cover out of some crates Mikal has out back," Karyn explained. "The trunk will just be a base." She was already positioning the trunk near the stove. She stood up and smiled happily. "In fact, this will also make a good cutting table. I won't have to move my sewing so often. I can leave the kitchen table outside."

"But then we will have to eat outside," Sophie protested.

Karyn nodded briskly. "Of course. It was cool enough this morning when you came to eat in the kitchen. But most of our eating and as much cooking as possible is done outside. It keeps the house cooler." She smiled. "Did you notice that even my sewing machine is outside? Sophie, you will get so much good, fresh air here, I am certain your health will improve. You will be the owner of your own business in Millersburg in no time." Enthused by the thought of Sophie living in Millersburg, Karyn added, "You won't regret coming to America, Sophie."

Karyn rolled up her feather tick and headed for the door. "Come and see the rest of the homestead." On the way down the slope to the corral, Karyn pointed out her seedling trees. "Mikal was gone for three weeks. He hauled lumber from Kearney and then built Cay's new store. While he was gone, the Delhommes helped me plaster the inside of the house and make a floor that I can sweep. I transplanted seedlings from the bank of the creek." As she spread the feather tick on the corral fence she said proudly, "Mikal was very surprised when he got back and saw what I had accomplished."

Sophie was amazed. "You mean it looked even worse than this when you first came. And you stayed here? Alone? Weren't you frightened?"

Karyn shook her head. She leaned against the corral fence for a moment as she spoke. "I was a little nervous the first night, but I soon became accustomed to the sounds of the various night creatures. The nights really are lovely here. The sun goes down and the sky is a rainbow of peach, then apricot, then there is the most stunning violet . . . and then the moon and the evening stars appear. The air is cooled, and more stars appear overhead like a vast garden of diamonds." She joked, "Of course, I was reassured by having Mikal's rifle with me."

Sophie nodded. "Then he knew not to worry about you."

Karyn grinned mischievously. "Oh, I didn't think it was necessary for him to know everything about me right away. I told him Papa likes to hunt, and I left it at that."

Sophie laughed. "Well, I hope I am there when he discovers that you are probably a better shot than he is."

Karyn led Sophie inside the tiny dugout.

"He lived in here for two entire winters?" Sophie looked about her in disbelief. Karyn nodded proudly.

Sophie shivered. "I would have gone mad." She headed for the doorway and the sunlight, promising herself that she would have her business established in Millersburg long before winter.

103

"Tell me more about the Delhomme family," Sophie asked as they walked back up the slope toward the soddy.

Karyn recounted the details of her meeting with Celest and Emile. She told Sophie about the dance they had hosted, concluding with, "I see Celest as often as I can. She is our nearest neighbor. Only a few miles away."

Sophie sighed. "I'm glad you are so happy, Karyn." She looked about her. "I can see that you and Mikal are working very hard, but"—she stopped short, then plunged ahead—"I thought it would be a good joke on you to arrive unannounced." She looked towards the soddy and sighed. "But I should have waited until Papa was ready to come." She smiled. "He believes all the stories about people coming to America and having their health restored."

"Have you been very ill, Sophie?" Karyn asked, heading back up the slope toward the house.

"Oh, nothing really serious," Sophie said quietly. She reached up to lay one hand at her throat. "It just seems that I never have energy." As if to illustrate her point, the moment they arrived at the door of the soddy Sophie sank into the chair beside the sewing machine, breathless. "I'm always so tired." Her blue eyes grew dark and serious. "Sometimes I think I won't live long, Karyn."

Fighting her resentment of Sophie's dramatics, Karyn patted her on the shoulder and said, "Don't be discouraged. We will visit Celest. She knows about remedies from the Indians. I'm sure you'll feel better soon."

Sophie looked up, frightened. "Indians?"

Karyn laughed. "There haven't been any Indians about that I know of, Sophie. Mikal says they are all farther to the west now." She shielded her eyes and glanced toward the sun momentarily. "Come now. You take a nap. Mikal has forgotten his lunch, and it's time I take it to him. Then, I must get to my sewing."

Sophie followed Karyn inside the soddy and sank onto the bed with a sigh. Karyn put half a loaf of bread, a chunk of butter, and a sausage in a sugar sack. While she worked, she explained, "Mikal is plowing the northwest quarter of our section. I won't be gone too long." There was no answer from the bed. Sophie had fallen asleep.

Mikal was waiting with a big smile and a hearty thanks when Karyn rode up and handed him his lunch. He took off his hat and wiped his brow. "I wouldn't have blamed you for letting me go hungry, but I'm glad you didn't. I brought water for the horses, but in all the excitement I forgot about feeding myself." Mikal opened the sack with his lunch in it. He took a bite of bread and then set the sack on the ground.

"Sophie's arrival was quite a shock, wasn't it?" Karyn said quietly. Frowning a little she said, "I'll do my best to see that she is not a burden to you."

Mikal protested, "How could such a little thing as Sophie be a burden?" He looked up at Karyn. "She will be good company for you and good help with the sewing, too. I'm glad she came. In fact, I was thinking as I plowed this morning that it might be better for you if she stays with us for a while instead of moving into Millersburg. Although I am certain Cay will be eager to rent her the rooms over his new store." He asked abruptly, "Can you stay while I eat?" He didn't wait for Karyn to answer. Reaching up he put his hands about her waist and lifted her to the ground. In the process, he bumped against the broad brim of her bonnet, pushing it back off her head.

Blushing, Karyn turned away from him and fumbled with untying another sack containing a corked jug full of fresh water. She left the bonnet as it was, draped about her shoulders, un-aware that Mikal was admiring the way the sun put red and gold highlights in her rich brown hair. When she handed the jug to Mikal he took a drink. Then, stepping away from Karyn, he removed his hat and poured the cool water over his head. Water plastered his flowing hair to his head, ran down the back of his neck, and soaked his shirt. He shook his head like a horse. Drops of water flew in all directions as he clamped his hat back on his head.

After Karyn had put the empty jug back in its bag and tied it to the saddle horn, she raised her hand to her brow and squinted toward the far end of the line of broken sod. "The new team is making a difference, yes? Already today you have much plowed."

Mikal lowered his voice and cleared his throat. "Do you think—I mean, now that Sophie has come, it should be easier for you here. Not so lonely." He took his hat off and wiped his damp brow with his forearm before continuing. "I was hoping that the planting of the garden meant that you were thinking of extending our agreement. But I haven't had the courage to say anything. It seems we never have opportunity for talking—just us two."

Looking up into Mikal's blue eyes, Karyn felt her heart begin to pound. Self-consciously, she bent to retrieve his lunch from where he had set it on the ground. As she handed it to him she said, "I have been thinking about harvest. Celest speaks of our working together to can and dry our garden produce."

Mikal seemed to have forgotten about eating his lunch. He held the sack in one hand, but his blue eyes never left hers as he said, "I don't think I can manage to build another room onto the house this year. Do you think you and Sophie could stand a Nebraska winter in the soddy? You remember my tales of my two winters here. It will be much colder than Brandenburg . . . much more severe." He quickly added, "Of course I can manage in the dugout."

He wants me to stay through the winter. Karyn straightened her back and answered firmly, "I'm not frightened by tales of blizzards and cold, Mikal. We can manage just fine. With or without Sophie." *Please, God, without Sophie.*

Mikal took note of Karyn's reference to "we" and nodded happily. "Then it's settled. I promise never again to hint that you might not be able to persevere, and you promise not to speak of leaving Nebraska."

Karyn nodded. She gathered up Sugar's reins and mounted, preparing to leave. Mikal thanked her again for bringing out the lunch, which he still had not eaten. Karyn urged Sugar forward, but the little mare had taken only one step when Mikal called Karyn's name. She pulled Sugar up.

Mikal reached out and put one giant hand over Karyn's. He

squeezed gently and said, "I don't say much, Karyn, but it's good to have you here in Nebraska. In my life."

Looking down into Mikal Ritter's gorgeous blue eyes, Karyn was suddenly filled with happiness. She said, "And it's good to be in your life, Mikal."

Mikal nodded. Clearing his throat he pulled his hand away and said, "Sophie will be wondering what has become of you."

"Yes," Karyn said. "I should be getting back to Sophie." She urged Sugar forward and rode off at a smart gallop.

Karyn had unsaddled Sugar and turned her into the corral, picketed Ella in a lush stand of buffalo grass, watered each seedling tree, and was seated at her sewing machine before Sophie woke from her nap.

When Sophie appeared yawning and blinking against the bright sun, Karyn said, "Bring a chair outside, Sophie. I want to hear everything about home. You can hem this dress for me while I set in the sleeves on another. You always could do the hemming so much more quickly than I."

Sophie came outside. "I brought something for you." She handed Karyn a photograph of herself with Vroni and Jette. Sophie joked, "We wanted to make certain you didn't forget us now that you are a rich American." She sat down and began to stitch and chatter about their friends and acquaintances in Brandenburg while Karyn pushed the ornate foot pedal on her sewing machine faster and faster.

"Does it disturb you to hear me speak of the Gilhoffs, Karyn?" Sophie asked suddenly.

Karyn stopped sewing. She leaned back in her chair and stretched, bending her neck from side to side and reaching up to rub her shoulder before she answered. Finally, she said, "Hans is not coming back to this earth, and I have a new life here in America. I intend to make it a useful one. Mikal is a good man. He's very different from Hans, but he is suited to this life." She turned her head and looked across the vast tableland that stretched toward the east. Remembering Mikal's hand on hers only a few hours earlier, she said sincerely, "I'm content."

"But what of love, Karyn? Have you given up thoughts of love?"

Karyn considered the question, looking soberly over the shiny black top of her sewing machine. "I thought I loved Hans. But I was just a foolish girl play-acting a romance: Handsome Boy Goes to War and Swears Undying Love." She looked down at her hands. "Celest Delhomme says that true love is standing by someone in sickness and trouble as well as in happiness." She began to stitch very slowly. "Mikal Ritter is the kind of man who stands by his friends in sickness and in trouble and in happiness."

"Well," Sophie blustered, stabbing the dress hem energetically, "if I were in your place, I would want to be much more than his friend."

And I do. Karyn blushed and changed the subject. "Mikal says he knows many men who have come here from the east because of poor health. Most of them find that the hard work and the good air improve their health." She smiled. "We must hope that you find the same result, dear sister."

Sophie tied off her thread and looked towards the horizon. After a long moment, she murmured, "There is not even a thing one can hide behind." A moment longer and Sophie's face brightened. "Well, Karyn, until I can find a little room in Millersburg, perhaps I can be of some use to you. Heaven knows I have been too ill to be much help to our dear mother. But if what you say is right about America, things will improve."

Karyn finished setting the sleeves into the dress in her lap and stood up. "I must get to the weeds in the garden, or my poor little cucumber patch is going to disappear and die."

Sophie jumped up. "I can help."

The two sisters walked together to the garden. Karyn recited what she had planted, teaching Sophie the words for each plant. "Tomatoes here. Cucumbers there. Cabbage here. Turnips and beets over there." She handed Sophie a hoe. "When I first came, this was only a square of tall grass. You would not believe the work it is to plant in virgin sod. I did it while Mikal was gone." She straightened up for a moment. "And then he put the sod wall around to keep wildlife out. I never imagined things would grow so well the first year. Mikal says the soil is unbelievably rich. We won't hoe along like we do at home. Only chop out the tall weeds."

They had finished only half a row when Sophie stopped to wipe the sweat from her brow. She leaned heavily on the hoe, shaking her head. "I am sorry, Karyn, but I fear I am too weak—" The words were barely out of her mouth when Sophie crumpled to the ground.

Karyn ran to the well. Soaking a cloth in cool water, she ran back to Sophie. Cradling her head in her lap, she wiped her brow, shading her from the sun with her own body.

Sophie opened her eyes and smiled softly. "You see, Karyn, how the old ways have followed me even here." She sat up and looked about her, blinking her eyes.

"You had better get out of the sun, Sophie."

Sophie nodded. "Yes. I am afraid you are right."

"It's cool in the house. Go in and rest for a while. If you feel better, you can finish hemming the blue dress."

Karyn helped her up, and Sophie made her way to the sod house, weaving uncertainly as she walked. As she disappeared inside, Karyn grabbed the hoe Sophie had been using and tossed it toward the garden wall. Then she returned to her own work, striking at the offending weeds in her cucumber patch with unusual vigor. *So. This is how it is to be.*

The Diary
June 30, 1880

Sophie arrived today. Such a surprise! She speaks—in English—of a dressmaking business. May God grant her renewed health. Mikal asks that I stay through the winter. It will be strange having Sophie in the house. Mikal says the dugout is fine, but I wish it did not have to be this way. How I have changed, from longing to have people around me, to longing for time alone. But no, not really alone.

CHAPTER 9

Red, White, and Blue Ribbons

For the lips of a strange woman drop as an honeycomb, and her mouth is smoother than oil.
Proverbs 5:3

"But you *must* wear it, Karyn," Sophie begged, holding the blue silk gown up for Karyn to inspect. "I brought it all the way from Brandenburg." She wheedled, "You'll look so pretty. It will be a wonderful surprise for Mikal to see you in a new gown. He won't be able to take his eyes off you."

Karyn stubbornly shook her head. "No. I appreciate your bringing it. It's truly lovely. But I cannot wear it."

"Why not?" Sophie actually stamped her foot. "Surely you can see it's much better suited to your coloring than that old green thing you brought with you."

"As it happens, Sophie, I don't have 'that old green thing' anymore. But even if I did, I wouldn't be wearing it."

"What do you mean you don't have it anymore?"

"I gave it to Ida the night before the meeting in the church."

"Karyn Ensinger! You didn't! Why, Ida Gerstenschlager never had a silk gown in her life!"

"She deserved to feel just as pretty as the rest of us, Sophie." Karyn smiled, remembering Ida's shy smile when she saw herself in the hotel mirror the morning of her meeting with her prospective husband. While Sophie fumed, Karyn went on to recount

110

her experience at the Delhommes' social. She concluded, "I absolutely cannot arrive in a new silk gown. Not one of the dresses I made for this celebration was silk. I will not have the women thinking I purposely tried to best them. It would be cruel. I will be much happier in the red calico." She pulled some red, white, and blue ribbons from a box on her trunk and held them up. "I am going to braid these ribbons you brought me into my hair. I will look just like the American flag!"

Sophie sniffed impatiently. "Well, *I* am wearing a silk gown, and I will *make* them like me whether they want to or not."

Indeed. Karyn reached for her red calico dress. She sighed a bit wearily. She had risen almost in the middle of the night and spent the entire morning baking and cooking. She had two baskets each of corn bread and rye bread. Mikal had shot half a dozen prairie chickens and a particular prize—a wild duck. Karyn had spiced their last treasured crock of dried apples, adding vinegar and the last of her white sugar to create *eingamachcte Apfel,* something Mikal had once mentioned that he missed from his homeland. There was a platter of blina pancakes, to be served with sausage and beet syrup, the latter to be provided by Celest. As they loaded the wagon, Karyn blushed with pleasure at Mikal's praise for the bounty she would add to the tables at the celebration.

The closer they got to Millersburg, the more excited Sophie became. She moved her slippered feet in a little dance as they rode along, exclaiming happily as they approached Millersburg and saw that the little hamlet was already crowded with wagon after wagon. Children dressed in fanciful costumes ran everywhere, and small clutches of women moved up and down the street complimenting one another's new dresses and trimmed bonnets.

Cay Miller and Luc Delhomme had erected a dais on the front steps of Miller's store. The store itself was bedecked with red, white, and blue bunting. Lacking a cedar pole long enough to serve as a flagpole, Cay had unrolled a huge American flag from the second story roofline of his store. Loud popping noises came from behind the blacksmith's shop where a group of young men had gathered to fire their guns and pound powder on the black-smith's anvil.

Across the street from Cay's store, a long row of tables stretched along the entire length of the Kruger house. There were massive quantities of fried chicken, potato salad, sandwiches, something Celest later identified as "brownstone front cake," and gooseberry and raspberry pie, a testimony to the diligence of both women and children in gathering wild fruit from creeks and canyons.

There were four huge barrels of fresh lemonade. Someone Karyn didn't know was producing a precious chunk of ice from a gunnysack. Wiping off the strands of insulating straw that had kept it frozen since the previous winter, he began to chip it into four chunks. Seeing the ice, Karyn wondered if the rumor was true that there would be real ice cream at the dance that night.

Karyn was carrying her platter of blina to the tables when Celest caught up with her. "Already I have heard from six women who tell me that you made their dresses." She squeezed Karyn's arm affectionately. "See, I told you you would have all the work you desired."

Karyn set down the platter of blina. "I have news, Celest. My sister has come."

"What? Which one?"

"Sophie. There." Karyn pointed across the street to where Sophie was standing next to Mikal. As Celest and she watched, Sophie smiled and shook Emile's and Luc's hands. Something was said, and Remi and Serge pressed forward, laughing and shoving one another. Sophie lifted her hands and waved them toward the boys, then turned and headed for the wagon where she retrieved a basket of biscuits and headed toward Celest and Karyn.

"You must be Celest," Sophie said. "Already I have met the charming men in your family," she said, nodding back over her shoulder. She set the basket of biscuits down on the table and turned toward Karyn. "Mikal says that we are to leave him to get the rest of the food. He has our chairs unloaded, and they are to begin the speeches soon." She leaned toward Celest and whispered, "And I do hope the men in America are not like the long-winded orators in Brandenburg." She stepped between Karyn and Celest, tucked one tiny hand under each woman's arm, and pulled them toward the chairs.

Every family in the surrounding area had brought chairs from home. There were rockers and straight-back chairs of every imaginable style. While some left their chairs in their wagons and sat at a distance from the podium where Cay Miller was just announcing the first speaker, others, like the Delhommes and the Ritters, arranged their chairs in theater fashion before Miller's store. In only a few moments, Germans and Danes, Irish and Swedes, English and Easterners, sat side by side, listening reverently as Cay Miller read the preamble to the Constitution of the United States. When he finished, the crowd stood to sing *America* and *The Star-Spangled Banner,* and then once again settled in their chairs for an afternoon of speech-making by various county dignitaries. Speeches were interspersed with songs. Women fanned themselves while their husbands smoked. Children alternately sat in their mothers' laps and trotted away to filch biscuits from the supper table.

When the speeches were finished, the afternoon of contests began. There was a horse race pitting Cay Miller's thorough-bred against Emile Delhomme's favorite saddle horse, followed by a baseball game in which the Millersburg Nine played the Olive Creek Gang. The Delhomme family contributed over half of the Millersburg Nine team. Luc Delhomme convinced Mikal to pitch. "With that arm," he said hitting Mikal playfully, "we'll be sure to win."

Mikal grinned. "Well, that's a strong arm, all right"—he pointed to his head—"but I don't understand that American game at all."

"You don't need to understand it, Mikal." Luc laughed. "Just throw the ball as hard as you can. We'll tell you what comes next."

Mikal threw the ball as hard as he could. Unfortunately, his control was lacking, and the Millersburg Nine nearly lost the game. But Remi and Serge saved it in the last inning with colossal hits judged to be home runs by virtue of the fact that each baseball landed in a patch of switchgrass just behind the black-smith's shop.

Sophie kept her promise to make the women like her in spite of her silk dress. Had she not been Sophie's sister, Karyn would have been tempted to think Sophie's behavior a bit contrived. Still, her mention of having been ill so much, her sighs for home, her exclamations of humility when women admired her gown, all seemed to endear her to the community.

In Karyn's eyes, Sophie's charm, which had worn thin as the day advanced, became positively annoying by the end of the baseball game. Mikal was coming toward her, his face wreathed in smiles, when Sophie felt faint and Mikal hurried off to get her a glass of lemonade. Karyn scolded herself for her lack of concern for her sister.

When Mikal encouraged her to join Celest and another group of women inspecting the new bolts of calico that Cay Miller had just received, she obeyed him. Looking through the window of the store, Karyn could see that Sophie had made a remarkable recovery. She was standing on tiptoe, wiping the sweat from Mikal's brow with a lacy handkerchief.

Finally, the sun set and the music began. Everyone moved their chairs from the front of Miller's store to the bowery where dancers could rest and talk between numbers. Cay Miller danced with Sophie for nearly half an hour before reluctantly allowing Serge Delhomme to cut in. Emile and Celest Delhomme waltzed beautifully to a rendition of "The Blue Danube." But much to Karyn's disappointment, Mikal gave no sign of interest in dancing with his wife. He joined the conversation with the new settlers, seemingly impervious to the music.

Mikal had just sat down by Karyn when Luc joined them. "Mikal," he said, "knowing you as I do, you are at this moment wondering how to tell your lovely wife that you dance with all the grace of a bull. So I have told her for you. And now I ask your permission to dance with your wife."

Mikal looked sheepishly at Karyn. "I'm afraid what he says is true." Obviously embarrassed, he nodded toward Luc. "Thank you, Luc."

"But everyone loves to dance, Mikal," Karyn insisted.

He shook his head. "Not me."

"But—" Karyn started to argue when Luc interrupted.

"Save yourself, Karyn. Believe me, you do *not* want to entrust yourself to this man. He'll break you with one giant step forward right onto the top of your foot." Luc grinned. "Sometime you must ask him to tell you about the evening my mother insisted that she could teach anyone to dance."

Mikal shook his fist at Luc and growled with mock ferocity.

Luc ducked away, defending himself with, "I promise I won't tell her the details, Mikal. But really, you should have let her know before she agreed to come out here, that while we have many, many dances, there is absolutely no possibility that she will ever actually dance with her husband!"

Caught between Mikal and Luc's easy banter, Karyn felt a surge of happiness. It was obvious that the two men were once again friends, and that any jealousy between them had been resolved.

"It's all right, Mikal," Karyn reassured him. "To tell the truth, Sophie is the dancer in our family." She turned toward Luc. "Why don't you find her, Luc. She's a much better partner than I." She longed to reach out and hook her hand in Mikal's arm, but something held her back. She could not bring herself to make a public display of something that did not exist in private.

Luc pulled her gently toward the bowery. "Just one dance, Karyn," he urged.

"Oh, all right then," Karyn agreed. With a glance at Mikal, who was nodding his encouragement, she followed Luc onto the dance floor.

Karyn danced with Luc, with Emile, with Serge, with Remi, each time returning to stand beside Mikal. He seemed content to have her dance with his friends, and she was content to bask in his gaze as he watched her move across the dance floor. It was nearly midnight when Karyn realized that Mikal had disappeared.

She went to look for him. She thought she saw shadows in the moonlight behind Miller's new store. Thinking that some of the older boys might be up to some mischief, she went to investigate. But instead of mischievous boys, Karyn discovered Sophie in Mikal's arms.

No, she reasoned later, *they were not really embracing.* She could hear what Sophie was saying. She was instructing him in a dance. Karyn was devastated. She had done everything in her power that night to convince Mikal to do even part of a dance with her. He would not concede. *How is it,* she wondered, *that Sophie, so recently arrived, has such power over him?*

"Karyn!" Sophie called happily. "See how I have convinced Mikal that he can dance, after all."

The moment Sophie spoke, Mikal wheeled about to face Karyn. He said sheepishly, "I thought perhaps I could learn, after all."

"Yes," Karyn said. "I see." She backed away. "Well, I think I'll be loading up the remains of our supper. Perhaps there will be enough that I won't have to cook so much tomorrow." She wheeled about and headed toward the outdoor tables. In the moonlight, she covered the plates. Mikal appeared beside her. Without a word, he took things from her hands and returned them to the wagon. When they had finished, he spoke up. "She said she could teach me. I thought I might surprise you by asking you to dance before we go home."

"It is all right, Mikal. Please don't make such an issue of it."

When Mikal finally suggested it was time to go, Karyn pleaded a headache and went to lie down on the feather tick she had originally put in the wagon for Sophie. By the time the wagon pulled into the yard in front of the soddy, Sophie had fallen asleep on Mikal's shoulder.

The Diary
July 4, 1880
  My first Fourth of July in America. Such a celebration they have! Speeches and food, games and more food, dancing and more food. We ate until our eyeballs ached. Almost everyone is learning English, and listening to the chorus of voices and the accents made me so proud of this country,

*which offers an equal chance to all who will work hard. I
have much for which to be grateful, and I must dwell on
this rather than being tempted to worry over things of no
consequence.*

CHAPTER 10

A Rattler's Tail

Thou shalt not be afraid for the terror by night . . .
nor for the destruction that wasteth at noonday.
Psalm 91:5–6

A faint light in the east promised the coming dawn by the time the Ritters arrived at home. "What a wonderful time!" Sophie exclaimed as Mikal lifted her down from the wagon. He took a step toward the wagon box, but Karyn jumped to the ground from the opposite side of the wagon. Reaching for a basket of leftover food, she headed for the house.

Sophie lingered in the predawn light, looking up at Mikal with shining eyes. Mikal didn't notice. He was looking toward the house even as he lifted the chairs down from the wagon box. He carried two chairs inside, setting them down near where Karyn stood with her back to him, unloading the contents of the basket. When she didn't turn around, he took a step toward her. He was about to put one hand on her shoulder when she wheeled about briskly and, brushing past him, went back outside.

Mikal heard Karyn saying to Sophie, "I'll get the other basket of food. You must get to bed. You are exhausted, and you don't want to be ill."

Sophie giggled. "An evening of dancing could never make me ill, Karyn!"

From the doorway Mikal watched as Sophie whirled around happily. She said, "Wasn't it wonderful? Serge and Remi promised to help me with that American dancing soon. I don't know if I'll ever be able to keep up with the calling."

She looked past Karyn and at Mikal. "You must help me with my English. I want to learn to speak without such an accent."

Mikal stood to one side to let her go in, then he went to the wagon for the other chair, which he set beside the sewing machine outside. "There was talk of a literary meeting this Friday, Karyn. I have never cared to go alone, but perhaps we could attend together."

Yes, now that Sophie is here he finds time for such things. Karyn answered coldly, "Whatever you wish, Mikal. Good night." Thus dismissed, Mikal turned to go.

Inside, Karyn slipped out of her dress and into bed.

"Karyn—Karyn, listen. What is that?"

Karyn ignored her, but Sophie was persistent. She reached out and jostled Karyn's shoulder. "Karyn, wake up. I don't like the sound of that."

"It's only a cricket, Sophie. Go to sleep."

Sophie was quiet for a few moments, then she whispered loudly, "I think I hear someone talking. Is someone outside?"

Lifting her head from her pillow, Karyn listened carefully. "Coyotes. They look like small wolves. They will do us no harm, and Mikal will guard his sow and Ella and the calf. Now go to sleep."

"Who can sleep? That may be coyotes *outside,* but I still hear something *inside,* and I do not think it's a cricket." Sophie shivered. "What if something crawled in through the doorway while we were gone?" She muttered, "I cannot believe you live without a front door." She slipped out of bed. "I am going to get Mikal."

Karyn sat up abruptly, managing not to shout but still letting Sophie know that she was very angry. "Don't be ridiculous. We cannot be bothering Mikal every time we hear a little sound. You must remember that *he* cannot sleep late tomorrow." Motioning for her sister to get back in bed she said firmly, "He deserves at least one hour of sleep before his day begins."

"And do we not deserve to sleep, too?" Sophie insisted. She hurried outside while Karyn lay in bed fuming.

Mikal appeared at the doorway, his shirt half buttoned, only one strap of his overalls fastened. "What is it, Karyn?" he asked wearily.

Karyn didn't even turn over to look at him. "I told Sophie not to bother you. I will take care of it in the morning."

But Sophie persisted. "Something came in while we were gone. I am sure of it. I could hear it"—she pointed to the corner of the room—"over there."

Holding his lantern before him, Mikal dutifully inspected the corner Sophie had pointed out. "There's nothing there." He reassured her, "Everything seems louder at night. I'm sure it is nothing. Even with such fine housekeeping as Karyn's, unwelcome guests visit. Go to sleep. It's too dark to look anymore tonight. Tomorrow is Karyn's cleaning day. You can solve the mystery when the sun comes up."

Mikal left. After perching on the side of the bed for a moment, Sophie relented and snuggled under the quilts again.

While Sophie snored, Karyn lay awake replaying the evening's events. She wrapped herself in a cloak of self-pity for as long as possible. For nearly an hour she managed to justify her feelings. But then she considered Mikal's response to Sophie's pleas for him to look for a mere cricket. He was exhausted, but he had come back up the slope with his lantern. Instead of scolding Sophie for her silliness, he had inspected the soddy. He had been patient and reassuring. He had even complimented Karyn's housekeeping.

Over and over again Karyn thought through the awful thing that Mikal had done at the dance the evening before, but try as she would, she finally had to admit that she was the author of her own misery. When Mikal had been jealous over her dancing with Luc, she had been angry. And now she was guilty of the same offense!

But she could not admit that to Mikal. Why, she would have to admit that she always felt clumsy and plain around Sophie, that she had to fight against resenting Sophie's charm. Worst of all, she would have to admit to feeling possessive about Mikal—

even jealous! Admitting that would include revealing that she was beginning to have feelings for him, which went far beyond their spoken agreement to be partners in the business of creating a successful farm. Mikal had said that he was glad that she was in his life, but he had given little indication that he had plans for them to ever be more than good friends. He was a forthright man. Unlike Hans, he was not given to flirting and to clever, romantic speech. If she raised the issue of feelings about Sophie and Mikal, he might well take the opportunity to say that he found Sophie attractive. No, she definitely could not talk to Mikal about being jealous of Sophie.

Lying in the dark, listening to the rustling of something that she knew was not a cricket, Karyn decided that tomorrow she would clean the soddy, she would clean Mikal's dugout—and she would find a way to apologize to him without words.

By the time Mikal emerged from the dugout the next morning, Karyn was bent over the outdoor fire pit cooking his breakfast. By the time he fed the livestock, she had disappeared. He went up the slope to look for her, but stopped when he saw a steaming cup of coffee and a plate of cakes sitting on one of the stumps beside the fire. Beside the stump a sugar sack held his lunch. Obviously, Karyn had no intention of discussing the previous night's events. With a sigh, Mikal settled down to eat. He had downed nearly half a plateful of pancakes before he saw Karyn making her way toward the creek with a basket over her arm.

As soon as she saw Mikal drive the team out of the corral and head toward the tree claim, Karyn began cleaning the dugout. She pulled his feather tick and comforter outside and stretched them across the corral fence. She was careful to put the comforter bright side down so that the relentless sun could not fade the colorful fabric used for the top. She swept the floor vigorously, sneezing amid the clouds of dust and thanking God that her house had a hard floor. She wiped down the few pieces of furniture in the room and cleaned the little stove in the corner. Then, she put a bouquet of wildflowers where Mikal would see them as soon as he returned from the tree claim.

Karyn was on her way up the slope toward the soddy when she heard Sophie shriek, "Karyn! Karyn, where are you! A snake! It's a snake!"

Karyn ran to the doorway of the soddy where she stopped, staring with horror at a huge brown snake coiled up at the foot of her and Sophie's bed. It was a hideous thing with an odd diamond pattern running down its back. Its tail rattled.

"Don't move, Sophie."

Without taking her eyes from the snake, Sophie whispered, "I can't move, Karyn. I'm too—too—" She didn't finish; she just sat wide-eyed, staring at the snake.

Karyn took a step backward and whispered hoarsely, "I'll get—something—" She wanted to scream for help, but she knew that even if Mikal heard her, he was too far away to get there in time to stop that hideous thing from striking out at Sophie.

The thought of defending Sophie melted the last vestiges of resentment over her flirting with Mikal. It also spurred Karyn to action. She hardly knew what she was doing, but one moment she was backing out of the soddy and the next she was headed back inside, walking calmly toward the snake and grasping a hoe poised to strike it.

Sophie's eyes grew wider. "Karyn—what if you miss?"

"I won't—miss." In the seconds she had paused between the words, Karyn struck at the snake. Miraculously, she pinned the ghastly head of the creature against the quilts. It thrashed about with deadly force, flailing the three feet of its length about in a vain attempt to escape the pressure of the hoe against its neck.

Terrified, Karyn bore down with all her might. What seemed like hours passed before the snake was finally dead, its head partially severed. Karyn reached down to pick it up by its tail. It was a meter long, but she laughed nervously. "Not so big." She dragged the dead snake out of the house, tossed it aside, and went back inside to comfort Sophie.

Sophie cried for a long time, clutching desperately at her sister. "How did you do it, Karyn? Weren't you afraid?"

Karyn hugged Sophie. "I couldn't stand idly by and watch my Sophie be hurt, now could I?"

"Well, I couldn't have done it. I would still be sitting there staring at that hideous thing or suffering from the effects of the poison. I heard the men talking about rattlesnakes at the celebration. A child was bitten last week. He suffered horribly before he died." Sophie, who had begun to calm down, began to cry again.

"Come now, Sophie. Don't let it make you ill. Get dressed. We don't have to look for an intruder anymore, but I still want to clean. We must wash the shelves in the kitchen, air the quilts and the feather tick, sweep, dust—" She smiled. "Work will take our minds off our little ordeal."

Sophie got dressed and went through the motions of helping Karyn clean, but it wasn't long before she pleaded weakness and had to sit down. Karyn was not to be deterred. She accomplished her tasks alone, humming happily to herself while Sophie sat on a chair just outside the door, pretending to sew.

When at last Mikal arrived home, he was greeted by the aroma of cabbage soup cooking over the fire. With renewed vigor, he turned the horses into the corral and made his way up to the house.

Karyn emerged from inside with a plate of biscuits in her hand just as Mikal bent over to inspect the dead rattlesnake.

"You did not tell me that Nebraska has this variety of cricket, Mr. Ritter."

Mikal was speechless.

Karyn continued, "The ungrateful creature was willing to share the warmth of our bed, but quite unwilling to depart without threatening violence to poor Sophie."

Mikal looked toward where Sophie was sitting. At the question in his eyes, Sophie nodded. "I awoke this morning to the specter of that creature coiled at the foot of the bed, preparing to strike me down." She described Karyn's performance with the hoe. "She saved my life, Mikal. She saved my life." Sophie burst into tears.

He frowned. "I should have warned you, Karyn. It is one of the bad things about Custer County. We wage a constant war against the rattlesnakes."

"You mean," Sophie cried out, "you mean there are more—

nearby?" She clutched the dress she had been hemming to her breast in a dramatic show of horror.

Mikal shook his head. "Probably not many now. I killed thirty-five during spring plowing. Emile and the boys killed more earlier, when they had just come out of their burrows. They've scattered now." His voice shaking, he added, "Thank God you weren't hurt."

Was that tenderness in his voice? Karyn blushed. "Yes, thank God and"—she looked down at the plate of biscuits—"and have a biscuit." She thrust the plate at Mikal and hurried toward the fire where she began dishing up soup.

"Come, Sophie," she called. "You've had the entire day to recover from our excitement over the snake. Come. Eat."

The morning after her introduction to the prairie rattlesnake, Karyn awoke before daylight to the sound of the wagon being driven out of the yard. Hurrying to the door, she watched in dismay to see Mikal headed toward Millersburg. In light of the previous day's excitement, she would have expected Mikal to invite her to ride along.

"Sophie, wake up!" Karyn called over her shoulder. "Mikal has gone to town without us. What do you say to a visit with the Delhommes? If we take our time, we can ride double on Sugar."

A few hours later Karyn and Sophie rode up to the Delhommes' house just in time to help Celest prepare lunch. After a meal during which Sophie once again exercised her dramatic talents recounting the story of the rattlesnake, the women made their way across a pasture to a small thicket of chokecherries. They collected the deep red fruit until their baskets were brimming. The rest of the day was spent washing and pitting chokecherries. They made four pies for Friday's literary meeting, then canned the remaining fruit. Shortly after supper, Mikal rode up on one of the draft horses.

"You didn't leave word where you were." He was obviously upset. "I was worried."

"Well, you didn't leave word where you were going, either," Karyn retorted. "I didn't think we needed to wait meekly for your permission before going to help a neighbor harvest chokecherries."

Mikal grinned. "Of course you don't need my permission." With a look toward the horizon, he said, "Those clouds may be here before we can get back, but I'd like to try and beat them. I have a surprise for you at home."

He was obviously quite pleased with himself. Karyn's heart beat a little faster when he said, "You ride with me, Karyn. Sophie can manage Sugar."

Mikal pulled Karyn up behind him, and they set out for home. When they finally rode up to the soddy, it was dark enough that Karyn saw no evidence of Mikal's trip to Millersburg. Mikal kicked one leg over his horse's mane and slid to the ground, and as he did so, Sophie, who had jumped down first, squealed with delight. "A door, Karyn. Mikal has given us a door!"

Karyn laid one hand on her husband's arm. She took her hand away, blushing. "It's so good of you. I hope you didn't feel pressure from us." She frowned. "I would never want you to have to go in debt for anything so—"

Mikal interrupted her. "I made a very satisfactory arrangement with Cay. Don't be concerned. When I told him what had happened, he dropped the price of the door. I will have it paid for by next week. In fact, he threw in a large bell, which I will position at the top of a pole here in the yard." He leaned toward Karyn. "And the next time there is an emergency, you will be able to ring the bell for me."

From inside the house Sophie called good night, leaving the two of them alone. Karyn said hopefully, "Would you like some coffee, Mikal? It won't take long to stir up the fire."

He thanked her. "Just let me take Lena down and turn her into the corral. I'll be right back."

It wasn't long before the two of them were seated around the fire. Mikal sipped coffee and said, "Thank you for the flowers, Mrs. Ritter."

Karyn blushed and spoke once more of the debt at Miller's store. "How much do we owe, Mikal? Cay mentioned wanting me to make shirts to sell at his store. If you can get me the cloth he wants me to use, I can help with the bill."

"Really, Karyn, it's no problem. Cay offered a very satisfactory solution." He chuckled softly. "When I asked for credit, he answered, 'Credit I would gladly give you, Mikal. But you don't need credit. If you will arrange for me to sit by Sophie at the Literary Society meeting, I will consider it a fair trade for the door. In fact, if you can get Karyn to invite me to dine with you sometime soon, I will include that large bell so that Sophie and Karyn have a way to summon help in future emergencies'."

"So that's how it is," Karyn said softly.

"Yes, that's how it is." After a brief pause, Mikal said, "You know, Karyn, as the founder of Millersburg, Cay has a very promising future. Once the railroad comes, he will be able to relax and enjoy life. He has enough investments already to provide him with a good income. He only lacks a wife to share his future." He added pointedly, "And one thing is certain. Cay Miller's wife will have an easy life."

Karyn and Mikal drank coffee and talked until long after the little fire died down. Mikal finally said good night, unaware that Karyn was watching him retreat down the slope. He lay in bed looking at the wildflowers Karyn had put on his table for a long time before finally getting up and going back outside, where he leaned against the corral fence. He heard the hinges of the new soddy door creak and looked up to see Karyn come outside. A faint golden light from a lamp illuminated the back of her silhouette. She had taken her hair down. Dressed in her nightgown, she stood under the porch for a few moments, looking up at the sky before turning around and going back inside.

Standing in the dark, looking up toward his house, Mikal thought of Cay Miller and smiled. Perhaps, just perhaps the way had been provided for him to once again have the life he longed for, the privacy he and Karyn needed.

The Diary
July 6, 1880
  I killed a rattlesnake. Horrible creatures. God protect my Mikal from them. He said that he has killed thirty-five al-

ready this year. Sophie and I helped Celest can chokecher-
ries and make pies for the literary. We have a new front
door. I will use the old quilt to stuff another comforter for
Mikal. There is a plot between Cay Miller and Mikal re-
garding Sophie. I must invite Cay to dinner soon.

CHAPTER 11

A Literary Society Programme

God thundereth marvellously
with his voice; great things doeth he,
which we cannot comprehend.
Job 37:5

On Friday, Karyn decided to roast six prairie chickens for the supper preceding the literary society meeting. Since only three hens would fit into the roaster she used in her outdoor oven, Karyn fired up the indoor stove. Firsthand, she learned the excellent insulating properties of sod walls. Not only the hens, but also anyone inside the soddy, roasted. Even Sophie spent the day outdoors.

After lunch Karyn went to tend the garden. Sophie, who could not bear the hot sun, meandered down the slope of the hill to where Mikal sat outside the dugout mending harness. At sight of her, he smiled and nodded. He didn't look up from his leather-working when he said, "It's about time Ella was moved to fresh grass." He nodded toward where the heifer had been picketed between the creek and the corral.

Sophie sighed. "I'm sorry, Mikal, but I'm afraid of cows."

He looked at her levelly. "Some say that the best way to overcome fears is to face them. Ella is very gentle. She'll follow you like a puppy." He nodded back up toward the garden where Karyn was hard at work. "It would help us both if you could take charge of Ella. I can teach you to milk. Perhaps you and Karyn could work out a way to share the butter-making. Then you could begin to save money toward your business in town." He paused meaningfully. "It shouldn't tire you out too much. Try it."

Sophie marched off to move Ella, indignance evident in the tilt of her head and her unusually energetic gait. She snatched up Ella's picket rope, screeching when Ella tossed her head to flick away the flies. When Ella's calf butted her playfully, Sophie was caught unawares and sprawled on her back. She lay there for a few moments, waiting for someone to help her up. But no one came, and the calf showed an inclination to lick her face, so Sophie picked herself up. Shoving the picket stake as far into the earth as she could manage, she marched back up to the house.

Mikal covertly watched the entire display, smiling to himself. Obviously, Sophie's health was improving. The brisk walk back up to the house didn't seem to have left her short of breath.

When he saw Karyn come around the side of the house and head for the well, Mikal set aside the harness and started up toward the soddy. Sophie went inside, but not until she was certain he knew that she was purposely avoiding him.

Karyn was pulling up a bucket of fresh water when Mikal reached from behind her and took over the hoisting of the rope. "It won't be much longer, and I'll have a windmill," he said. "Then I'll build a slurry to carry the water down to the trough at the corral. I'll add a valve so you can collect water without having to hoist it up."

He dipped a tin cup into the bucket and held it out to her. "I hope you won't think I am interfering in the way you manage things, but I suggested that perhaps Sophie could take over the care of Ella."

"Yes." Karyn nodded. "She told me."

"I thought it would be a way for us to help her realize her goal of a shop in Millersburg. That is still her plan, yes?"

Karyn nodded. "I think so."

"Cay mentioned your making shirts for his store. Perhaps Sophie could talk to him about that at tonight's meeting. It would be a good way for her to get started with her own sewing business. She could have her name established before she moves to town."

"It's a good idea. I hate to turn down the work, but I was wondering how I would manage." Karyn set down the tin cup. "The hens should be just about cooked. When do you want to leave?"

Abruptly, Mikal said, "Let Sophie check on the hens. Walk with me."

Karyn walked to the door of the house. "Sophie," she called. "Would you check on the hens, please? Just see if the leg bone is loose like I showed you. Mikal and I"—her heart gave a little jump as she said it—"Mikal and I are going to take a walk together."

Sophie was lying on the bed, panting from the heat. She lifted her head weakly. "Of course, Karyn. In a few moments."

"Don't wait too long. We don't want them to burn." Karyn reached up to push her hair back under her bonnet, hurrying to catch up with Mikal who was already walking toward the creek. When they reached a place where a formation of rocks jutted out over the creek bed, he motioned for Karyn to sit down. Instead of sitting beside her, Mikal walked to the edge of the creek. Stooping down, he picked up a flat rock and skipped it across the surface of the water. "I am worried for Sophie. She doesn't seem to be getting much better. Cay is hoping to attract a doctor to Millersburg soon. If it works out, we must take Sophie to see him."

Karyn smiled. "You are very kind to be so concerned, Mikal. But Sophie has seen many, many doctors. None seemed to be able to find an exact cause for her spells."

Mikal tried to empathize. "Surely she cannot be happy not being able to participate more fully in life. *Arbeit macht Leben suss.*"

Karyn nodded. "Yes, work makes life sweet." She explained, "But from the time when she was very young, it seems that Sophie has always been either just recovering from something or being threatened by a new illness. A little at a time, she withdrew from the daily chores. I think that by the time she was eight Sophie's work had already become entertaining the rest of us while we did the work. She read to us, sang to us, made us laugh. My sisters and I shared her duties. No one seemed to mind." She looked up at him. "I don't think she planned it. It just happened. You know how it is. Every family seems to have one child that everyone enjoys spoiling. For us, it was Sophie."

Mikal sat back on the ground. Resting his elbows on his knees he looked up at her and shook his head. "There were five of us, and we were all expected to work hard. I was six years old when my father decided he was tired of the responsibilities of his family. He left my mother with five small children and a sixth on the way. Without one word of complaint, she took up the farming. Then, she began to take in laundry from the nearby village. My older brothers cared for the livestock; my sisters did the gardening. And I took orders from them all. It didn't matter if we felt sick or not. We all had to work."

Once again, Karyn's attentive listening encouraged him to share more than he had planned. "Mother used to leave us locked in the house when she had to go to the village. We had a big black dog like Celest's Frona to guard us. Unfortunately," he added, chuckling, "our Magda did nothing to guard me from my own brothers. They introduced me to tobacco . . . and entertained themselves by hanging me out the window by my suspenders."

Karyn laughed. "And they no doubt howled with remorse when your mother found out!"

He shook his head. "Oh, Mother was far too busy to know about any of that. And I knew if I said anything it would only get worse the next time she had to be gone." He chuckled. "They weren't cruel. Just normal boys having fun. They tormented me themselves, but if anyone else would have tried to harm me . . ."

Karyn nodded. "That's how we felt about Sophie. Sometimes we suspected she was play-acting. But let anyone else accuse her, and we united in her defense."

Mikal took his hat off and ran his hand through his hair. With a glance toward Karyn, he continued. "The spring after my father left, Mother was trying to harness our horse when he kicked her. She fell back, and her skirt got caught in the plow.

That horse dragged her halfway across the field before my brothers could get it back under control. They managed to carry mother in and run for the neighbors. Our little sister was born four days later. She lived one day. My mother was never the same after that."

"Oh, Mikal, I'm so sorry."

Mikal gave a little half-smile. "She had a strong faith in God. She carried on in spirit as though nothing had happened. I never heard her complain of all the work. And I never heard her say a bad word about my father. In fact," he said smiling with the memory, "after every supper, we joined hands to recite a blessing she had taught us. What still amazes me is that Mother never failed to close each of those prayers by asking God to bless our absent father." He stopped short and looked at Karyn. "You know, Karyn, in many ways you remind me of her—always working hard, never complaining."

Karyn blushed. "Your mother sounds like a saint. You can be sure I wouldn't be praying for a man who left me in such a situation."

"It took me a long time to understand that myself. Her good example didn't rub off on me until I had lost Marie-Louise and spent an entire winter alone with God. I think I understand a little of it now. She used to say over and over again, whenever anything bad happened, that we must simply trust and obey; obey by doing the little thing before us that God had provided to do, and trust in Him for the rest. When Marie-Louise died, the words *trust and obey* came back to me, but they were of no comfort. I did not trust God, and I had no idea why I should obey Him after what He had allowed to happen. It was years before I realized that I had two choices. Either I could trust and obey God, or I could spend the rest of my life being bitter about what had happened. I had had quite enough of bitterness. So I decided to try my mother's way."

"Your mother must have been so happy to know that you found peace, Mikal," Karyn said softly.

He blinked back tears. "Mother died long before I came to America." He stood up, brushing dust off his overalls. "Again, I begin talking, and you are so quiet I go on and on." He returned to the topic of Sophie. "I don't mean to be unkind about Sophie, Karyn. Don't misunderstand. Your entire family is welcome to come to America and to stay with us until they can find a homestead." He had reached out to put his hand on Karyn's shoulder when Sophie screeched, "Help! Help!"

Mikal was the first one to reach the soddy. Smoke was rolling out of the window and the doorway. Inside, Sophie was wrestling the charred remains of three prairie chickens out of the stove. She was covered with soot and crying angry tears.

Karyn came up behind Mikal and shooed him away. "I'll take care of it. You need to get the team hitched."

Mikal backed out of the way. He heard Karyn tease, "Well, Sophie, I think they are cooked now."

At the sound of Karyn's laughter, Sophie spat out, "Don't you dare laugh at me." Mikal heard something slammed down on the stove top with great force. Then, Sophie said, "How could any woman possibly be happy in this hovel? You should have married Hans! You'd be living like a queen on his estate right now, the widow of a war hero. Instead, you work yourself to death in the middle of the Great American Desert!" She burst into tears, unaware that while her words had been directed at Karyn, they had struck Mikal Ritter.

Mikal walked down the slope to hitch up his team, and although he had not done anything particularly tiring that day, his shoulders slumped beneath the weight of a great load of unhappiness and self-doubt.

In July of 1880, Millersburg, Nebraska, was perceived as either a hamlet on its way to becoming the county seat or a sad collection of hovels on its way to oblivion, depending on one's inclination to believe Cay Miller's insistence that the railroad would, indeed, come through Millersburg. He had convinced enough men to believe him that next to his store, along the dirt clearing he referred to as "Miller Street," were a hardware store, a blacksmith shop, and a saloon. Isaac Kruger's harness shop across from his store and a growing number of houses attested to Cay Miller's persuasive talents.

As the community founder, Cay was expected to preside over

the Literary Society meetings. Anticipating the arrival of Sophie Ensinger, he took special pains with his preparations that evening. He donned a well-tailored new suit and positioned himself by the door. When Sophie arrived, he ushered her to a seat near the front of the room. Everyone's contribution to supper was arranged on the store counters.

Cay opened the meeting with a brief speech. "You all know that my faith in and hopes for this fine community know no bounds. Later in the evening, after supper is served, I invite you to inspect my new rooms upstairs. I hope to have them rented soon, with at least one business that will be of special interest to the female population." Cay looked meaningfully in Sophie's direction. He went on, "This evening I also want to raise the subject of our need for a social hall."

Celest Delhomme spoke up. "I have some ideas about that, Mr. Miller." She stood and turned to look at the crowd. "In fact, if the women in attendance are in agreement, we can meet upstairs during the refreshment break and form a committee."

Everyone nodded, and Celest sat back down.

Cay introduced the first event of the evening—a debate between Luc Delhomme and Isaac Kruger on the subject "Resolved: That the Capital of the United States Should Be Removed to a More Central Location, i.e., the Great State of Nebraska."

Cay took his seat beside Sophie. The debate was followed by a spelling bee among the men, many of whom were just learning English, and their attempts at spelling made for quite a bit of laughter, even among the contestants themselves.

After the refreshment break, Cay led a group out the front door and up the long outdoor staircase leading upstairs. Sophie ascended the stairs on Luc's arm. Karyn decided to forego Celest's meeting about the social hall in favor of lingering downstairs with Mikal. While some of the men admired Cay's pipe display, others crowded around the table at the back of the store, drinking coffee. Mikal and Karyn made their way outside and sat together on a bench just outside the door.

Karyn said, "I've invited Cay for Sunday dinner."

Mikal nodded. "Good. He and Sophie seemed to enjoy each other's company this evening."

Karyn nodded halfheartedly.

"What's wrong?" Mikal wanted to know. "Did I miss something? Doesn't Sophie like Cay?"

"Of course she does," Karyn said. "Cay is very nice."

"But?" Mikal encouraged her. "Tell me."

Karyn felt awkward. "Oh, it's just that, compared to Luc, Cay isn't very—"

"Compared to Luc." Mikal thought for a moment. "Yes. I see." He said quietly, "But Luc Delhomme wants to be a *musician*. However handsome he may be, he can't offer nearly the future that Cay can. I guess for someone like Sophie it might seem romantic to share a musician's life, but she is just not the kind of woman who can adapt. She'd live to regret such a choice."

Although Karyn had virtually the same opinion as Mikal, she was not prepared to give someone outside the Ensinger family free rein to criticize her little sister—and certainly not when Sophie was not present to defend herself. She stood up. "Well then, Mr. Ritter, since you understand Sophie so well, and since you know the correct future for her, we should hurry upstairs so that you can order her to have feelings for Cay Miller." She folded her arms and added, "Before you do, however, don't forget to remind her to ignore Luc Delhomme's blue eyes and square jawline."

Mikal held up his hands and tried to make peace. "Karyn, I didn't mean—"

But Karyn interrupted him. "You need to realize, Mikal, that most women find it difficult, if not impossible, to simply order themselves to feel a certain way about a certain man." Karyn wished she could pull her words out of the air and stuff them back down her own throat. Mikal looked at her with an odd little smile. To hide the color she could feel creeping up the back of her neck, Karyn wheeled about and headed for the stairs. *You idiot,* she chastised herself. *What do you suppose Mikal thinks now of his little arrangement with you? You just managed to tell him there is little possibility of romantic feeling between the two of you.*

At the foot of the outdoor staircase, Karyn stopped. She wheeled back around, relieved to see that Mikal was following her. She grinned sheepishly. "Remember when I told you how the Ensinger sisters always rallied to defend poor little Sophie? You just got a demonstration. I'm sorry. I know you mean well. Please don't be angry with me. It's just—"

He looked up at her and flashed a smile. "I'm not angry. Just a little confused. But we can discuss that later. At the moment, I'm worried about that." He pointed toward the northwest.

"That little cloud?"

"I don't like the looks of that. If it turns out to be hail—"

"It's just one little cloud, Mikal."

"You're probably right." He smiled at her and turned his back on the clouds. "Can't we at least *try* to help Cay?"

Karyn opened her mouth to answer when a huge clap of thunder made her jump.

Mikal wheeled around and groaned, "Oh, no."

Dark clouds had appeared and were racing to overspread the entire sky to the northwest. In no time, the colors of a beautiful sunset were completely blotted out. Rain began to fall. Mikal and Karyn ducked back inside the store.

A dozen heavy boots clomped down the outside stairs. Men rushed inside the store, each one wanting to be near the window. Mikal put a protecting arm about Karyn. Outside, raindrops changed to small drops of ice. Then marble-size hail began to fall, sending up a chorus of groans from the room.

Just as someone said hopefully, "Maybe it won't be too bad—" a bolt of lightning landed in the street right outside Cay's store. The blinding light made Karyn see stars. She blinked rapidly, rubbing her eyes. When her vision cleared, the first thing she saw was a horse lying dead in the street, smoke rising from its carcass. Hail the size of lemons pounded at the horse's body, slashing its hide. Mikal pulled Karyn away from the window just as the wind shifted and threw hailstones against Cay's storefront, shattering every one of his new windows.

Karyn heard Sophie scream. Mikal kept her from running out into the storm. "Cay's with Sophie. She'll be all right."

Outside all was chaos. Terrified horses broke away and tore wildly down Miller Street. Men who ran out to try to calm their teams came back inside, cut and bleeding. Luc Delhomme staggered in with a bad gash on the back of his head.

Karyn grabbed a bolt of muslin off of Cay's shelf, ripped off a length, and made a temporary bandage, which she hastily tied around Luc's head. She pulled him toward the back of the store and lit a lamp. Holding the lamp high she demanded, "Let me see." She gently lifted the bandage away from the cut. Blood flowed down the back of Luc's head, staining his shirt collar. Wincing, Karyn looked up at Mikal. "You said Celest does a lot of doctoring. She needs to see this. I can sew it up if I must, but she can probably do a better job."

Mikal grabbed an iron pot off the stove to hold over his head and dashed outside and upstairs. He came back without Celest. "She says just put pressure on it. She's busy with Sophie at the moment." Luc went white and began to weave uncertainly.

"Luc," Karyn ordered, "don't you faint on me. Sit down. Lean your head over on your arms. There. You're going to be fine." She clamped a fresh piece of muslin over the wound, refusing to let herself think about the fact that Luc's skull was showing beneath a jagged piece of flesh. Handing the bolt of muslin to Mikal she ordered, "I'll need more pieces of this ripped off," and then in the same breath asked, "Is Sophie all right?"

"Just a small cut from the broken window. She fainted momentarily. There's a bump on her cheek."

Blood was seeping through the cloth on Luc's head. Karyn pressed down firmly. Luc had fallen asleep. Karyn frowned. "You'd better go get Celest. I'll see to Sophie as soon as Celest gets down here."

It had stopped hailing. Celest came rushing in. When Karyn lifted the bandage from the back of Luc's head, Celest's mouth set in a firm, thin line. "Let's boil some water."

Celest's serious manner banished all thought of Sophie and her little cut from Karyn's mind. She was lighting the stove when Celest said, "I'm going to need another pair of hands. Can you do this? I can't have anyone fainting in the middle of it."

Karyn nodded. "I would have done it myself, but I know you'll leave a neater scar."

Celest looked up at Mikal. "Can you ask Emile to come down? And Cay?"

Mikal left again. Every few moments Celest lifted the bandage to see if the bleeding had stopped enough for her to work.

Emile came in, covered with mud and breathing hard.

"It's all right, dear," Celest said calmly. "Karyn and I will get him sewn up in no time, and then I'm putting him to bed—" She looked at Cay who was standing just behind Emile. "If I can impose?"

"Of course," Cay said.

Celest turned back to Emile. "It's better if we don't move him tonight. Is the team all right?"

"Battered and scared to death, but nothing serious."

"I know you're wondering about the wheat. Why don't you and the boys go on home?"

"Should Remi go for a doctor?"

Celest shook her head. "I don't think so."

Emile called toward the front of the store where Remi and Serge were beginning to pick up shards of glass from Cay's broken windows. "Remi. Stay with your mother and Luc. If there's need for a doctor, you go. Serge and I will drive the team home and check on things."

Mikal came in, a very shaky Sophie leaning on his arm. A length of petticoat had been wrapped around her left forearm. A bump on her left cheek was beginning to turn blue.

"Cay," Celest called out. "I need a needle and thread."

Sophie paled. Her eyes widened as she slumped into the chair across from Luc. She lay her arm on the table and whispered hoarsely, "I thought you said it was just a little cut—"

"The needle and thread are for Luc," Celest said shortly. At that moment, Karyn lifted a kettle of hot water onto the table. Celest replaced the cloth on Luc's head, sliding a bloody one into the hot water.

With a glance at Sophie, Karyn said impatiently, "If you feel faint, Sophie, you'd better move."

Mikal helped Sophie to the front of the store, where she slid gratefully into a rocking chair. There was a conference between himself, the Delhomme men, and Cay. Emile walked back, patted Luc on the shoulder, kissed Celest, and left. Mikal returned to watch Celest and Karyn.

Karyn handed a razor to Celest and sopped up blood while Celest used a tiny pair of sewing scissors to clip blond hair away from the edges of the jagged wound. Once again applying pressure to stop the bleeding, Karyn waited while Celest threaded a needle. Then, as Mikal looked on, she took up a pair of tweezers and pulled the gaping flesh together while Celest stitched. Mikal winced. Luc gave no indication of feeling anything.

"It's good he's asleep," Mikal commented.

Celest tied off her last stitch and stood up. "No. Actually, it isn't. I wish he were awake and yelling. I don't like it." Her hands trembled as she wrapped Luc's head with clean strips of muslin.

Cay came back in. "Use my quarters as an infirmary. I've set up a cot for you, Celest. Remi and I can sleep in here. We'll be nearby if you need anything."

"That doctor you've been trying to get to come," Celest asked. "How far away is he?"

"It's a she. She's in Lincoln."

Celest shook her head. "Too far."

"I can go for Doctor Westerville," Mikal offered.

"If he's been drinking he'll be worthless." Celest sighed and looked down at Luc. "He's a hardheaded boy. Perhaps I'm worrying too much."

Mikal hoisted Luc into his arms and carried him into Cay's quarters. Celest reached for the pot of water, but Karyn pushed her hand away. "Sit. I'll clean up."

Gratefully, Celest sank into her chair. "You're a good assistant, Karyn."

Only after things were cleaned up did anyone think of Sophie. She had curled up in the rocking chair and gone to sleep.

Mikal came back into the store. "What else can I do for Luc?"

"Nothing but pray."

He turned to Remi. "Let's see what we can find to board up the windows."

While Remi and Mikal worked, Karyn lit several lamps and swept up broken glass. When they had done what they could to resurrect Cay's store from the storm, Mikal went to hitch up the team. Sophie woke up. She reached up to touch the bump on her cheek. "Oh, what a headache I have!" she moaned. "Can we go now?"

Mikal drove up outside. Sheltered in Cay's sod stable, his team had escaped injury. All along the street, farmers were tending their cut and bleeding horses. Celest came outside, needle and thread in hand, and went to help where she could. Cay brought a fat feather tick outside and spread it in the wagon for Sophie's comfort. Karyn climbed up beside Mikal, wondering at the four inches of hail that covered the earth as far as she could see.

As they drove out of town, Karyn longed to put her hand in Mikal's, to lay her head on his shoulder, to do something tangible that would say, "It will be all right. We will face it together." But just as she found courage to reach toward him, Sophie bounced up behind them. Seemingly impervious to the tragedy they were about to encounter back at the homestead, she chattered away about the Literary Society meeting. When she finally lay back down, Mikal pulled his hat down so far that Karyn could barely see his eyes. She took it as a sign that he wanted to be left alone.

It was still dark when the interminable ride back to the homestead ended. Mikal left Karyn and Sophie at the door of the soddy and drove off without a word. Sophie half staggered into the soddy and fell into bed without undressing. Karyn lit the lamp and went back outside. She crept along the front of the house and around to the garden where she lifted the lantern high. Shredded vines, broken stems, scattered unripe tomatoes were visible among the mounds of melting hailstones.

The last of the clouds cleared and a full moon came out,

illuminating the remains of the garden. As tears of frustration and disappointment pressed against her eyelids, Karyn turned to look toward the dugout. Mikal was coming from the direction of his wheat field, his hands stuffed in the pockets of his overalls, his shoulders slumped.

At times like this, there were no words. At times like this, a woman could only put her arms around a man and hold him. Karyn had taken her first step toward the dugout when Sophie called for her. "Karyn, oh Karyn, my head hurts so . . ."

Karyn looked toward the dugout, sighed, and went in to see about Sophie.

At that moment, Mikal looked up the slope toward the house. In one day, his world had fallen apart. A few hours ago he had learned that Hans Gilhoff was more than just a boy going off to war. Had she married him, Karyn would at that very moment be living as the mistress of an entire estate. Given that reality, what woman on earth would want a few acres in Nebraska with a ruined wheat field? Why, hadn't Karyn as much as told him that very evening that she couldn't love him? Her words came back to him: "Women find it difficult to order themselves to feel a certain way about a certain man." Was that her way of telling him that she had come to his homestead with good intentions, but she just couldn't make herself care for him?

Mikal sighed. Karyn would have been amazed to learn that his unhappiness had little to do with the loss of his wheat. Standing in the dark, looking up toward his house, Mikal Ritter was praying that in spite of all the obstacles, God would show him how to go about winning the heart of his wife.

The Diary
July 11, 1880

Hail has ruined Mikal's wheat. Everyone was gathered for a pleasant evening in Millersburg when the storm came up, and in moments all was lost. I do not know what we will do. The garden is a complete loss. Worse than all this is that I am unable to comfort Mikal. No, worse than all this is that Mikal does not seek my comfort.

CHAPTER 12

Grains of Wheat

The simple believeth every word:
. . . but the prudent are
crowned with knowledge.
Proverbs 14:15, 18

In the three and a half months since her arrival in America, Karyn Ritter had learned that no matter what she expected, both the land and the inhabitants of Custer County, Nebraska, would surprise her. Her desire to succeed helped her adapt to most surprises. Thus, when an unexpected hailstorm destroyed her garden and Mikal's wheat, Karyn summoned strength and prepared to help her husband. But the morning after the hailstorm presented yet another surprise for Karyn, for Mikal did not seem to be in need of comfort.

Karyn made breakfast that morning with an aching heart. The rising sun revealed the condition of her garden to be even worse than she had imagined from her brief inspection by moonlight. *If I feel this way about my little garden, how must Mikal be feeling? What will I ever say that can make him feel better?*

When Mikal came up for breakfast Sophie was still sleeping. He settled by the morning fire and drank a cup of coffee. When Karyn offered him a second serving of sausage, he shook his head. "I'm sorry. I'm just not very hungry."

And who could be hungry on such a day? Karyn thought.

Mikal patted his stomach. "I ate far too much at the social

last night." Then he looked up at the sky. "It will be hot today. The sun will dry up all this mud in no time." He sipped coffee for a moment before announcing, "I'm going to ride over to Emile's this morning and see what the hail did there. There might be a way to salvage some of the crop. Maybe we can gather some by hand and then dry it in the sun." He grinned. "I may have to change my name to Boaz."

"Boaz?"

"The book of Ruth. Remember?"

Karyn nodded vaguely. "Oh, yes . . . of course."

Mikal went on, "Emile might have much worse damage than I, and with Luc hurt, an extra hand will be welcome." He hesitated. "Of course, they might have been completely spared. In that case, I'll probably meet them on their way to help me. One thing I've learned about the prairie—the weather changes in an instant, and two places five miles apart don't always get the same weather." He stood up and smiled at Karyn. "I'll try to be back by tonight, but if I'm not, don't worry. If there's anything at all to save, it could take longer than just today."

When Karyn still didn't say anything, Mikal said, "I'm sorry, Karyn. I didn't even ask about your garden, did I? Let's have a look."

Karyn shook her head. "There's no need. I checked it when the moon came out last night." She sighed. "The root crops will probably recover. But the tomatoes and vines—"

"Can you replant?" Mikal wanted to know.

Karyn shrugged. "Maybe some things. It depends on when it frosts here in Nebraska."

"Well, if Sophie feels up to it, why don't you two head back to Millersburg later this morning. Cay is a good friend in a crisis. He'll extend enough credit for a few garden seeds. And he can advise you on what's worth trying."

"What about your wheat, Mikal? What will you do?"

He shrugged. "I'll gather up what I can and hope to salvage enough broken heads to replant next spring. Although God might already have done next year's planting for me. Enough might have scattered to give me a good crop next year without planting." He smiled at her. "Don't worry so much, Karyn. As long as there's good *rain*fall instead of good *hail*fall, there will still be some corn. From the twenty acres I could get eight hundred bushels of corn. That's a good mountain of cobs for fuel, which means we'll need fewer chips." He grinned. "I think Celest had a cookbook titled *Thirty-three Ways to Cook Corn.* You may want to borrow it."

"How can you be so—so calm about this? I hardly got a moment's sleep last night worrying about you. Worrying about everything."

Mikal pushed his hat back off his forehead and thought for a moment before answering. "Well, I believe that God knows everything, and that God can do anything. This means He knew it was going to hail. And He could have stopped it. But He didn't." Mikal thought for a moment before continuing, "I don't think God is up in heaven today saying, 'Oh, my goodness, look what happened to Mikal Ritter's wheat! How am I going to get him through the winter?' There is a verse that says all things work together for my good . . . and in many places the Bible assures me that God cares for me. So, I accept that in some way I do not understand, hail on my wheatfield is part of God's plan for my good."

"Where did you get such ideas?" Karyn asked.

"That very long winter in the dugout when I spent a lot of time trying to understand life. I kept asking the same questions and most of my questions involved God. I just kept reading the Bible Celest had given me, looking for answers."

"You seem to have found them," Karyn offered.

Mikal grinned. "Well, I found *some* answers . . . which I had to memorize so that in the face of things like ruined crops, I would be able to remind myself of what I believe!"

Karyn shook her head. "I don't remember our minister at home ever talking about God the way you do. You make Him sound so—personal. I believe He exists, but—"

Mikal interrupted her. "But when the wheat field is smashed"—he looked at her gently—"or the person you love is dead—what really matters is that He is *here*." Mikal patted his chest. He stopped abruptly. "And now I am beginning to preach to you when all you asked was one little question." He poured some water over the fire and turned to go. "Tell Sophie I hope her head is better this morning."

"I will."

"And Karyn . . ." he hesitated momentarily before saying, "Those verses I told you about memorizing. I underlined them in my Bible. If you're interested, you can read them for yourself."

Karyn and Sophie spent the rest of the day trying to resurrect the garden. They picked hundreds of small green tomatoes off the ground, sliced them, and laid them in the sun to dry. Even when the sun came out, Sophie did not complain of the heat. When the two women had finally done all they could in the garden, Karyn mentioned trying to pick up some of the broken wheat.

"We can't possibly glean all those acres by ourselves, Karyn. Mikal will bring back help, and the men will get it done in no time. You said Mikal mentioned our getting more seeds in Millersburg. Wouldn't it be best to do that?"

"And why are you so anxious to go back to Millersburg? It will be a hot, miserable ride." Karyn smiled knowingly. "So, tell me. Is it Cay or Luc? Because I invited Cay Miller for Sunday."

Sophie didn't try to hide her disappointment. "That will be all right, I guess."

"Only 'all right'?"

"Cay Miller is very nice." Sophie sounded noncommittal.

"Yes, he is," Karyn said. "And he's already quite prosperous."

"Yes."

"But?"

"Why must everyone assume I am looking for a husband?" Sophie complained. "Just because *you* came to America to be married doesn't mean that I want to do that."

"Did you look around on the Fourth of July, Sophie? Or last night? The joke here is that every dance and social is attended by five hundred men and three women. You're a lovely girl, and you can't blame the single men for hoping that you will marry one of them."

Sophie sighed. "But, Karyn, what choices! First, there is Cay Miller. He is prosperous. But he's just not very attractive. Then there's Luc Delhomme. He is handsome enough, but he's going to be a musician. There's no money in that. If Remi and Serge inherit their father's land, they will do all right. But they act like overgrown boys. I want to be taken care of, not mother some fool. That's four of the eligible single men, and there's really not a perfect prospect among them." She added, "And besides that, I don't want to get married for convenience. I want to fall in love first instead of trying to fall in love afterward."

"You never know, Sophie," Karyn replied. "Falling in love afterward might not be so difficult." She blushed in spite of herself. "Celest says that love comes when you act out of love for another."

"That doesn't seem to be working for you," Sophie said bluntly.

"Celest says that it takes time."

"Well just how long does it take? I don't see any evidence of love blossoming between you and Mikal. Does he ever hold your hand? Has he kissed you even once?" Sophie waved her hand. "Oh I know, I know. We aren't supposed to speak of such things. And it isn't any of my business."

Sophie stood up abruptly. "I have to bring Ella in for milking." She had stepped out from beneath the porch when she turned around and said, "But, Karyn, I can assure you that if a man like Mikal Ritter took me home to be his wife, he wouldn't still be sleeping in the barn. Not after one *week,* let alone an entire summer." She laughed nervously and blurted out, "Sometimes I think I should just wait and scoop Mikal up if it doesn't work out between you two. Income and status wouldn't matter much if a woman knew Mikal Ritter loved her."

Karyn rode to Millersburg alone. Sensing that she had said too much, Sophie pleaded a headache, and Karyn was glad to get away from her. All the way to Millersburg she tried to downplay Sophie's comments about Mikal. She was still in turmoil when she put Sugar in Cay's barn and hurried inside the store to ask Cay, "How is Luc?"

From the doorway to Cay's quarters came a shaky answer, "Better, thank you." It was Luc, leaning on his mother's shoulder while Celest helped him to the table at the back of Cay's store.

"No Sophie?" Luc said, looking disappointed.

"No, no Sophie," Karyn said. "She had a headache."

Cay called from the front of the store, "Are you sure she's all right alone?"

"She'll be fine," Karyn assured him.

Luc smiled. "Well, tell her both Cay and I asked for her." He leaned over and whispered, "Apparently we are to be rivals in the matter of Sophie."

"Your wheat?" Celest asked abruptly.

Karyn shook her head. "The garden, too. All shattered. Mikal sent me to get more seeds. He rode to your place this morning to help Emile."

Celest sighed. "I know that God is in control, but sometimes I am hard-pressed to understand His purpose. Which reminds me of something I wanted to discuss with you." Celest got up and poured Luc a cup of tea. "Drink this, Luc. I want to talk with Karyn about something." She called out, "Cay, when Luc finishes his tea, can you get him back in bed for me?"

With Cay's promise to help Luc, Celest led Karyn outside to a spot of shade on the north side of Cay's barn.

"Karyn, I hope that you won't misunderstand me, but I must broach a rather awkward topic. Luc speaks much of Sophie. I have been observing her." Celest reached out to take Karyn's hands. "Underneath her flirting and her smiles, I don't think Sophie is very happy. Not being able to participate more fully in life would make anyone feel unsettled. Does she *never* feel well enough to work? I wonder, Karyn, if Sophie should see a doctor."

Karyn smiled. "You're very kind to be so concerned, Celest. But, as I have told Mikal, Sophie has seen many, many doctors. None seemed to be able to find the exact cause for her difficulties. Underneath the pouting and her little spells, Sophie is a good girl. She came to America hoping to get well. I think she is better. Perhaps you don't see it, but she is helping more."

Celest nodded. "I'm going to be blunt, Karyn. Luc is going to be a musician. He is very talented and, in time, I think he will do well. But at first he will need a strong woman who can go without fine things, someone who will support him without complaint. Frankly, I don't see Sophie being able to do that."

Karyn tried to reassure Celest. "I don't think she's purposely difficult." She shrugged. "My family spoiled Sophie. But since she's been here, she has taken over the milking, and she helps me with the sewing. Mikal and I have discussed her making shirts for Cay's store." Karyn paused. "She really is trying to do better. She offered to stay at home alone while I came to Millersburg. She even urged me to stay the night—to have a good visit with you. She said not to worry, that if he gets home, she would make Mikal his lunch."

Celest frowned. "Karyn, if Sophie is helping you more, that is good. But she needs to help you more and talk and laugh with Mikal less." She looked at Karyn meaningfully. "Mikal is a good man, but he is a man, and Sophie"—she put her hand on Karyn's shoulder and lowered her voice—"is Mikal still in the dugout—alone?" When Karyn began to redden, Celest scolded, "I'm the mother of five boys, Karyn, and they didn't just sprout up under the cabbages in the garden. So stop blushing and answer me."

Karyn still didn't answer. Celest nodded. "I see." She asked, "You are in love with Mikal, yes?"

Karyn blinked rapidly, then nodded. "Yes, I think so. But he—"

"—he needs to be encouraged. That's all." Celest took a deep breath. "My goodness, child. What is difficult about this? You are already married. What is keeping you from one another?"

"Sophie." Karyn said the word, stifling tears.

"That is easy to solve," Celest said quickly. "If your sewing machine suddenly broke down, Sophie would have to come to my house to borrow my machine. She could stay with us for a while."

"It's not so simple as that," Karyn said. She looked at Celest, finally making herself speak of it. "You know what I mean, or you would not have said that Sophie needs to help me more and laugh with Mikal less." Karyn looked away and swallowed hard before whispering, "As you said, Celest, Mikal is a man . . .

148

and it takes very little wisdom to know which of the two women living in his house is more attractive, more able to make him laugh—"

Gently lifting Karyn's chin, Celest said, "God chose *you* for Mikal's wife, not Sophie. *You* are the one who had the courage to come to America alone. *You* are the one who plastered the walls, and sweeps the floors, and cooks the meals, and tends the garden. That's why God chose you for Mikal. And God does not make mistakes, Karyn!"

Karyn turned away. "You and Mikal. You seem so certain that God has His hand in everything."

"And you aren't?"

Karyn sighed and leaned against the sod wall of the barn. "I don't know. I haven't thought about it very much. We went to church, and I was confirmed. I believe the catechism. But I never thought about applying it all so personally—to everyday things."

"My dear, dear child," Celest soothed, patting Karyn's arm. "Such a good Lutheran girl you are. You know that God loves you so much that His beloved Son died for you, yes? Well, if He loves you so much as that, do you not know that He cares about this little matter with Sophie and Mikal and you? God is the Author of love, dear Karyn. He has given you the love for Mikal that grows in your heart. He means it for your good. You will see."

As Celest had predicted, Karyn soon had opportunity to see how things were. But she didn't see God working to bring herself and Mikal closer together. Instead, she saw Sophie's blue eyes sparkle when she looked at Mikal. She saw Sophie's dimple when she laughed with Mikal. She saw how every night, Sophie seemed to know just when Mikal came around the corner from the corral and started up the slope to join them for supper.

In the evenings, Sophie always had some mending in her smooth, white hands. There was never any dirt under Sophie's immaculate, smooth fingernails. Karyn saw that her own hands were growing weathered and freckled, her nails cracked and stained with chokecherry juice and elderberry jam.

Karyn saw Mikal's concern for Sophie's comfort. When Sophie mentioned how hot it was outside, Mikal moved the sewing machine inside. He positioned it by the window where there was plenty of light. He even bought screen for the window so that Sophie could enjoy a breeze while she sewed.

When Sophie mentioned missing the regular church services at home, Mikal began to read aloud from his Bible at every supper. He had the three of them hold hands and recite the blessing his own family had recited. It became his habit to ask Sophie and Karyn to sing a hymn together, laughingly excusing himself. "You don't need my off-key bellowing to ruin your music."

On the Sundays Cay Miller joined them for lunch, Karyn saw that Sophie was polite, but she didn't sparkle for Cay as she did for Mikal. Only for Mikal did Sophie turn on all her charms.

Each time Karyn thought that she and Mikal might have time to grow closer, something happened to draw their attention elsewhere. Ella got sick, and Mikal had to go to Emile for advice. The plums ripened, and for several consecutive days Karyn was gone half the morning gathering. One of the horses got a bad gash on its leg. In the midst of all the little crises, there was work and more work.

Sophie's "work," except for tending to Ella, seemed to be staying near the house, sewing and singing to herself. More and more women were bringing in sewing, and Cay Miller asked again for shirts for his store. Sophie could not keep up with all the sewing, let alone help Karyn with other chores. She did manage, however, to make Mikal a straw hat. By plaiting some of the hail-damaged wheat and soaking the long braids in water, she made them soft enough to sew 'round and 'round into a hat.

Karyn labored from dawn until sunset, falling into bed so exhausted she fell immediately asleep. Every time she thought of some little thing she might do for Mikal, she found herself either too busy or too tired to realize her plan.

The second week of August Mikal began to talk of making a trip to the cedar canyons. "Cay Miller wants to stockpile fence posts. He says that once the settlers have built their homes, they will turn their attention to fencing in their property to keep the ranch cattle out of their fields. He will buy all the posts I can cut and pay eleven cents each for them. Luc will probably want to come with me."

Sophie pouted. "You men are always going off somewhere and leaving us alone."

"You won't be alone. Cay will keep an eye on you."

Sophie rolled her eyes and stabbed ferociously at the shirt lying in her lap.

Mikal turned toward Karyn. "Remember when I said that God would provide for us, Karyn? I can earn enough money from this to more than pay for the winter wheat I want to try. And you will be able to stock up on groceries."

On the day that Mikal was to leave, Karyn got up early to get her gardening finished. She had been surprised at her own feelings of dread at the prospect of his leaving. He had said that he and Luc would be gone for at least two weeks. *If it weren't for Sophie, I could have gone along.*

Karyn decided that elderberry sauce would taste delicious poured over the fried cakes they always ate for lunch. It would be a nice treat for Mikal and a nice way to send him off on his trip to the cedar canyons. She set aside the morning of chores she had planned and hurried to a stand of elderberries a quarter of a mile from the soddy.

Mikal's team was already hitched up and waiting outside the soddy when Karyn got back from her berry-picking. *It's a good thing I already rinsed these off in the creek. If I hurry I can still have his surprise ready.* Intending to slip behind the house, Karyn stopped short when she heard Sophie giggling. *I'm not eavesdropping. This is my home. I can enjoy the fresh air for a moment or two if I wish.*

"We can't send you off with a tear in your shirt, Mikal," Sophie was saying. "I can mend it in just a moment. In fact, why not let me get your measurements now, and I can make you a new shirt while you are gone?"

Hearing Sophie's tone of voice, Karyn knew the exact expression that was on her face. She had pursed her lips in a charming little pout. "Come now, Mikal. All seamstresses do fittings for their customers. You don't want a shirt that won't button, do you? Don't be shy. Just take the shirt off so I can get accurate measurements. There's so much sewing to do, and I don't want to waste my time making something that won't fit." She sighed. "There's so little I can do to be of help to Karyn. She works so hard every day. Why, she's ruining her skin while I lounge indoors." She coaxed, "The thought of her growing stooped over like an old woman while I cannot help . . . sewing is a way I can help her, Mikal. Don't you see? If I can take the sewing off her hands, then—"

There was a long pause, and then Sophie said, "Yes. That's it." Sophie cleared her throat. "Chest—123 centimeters. Neck—49 centimeters. Now the sleeve length. Yes, I see. It's a good thing you let me measure, Mikal. I never guessed you were so broad-shouldered."

Karyn finally went to the door. Mikal was standing near the stove with his back to her. Karyn caught her breath as she took in the sight of flawless suntanned skin, broad, muscular shoulders . . . and Sophie's small white hand on Mikal's arm. Sophie noticed Karyn and dropped her hand. "Karyn—you see that I have convinced your shy husband to let me get proper measurements for my sewing."

Mikal wheeled about, grabbed his thermal undershirt, and pulled it quickly over his head.

Sophie broke the awkward silence between them. "And now I will be able to do something to help you even more, dear sister." She clucked her tongue. "We'll have to get extra fabric from Cay. This giant you call your husband is going to require much larger shirts than I anticipated." She flashed an admiring glance up at Mikal.

"I'll ride into Millersburg as soon as Mikal has his lunch," Karyn said mechanically. She swallowed hard. Looking down at the basket of elderberries she whispered hoarsely, "I was going to make something special, but . . ."—she looked at Mikal—"I see that the team is already hitched up. You need to leave. You probably won't want to be bothered with my little surprise." She blinked back tears and pushed by him. Karyn took no notice of the project Sophie had laid out on the makeshift table next to the sewing machine. She set the basket of elderberries down on top of it. Reaching for a covered crockery bowl that stood on the kitchen stove, she mumbled, "I already have the batter mixed. It won't take long to fry some cakes for you. Then you can be on your way."

In only a few moments, Karyn was handing Mikal a plate piled high with fried cakes. She had fresh milk for him to drink and plenty of butter for the cakes. There were even two fried eggs. But Sophie was the only one who truly enjoyed the small feast. Mikal pretended to eat, all the while watching Karyn from under the brim of his hat. Karyn drank cup after cup of strong coffee. She busied herself with tending the fire and a thousand little things that didn't need to be done.

When Mikal finally stood up to go, Sophie stood on tiptoe and demanded that he bend over so that she could kiss him on the cheek. Karyn turned to go to the well for wash water. She had a bucket of water near the top of the well when Mikal reached from behind her and hoisted it up.

"Thank you." She added mechanically, "I hope you have success these next two weeks. I—" She wanted to say she would miss him, but something held her back.

As she turned to reach for the bucket of water, she felt the pressure of Mikal's hand on the small of her back. Quickly, he leaned down and kissed her on the cheek. He didn't even take off his hat, and the kiss itself was nothing much. It only took an instant. Mikal didn't say a word, and Karyn didn't dare look at him. She stood with her hands on the curbing of the well, listening as he drove away.

The Diary
July 31, 1880

Hot and clear. Mikal is gone to cut fence posts. He says it will yield enough for red wheat and a load of groceries. The wheat lies beneath the snow all winter and ripens in summer. In spite of my efforts here, I begin to think it might be best if I do not expect to see the results of planting this new crop.

CHAPTER 13

A Pocketknife

And call upon me in the day of trouble: I will
deliver thee, and thou shalt glorify me.
Psalm 50:15

The evening that Mikal left, Karyn and Sophie ate a cold supper in relative silence. Knowing she had carried her flirting with Mikal too far, Sophie did not have the courage to reach over the wall she had built between herself and her sister. Karyn had the courage, but she didn't have the energy. So, the two women spoke in half-sentences about things that didn't matter.

After the meal, Sophie insisted that Karyn let her wash the dishes. "And I've already washed the elderberries, so don't worry about them. I think I'll try making some jam tomorrow. And I don't want you to help. I want to try it myself. Why don't you try to sleep late tomorrow, Karyn? You've been working so hard lately. I can feed the sow and get breakfast."

There was the sound of yelping near the corral. Karyn got up. "I'll go check on that. Those coyotes seem bent on getting at Ella's calf. I might walk out toward the ridge. Light the lamp and set it in the window. I don't plan on getting lost, but it never hurts to take precautions." She retrieved Mikal's rifle from inside the soddy and headed down to the corral, where she fired two warning shots in the direction of the coyotes' yelps.

Karyn watched until the lighted lamp appeared in the win-

154

dow. Then she made her way around the edge of the corral and toward the north. She walked in an ever-widening semicircle. Finding no sign of the coyotes, she finally made her way back to the corral. But instead of heading up the slope for bed, she went into the dugout.

Mikal's Bible lay on a table next to the bed. Karyn sat down on the bed, sinking into the feather mattress. She picked up the Bible. In the waning light, she couldn't make out very much, but she could tell that Mikal had, indeed, underlined many, many verses between the worn covers of the book. Resentment and hurt flickered. If he knew so much of this book, then why did he behave as he did with Sophie? Didn't he know it hurt her terribly?

She heard Sophie calling for her. Sighing, Karyn put the Bible down and went to the door of the dugout. "I'm all right, Sophie," she called. "I'm coming." She plodded up the slope.

"I was worried about you," Sophie said. "Come to bed, Karyn. I don't hear any coyotes yelping now."

It wasn't long before Sophie fell asleep. Karyn slipped out of bed, picked up the lantern, and went back down to the dugout where she sat for some time thumbing casually through Mikal's Bible. When she grew sleepy, instead of going back up to the soddy, Karyn stretched out on Mikal's bed.

As shadows flickered on the walls of the dugout, Karyn let her mind go back to the first time she had seen Mikal Ritter. Could it possibly have been four months ago? It seemed like only yesterday. He had half frightened her, with his huge hands and startlingly blue eyes, his mane of wild black hair. *But I never back down from a challenge,* Karyn thought. *So when he asked, I said yes.*

She thought through the ensuing weeks when she had struggled so to deal with the harsh realities of life in Custer County. What had made her try so hard? Why hadn't she just packed up and left? With her sewing, she could make a living anywhere. *But it wasn't really a living I was looking for.* Finally, Karyn admitted to herself that yes, she had come to America hoping for love. And yes, she had grown to love Mikal Ritter. Just exactly when it had happened, she was not certain. But love him she did. And she could tell a thousand reasons why.

Then, as Karyn thought back over their weeks together, she looked for reasons to be hopeful that, even after being married to someone like Marie-Louise, Mikal Ritter might love someone like herself. *I work hard for him.* But a thousand women would work hard. It was expected. Working hard couldn't make a man love a woman. *I'm not so bad looking.* But even in the poor light in the dugout, Karyn could see the effects of all the hard work on her hands. She could feel that her skin had grown rougher. And she hardly ever had time or energy to put her hair up in that coronet that looked so attractive. *We can have fun at the socials.* But socials in general and dancing in particular didn't seem important to Mikal. Thinking back, Karyn could remember only two times when she had been fairly certain that Mikal felt attracted to her in a way that might end in love. He had been upset when she danced with Luc. And he had squeezed her hand that day when they were alone in the fields. *But lately he hasn't seemed to care much at all. He is much more solicitous of Sophie than of me. He's very concerned for her health . . . and he does so many things to make her life easier.*

No matter how many times Karyn considered the situation, she came to the same conclusion: Mikal Ritter was too honorable a man to admit it, but he had fallen in love with Sophie. As for the little kiss he had given her earlier that day, it wasn't hard to explain. It was only Mikal's way of telling her that he would be true to his marriage vow.

Celest had said that God had chosen her, Karyn, to be Mikal's wife. Celest had said that things would work out. *Well, Celest,* Karyn thought. Then, she raised her heart higher. *Well, God in heaven. I have been patient. I have done what I can. And now, what am I to do? Do I stay here and serve Mikal, all the while knowing that, while he likes me as a friend, he has much deeper feelings for Sophie?* Karyn took a deep breath. *I don't know if I can do that. Celest says that You care about things like this. Celest says that I must trust You and that You will work it out.* Karyn swallowed hard, fighting against the lump in her throat. *If You are the Author of love, then can You not make Mikal love* me? Karyn buried her face in Mikal's pillow and wept.

As Mikal had suspected, Luc was delighted with the idea that he drive an extra wagon and help cut wood. While Luc went to the corral to hitch up a second team, Emile drew Mikal aside. "You boys be careful up there. Fred Smith was by yesterday and said they finally found what happened to the old settler who headed up there last year and never came back. A storm washed what was left of him out of a thirty-foot hole. Fred said the sides of the hole were charred. Lightning must have struck one of the older trees and burned completely down into the roots. The poor old fellow must have slipped into the hole. I'm glad you won't be going alone."

Mikal assured Emile that he and Luc would stay together. He stooped to where his grub box sat waiting to be loaded onto his wagon. Pretending to check over its contents, he said, "I wanted Karyn to go. But I didn't know how to ask her. With Sophie there—"

Emile raised one eyebrow and asked, "Do I detect a little negative feeling toward Sophie's presence?"

Mikal shrugged, closed his grub box and hoisted it to its place under the wagon seat. "Oh, Sophie's all right. I owe it to Karyn to make her feel welcome. It's just that—" He took his hat off and ran his fingers through his hair.

Emile leaned against the wagon. He put his hand on Mikal's shoulder. "You know, Mikal, even the wise patriarch Abraham had difficulty managing a household that included two women."

Mikal wiped his forehead with his sleeve. He nodded agreement. "Yes. But what can I do? She's Karyn's sister."

The men lifted two jugs from the back of the wagon and headed for the well. As Emile pulled a bucket of fresh water up he asked, "Does Karyn know how you feel?"

Mikal shook his head. "I don't know. We were getting along well, but since Sophie arrived there seems to be something between us. I don't know how to get around it. There's never a moment when Karyn and I can just—talk." Mikal shook his head. He filled the two jugs with water. "She's strong-willed. She doesn't back down from a challenge, and I admire her for that. But I can't tell how she feels about me. And this morning I let Sophie talk me into something." He recounted the incident of the shirt-fitting. "I've never claimed to be the most intelligent man in the county, but looking back on that, I can't believe I was so dense. It was totally innocent. I was only thinking that here was another way to encourage Sophie to do something constructive. But then Karyn came in. Seeing it through her eyes, it must have looked terrible. Who knows what it made her think? She just pulled it all inside, made my lunch, and said good-bye. I kissed her on the cheek. I meant it as an apology, but I might as well have been kissing a tree for all the response I got."

Emile frowned and shook his head. "I think you may have to come up with something better than a kiss on the cheek to make up for that one, Mikal. Since you brought this up I will tell you that Celest has been concerned that Sophie is too—familiar—with you."

Mikal nodded. "I know. I've been telling myself not to be vain and think more of it than I should." He shook his head. "But really, Emile. I passed over a dozen girls like Sophie in Grand Island the day I met Karyn. Girls like Marie-Louise. I made that mistake once. I wasn't going to make it again. The more I see of Karyn, the more I like." Hooking a finger through the handle of each water jug he started back toward the wagon. He stopped abruptly and corrected himself. "The more I see of Karyn, the more I love." He looked at Emile. "But then that wall, whatever it is, looms between us. I say the wrong thing, she doesn't say anything." He sighed. "I don't know how to fix it."

Emile followed Mikal back to the wagon where he set the two water jugs behind the wagon seat. Then Emile asked, "Is there something besides Sophie between the two of you?"

Mikal leaned against the wagon box and thought before answering. "Maybe. Karyn told me there was someone in Germany who got killed. She made it sound like it was nothing. But Sophie has let it be known more than once that he was refined, educated, wealthy." He shook his head. "If she's comparing me to him, I don't have much of a chance." He paused. "But I'd sure like to have some time alone with her. Time to talk things out."

"It might take more than talking, Mikal," Emile reminded him.

"I could manage that, too," Mikal said quietly.

"Well, Mikal, here's what I suggest. While you are gone, make it a matter of prayer. Then, if you still feel the same way when you get back, you say something like this: 'Karyn, I am in love with you. Let's send Sophie to the Delhommes' for a visit.'" Emile chuckled. "I'm certain Celest can think of a reason why she needs Sophie's help. By the time you get back, I'll have her convinced. She doesn't approve of Sophie, but if I tell her that it's for Karyn, she'll be more than willing to help. Luc can bring Sophie here."

Luc walked up. "I only heard the last sentence. But I like the plan, whatever it is." He put one hand on his father's shoulder and one hand on Mikal's. "If Sophie came for a visit, perhaps Mother would change her mind."

Emile defended his wife. "Your Mother—and I—want what is best for you, son. If you are to fulfill your dream of teaching music, you must have a wife who supports you in every way. She must be willing to get by on very little during your years of study."

"How can you be so certain that Sophie would ruin me?" Luc's voice rose a few decibels. "It should be obvious to both of you that she doesn't belong here. She was never meant for this life. If she were living in an apartment in Philadelphia with me, she'd be a different girl. I'm certain of it. Don't be so judgmental."

"And don't be so defensive, Luc," Mikal said. "If you can win Sophie's heart, please do so. And sooner rather than later."

Thanking Emile for his advice, Mikal nodded at Luc. "So let's be going. I'm in a hurry to get home."

All day, every day, for the next week, Luc and Mikal cut wood. While they cut, Mikal prayed about Karyn, and Luc talked about Sophie. A week of praying had made Mikal even more convinced that Karyn was the woman God wanted for him. If only he could convince Karyn of the same thing. Finally, the two men had both wagons filled with fence posts.

"Eleven cents a post," Mikal said as he loaded the last post into his wagon. "That's enough for me to buy that new red wheat I want to try and a few groceries. We should make another haul if we can. I'm hoping Karyn won't have to cook the entire winter with only cornmeal. Another seven dollars would buy a hundred-pound bag of flour."

Luc teased, "I don't know about you, Mikal. One minute you're wondering if Karyn cares about you at all. The next you're assuming she'll be here through the winter."

"She already agreed to stay through the winter," Mikal said.

Luc shook his head. "You better think of something more romantic to buy her than a bag of flour, Mikal. Or have you already decided to spend another winter in that dugout?"

Mikal changed the subject. "I think if I head south across East Table I can get this load to Cay sooner. After you get back to your place, would you ride over and tell Karyn I'll be home in a few days?"

The two wagons headed off, Luc to the southeast toward his own farm, and Mikal into unfamiliar territory. Traversing Pleasant Valley, he made his way across East Table.

Mikal's trouble started after nightfall when the team descended a steep incline and approached the north branch of Mud Creek. There was a full moon, but nowhere did a pinprick of golden light shine through the darkness to lead him to a house. He was lost. On a ridge just ahead, a dark shape loomed up. Hoping to find shelter for the night, Mikal headed up the ridge. The shape proved to be a fallen-in sod house. In the moonlight, Mikal thought he saw a wagon track leading south. *That's it, that's where I should have been all along.* Thinking he had found his way, Mikal turned the team and was heading down the track when Lena faltered. She seemed to have stepped into a hole. She lunged sideways against Grace and stood trembling in the dark.

"Whoa there, Lena," Mikal called out to calm her while he jumped down from the wagon and made his way alongside her.

"Maybe we should just camp over near that house and wait until daylight. Let's see, girl—is your leg all—"

Mikal never finished that sentence. As he came even with Lena's flank, he was plunged downward into what he now realized was an old well. Feeling suspended in time, he flung his arms up over his head and slapped his boots together. "God!" The moment he cried out his one-word prayer, Mikal hit the bottom of the well. Several feet of mud and water saved his life.

He was covered with cold water, the entire lower half of his body buried in mud. Choking and sputtering, he managed to flounder about in the mud enough to get his face out of the water. Then, with another prayer for help, he tried to calm himself and get his bearings.

His right knee was twisted, and he suspected his ankle might be broken. Thankfully, his arms were all right, but every breath confirmed that at least one rib had been broken. Looking up, Mikal thought, *It's a miracle I didn't break my neck.* The mouth of the well was barely visible above him. The full moon cast shadows down into the well. When his eyes finally adjusted to the dark, he estimated that at least one hundred feet of earth separated him from escape.

He began to shiver. *I've got to get up out of this water.* The wooden curbing around the bottom of the well was too slimy for him to get hold of, but he managed to break off a loose board. By bracing the board across the top of the curbing, he made a small shelf. As he tried to lift himself onto the shelf, the mud sucked his boots off. With a shout against the pain of the broken rib, he pulled himself onto the little shelf. He leaned against the side of the well until morning.

"Lena—Grace—are you there?" Sunlight was pouring down into the well. Blue sky shone overhead. Mikal called again, "Lena—Grace!" An answering whinny brought a sigh of relief. *God, please send someone this way. Let them see the wagon. Send someone.*

No one came. The mud caked from his waist down had begun to dry. His stomach growled. Mikal looked up again. In the daylight, it was easier to see how the well was built. There were large sections completely surrounded by wood curbing. Then there would be three or four feet where there was no curbing at all. As far as he could see, everything was in good condition. *At least it's not going to cave in on me.*

Mikal managed to brace himself against the sides of the well and stand up on his good foot. Even with his long arms fully extended he was still at least two feet from the top of the next section of curbing. *Well, Father, what do I do now?* The answer to his prayer came in the form of the pocketknife in his back pocket. *Thank God it didn't disappear into the mud down there.*

Over the next few hours, Mikal laboriously cut wedges into the side of the well. When he was ready to climb up, he removed his socks. Then, he undid his overalls and tied the long straps around the board he had used for a shelf. Tentatively he crept up the side of the well, breathing a sigh of relief when the board was dislodged and dangled below him, held fast by his overall straps. At the top of the next section of curbing, he let go with one hand, worked along the denim straps until he had the board in his hands. Then he positioned it across the top of the curbing. Again he perched on the board.

It was late afternoon. He called again to his horses, rejoicing when Lena's head appeared at the top of the well. She whickered softly. A few stalks of dried grass fell out of her mouth and wafted down the well shaft past Mikal.

"Good girl, Lena, good girl. You stay nearby. God will surely send someone after me."

Mikal rested on the board. His ankle was swollen. His knee hurt worse. Every breath sent sharp pains through his midsection. For the first time, he considered the possibility that he might not have the strength to get out of the well alone. He dozed off, jerked awake by the awful sensation of falling every time his head nodded forward.

During his second night in the well, Mikal listened to coyotes yelping near the abandoned farmstead. In spite of his earnest pleas to God, the coyotes came nearer and nearer. Mikal called out to the team trying in vain to keep them calm. But finally the coyotes sounded right above the mouth of the well. With a shrill whinny, Lena and Grace charged off.

Listening to the crashing sounds as his wagon bounced along behind the terrified team, Mikal realized that there was no chance Lena and Grace would run home. They couldn't possibly know the way. They would run at will, scattering his load of cedar posts across the empty prairie. If they came to a canyon they would plunge to their deaths. Exhausted, Mikal contemplated the loss of his team, the loss of his income, the loss of his own life. Discouraged, wet, and hurting, he brushed angry tears off his face.

Lena and Grace might well have leaped off a canyon ridge had it not been for a wide creek that brought them up short. Foaming at the mouth, their sides heaving, the mares finally stopped running. They drank deeply, lifting their heads to look about them, flicking their ears back and forth. They began to graze. They grazed along the banks of the creek for several hours before Lena lifted her head, pricked her ears, and began to walk east. Grace followed willingly, munching huge mouthfuls of grass. In less than an hour Lena and Grace pulled their empty wagon up to a familiar barn. It was dark. The mares helped themselves to a pile of hay outside the barn.

Daylight finally trickled down into the well, making it easier for Mikal to look around him. He had spent his second night in the well. His strength was waning, and he knew that if he was to survive, this must be the day he reached the top. All day he inched his way up the side of the well, laboriously carving footholds and handholds with his pocketknife. By the end of the day he had made his way to the last curbing. He was only about sixteen feet from the top of the well. But when he examined the last layer of curbing he realized that it would take a miracle for him to make it out. Earth had washed away behind the curbing. If he put his full weight on it, it would hurtle to the bottom of the well and take him with it.

The only way was to burrow behind the curbing, cut toeholds, and pray that by some miracle the earth would hold long enough for him to scramble to safety. Every inch was agony now. He held his breath and reached up, trying to ignore the stabbing pains in his side, his knee, his feet and ankles. He managed to scrape earth away. It took most of the rest of the day for him to hollow out a place big enough for his entire body. *For once I wish I were Cay Miller's size,* he thought grimly.

Within six feet of the top of the well he struck slippery clay. With one last monumental effort, he pulled himself from behind the top of the last curbing. Grimacing with pain he groped upward. He could barely reach the mouth of the well. With a prayer for a miracle, he put the foot that could bear weight on the curbing he had just tunneled behind. He could feel it giving way. With a mighty push, he propelled himself upward, even as the curbing crashed to the bottom of the well. He heard it hit the water just as his upper body cleared the mouth of the well. He dangled there for a moment, unable to force his sore knee to make any more effort.

Finally, with a combination of pulling and scrambling with his knees, Mikal pulled himself up. He was above the ground for the first time in two nights and nearly two full days. He thought of the dead settler whose remains had been washed out of the hole in the cedar canyons. Looking back down into the black hole behind him, Mikal shuddered. Ignoring his twisted knee, he knelt and thanked God for the miracle of life. Exhausted, he crawled inside the abandoned soddy and fell asleep.

It was almost night when Mikal awoke. He was alive, but his ordeal was far from over. He was thirsty and hungry. He couldn't walk. And he was lost. *If two days and two nights in a well didn't kill me, crawling across the prairie won't, either.* He headed out, following the trail of cedar fence posts left by Lena and Grace's wild dash away from the coyotes.

Celest Delhomme was always the first one up in her household. She prided herself on having her stove fired up and breakfast in progress before the men got up to do their morning chores. It was before dawn when Celest hurried toward the henhouse to gather eggs for breakfast. She rounded the edge of the barn and stopped short at the sight of Lena and Grace and Mikal's empty wagon.

Barely half an hour after Celest found Lena and Grace, the four Delhomme men had saddled horses and were loping across the prairie in the direction they guessed the wagon had come. In the early morning light, it was difficult to follow the trail, but as the sun came up the trail became more evident. They found the spot where the mares had stopped to drink at the creek. From there, a trail of cedar posts led them to where Mikal lay unconscious in the middle of the prairie. He was barefoot and covered with dried mud from his waist down.

Luc knelt over Mikal. "His ankle is broken," he called up to his father.

Together, the men turned him over. Remi pulled Mikal's head into his lap and began to trickle water from a canteen into his mouth. When he finally began to stir, he drank greedily.

"Karyn?" he asked weakly.

The men laughed with relief. "Well, God knows where he has been in reality, but I guess we all know where he has been in his dreams."

The sound of masculine laughter brought Mikal fully awake. He started to sit up, but Emile pushed him back.

"Whoa there, Mikal, your ankle is broken. Don't move too much until we check you out."

"Just the ankle. Maybe a rib. My knee is twisted. Otherwise, I'm all right."

"What happened?" Luc wanted to know.

"Lena stumbled in a hole in the night. It turned out to be an old well. I got out to check on her and went down the well. The team ran off. Coyotes." He sat up slowly, wincing and laying one hand over his side.

Luc explained, "Mother went out this morning to gather eggs and found them standing by the barn."

Emile broke in, "Can you ride, Mikal? We can go back for the wagon if you need it."

"I can ride. Just get me home."

Emile shook his head. "You are in no condition to go far. Your ankle must be set and Celest must supervise that." Emile looked up. "Luc, you ride to Mikal's and get Karyn and Sophie. We'll meet you at home."

165

The Diary
August 9, 1880
    Mikal still gone. I'm glad Luc is with him. I worry less.
Hot and clear. The coyotes are growing more determined to
get Ella's calf. I am more determined that they won't.
Sophie helps more.

CHAPTER 14

Overall Buttons

For I will pour water upon him that is thirsty,
and floods upon the dry ground.
Isaiah 44:3

Karyn was working in Mikal's ruined wheat field when Luc
Delhomme rode up.

"What's happened?" she asked abruptly, trying to keep her
voice from shaking.

"He's all right," Luc said. "But he took a bad fall down a
well. Then Lena and Grace were frightened by coyotes. By some
miracle they came to our house. We found Mikal today. His
ankle is broken—"

Karyn reached up. "Pull me up behind you. We'll have to get
Sugar. Sophie will want to come." When they reached the corral, Karyn hopped down. "I'll saddle Sugar. You go on up and
tell Sophie. Tell her to pack a bag with clean clothes for both of
us. I'll get some of Mikal's things from the dugout." She slid
down and hurried into the dugout where she collected Mikal's
only other pair of overalls and his Bible. With a grim smile, she
realized that it was a good thing Sophie had made Mikal a new
shirt.

Luc rode up the slope and dismounted at the soddy where
Sophie sat under the wide porch sewing. Her bright smile faded
the moment she saw Luc's face. She reached out to grab Luc's

arm. "What is it? Is it Mikal? Is he—is he dead?" Her voice went up with each word until she sounded nearly hysterical.

"Calm down, Sophie. He's had a bad fall. But by now Mother probably has him bandaged and drinking tea. Karyn said to tell you to pack a bag for the two of you. We'll ride over right away."

Karyn had saddled Sugar, packed Mikal's bag, and ridden up to the house to join Luc when Sophie rushed outside with Karyn's carpetbag.

"Get your bonnet, Sophie," Karyn reminded her. "And Mikal's new shirt. And calm down. Luc says he is all right, and we'll see for ourselves soon enough. He's in good hands."

Karyn urged Sugar forward. Luc extended his hand toward Sophie. "Ride behind me, Sophie."

On the way to the Delhommes', Luc told what he knew of Mikal's adventure.

The moment the trio arrived at the Delhommes', Sophie slid off Luc's horse and started to rush inside. But Celest intercepted her, pulling her back by her sleeve. She spoke to Karyn. "Serge and Remi helped me set the ankle, and I've wrapped his knee. I hope you brought clean clothes. We did what we could, but none of my men's things will fit him. He couldn't even button Serge's shirt."

Karyn held up the bag of Mikal's things. Celest nodded, finally looking at Sophie to include her in the conversation. "Now listen, girls, he looks terrible. He's bruised and scratched, and it hurts every time he moves. Just remember that in spite of appearances and the grimaces and groans, he's come out of this in amazingly good condition. It's a miracle he survived. Emile helped dig that well a few years ago. He said it's at least 140 feet deep."

Celest dropped her hand from Sophie's arm, and she rushed inside ahead of Karyn. "Oh, Mikal," Sophie cried out, falling to her knees beside him. "You poor, poor, thing. What an ordeal!"

Mikal smiled weakly. "I must be a sight." He was patting Sophie on the head, reassuring her, when Karyn and Celest came in.

Karyn froze in the doorway.

Celest frowned. "Sophie, would you come with me? Karyn and Mikal should have some time alone."

Even with Sophie gone, Karyn didn't trust herself to say anything. She was too afraid of embarrassing both herself and Mikal with unwelcome emotion, so she merely leaned against the kitchen table, her hands clasped before her.

Mikal made an attempt at humor. "Some stupid husband you have, Karyn."

"You need to rest," Karyn said. She felt a sudden need to escape lest she succumb to the temptation to engulf Mikal in her arms. "I'll call one of the boys to help you upstairs."

"Karyn," Mikal said softly. "That business at the house with Sophie. And the shirt."

Focusing on Mikal's broken ankle, Karyn forced herself to say calmly, "What is important right now, Mikal, is that you are all right. We can speak of other matters later." She laughed grimly. "It's a good thing Sophie made that shirt." She produced the bag of clean clothing. "I have your other overalls, too. Tomorrow I can go to Millersburg and get new boots."

"But, Karyn—" Mikal cleared his throat, wincing as he shifted his weight in his chair.

"Please, Mikal. Don't speak of it. Not now. We'll talk another time. You must be very tired. I'll get one of the boys to help you upstairs to bed." She hurried out of the room.

Celest and Sophie were coming back from the henhouse. Two plump chickens had met their demise and were dangling from Celest's hands. Luc walked up and began to tease Sophie about her cleaning the chickens for supper.

"Luc," Karyn said shakily, "would you help Mikal upstairs? He needs to rest." Without waiting for Luc to answer her, Karyn turned and walked toward Celest's garden.

Sophie started to follow her, but Celest pulled her back. "No," she said firmly. "You go on inside. Scald the chickens and get them plucked. I'll see to Karyn."

Sophie looked down at the dead birds.

Celest held the chickens out to her. "Just be sure you get all the pinfeathers singed off."

Sophie looked up with pleading eyes. Something in the older

woman's expression told her this was not a good time to feel faint. With a grimace, Sophie took the chickens. "Yes, ma'am." She headed for the kitchen.

Smiling to herself, Celest went to look for Karyn. She found her in the garden, sitting where she could lean against the sod wall.

As Celest settled beside her, Karyn smiled weakly and wiped her face on her apron. "I've always been this way. I do very well when the crisis is at hand, but once it's over, I have to sneak away somewhere and have a good cry."

"Ah, but I think this little cry is about more than today's crisis."

Karyn began to cry again. Words tumbled out. "You told me that God had chosen me to be Mikal's wife. You told me to talk to God about it. Well, I have. And the only thing that has happened is that I have had the pleasure of watching my sister throw herself at my husband and my husband succumb to her charms." Karyn described the incident the morning before Mikal left to cut wood. By the end of the story, she had begun to cry again.

Celest said quietly, "Things are not always as they seem, Karyn. It seems to you that Mikal cares for Sophie. It seems to you that God has not answered your prayers. But perhaps Mikal was only trying to humor Sophie into doing something productive." She paused, adding thoughtfully, "Perhaps God withholds the very thing you want most, so that you will realize that you need Him much more than you need Mikal Ritter."

Celest reached out to take Karyn's hand as she said, "Do you remember the first day we met? I could see that you had been crying when Emile and I rode up. But I could also see that you were determined not to let disappointment beat you down. Since that day, over and over again, I have seen how bright and intelligent and strong you are. You have found a way to overcome every disappointment that has come your way thus far, seemingly without much help from God. But now something has come into your life that has brought you to the end of yourself." She patted the back of Karyn's hand and sighed. "People who depend on other people for their happiness can never be truly happy, Karyn. We poor humans always disappoint one another."

Celest continued. "Let us suppose that Sophie never came. Right away, you and Mikal fell in love." She turned and looked Karyn directly in the eyes. "But one day Mikal goes out to cut wood and is killed in a terrible accident. What then?" Celest could see she was having an impact. She said slowly, "Stop putting Mikal Ritter on the throne of your life, Karyn. Only God belongs there."

Karyn took a deep breath. "I don't see how a relationship with God will solve this mess with Mikal."

Celest answered, "One of my favorite Scripture verses is in the Psalms. It says, 'Delight thyself also in the LORD; and he shall give thee the desires of thine heart. Commit thy way unto the LORD; trust also in him; and he shall bring it to pass.' That does not mean that God gives what we ask, Karyn. It means that He changes our hearts to desire His will."

"But I can't change wanting Mikal."

"And you don't have to. Your part is to delight in the Lord and to commit your way to Him. His promise is to give you right desires and to accomplish the best for you. Leave your heart and Mikal's heart in God's hands. Only God rules men's and women's hearts."

Finally, Karyn admitted, "I know you're probably right. But I still don't think I can do it."

"A girl as strong-willed and independent as you? I know you, Karyn. You can do anything you set your mind to do. And in this matter, you will have God's help." She put her arm around Karyn's shoulders. "And even with our help you are going to be very busy taking care of things while Mikal's ankle mends."

"How long will that take?"

"I'd like to keep him here for at least two weeks. We could take him home in the wagon, but if he's there, he'll be up trying to do things long before he should. If he stays here, I'll see to it that he behaves himself."

She put her arm through Karyn's. "While you are taking care of Mikal's farm, you can grow your relationship with God. You don't have to be a scholar to understand what God says about

171

Himself. Just pick up that little prayer book you have and read the Psalms. Much of God's character is revealed there."

"Mikal suggested I read his Bible."

Celest chuckled. "Through two different people God has told you that He wants you to get to know Him better, Karyn. Wouldn't you say it's time you listened?" She stood up, pulling Karyn to her feet.

"All right, Celest," Karyn said. "I'll do what you say." She took a deep breath and headed for the house. "Sophie and I will leave in the morning."

Celest shook her head and smiled. "I think you need this time alone with God. Leave Sophie with me. It's time she and I got to know one another better."

"Of course I'm driving the team home," Karyn insisted that evening at supper. "I'll need them. There's still at least one wagonload of wheat to be picked up. And if I'm driving to Millersburg to get your boots, I can take the shirts Sophie finished for Cay's store. There will be more bolts of cloth to bring home. I need the wagon."

It was suppertime, and as the Delhommes, the Ritters, and Sophie sat around the table laden with bowls of fried chicken and baked potatoes, Celest had raised the idea of Mikal and Sophie remaining with her while Karyn carried on at the homestead.

Again, Mikal expressed doubt. "You might get hurt."

"How? There aren't any abandoned wells between here and Millersburg," Karyn joked. "The wagon trail is well beaten down. I can't get lost. What could possibly happen?"

"What if a snake spooks the team? What if someone bothers you? Custer County has its share of horse thieves and bandits."

"I'll take the rifle."

Mikal opened his mouth to say something, but Sophie interrupted him. "Karyn," she said, "I think it's time you let Mikal in on your little secret."

"I wouldn't be defenseless," Karyn said, reaching for a biscuit. "I know something about rifles."

"Don't be so modest, Karyn," Sophie said. Karyn buttered

her biscuit while Sophie bragged. "Karyn hunted with Papa from the time she could walk. Last year in Brandenburg she won a shooting contest—in spite of the fact that one of the contestants was a retired military marksman."

Mikal still shook his head. "You've never driven the team. Remi can harness them here, but you'd have to manage at home. It's too much."

Sophie leaned over and patted him lightly on the shoulder. "Dear Mikal, there are many things you have yet to learn about Karyn. At home she drove Papa's delivery wagon. She knows all about harnessing and unhitching."

Serge interjected. "Give it up, Mikal." He raised his glass high. "To Karyn Ritter. Long may she reign."

So it was settled. Karyn would drive the team home, leaving Sugar for Sophie.

Karyn spent the night in a chair in the corner of the bedroom she shared with Mikal. She dozed fitfully, waking to the sound of Mikal groaning every time he moved in bed. Long before dawn, she rose to go downstairs. She had already opened the door when she turned back. She went to the bedside and looked down at Mikal. Impulsively, she reached out to touch his hair. Then, she leaned over to kiss his cheek. When she turned again to go, Mikal grabbed her hand and squeezed it.

"I was just going, Mikal," she whispered. "Go back to sleep." She heard the floor creak behind her. Sophie was standing in the doorway with an odd expression on her face. Karyn brushed by Sophie, pausing to say, "I'll heat water. If he wants some tea, it will be ready."

Karyn was only halfway down the stairs when she heard Celest say, "Good morning, Sophie. I'm so happy to see you feel well this morning. Come. You can help me gather eggs."

Karyn had been home only a few hours when Cay Miller drove up in a new carriage. He was dressed in an impeccably tailored suit and sported a stylish top hat.

"Oh, Cay," Karyn said. "I'm so sorry. Sophie isn't here. Mikal has had an accident. He broke his ankle, and he's staying where Celest can take care of him for a few days." Karyn almost choked on the next words, but she forced herself to sound casual. "I left Sophie there to help."

Cay frowned. His voice was warm with concern as he asked, "Is Mikal all right?"

As quickly as she could, Karyn recounted Mikal's story.

Cay shook his head. "We *must* get a campaign going to get those old wells filled in."

Karyn laughed. "Well, as soon as Mikal's ankle heals, I know one well that will be filled in. He vowed to personally drag that soddy down and use the sod to fill in the well."

"You tell him to come see me before he does it. I'll get the county to pay him. He'd be doing the community a great service. Imagine if a child had fallen in!" Cay set his top hat on the seat beside him and asked, "What can I do to help you, Karyn?"

Karyn reached into her apron pocket and withdrew a piece of paper on which was traced the shape of a man's foot. She held it up to Cay. "Get Mikal a new pair of boots. His are still at the bottom of the well."

Cay nodded. "Done. What else?"

"Would you take a look at the wheat? Mikal seemed worried about letting it lie any longer."

Immediately Cay jumped down from the carriage. Tying his horse to the post that formed a corner of Karyn's porch, he headed down the hill. Karyn followed, smiling to herself as the little man swaggered ahead.

At the bottom of the hill, Cay waited for Karyn and together they walked to the nearest field. Adjusting his eye patch, Cay bent down and examined the wheat that had been partially shattered and flattened to the earth. Gathering a small bunch of it, he held it up and breathed in deeply. Then, he examined a single stalk closely. Finally, he said, "It's still dry. If you get it picked up and stacked before it rains, you could have a lot of fuel this winter."

"Fuel?" Karyn asked. "I thought that's what we collected chips for. And Mikal still has great hopes for the corn."

"If it's a bad winter, you'll need all the fuel you can get. Wheat straw burns well if you know just how to twist it," Cay offered.

174

"Can you show me?"

Cay nodded. They walked back to the dugout where Karyn had piled up some straw the previous week. Cay demonstrated, quickly twisting the bundle and tying it with more wheat.

Karyn watched carefully, then tried and failed. She tried again. On her third try, Cay approved. She smiled. "Good. I can work on that. I'll put the tied bundles in the dugout."

"I'll drive back in the morning in my work clothes and help you pick up the last of your wheat. Isaac Kruger will be glad to watch over the store for me. We can probably finish in a day or two."

Karyn smiled at him, her dark eyes glowing with appreciation. "Thank you, Cay. Remi and Serge promised to come by in a couple of days. But with your help perhaps I can have the job nearly finished before they arrive."

Cay frowned. "I suppose Luc will want to stay close to home now that he has Sophie right under his own roof."

"Don't give up so easily," Karyn encouraged him. She asked, "Can I make you an early supper?"

"I don't want to be any trouble," came the reply.

"It's no trouble. Actually, I'd welcome help unharnessing Lena and Grace. At home I drove my father's delivery wagon, but his old mare was barely alive compared to those two giants. They scare me a little. And I think they know it."

Cay smiled. "Draft horses are very gentle, Karyn. You've nothing to fear from them. You're more likely to get bucked off by Sugar than to have Lena or Grace hurt you. You'll see."

Watching Cay handle Lena and Grace helped Karyn relax with them. Cay was fully two inches shorter than Karyn, and yet the mares showed no signs of willfulness when Cay lead them into the corral. He showed Karyn how to undo the massive harness and hang it so that none of the straps tangled. Then, while he worked at cleaning Grace's gigantic feet, Karyn followed suit with Lena. By the time the mares had been curried and bedded down in the stalls inside the dugout, Karyn felt totally at ease handling the horses.

Over supper, Cay regaled Karyn with stories of his war experiences and his plans for Millersburg. When he finally rose to leave, he said, "You tell Mikal that as soon as his ankle heals, if he wants to cut more cedar, I'm paying twenty cents a post right now. I think that's about double what he expected." Cay shook his head. "It's too bad he lost that load."

"Why don't you tell him yourself?" Karyn wanted to know. She looked at Cay meaningfully. "He really could use those boots."

Cay grinned at her. "Well, since you can't take them over, and since he's in such a hurry, I guess I will be forced to deliver them myself."

"That would be really good of you, Cay. And be sure to tell Sophie I send my love." Karyn winked at him.

As Cay drove off, Karyn lit the lamp and put it in the window. Then, she took Celest's advice. Opening the little prayer book that Tilda Stoddard had given her weeks before, she turned to the back and began to read the Psalms. Even though what she read wasn't of any particular significance at first, she felt better knowing that she was fulfilling Celest's wishes. Celest had said that she should read and pray and leave the rest to God. She had determined to try it for at least the two weeks that Mikal and she were apart.

Once in bed, she recited a childhood prayer. But she couldn't sleep. Finally, she spoke into the darkness, "All right, God. I don't want to do this, but I am going to do it anyway. Sophie is a selfish, foolish girl, and I don't want her to have my Mikal. But I'm going to pray for her anyway. Please, God, help Sophie to be happy."

Karyn slept.

Over the next few days, Karyn thought about Mikal, worried over Sophie, and tried her best to trust God. She spent her evenings reading the Psalms. Nothing dramatic happened as a result of her reading. Still, it wasn't long before she began to notice certain themes in what she read. Fulfillment and true happiness were promised to those who turned to God, trusted Him, and served Him first instead of worrying about themselves.

She kept thinking about the cedar logs scattered on the prairie. *Twenty cents a piece. That's the same as if I sold Cay almost ninety pounds of butter.* But even as an idea began to form, she argued with herself. *Don't be ridiculous. You'll never find them.* Then she answered back, *But if I could find them . . . if I could load them . . . it would be a wonderful surprise for Mikal.*

Finally, Karyn tacked a note to the door: *Remi/Serge—Tell Mikal everything is fine. Wheat gathered. Twisted what I could and put in dugout. Gone to Millersburg.*

In Millersburg, Karyn got news from Cay that Mikal was acting like a caged bear.

"And Sophie?" Karyn asked.

Cay smiled. "Sophie is taking cooking lessons from Celest Delhomme. And learning to spin wool and do a million other things." He added happily, "She says she hasn't had a weak spell since she got there."

"That's wonderful!" Karyn said. She didn't ask any more, afraid of what she would hear. Instead, she asked Cay to bring her account up to date and pay her with boots, overalls, a shirt, and a hat. When Cay turned to fill her order, she said, "No, Cay. I think I only need a medium size. And here"—she rummaged in her basket—"I drew around my foot so you can guess at boots while I try on the overalls." She hurried to explain, "I'm going after that load of cedar posts Mikal lost."

"Oh, no, you're not!" Cay insisted. "That's a man's job. Those posts are heavy. You can't possibly—"

Karyn glowered at him. "Cay Miller, if you are going to court my sister, then you had better learn one thing about the Ensinger sisters. One thing you do *not* do is tell us what we cannot do." She added, "And if you are going to be my friend, you had better learn something about me. You can't tell me not to do something 'because it's a man's job.'" She set her basket on Cay's counter and stared at him. "I am going after those logs. I need gloves. And supplies for the grub box. Here's my butter and another shirt for you to sell. Now, you said you knew exactly where that old well is. Draw me a map."

Cay put his hands behind his back. "I can't, Karyn. Mikal would kill me."

"He will not kill you," Karyn said. "He doesn't even have to know, if you're that worried about it. I'll tell him I tricked you into telling me where the abandoned well was. That you didn't know I was planning on going there. That I sneaked the clothes off the shelf when you were back in your own quarters." Just talking about the adventure made her more determined than ever to do it.

"But you're afraid of the team."

"I drove them over here, didn't I?"

"Why don't you ask Remi and Serge to go? How do you know they haven't already gone after that load?"

Karyn shrugged. "I don't." She pleaded, "Please, Cay. I want to surprise Mikal. If I get that load of posts Mikal will be able to pay for both the red wheat and most of the winter's groceries." She leaned across the counter and whispered, "Just draw the map, and you'll have a standing invitation to Sunday dinner."

"Sophie is at the Delhommes'," he grumbled. "I doubt I have much chance with her."

"Why not?" Karyn said, praying that Mikal's name was not about to be mentioned. "Wasn't she nice to you when you took Mikal's boots out?"

"Oh, she was nice enough," he muttered. "But I know where I stand. I may only have one eye, but I can see very well how I compare to the handsome Mr. Delhomme."

"But you can offer a woman a future far better than Luc's." Karyn reached across the counter and patted Cay's hand. "I said it before, Cay, and I repeat: Don't give up so easily."

Cay grinned. "All right. I won't." He pulled a piece of white paper off the roll bolted to his countertop and began to draw. "Stay on the east side of Muddy Creek. About five miles from here, it branches to the west. Don't follow that. Instead, go up the valley three miles. There will be a long ridge on your left. You'll see the soddy tucked against the ridge just after you pass a boulder the size of your house jutting out of the ridge." He reached behind the counter and collected a pair of overalls, shirt, hat, and gloves. "Try these on in my quarters. I've never fit a woman before."

Karyn walked back to Cay's quarters and reemerged in her stocking feet.

At the sight of her, Cay repeated, "Mikal will kill me if he ever finds out about this."

Karyn laughed. "Well, it's either be killed now by a very angry woman or later by Mikal. Either way, you're dead. Unless, of course, I come back with a full load of cedar fence posts. In which case Mikal will be very, very happy with both of us. Please tell me you have boots that will fit."

Cay tossed a pair of boots to her. "I'll stock the grub box while you put these on."

When Karyn exited his store, Cay followed her out to the wagon. "If you are not back by Friday, I am coming after you."

Karyn nodded. "Good. That way if I fall in a well somewhere, I will be rescued." She laughed. "Don't worry, Cay. I'll be fine." As she clamped on her new hat, she caught sight of Amalia Kruger. The old woman was standing in the doorway of Kruger's Harness Shop squinting at her in disbelief. Karyn called out a greeting, but Amalia pretended not to hear her.

Karyn had no difficulty following Cay Miller's map. She located the homestead, shuddering as she crawled to the edge of the well and peered down into the hole. She could see where Mikal had dug toeholds and handholds near the top. *Thank You, dear God. Whether he belongs to me or not, thank You that Mikal didn't give up.*

Karyn found the first cedar posts about a hundred yards from the well. Pulling the team up, she jumped down and hefted a post into the back of the wagon. After she had loaded only a few, she had to stop to rest. By the end of the day, she was exhausted. She had recovered all sixty-five posts. She unhitched Lena and Grace and walked them to the creek for a drink. As it grew dark, Karyn opened the grub box and ate a hearty meal. She tethered Grace and Lena where they could graze, stretched out under the wagon, and fell instantly asleep.

Dawn found Karyn headed back toward Millersburg with her full load of fence posts. She had barely started the drive along the edge of Mud Creek when two voices shouted, "Hey, you there! Stop! You've got our fence posts!"

Karyn pulled the team up and turned around to see Remi and Serge driving up in an empty wagon. She pulled off her hat, thoroughly enjoying the two young men's open-mouthed amazement.

"Karyn?" Remi sputtered, then broke out laughing. "I don't believe it!"

Karyn blushed. "I wanted to surprise Mikal."

"Well, he's going to be surprised, all right."

"Don't tell him. Please," Karyn pleaded.

"Well, how are we going to explain our empty wagon?"

"Tell him the truth. Someone had already picked up all the fence posts."

Remi nodded. "All right. That's fair." He chuckled. "Are there any more sisters at home like you?"

Karyn laughed. "No. The rest are sweet and charming. And pretty, like Sophie." She was suddenly serious. "And how is Mikal? Is he mending?"

"He's going crazy. He wants us to make him a crutch. Mother says we're going to have to tie him to the bed before too much longer. His knee is better. And I think he actually managed to get out of bed this morning without sounding like a wounded bull because of that broken rib. He is mending. He misses you, though."

Karyn blushed. "Well, I'm sure Sophie is doing a good job taking care of him."

"Actually," Remi said pointedly, "Mother and Luc are keeping Sophie too busy for her to have much to do with Mikal."

Karyn's heart missed a few beats. Sophie wasn't spending much time with Mikal. Mikal missed her. *Let God handle Mikal's heart, Karyn.*

Serge and Remi escorted Karyn back to Millersburg. As they pulled up in front of Cay's store, Amalia Kruger came to the door of the house across the street. Karyn waved at her again before insisting that she help Remi and Serge unload the fence posts. When the wagon was empty, Cay tried to pay Karyn

$13.00. She refused. "I just want Mikal's sack of red wheat. Put the rest on his account. I don't need anything right now."

"I suppose you're going to plant that for him, too," Remi joked.

"Not until I get a good night's rest," Karyn joked back.

At that moment, Amalia Kruger crossed the street. "Mrs. Ritter," she said shortly.

When Karyn turned around, Amalia muttered, "You must be very tired. You are welcome to stay with me tonight. A woman should not be out alone on the prairie after dark."

Karyn looked at her in amazement.

Amalia barked, "You don't want my help, I suppose," and started to shuffle back across the street.

"No, it's not that, Mrs. Kruger. I'm just surprised, that's all."

Amalia looked her up and down. "I have always liked Mikal Ritter. I am glad to see he finally got some sense and picked a woman who would last."

"Go ahead, Karyn," Remi said. "We'll take care of the team. You must be exhausted."

Karyn followed Amalia into her son's immaculate little house.

"My son and his wife are gone to Grand Island. Of course, they did not invite me along. You can have their bed. I put on clean sheets today. And the best quilt."

Karyn undressed wearily. Amalia brought her a cup of tea, but Karyn was already asleep. Peering at Karyn, Amalia smiled in spite of herself.

The Diary
August 16, 1880

Mikal recovers at Celest's from a terrible fall. The tale of it will no doubt be told for some time to come. As Mikal said, it is proof that God can help even when all hope is gone. If only I can apply that to other matters. I have shocked a few people by dressing like a man and retrieving Mikal's lost fence posts. I like knowing that I am helping.

CHAPTER 15

A Butter Stamp

----

*Let my cry come near before thee, O LORD: give
me understanding according to thy word. Let my
supplication come before thee: deliver me
according to thy word.*
Psalm 119:169–170

Karyn woke the next morning to the aroma of fresh coffee.
She hurried to dress, intending to leave immediately. When she
reached the kitchen, Amalia was standing with her back to
Karyn at the stove. Something in the way the wizened old
woman held her head reminded Karyn momentarily of her own
mother. Amalia moved deliberately, as if she carefully thought
out every movement. In truth, Karyn wondered, looking at
Amalia's crooked fingers, perhaps she had to do just that so her
arthritic hands and wrists would obey her.

As Karyn watched, Amalia bent to take a pan of fresh biscuits
from the oven. She grunted softly with the effort of stooping,
reached for the pan of biscuits, and slid it onto the stove top.
Closing the oven door evoked another soft grunt. When Amalia
rested a trembling hand on the top of a nearby chair for a moment, Karyn's heart softened.

Amalia reached to a shelf near the stove and took down two
plates. When she turned to set them on the table, she saw Karyn
and nodded. Her voice sounded weary. *"Bitte setzen Sie sich."*
Before Karyn could cross the large room to obey Amalia and sit
down, Amalia was lifting a pot from the back burner of the

stove and pouring strong black coffee into a huge brown cup beside Karyn's plate.

While she slathered a biscuit with butter, Karyn considered the room around her. Someone had tacked lace-edged paper along the shelf that held the dishes. There was only one plate and one cup on the shelf, which meant that the entire china supply of the Kruger household amounted to three plates and three cups. But they were china instead of tin like the ones Mikal used. The room was immaculate. From the wood puncheon floor to the rafters, there was not a speck of dust, not a cobweb, in sight. The panes of the window in the far wall sparkled in the morning light.

"You have a nice home, Frau Kruger," Karyn offered while she slathered a biscuit with butter.

"It is not mine. I am reminded of that often by my son's wife." Amalia sighed deeply. "Although she does not seem to mind that I clean it as if it were my own." Without getting up, Amalia reached for the plate of biscuits that she had left warming on the stove. She offered one to Karyn.

Karyn gulped coffee and said, "*Danke.* Having someone cook for me is a nice treat."

Amalia shrugged. "I am not worth much anymore. But I still make good biscuits."

"How long have you been here?" Karyn asked.

"Here? Where here? Here in Nebraska or here in America?"

"America," Karyn said.

"Fifteen years," Amalia said. "Fifteen years of regret and unhappiness." She peered over her tiny oval glasses and blurted out, "Be glad you came to America when you are so young. For young people it is simple. They come to America, they take off their German coat. They put on an American coat. Is done. Just so."

Karyn disagreed. "It has not been that simple for me."

"Already you are speaking English better than I, who have been here for many years." Amalia snorted softly. "Humph. Even that sister of yours speaks better English than I."

"Sophie was always a brilliant student," Karyn said. "I think God gave her that to compensate for her being ill so much. As for me, I had help from some children while their father worked with Mikal." She told Amalia about Tilda and Sten Stoddard.

"The daughter and son were about seven and nine years old—the wagon pulled by a team of skinny white horses?" When Karyn nodded, Amalia said, "I was in Miller's store when they came in. Stoddard was selling everything to go back to— Ohio I think it was." Her expression softened. "Your Mikal bought those children candy." Amalia shook her head. "Tilda Stoddard could have spent an entire year trying to teach me. It would have made no difference. I have no ear for languages." She grimaced. "*Ach*. No matter."

Karyn took another biscuit.

Amalia chuckled. "It is good to see a woman with an appetite." A smile slowly took over the wrinkles on her face, willing them to fold back and transform her usually dour expression into something more pleasant. "As soon as you left yesterday morning, I went over to Cay Miller's. It did not take long to get him to tell me the story of where Karyn Ritter was going dressed like a man." She lowered her voice. "I wish I had been so determined when I was young. I would have had a happier life."

Karyn was wary of Amalia. Still, it was good to be speaking German again. She couldn't resist asking, "What do you wish you had changed?"

"Everything," came the answer. "Everything." Amalia studied Karyn carefully for a moment or two. Then she got up and poured them both another cup of coffee, while she asked, "You are from Brandenburg? Do you know Oelde?" When Karyn shook her head no, Amalia smiled. "*Das schone Oelde.*" She described a charming city overshadowed by a castle in the midst of thick woods. "My father was mayor of Oelde. When my mother died, I was thirteen." Amalia set the coffeepot back on the stove, but she didn't sit back down. She stared out the window and from her expression Karyn could tell that Amalia was back in Germany. "I was sent to live with my married brother in Munster. He was an independent thinker. So, unlike most German girls of my day, I was educated. We took trips along the Rhine, we attended dances and balls, we participated in musical clubs. We discussed philosophy and art with the same familiarity, the same fervor, as the farmers here discuss what kind of wheat to plant."

"Why did you leave?"

Amalia waved her hand in the air, shook her head, and plopped back in her chair. "For the same reason as you, and a thousand other women like us. Because of a man. My betrothed, Jacob Kruger, was a physician with a good practice and a promising future. I never dreamed he would do anything but practice medicine in Munster. But the fever to emigrate set in." Amalia sighed. "Suddenly, he could speak of nothing but America. Cheap land in America. Future riches. He said he was going to a place called Kansas." Amalia shrugged. "I threatened not to come—to break our engagement. But it was an empty threat. Women could not enter the professions in Germany. My brother would never have supported me. And besides"—Amalia smiled bitterly—"I loved Jacob. So, while my heart was breaking at the thought of leaving, my heart was also breaking at the thought of losing Jacob. He was so determined; so certain that America held the promise of wealth. So we married and came to America."

Amalia grunted. "We lived in a dugout. There was no other woman within ten miles of our little hovel. With his practice, Jacob was gone much of the time—and I was left alone. He learned English readily. But no Tilda Stoddard came along to help me." Amalia clucked her tongue against the roof of her mouth. "And there was no Celest Delhomme with whom I could share my troubles. There were no fences or walls within sight of my one-room house, but I still felt as though I was in prison."

"Such loneliness would be a kind of prison," Karyn empathized. "It must have been dreadful. But at least you knew your husband loved you."

Amalia looked at Karyn. Her eyes narrowed as she said, "Love does not always make the difference in every circumstance. It was still dreadful. There were days when I woke with the determination to take my own life and end my misery. But Jacob always kept his gun with him. And there was not even a

185

tree from which to hang myself." She sighed. "Of course once there were children, I had to stay for them."

Karyn tried to encourage her. "Having children must have been a comfort."

Amalia looked at her keenly. "I thought it would be. Until I had to bury five of my babies there in Kansas."

"Oh, Amalia—I am so sorry." Karyn was beginning to understand why Amalia Kruger was so unhappy. Karyn wondered if she would have fared any better, given Amalia's circumstances.

Amalia shrugged. "It is in the past. Enough talking about me. My Jacob is dead. Ida and Isaac remain. I never hear from Ida, and the woman Isaac married does not really want a difficult old woman like me around." She looked at Karyn. "I understood Marie-Louise Ritter's unhappiness. I wish I could have helped her more."

Amalia sipped coffee while she thought. Then, she said, "I know I do not have pleasant ways like Celest. But that day I met you and told you about Marie-Louise, I *was* trying to help you." Suddenly she reached across and patted Karyn on the hand. "Learn from my mistakes so that you do not end up like me."

When Karyn was silent, Amalia said, "You do not believe me, do you? You think if only Mikal Ritter loves you, then everything will be wonderful."

Karyn said, "Celest advised me to stop worrying about Mikal so much and to spend my time working on the things I can do something about—the duties at the homestead." She added timidly, "She thinks I am trusting too much in other people and not enough in God."

Amalia looked at Karyn soberly. "If you have a strong faith, so much the better. Perhaps, if I had known God's love years ago, it would have made a difference for me. I do not know. But strong faith or no, a woman must still determine to fight for what she wants. She must not give up." She paused, emphasizing each word of her next sentence. "Even if her own sister succeeds in stealing her husband away from her."

As the meaning of what Amalia was saying sunk in, Karyn protested. "*Was du nicht sagst!*" She wiped her mouth, put both hands on the edge of the table, and started to get up, but Amalia wasn't finished.

She grabbed Karyn by the wrist. "I know what has been going on. I have been watching. "Her voice took on a surprisingly kind tone as she said softly, "*Das Wichtige siehst du nicht.* You are worth a hundred Sophies, Karyn. You remember that. And if Mikal Ritter is such a fool as to fall for another woman like Marie-Louise, he deserves what he gets. You must not allow it to turn you into an unhappy old hag like me. *Sie haben es gut.* In America life can be good for a woman, whether she has a man or not. And Celest's idea about learning to trust God may not be so bad, either." Amalia stood up and shooed Karyn toward the door. "Now, go. You have a cow to milk and a sow to feed. And I have work to do."

Automatically mumbling thanks for Amalia's hospitality, Karyn headed out the door and toward Cay's barn where Lena and Grace had been stabled for the night. She was only a few feet away when Amalia called, "You know, Karyn, here in America a woman can own land. That Herr Stoddard has abandoned his claim. Cay could tell you how to find it." When Karyn turned around to respond, Amalia had already retreated back inside the house.

In spite of Amalia's warnings and implied advice, Karyn had absolutely no intention of looking for Doane Stoddard's homestead. She would return home, work hard to keep things in order for Mikal, and try to trust God.

Her return home found Karyn too busy, too exhausted, too challenged to spend much time worrying over what might be happening between Mikal and Sophie. Weeding and replanting the garden, drawing bucket after bucket of water for the livestock, picking wild fruit and preserving what she could, milking and making butter and cheese, sewing and cleaning, kept her so busy she had not one moment of idle time from sunrise until she collapsed, exhausted, into bed at sundown. It was all she could do to keep her promise to Celest that she would read from the Psalms. Most evenings, she nodded off long before she had read even half a chapter.

Any energy that might have been left after a day of chores was sapped by Nebraska's relentless summer heat. Accustomed to the moderate climate of Brandenburg, where summer temperatures were rarely uncomfortable, Karyn was dismayed when by midmorning sweat was pouring down her face and soaking through the back of her dress. Time and again, she squinted into the distance thinking someone was coming, only to realize that she was being tricked by heat waves.

She began to get up earlier, trying to do as much work as possible before the sun climbed very high in the sky. By noon of the third day of the searing heat, she sought out the shelter offered by the interior of the soddy and began to cut out fabric to make some shirts for Cay's store. She smiled at the fact that thanks to Sophie's flirting she knew Mikal's measurements and could surprise him with another new shirt.

The nights remained so hot Karyn would lie as still as possible, trying to conjure an imaginary breeze. She was grateful she was alone. It meant she didn't have to cover herself with layers of nightgown. One night she took a blanket outside and lay on the ground beneath the porch. The air was slightly cooler there, but mosquitoes and fleas attacked, and she soon fled back inside. The insects followed her. She made a mental note to ask Cay about the cost of a screen door.

The livestock suffered terribly from the unrelenting heat. Karyn watered the seedling trees faithfully, thinking how wonderful it would be if the corral were shaded. She led the mares to the creek and picketed them where one big cottonwood afforded shade. They grazed halfheartedly, their heads hanging down as they munched on the increasingly dried grass. Much of the time they just stood in the shade nose-to-tail, trying unsuccessfully to keep the unrelenting flies away.

Ella grew cross, balking when Karyn tried to move her picket. One morning when Karyn fumbled awkwardly during milking, Ella kicked at her angrily, sending both the milk pail and Karyn flying. Karyn picked herself up out of the dust, tears of frustration stinging her eyes.

The heat presented other challenges—among them finding a way to keep her butter from going rancid. She rode into Millersburg on Saturday to trade, but by the time she arrived, her few pounds of butter were ruined. Before leaving town, she stopped by Amalia's. The old woman welcomed her with surprising friendliness.

Amalia smiled when Karyn mentioned the problem of the butter. "I know how to fix that. Let me tell you what I did in Kansas. . . ." She described a way for Karyn to save her butter and gave Karyn a small wooden stamp that would leave the design of an acorn and oak leaf in the top of her squares of butter. "I used it all my life," Amalia said. "I want you to have it."

Before leaving town, Karyn returned to Cay's store and asked for four six-gallon crocks. Returning home, she spent the rest of the day creating what Amalia called a "larder" at the back of the dugout. It was after dark before Karyn had dug a trench deep enough to hold the four crocks, but surveying her work by lamplight, Karyn smiled with satisfaction.

As soon as the bucket in the well was filled with blocks of fresh butter, she would salt each block well, then wrap it in muslin and tie it securely with string. Each block of butter would be packed tightly into the crock. When the first crock was full, she would set the lid down on it and cover it with another cloth, tied securely in place. Then, she would cover the crock with several inches of earth to keep it cool. As soon as the heat lifted, she would present Cay with as much butter as he could use. Why, he might pay as much as ten cents a pound for such a fine product!

Karyn stepped outside the dugout and watched the moon appear in the eastern sky. No breeze wafted over the prairie to cool her face. The heat of the night melted her sense of accomplishment, sending rivulets of sweat running down the back of her neck. When she reached up to wipe it away, she could feel grit from her filthy hands scraping against the soft skin at the nape of her neck.

She walked toward the corral, listening for the now-familiar sounds of night on the prairie. But the heat had silenced even the creatures in the tall grass. Leaning against the corral fence, Karyn looked down toward the creek where a few inches of water still flowed, fresh and cool from a spring that bubbled out of the earth less than a mile away. *If Cay Miller ran a hotel I think I would ride all the way to Millersburg by moonlight just to have a real bath.* Articulating the thought gave Karyn an idea. By moonlight she slipped down to the creek and out of her dress and petticoats. She took her hair down and lay in the water. For the first time in what seemed like months she felt cool and clean.

Karyn slept in the dugout that night, waking several times to fire warning shots to keep the increasingly determined coyotes away from Ella's calf. Tomorrow was Sunday. Tomorrow she would ride to the Delhommes'. Mikal would be proud of all she had accomplished. The image of Sophie made her determine to wear her nicest dress. And she would take care with her hair tomorrow morning, as well. In fact, she would take the time to arrange it just the way she had worn it the day she and Mikal met.

Early Sunday morning, Karyn picked the last of the ripe elderberries growing in a thick patch about a half mile from her home. She built a fire, cooking the elderberries and pressing them through a sieve until she had a quart of dark purple juice. Adding water and sugar to the juice, she strained the liquid through cheesecloth. Then, she poured the concoction into a gallon jar and added yeast. While she worked, she pictured herself and Mikal at Christmas, toasting one another with elderberry wine. Sophie was not a factor in her imagined setting.

Karyn had decided not to take the time to hitch up the wagon. She would ride Lena to the Delhommes', surprising Mikal with her early arrival. She would report that things at home were fine, that she had found a way to keep the butter from going rancid, that she had made three shirts for Cay to sell, that Ella and the calf were fine, that the sow was almost big enough to butcher . . . and that for Christmas they would have elderberry wine.

Plodding along astride Lena's broad back, Karyn smiled to herself. Her mother would be shocked to see her own daughter riding a horse like a man instead of perched atop a sidesaddle like a proper lady. But then, everything about life in Custer

County would probably shock Mama, who, like Karyn, had imagined Karyn's future in a little cottage "in the countryside."

Bending down to pat Lena on the neck Karyn said aloud, "You know, Lena, Mikal is going to be upset that I'm not bringing the wagon. I'm certain he has it in his mind to insist that he come home today. But I'll tell him he has nothing to worry about, that his ankle must heal . . . and then while he stays at the Delhommes', perhaps you and Grace can help me plant at least one acre of that red wheat." She smiled happily. Surely living in Custer County was difficult, but a woman could do just about anything she set her mind to here. Why, Cay Miller had said they might get a woman doctor in Millersburg. That could never happen in Germany. And Amalia said women could own land. Karyn didn't want a profession. Being Mikal's wife was becoming increasingly fulfilling. And she didn't care to own land—unless Mikal wanted to expand his holdings. Still, it was good to be in a country where even women were free to make choices.

She took a deep breath and began to sing an old German hymn. By the time Lena climbed up the steep incline that led them onto French Table, Karyn was ready to urge her to a canter. "I know it's hot, Lena, but I'll give you plenty of fresh water and hay . . . I just can't wait any longer to see Mikal." *I'm so glad I came to America. I'm not going to let anything ruin today. Not the heat, not doubts about the future—and certainly not Sophie.*

When she arrived at the Delhommes', Karyn led Lena inside the sod barn where she would be cooler. True to her promise to Lena, she pumped a fresh bucket of cool water and forked a mound of hay into the corner of the stall. She reached up to pat the gigantic mare on the neck. "Now, Lena, you enjoy your day of rest in this cool barn."

Next, Karyn turned her attention to readying herself to see her husband. She smoothed her hair and patted her face and the back of her neck with fresh water. She washed her hands, now regretting the morning's session with the elderberries. Hopefully Mikal wouldn't notice the purple stains on her hands. She had just started for the house when Celest came out the front door, dressed in her riding breeches and carrying riding gloves and a crop in her hand.

"I've been watching for you all morning!" Celest said. "I told the family I'd stay behind and make sure Mikal stayed put until you got here. There's to be a church service in Millersburg today. Everyone else has gone on ahead. If I hurry I think I can at least join them for the hymn sing they were planning after lunch." She winked at Karyn and nodded over her shoulder toward the house. "Beware the bear, dear. He's impossible." Celest headed for the barn.

Karyn ran to the house. Then, she stepped across the threshold and forced herself to walk calmly up the stairs to Mikal's room. He was sitting in a chair by the window, his foot propped up on a footstool, his open Bible in his lap.

"Why didn't you bring the wagon?" He was frowning as he closed his Bible and tossed it on the bed.

"Hello to you, too, Mr. Ritter." Karyn felt herself blushing. She had forgotten the exact shade of those blue eyes.

But the blue eyes were glowering at her. "Why didn't you bring the wagon?"

She sat at the foot of the bed and tried to tease him. "If I brought the wagon, you would insist on going home. Celest says you're to stay off the ankle for at least two more weeks. So, unless you can fly, you're going to have to be a good patient."

Mikal would not be humored. He barraged her with questions and warnings. Instead of praising her for her diligent work, he seemed intent on pointing out how she should have done things. It seemed to Karyn that as the moments went by, she steadily lost ground in Mikal's eyes.

Karyn did her best not to overreact to Mikal's criticisms. *After all,* she told herself, *he's had a hard week.* "It's nearly time for lunch," she said when there was a pause in the conversation. "I'll make us something to eat."

She headed downstairs to the kitchen, thankful that Mikal couldn't follow her. Being alone for a few moments would give her time to collect her thoughts and to calm down. Quickly she made biscuits and fried eggs. When the biscuits were finished, Karyn arranged Mikal's and her lunches on a tray. She served him and had barely sat down when he asked abruptly, "So. Tell me. What is it that Remi and Serge have been keeping from me?"

At Karyn's look of surprise, he leaned forward. "Did we lose the calf to the coyotes after all?"

Karyn shook her head. "The calf is fine. I told you that I've slept in the dugout the nights I thought there might be a problem."

"You should take Ella and the calf into the dugout. That's safer."

"All right."

Mikal hadn't eaten yet. He worried, "Well, if it isn't the calf, it must be the sow." Mikal shook his head and looked out the window. "I knew I should have warned you about this heat. They just can't stand heat." He muttered, "She would have given us a good supply of pork—"

"Mikal," Karyn pleaded, "why are you so certain that Remi and Serge's secret news is something bad? The sow is very comfortable—and very, very fat. We'll have to butcher her before long. If you think it should be done now, I'll get Remi and Serge to help." She explained, "I cut branches down at the creek and made a little roof for her pen. She's in the shade, and twice a day I pour a pail of cold water over her to cool her down." Karyn grinned. "She's come to anticipate it. In fact, if I don't get there at the usual hour with her bath, she squeals to get my attention. I think I actually recognize my name in 'pig' now."

Mikal didn't smile. Instead, he raised his voice. "Then what is it? What's happened?"

Karyn sighed. "I wanted it to be a homecoming surprise." She paused before finally telling him, "I drove the team out to that abandoned well and followed your trail of cedar fence posts." She smiled. "I found every last one of them and took them to Cay. And he paid twenty cents each for them. That's almost twice what you were expecting, isn't it?" She rushed ahead. "So the red wheat—which, by the way, has finally come—is paid for." She chuckled. "Amalia Kruger was so impressed she invited me to rest at her house overnight. She even made me breakfast. I'm not sure which news is more shocking—that your wife dressed in men's clothes and retrieved the posts, or that Amalia Kruger seems to have decided she approves of me."

Mikal glowered at Karyn. He almost shouted, "What possessed you to do such a foolish thing?"

"It wasn't foolish," Karyn retorted. She set her tray of food down on the bed. "It needed to be done, and I did it."

"Maybe you should be a little more like Sophie and a little less anxious to do everything you think needs to be done. You might live longer."

Karyn stood up, biting her lips to retain an angry retort.

Mikal rubbed his forehead briskly. "I'm sorry, Karyn. I shouldn't have said that." He looked out the window. "I don't know how to tell you what this week has been like. I'm afraid I haven't been very successful in handling this. A ruined crop— that I can do something about. But being trapped here, able to do nothing—" He sighed. "Things are a mess. With you. With me. And then there's Sophie—"

The moment Mikal mentioned Sophie, something happened inside Karyn that clicked off whatever Mikal was saying and set her mind to whirling. *Of course. I should have realized. That's why he's so unhappy. Here I am rattling on and on about how well things are going . . . and about the future . . . when he's trying to find a way to tell me about Sophie.* Karyn's dark eyes flashed. *But why didn't Celest warn me?* She reasoned. *Maybe she doesn't know. Maybe it all happened in private . . . while Sophie helped care for him here . . . in this room.*

Karyn interrupted whatever Mikal was saying. "Mikal, I think somewhere in that book you were reading when I arrived that it talks about speaking the truth in love. All you have to do is tell me the truth, Mikal." She backed toward the door. "In fact, since it obviously makes you uncomfortable to talk about it, you don't have to tell me. I'll save you that."

She left Mikal sitting by the window, an odd look of amazement on his face, and hurried down the stairs and outside. As she ran toward the corral, she prayed that Mikal would come after her, that he would tell her she was wrong. But he didn't.

She put the bridle on Lena, climbed up on a hay bale to slip onto the mare's broad back, and rode for the homestead. Once she thought she heard something—she stopped Lena and looked back toward the house, her heart thumping, hoping to see Mikal at the doorway, hoping to hear him calling her name. But whatever it was she had heard, it wasn't Mikal calling for her.

The Diary
August 24, 1880
   Psalm 37—of David, who also knew betrayal
"Fret not thyself because of evildoers, neither be thou envious against the workers of iniquity."
   —But I am so very envious of one tonight.
"Trust in the LORD, *and do good";*
   —I thought I was trusting. Was my motive impure?
"so shalt thou dwell in the land, and verily thou shalt be fed."
   —But not in the land I desire, or so it seems.
   To what land do I go now?
"Delight thyself also in the LORD; *and he shall give thee the desires of thine heart."*
   —Have my desires been so far from His?
   "Commit thy way unto the LORD; *trust also in him; and he shall bring it to pass."*
   —I thought I was committed and trusting.
"Rest in the LORD, *and wait patiently for him":*
   —I have tried to be patient. What good has it done?
"fret not thyself because of him who prospereth in his way, because of the man who bringeth wicked devices to pass. Cease from anger, and forsake wrath: fret not thyself in any wise to do evil."
   —May God help me to obey, for at this moment I find myself wishing evil on one whom I should love.
God give me strength to obey. I have read the psalm again and again. But I cannot do what it says. What a poor, pathetic creature I am. Lord, I do believe. Help my unbelief.

CHAPTER 16

Why art thou cast down, O my soul?
and why art thou disquieted in me?
hope thou in God: for I shall yet praise
him for the help of his countenance.
Psalm 42:5

Sitting at the base of the Delhommes' stairs, Mikal looked
about him. He rubbed his forehead with the back of his hand. It
was no wonder that Karyn had been angry. No wonder that she
had gone home. She had done the work of a man and received
nothing but criticism in return. It was a wonder that she had not
thrown an entire tray of food at him before she left the room
that morning. It was little comfort now, realizing that he had
intended to apologize. He had grabbed his crutch and tried to
follow her . . . he had meant to explain. But she had stormed
down the stairs and out of the house so quickly that he couldn't
catch her, and when he tried to hurry he had stumbled and
fallen headlong down the stairs. Mikal wondered if she had
heard the crash.

Slowly, painfully, Mikal inched his way along the floor until
he could reach the crutch that had been sent flying halfway
across the parlor when he fell. He half crawled across the floor
to a chair in the parlor and pulled himself into the chair where
he could see outside.

That morning, when the Delhommes' had announced they
were going to Millersburg to hear the circuit rider preach, So-

196

phie had volunteered to stay with Mikal, but Luc had talked her out of it.

Mikal smiled grimly at the sudden realization that Celest had finally found a way to allow him and Karyn time alone . . . and he had ruined it. He had finally had the long-awaited opportunity to declare his feelings . . . and instead he had only pushed Karyn farther away.

Once again, Mikal thought back over their short time together that morning. Karyn had ignored his surly mood at first. She had patiently reassured him, had recounted the details of everything she had done in his absence. And she had done so much. Conjuring up the picture of Karyn dressed in overalls loading cedar posts into his wagon made Mikal half angry again. It was too much. That was a man's job. She shouldn't have had to do it. And she didn't have to do it, did she? *She did it because* . . . Mikal wondered, *Perhaps she did it for us.*

The Delhommes and Sophie had taken all the horses. He would have to wait until they all got back from Millersburg before he could go after Karyn.

Mikal sighed, leaning his head back against the high back of the parlor chair. Dusk sprinkled the window ledge with golden light, making the geraniums that bloomed there glow. Karyn would be back at the homestead by now, milking Ella, tending the sow, perhaps baking biscuits for her supper alone. Was she angry or hurt? Had she cried? How would she react when he rode up? He had been waiting for her to show some sign of caring for him . . . but he was finished with waiting. Suddenly, Mikal knew that the time had come for him to convince her that he had held her at arm's length because he wanted so to hold her in his arms.

Taking up his crutch, Mikal hobbled outside and towards the corral, where he sat down on a small pile of hay, facing the direction from which the Delhommes would come. Off to the west the sky glowed with the eerie golden light of fire. It was far enough away that he didn't think it posed a threat. Sitting in the dark, contemplating the odd light in the distance, Mikal spoke with God about the prairie fire, about the heat, making request after request. He realized how fortunate he was that there was a spring-fed creek running through his section. He thanked God that it had never run dry, even in the hottest weather. He mentioned his desire to have a windmill so that Karyn wouldn't have to work so hard to get water. He thanked God for Karyn. Soon he was thanking God for His blessings instead of asking. And then he wasn't talking at all, but rather listening to a still, small voice. And the voice whispered hope, whispered peace, whispered love.

It was about midnight before Emile and Celest broke away from the impromptu social in Millersburg and went outside to stand on the front porch of Cay Miller's store. Emile put his arm around his wife. "I know what you are up to, Madame Delhomme."

"What are you talking about?"

"This little social isn't in the least bit impromptu. You made certain Fred Smith would be here. And that tale about wanting to bring the organ so that we could have a proper hymn sing today? Why, that was shameful bold-faced lying, Celest. That's all it was. You plotted everything so that Karyn and Mikal would be alone tonight."

Celest chuckled and looked up at the sky. "Well, looking at that beautiful, romantic moon, I would say God approves of my little plot. Now if only Karyn and Mikal will cooperate."

"They are probably in each other's arms at this very moment," Emile said, kissing his wife's cheek. They turned to go inside. Emile had seen the golden light to the west, but he didn't think it was anything to be concerned about. At least not tonight. There hadn't been any wind for days. If the glow was still there tomorrow, then they would have to make preparations. But there was time. As long as the air remained still, there would be time.

Karyn took nearly three hours to cover the eight miles between the Delhommes' and home. She let Lena set her own pace while her mind whirled with thoughts of Mikal and Sophie. She loved Mikal Ritter much more completely than she had expected to. She had begun to sense a physical response to his presence that half frightened her. Even now she blushed when she thought about him. The sense of loss that had washed over her when she heard Mikal say that he wished she were more like Sophie had caused an ache deep inside. Her greatest desire and her worst fear had come true all at once. Mikal had finally fallen in love. Only not with her.

She was grateful that she had determined not to be the first to speak of love. What if Mikal had responded out of a sense of duty? Karyn sighed. She had come to Nebraska planning just that kind of partnership—one founded on duty and mutual respect. But Mikal Ritter's blue eyes and strong hands, muscular shoulders and beautiful smile, had changed all that. She had begun wanting those blue eyes to light up when she came into view. Feeling Mikal's hands on her waist had made her long to reach out and put her arms around his broad shoulders.

Karyn imagined what the past week had been like for Mikal. He was an honorable man, and it had probably been hard for him, being more and more attracted to Sophie . . . knowing that on Sunday he would have to face Karyn. Tears stung her eyes as she thought back over the morning. All her cheerful chatter seemed so ridiculous, now that she understood. He had been waiting to speak of Sophie . . . and she had rattled on about how she had kept the sow cool.

Lena had stopped to graze, but Karyn barely noticed. Her mind whirled as the mare nosed her way through the tall grass. Perhaps she should have been more like Sophie, after all. Perhaps she should have flirted more and worked less. She would have had more energy for things like elaborate hairdos. She could have avoided work-worn hands and freckles. Perhaps if Sophie had not come, she and Mikal might have been happy together. Thinking back over the recent months, Karyn was convinced she could have learned to please Mikal. She would have tried with everything in her being to please him. Tears began to flow. Karyn let them stream down her face.

"Lena, let's go." Karyn pulled the mare's head up and urged her forward. She thought of Hans Gilhoff. She had believed that her grief would surely kill her when Hans died. But she had survived. She had even come to believe that she would be happier in the wilderness of America than she would ever have been on an estate just outside of Brandenburg. Was it possible that someday she would realize that her life was better without Mikal Ritter? She doubted it, but she would pray for grace to remember the happy times they had shared without bitterness. There was no use being bitter. No good would come of it. God forbid that she become an unhappy old woman like Amalia Kruger.

Karyn brushed away the last of her tears. Had not Celest warned her against demanding her own way? Had not Celest urged her to love God, to trust Him completely? Karyn smiled sadly. Perhaps Sophie could make Mikal happy. Perhaps things would turn out for the best, after all.

Karyn was brought back to the moment when Lena arched her neck, pricked her ears, and neighed loudly. The mare broke into a canter, quickly covering the ground to the corral where Grace paced up and down the fence, anxious for the return of her partner. Karyn turned Lena into the corral. She took Ella and her calf into the dugout and shut them into a stall.

Looking up the hill toward the soddy, she realized how much she had grown to think of it as home. Taking a deep breath, she forced herself to relinquish her own plans for her future. Slowly, a plan began to form, a plan that would make things easier for Mikal to have what he really wanted. Karyn leaned against the corral fence for a few moments, thinking. Once again, she began to replace her own expectations and hopes with reality. But this time, Karyn prayed for God's help in facing that reality. As she prayed, she grew calmer. God had not granted happiness and love in this place, but certainly He had given her much to be thankful for.

Looking up at her little sod house illuminated by the bright moonlight, Karyn knew what she must do. She went up the slope to the house and inside. She lit the lamp and tore a sheet of paper from her journal. After three failed attempts, she finally managed to write a note that, while not completely satisfactory, expressed some of her thoughts to Mikal. She weighted the note down with the crock that held the elderberry juice. Then, she began to pack. In only a few moments, she was ready. She lay down to rest, grateful for the breeze that stirred the night air. Before dawn she rose and harnessed the team by moonlight.

Mikal fell asleep waiting for the Delhommes and Sophie. Dawn was breaking over the eastern horizon when he started awake at the sound of approaching hoofbeats. He awoke, pushing himself up on his crutch and waving furiously at the approaching riders.

Luc called out, "What is it? What's wrong?" He pulled his horse up next to Mikal.

Grimacing against the pain in his leg, Mikal answered, "I am an idiot, and I have to go after my wife and tell her so."

Sophie had yet to dismount. She looked down at Mikal and scolded, "Don't be absurd, Mikal. You are in no condition to go anywhere."

Mikal looked up at her. "Sophie, you are Karyn's sister, and I have not wanted to say anything, but now I'm telling you. I have let you cause me a lot of trouble. I take the blame. And now I take responsibility to try to right it. I won't say any more as long as you act like the good girl I know you want to be and keep out of my business with Karyn."

Sophie blinked a few times. She looked about her at Remi and Serge and Emile. No one was looking at her. Even Luc was studying the dirt at Mikal's feet.

Emile climbed down from the wagon and said quietly, "Take the team, Mikal. It will be safer." He managed to joke, "Just promise me you won't go on a mad dash across the prairie and end up down another well."

Remi and Serge boosted Mikal up into the wagon seat.

Celest called out, "Give me ten minutes to restock the grub box, Mikal. I'll get some food together."

Luc nodded toward the west. "Make sure there are matches, Mother."

Mikal answered, "Yes, I've been watching." He lowered his voice. "Could you ride over tomorrow and help us burn out the strips between the firebreak?"

Luc nodded.

In moments Celest was back with a basket filled with provisions for the grub box. She laid a hand on Mikal's arm. "Get it right, Mikal. That girl is the best thing that has happened to you in a very long time."

Mikal nodded. "I know. And I will get it right."

Celest lowered her voice. "And Mikal, Cay Miller will be delighted to help Sophie begin a dressmaking business over his store. In fact, I discussed it with him just this afternoon."

Mikal pulled his hat down and slapped the reins across the backs of Emile's team. It took every ounce of self-control not to send them off in a mad gallop. As the sun came up in the east, Mikal felt a surge of anticipation. He couldn't help but ponder the possibility that he had spent his last night alone in a dugout.

Dear Mikal,

I have done my best to keep things going for you. I hope your ankle heals well. I do not know the laws in America.

Certainly we have plenty of witnesses to the fact that we were married in name only. Hopefully, it will be a simple matter. I will do whatever you wish. Leave word with Amalia Kruger, and I will contact her.

My things are at Amalia's. Grace and Lena and the wagon are with Cay. There is little to worry over in the garden. Don't forget the butter in the dugout.

I should have liked the opportunity to love you, Mikal. But I think I have learned more from not being loved. Perhaps that is what God wanted me to learn. It brought me closer to Him, so it accomplished its purpose in my life. I only write this to assure you that my experience as your wife will not be a cause for my becoming bitter, although I deeply regret that I failed to meet your expectations. Perhaps someday you will believe that I did my best.

The wine will be ready for Christmas. Perhaps you and Sophie will drink a toast to me.

Your ——————
Karyn Ensinger Ritter

She had scratched out part of the closing. Mikal could see that Karyn's trunk was gone. No fresh aprons hung on the post in the center of the house. He hobbled to the door. He lowered the tailgate of the wagon and pulled himself up into the wagon box. Then, he made his way up to the wagon seat. He drove the team down to the dugout where he saw that Karyn had fed the sow. Ella had been milked, and the trough was brimming with fresh water. He let Emile's team eat a little. Then, he drove them back up to the well. Once again, he got down from the wagon, hopped to the well, and drew water. As soon as the team had drunk, he repeated his unusual approach to the wagon seat, took up the reins, and headed for Millersburg.

Early that afternoon, Mikal sat on the wagon seat outside Cay Miller's store, listening as Cay explained, "She's only been gone a couple of hours. She asked how to get to Doane Stoddard's homestead. She made it sound like she had another surprise for you. I thought it was just a matter of her not understanding the land laws—that you have to live on the land to qualify for a preemption." Cay shrugged. "But I wasn't going to argue with her. I tried that when she went after those fence posts."

Cay wiped his hands on his shopkeeper's apron and tried to convince Mikal to come inside the store and rest. "Don't worry about her, Mikal. I made certain the saddlebags were well stocked with food. I loaned a gun to her and she has plenty of ammunition. She proved she knows how to use it by having me toss this in the air." Cay reached into the pocket of his apron and held up a coin with a bullet hole through it. "She should be back in a couple of days. Why don't you stay here until she gets back? Karyn won't want you taking any chances with your leg. That's probably at least part of the reason she slipped away without telling you."

Mikal shook his head. "No, Cay. I can't wait. We have had a misunderstanding, and I must find Karyn and resolve it. Now."

Cay peered at Mikal for a moment before nodding his head briefly. "Well then, at least go inside and let me hitch up Lena and Grace for you. You can leave Emile's team in my barn for now." Cay bustled about like an old maid, helping Mikal down from the wagon and inside his store and heating up coffee and biscuits before leaving to switch teams.

Mikal had practically inhaled two biscuits when the sound of a cane tap-tapping on the store's wood floor filled him with dread.

Amalia Kruger refilled his empty coffee cup. "I am glad to see you, Mikal. You are going after her. Right?"

Mikal looked up and nodded. "Of course."

"I told Karyn she is worth a hundred Sophies. I am glad to see you finally realized that."

Mikal frowned. He resented the fact that Amalia Kruger, of all people, seemed to know details about his relationship with Karyn. Didn't Karyn know this woman was a gossip and the last one she should trust with secrets? He said defensively, "I didn't just realize it, Amalia. I've known it all along."

Amalia thought for a moment. Then, she smiled. "I see. But, Mikal, Karyn does not know that you know." She chuckled. "Mikal, with you and Marie-Louise, it was all passion and no reason. With Karyn, you have been trying it the other way. And if Sophie had not come, I think that by now you would have realized that all reason and no passion does not work very well, either." She laid a hand on Mikal's shoulder and said kindly, "But I know you well enough to know that you will correct that as soon as you catch up with her." Amalia patted Mikal's shoulder. "God bless you, Mikal." Then, she turned to leave.

Mikal was so amazed by Amalia's kindness, he could only nod and mumble his thanks.

Amalia was halfway to the door when she turned around and said, "Karyn told me about reading the Psalms. But I discovered that the Proverbs are good, too. I read one about how lucky a man is who can find a virtuous woman. I think it said something like 'for her price is far above rubies. The heart of her husband doth safely trust in her, . . . she will do him good and not evil all the days of her life.' " Amalia paused a moment and then said, "It has been a hard road for you, Mikal. But you finally have a good woman. See that you do not lose her."

The Diary
August 27, 1880

  I am camping under the stars, like the pioneers who went to the far west only a few years ago. The moon is bright and a breeze is blowing. I cannot say that I am happy, but I am not weeping every moment. That is something. There is a golden light to the west that is very beautiful in an eerie sort of way. I know it is probably a fire of some kind, but I should be able to find the Stoddard homestead by tomorrow, and then I will head back to Millersburg. I have Cay Miller's big bay gelding. If we must, we can outrun a fire. I cannot return to Millersburg before I have a plan for my future.

CHAPTER 17

An Indian
Spearhead

Bow down thine ear to me;
deliver me speedily: be thou my strong rock,
for an house of defence to save me. For thou
art my rock and my fortress; therefore for thy
name's sake lead me, and guide me.
Psalm 31:2–3

Cay had warned Karyn that between Millersburg and the Stoddard homestead she would encounter a series of canyons and ridges that had made the area less desirable for homesteading. She was only a few miles from town when she rode down an incline and entered a round, flat valley. Across the valley, she started up a grassy slope to a high hill, finding herself riding along a rim of rock. She stopped the horse and pulled Cay's drawing from her saddlebags. *He said it was a steep descent off this ridge . . . but I didn't realize just how steep he meant.* Taking a deep breath, Karyn urged the gelding down the slope. She clung to the saddle horn and gave the horse free rein to pick his own way down. Finally at the bottom, Karyn breathed a sigh of relief. She looked back up behind her, dreading the return ride. *I'll walk up and lead the horse.*

She was at the bottom of the ridge now, and even though it was midmorning, the high bluff cast shadows along her way. From the other side of the bluff a spring bubbled from beneath a huge rock. All along the valley wild hemp and sunflowers grew in profusion.

Karyn was riding toward the mouth of the canyon when she

noticed a deeply cut wagon track. Thinking she had found Doane Stoddard's trail, she turned to follow it. A few yards later, she saw a spring from a wagon seat along the trail. Doane Stoddard's wagon seat had been missing a spring. A few feet beyond that, a horse had thrown a shoe. But then the trail led off to her left. She knew now that she was following someone else's trail. According to Cay's directions, the Stoddard place was a few miles to the north and farther west. But Cay had also said it was unlikely she would encounter any signs of civilization en route. Suddenly, she was glad she had decided to wear what she now thought of as her "work clothes." If anyone saw her from a distance they wouldn't know she was a woman.

Descending a low hill, Karyn passed along a ridge of rocks. Suddenly, she came upon a door set flush with the perpendicular bank. Someone had taken great care to camouflage it. From a distance, it would be indiscernible. Her heart beating, Karyn dismounted and tied the gelding's reins to a scrub bush. There were no signs of recent tracks nearby. Still, she cradled Cay's rifle in her arms before trying the door. It opened inward. When her eyes finally adjusted to the dim light, Karyn could see that she was in a room—a rather large room, containing a single sleeping bunk and an old rough board table, fully six feet long. On the table was a copy of *Harper's Weekly* dated June 1879.

At the back of the room there was a huge fireplace, blackened from frequent use. At one side of the fireplace another doorway was cut into the rock. Karyn called out. "Hello. Is anyone here?" There was no answer, so she walked to the doorway and looked into another room larger than the first. This room had feed stalls arranged along one side, and more sleeping bunks. There was corn scattered about.

Karyn went back outside. There were no signs of recent occupancy. The spring-fed creek bubbled along a few yards below the cave, but no paths or tracks led from the cave down to the water. She could have ridden within a few feet of the cave and never known it existed.

Untying the gelding, Karyn walked down to the creek. At the water's edge there was a block of wood about three feet long. It was staked in place with forked stakes. A person could stand upon it and dip water from the brook without getting muddy or wet. Karyn smiled at the ingenuity of the cave dwellers, and made a mental note to do something similar at home. *If I have a creek. Cay said there was a creek on the Stoddard place, didn't he?* She was still thinking of Mikal's place as home. It would probably be some time before she stopped doing that.

Karyn walked back up to untie the gelding and led him down to get a drink. While she waited for him to drink, she looked up to see a gray wolf trotting along the ridge above them. It paused momentarily and looked down at Karyn, then took off toward the east. The sight of the wolf sent a chill down Karyn's spine. She mounted the gelding and headed back to the north and west.

The next landmark Cay had mentioned was easily found. Jutting from the bluff above her was a curiously shaped boulder. Cay had called it "Pawnee Rock." It took little imagination to discern the silhouette of an Indian brave in the rock. She urged the gelding up a narrow trail around the rock and onto the tableland. Expecting to see Doane's soddy any moment, she urged the gelding to a canter.

Doane Stoddard's soddy was a windowless one-room hovel. Two bare sticks planted in the sandy soil of what would have been the front yard testified to Anna Stoddard's unsuccessful attempt with trees. Using one of the dead trees as a hitching post for the gelding, Karyn went to the door. Pushing it open, she peered inside. She didn't step across the threshold. This place could never be home. There was no well, no corral, not even the beginnings of a garden. Of course those things could be added, just as Mikal had. Karyn sighed. *But I don't want to add them. Not out here. Not alone.*

Karyn stepped back outside. Everything she saw made her long for her little soddy nestled against the ridge. Off in the distance, a herd of antelope were trotting along toward the east. It was getting late. She considered starting back, but the image of the wolf that had stared at her from high on the ridge made camping in the shadows of the bluffs less than desirable. She decided to spend the night beside the soddy and head back early in the morning.

As the sun set, Karyn got out matches to start a fire. Looking about her at the dry grass of the tableland, she decided to eat a cold supper. She took off the gelding's saddle and led him across the table to a clump of low bushes where a tiny spring bubbled up out of a rock. *I suppose if a person built a dam down below, you could create a sizable pond.* But Karyn didn't want to build a dam. She wanted to go back home.

Back at the soddy, Karyn hobbled the gelding and turned him loose to graze. Leaning against the front of the shack, she ate bread and cheese, smiling to herself when she discovered that Cay had packed candy for her. *Cay can give you advice of where you might be able to establish a successful dressmaking shop.* Grand Island wasn't such a bad place.

As the sun set, Karyn spread out her bedroll in the shadow of the shack. The wind had come up. Every few moments the gelding lifted his head and looked intently off toward the west. Karyn finally got up and looked around the corner of the soddy. The glow of the prairie fire was brighter. She would need to get an early start for Millersburg.

With a team and wagon, Mikal couldn't descend the steep trail down into the canyon after Karyn. So, while Karyn was investigating the mysteries of the cave in the canyon, Mikal was driving his team along the top of the ridge that edged the canyons. He saw the same wolf that had peered down at Karyn. In fact, he was increasingly seeing wildlife trotting off to the east. It worried him. He reached into the grub box and put the matches in his pocket. Every mile or so he looked about him to locate the place to set a backfire. He decided not to stop for the night, but to continue toward the Stoddard place.

Karyn had no business being in the wake of a prairie fire. Guilt pressed in upon him, and once again he determined that whatever else happened this night, he was going to see to it that Karyn had no further chance to misread his feelings.

Sometime after midnight Karyn woke with a start. What was it? The gelding was standing just to the side of the soddy, his nostrils flared, his eyes wild. He lunged against the hobbles and whinnied. Karyn leaped up and went to his side. She grabbed his halter and tried to soothe him. But as she looked toward the west, her own eyes grew wide. The fire burning far to the west was no longer just a golden light glowing on the distant horizon. She could see flames. The wind was growing stronger, and it carried the scent of burning grass with it.

Karyn ran for the bridle and put it on over the gelding's halter. She pulled the horse to the front of the soddy where he couldn't see the flames, tied his head low, and threw on the blanket and saddle as quickly as possible. She rummaged through the saddlebags for matches. She hesitated for a moment, wondering if she should just set a backfire, or burn off a section of prairie and wait for the fire to go by. But one look at the wall of flames bearing down on her and her heart was gripped with fear. She wouldn't be able to control the gelding. She would have to let him go . . . and then what?

She threw her saddlebags behind the saddle and rammed the rifle in its scabbard. But the gelding wouldn't stand still for her to mount him. Time and again he spun away from her, trotting nervously in a circuitous dance. Finally, she managed to scramble up on his back. Wildlife of every variety was running with them now. A sea of fire was rolling toward them, carrying with it black clouds of suffocating smoke. The horse was wild with fear. Karyn gave him his head. Looking behind her she clung to the saddle horn while the horse charged mindlessly toward the east.

She could hear the roar of the fire behind her. Could it possibly overtake them? The moment the thought occurred, Karyn was being hurtled headlong into the air. The gelding had stumbled and was sliding down the sharp incline that led down into the canyons they had come through before. Karyn rolled down a little hill and landed in a patch of bushes beside the creek. Above her flames were licking at the sides of the canyon, crawling down the ridge from tree to tree, making their way relentlessly toward her. She looked around her, but the horse was gone.

She stumbled out of the bushes and into a creek. Running along the edge of the creek, she wiped smoke from her eyes, looking desperately for a place where the creek would be deep enough that she could immerse herself in water. *Oh, God,* she prayed. *Oh, God, please. God, please. Help!*

In the dark, Karyn stumbled and fell. She had run into something—something hard. A block of wood? Suddenly, she realized she had found the watering place just below the mysterious cave. Could she find it in the dark? The flames were coming closer, sending waves of heat through the air. A burning tumbleweed flew by. A tree nearby ignited. With another prayer for guidance, Karyn stumbled up the hill toward the rock where she thought the cave door—

Just as a wedge of fire shot down the other side of the creek, she fell into the cave. On all fours she scrambled into the back room, as far as she could get from the flames. She stayed low, huddling in the dark, listening to the roar of the fire just outside the cave door. The door caught on fire, casting an eerie light around the room. In a panic, Karyn rushed forward and pulled with all her might to get the long table away from the door. If it caught on fire, too, then all the bunks . . . the stalls . . . everything would burn.

But the door had burned out. She would be safe. She stumbled back into the room with the stalls and curled up in a corner. Waiting in the dark, she listened to the roar of the fire just outside the cave. When the roar finally stopped, she couldn't bring herself to go outside. Exhausted and sore from her fall from the horse, she stretched out on one of the bunks and fell asleep.

Unlike Karyn, Mikal was not unprepared for the fire. He had watched its relentless approach throughout the night, praying that by some miracle the wind would shift and the flames would take a path other than the one across West Table. Near dawn, he pulled up Lena and Grace, tying them securely to an ancient cedar tree that clung to the edge of the canyon.

With the box of matches in his hand, he hobbled as far away as he dared from his team. Then, he knelt on the ground and opened the box. If he did it right, if the wind held, he could burn a patch of earth large enough to shelter him and the team from the flames. If he could control Lena and Grace, they would all survive, and then he could go after Karyn. His hands shook as he looked off to the west. *God, give Karyn wisdom to know what to do.*

The fire was coming closer. He struck a match. The wind blew it out. Tossing it aside, he struck another. It went out. Match after match failed. The flames were visible in the distance. A bobcat raced by only a few yards away, stretched nearly flat to the earth in its wild run to escape. Lena and Grace were beginning to move about restlessly. Sweat formed on Mikal's brow. There was one match left. *God, please. I have only one match left. You didn't let me die in that well. Save me again.*

His hand trembling, Mikal cupped his huge left hand about the precious last match. It flickered, then smoke rose from the grass. Mikal got up awkwardly and hobbled to where Lena and Grace were tethered. Behind him, he could hear the crackling of the dry grass as a line of small flame and smoke began to appear. Then, the flames grew larger until a row of fire was being blown away toward the east. Mikal and his team were now trapped in a section of dried grass between two fires. He watched as the original fire approached. It would be no use to run away. The flames were ten to twelve feet high and traveling faster than a horse could run. Mikal forced the image of Karyn and the gelding from his mind. He had work to do. First, he must survive. Then, he would find Karyn.

It seemed like hours, but really it was only a few moments before the fire he had set blackened a patch of prairie large enough for the team and wagon. Pulling off his shirt, Mikal tore it in half. He used each half to wrap the horses eyes so they couldn't see the flames. Then, hobbling along in front of them, he awkwardly led them toward the ever-growing width of burned-off grass.

Only moments after the team and wagon reached safety, they were surrounded by a high wall of flames and billowing smoke that threatened to smother them. Grace and Lena whinnied and plunged, trying desperately to escape. Mikal hung on to their harness, trying to calm them. But the mares screamed with fear, plunging and rearing with such force that they lifted Mikal off the ground again and again. He held on grimly, praying for strength to keep his broken ankle from slamming against the earth. Coughing and sputtering, he wondered if he would lose consciousness.

Then, as suddenly as the inferno had raged, it passed. The air cleared. Grace and Lena stopped plunging about, and stood trembling and snorting. Mikal praised them, patted their necks, kissed their soft muzzles with tears of relief running down his cheeks. He waited a few moments to remove the remains of his shirt from their eyes. When he did, the mares snorted and pricked their ears at the strange sight of the smoking prairie, dotted with the whitened bones of long-dead antelope and buffalo.

Mikal bent to pick up his crutch and made his way to the back of the wagon box again. At the back of the wagon he bent to pick up an Indian spearhead that had been hidden in the grass. Shoving it in his pocket, he lifted himself into the wagon box. By the time he reached the seat, he was shaking. He pulled the remnant of his shirt from his pocket and wiped his face. He sat for a few moments before picking up the reins. Then, he turned the team back toward the west, praying aloud to keep himself from thinking about what he might be about to find at Doane Stoddard's abandoned soddy.

CHAPTER 18

A Gold Coin

O LORD, thou hast brought up my soul
from the grave: thou hast kept me alive, that
I should not go down to the pit.
Psalm 30:3

Dawn illuminated Doane Stoddard's fire-blackened soddy looming in the distance. Approaching it, Mikal fought against the sick feeling in his stomach. He pulled his hat down over his eyes and squinted at the little soddy, hoping against hope that there would be no sign of Karyn. Looking at the black emptiness about him, he groaned with relief. He pushed his hat back on his head, swiped over his face, and sat shaking, taking deep breaths to try to control his emotions. Then he saw something plastered up against the front of the soddy.

Leaving his crutch in the wagon he got down and hopped over, bent down and picked up what appeared to be the charred remains of some kind of blanket. He realized with a shudder that it was part of the bedroll Cay Miller always used on hunting trips. Mikal slumped against the front wall of the soddy. Groping along the wall he shakily pushed the charred door open, thanking God for the empty room inside. Karyn had been here, but she had gotten away before the fire reached the soddy. Gripping the side of the wagon, Mikal looked back toward the east. Would she have run down into the canyons? He couldn't follow. Not with the wagon. Not with his broken ankle.

214

Tossing the fragment of Cay's bedroll into the back of the wagon, Mikal got back up into the driver's seat. He headed the team for the spring. While they drank, he opened the grub box and pulled out some bread and jerky and set them on the wagon seat. After a quick drink of water for himself, he turned the team east and slapped the reins, urging them to a trot. "Go along, girls, we've got to get some help now. Go along, hup!"

For the first part of his journey back to Millersburg, Mikal stopped every half mile at the edge of the canyon to search below for some sign of Cay's gelding. For a few minutes he would sit on the wagon box and call for Karyn. He grew hoarse from yelling her name.

For a few hours Mikal managed to fight off the specter of Marie-Louise's body lying lifeless on the prairie. Finally, the last time he yelled Karyn's name, he gave in to the dread that had been threatening to overwhelm him all morning. *God . . . not again. I can't go through it again . . . if she isn't alive, then don't let me find her . . . let someone else find her . . . I can't go through that again.* Tears began to flow as Mikal spoke silently to God. *She doesn't even know I love her, God. She doesn't even know I love her . . . give me a chance, God . . . to love her . . .*

While Mikal was driving along the edge of the canyon calling for Karyn, she was curled up in the back room of the cave asleep. When she finally awoke, it was midmorning and her stomach was growling for breakfast. She stepped outside the cave and into the morning sunshine and caught her breath. Everything in the canyon had been burned off. The air was heavy with the smoke that still rose here and there from felled logs and thick clumps of undergrowth.

Karyn went down to the creek and drank deeply. She splashed her face with water. Finally, she took down her hair. Lying on her back on the charred block of wood at the creek's edge, she leaned back until her entire scalp was in the water. As the cool water flowed through her hair, she looked above her at the blue sky, rejoicing that she was alive. *Thank You, Lord . . . oh, thank You, thank You!* She smiled, wondering who had made the cave that had saved her life. She suspected that he was not one of the more upstanding citizens of Custer County.

She wondered how far the fire had burned. Celest had once told her that a big fire would go on and on for miles . . . maybe half the county . . . and surely this had been a big fire. With a dull ache in her midsection she wondered about Millersburg, the homestead, the Delhommes.

The Delhomme men would have headed east toward the fire—toward Mikal's homestead. They would have set backfires against the main fire, filled wagons with barrels of water, and beat out side fires with wet blankets. Celest had said that sometimes they slaughtered a calf and dragged the carcass behind their horses to smother flames. Karyn shuddered to think about Ella and her calf . . . and the sow . . . Would they have reached the homestead in time? Karyn smiled in spite of herself, thinking of Mikal having to drive a water wagon and watch the others fight the fire. He would be so frustrated. She could see him now, his blue eyes flashing angrily, grumbling about what a bother a little thing like a broken ankle could be.

With a sigh, Karyn sat up. Rivulets of water streamed off her wet hair and down her back. Turning around, she pulled her boots and socks off and soaked her feet in the creek. They would have started a backfire. Surely they started a backfire. And the creek—but Karyn knew that the narrow creek just below her little house would have been an easy thing for the fire to cross. She forced herself to stop thinking about the fire and studied her feet. *I wonder how many blisters I'll have by the time I get to Millersburg. If the fire burned that way, they won't have time to worry about me today, that's for sure.*

She would be out here alone at least one night. Her eyes rose to the edge of the canyon where only yesterday a wolf had stood peering down at her. Except for the gurgling of the water, there was no other sound of life. All the wildlife had fled before the flames. She wouldn't have to worry over coyotes or bobcats or wolves today . . . or tonight, when she slept alone. If the moon was bright, maybe she would just keep walking.

She leaned over and spread her fingers out in the water. It was going to be a long walk home. *Home.* The word brought her thoughts back from the joy of simply being alive to the heartache of the moment. *Well, don't worry about that now. God must have something in mind for you. He certainly could have taken you just a few hours ago. But He didn't. Just do the next thing, Karyn. You've a long walk ahead of you.*

As her hands swished through the water, she reached toward a glint of gold in the sandy bottom of the creek, unearthing a gold coin. She put it in her pocket, pulled her socks and boots back on, tied her still-damp hair back out of her face with a strip of her bandanna. Her hat in her hand, she headed up the canyon toward Millersburg.

On the morning after Mikal had gone home to Karyn, Luc, Remi, and Serge Delhomme rode to his homestead intending to make short work of burning off the firebreak and then head toward the advancing fire and set a backfire. But instead of finding Karyn and Mikal, they found a deserted homestead.

"They must have gone to Millersburg. I don't know what to think. Karyn's trunk is missing." Luc frowned.

"If they left together, our team and wagon would be here," Remi offered.

"So Karyn must have been gone with Mikal's wagon before he arrived." Luc said, "That's it. Karyn had packed and left. Mikal has gone after her."

"I didn't think things were so bad between them," Remi said.

"Why not?" Serge interrupted. "Don't tell me you've been blind to dear little Sophie's tricks."

"Don't start about Sophie," Luc said angrily.

Remi intervened. "All right, boys. This isn't the time to talk about that. What are we going to do?"

The brothers decided to split up. Remi would take Ella and the calf back to the Delhommes' and report on what had happened while Luc and Serge headed for Millersburg. Without a wagon for transportation, Mikal's sow would have to be left. They let her out of her pen, and she immediately headed for the creek where she sank down into the water with a grunt of satisfaction.

"Could we board her up in the dugout?" Remi wanted to know. "I hate the thought of all that lost sausage."

Before they left Mikal's homestead, the boys drew bucket after bucket of water and sloshed it over the walls and roof of the soddy. They burned off the grass around the house and dugout so that the area around the house appeared as a blackened dot on the tan prairie. Even if the fire burned this far, the house would be saved. Then, they forced the sow out of the creek and into the dugout, boarding her up in one of the stalls with fresh water and straw. "She'll be hungry, but she'll be alive when Mikal gets back."

As they headed off, Luc called out to Remi, "Hopefully we'll meet Mikal and Karyn coming home on our way in. Tell Papa that if the fire still looks threatening, we'll hitch up the team and head off with the other settlers to help fight it here instead of heading for home."

As they covered the miles between the Ritters' and Millersburg and Karyn and Mikal did not come into view, Luc and Serge grew more and more concerned. By the time they galloped into Millersburg several settlers had converged on Cay Miller's store to organize a plan for protecting both the fledgling town and their homesteads.

Cay was helping load empty water barrels into the back of one of the wagons. When Luc and Serge rode up and asked about Mikal and Karyn, Cay explained, ending with, "He is only a few hours behind her. In fact, he has probably caught up with her by now." Cay spoke with more confidence than he felt. "Karyn was on my big gelding, and Mikal knows what he is doing. He will have already set a backfire up ahead. He'll know we are doing the same and keep them out of danger."

Luc nodded. "You're probably right. But after we help set this backfire we're going to head out after them."

"Then make certain you have full barrels in the back of that wagon," Cay urged. "You never know where the wind might carry those flames."

Luc and Serge put their horses in Cay's corral, hitched up their father's team, and pulled into line by Cay's well to fill the barrels in the back of their wagon with water. A settler who had been posted as a lookout about a mile west of Millersburg came thundering into town and reported that the fire appeared to be veering off toward the north. Still, everyone went to work wetting down the section of prairie directly west of town. Then, they set a backfire.

Once a stretch of grass was sufficiently blackened to protect Millersburg from danger, the settlers replenished their supply of water from the town well and headed north and a little east, ready to beat out the onslaught of sidefires with wet sacks and blankets. Luc and Serge filled the barrels in their wagon and headed across the scorched prairie after Mikal. Finally, early in the afternoon, a speck of movement on the horizon caught Serge's attention. He stood up in the wagon, waving his hat and calling out. Luc urged the team to a gallop.

When Mikal saw another team coming toward him, he urged Lena and Grace to run. His hat came off, and with his long hair hanging in his face, he looked half mad. He pulled up alongside Luc and Serge and in short, desperate bursts, he half sobbed, "I can't find her. I know she got away from Stoddard's. Before the fire." He willed himself to take a breath and with a shudder nodded toward the scrap of burned bedroll in the back of the wagon. He wiped his face with his hand, smearing soot across his forehead in a vain attempt to calm himself. "I was hoping she was back in Millersburg."

Luc shook his head. "No. At least not when we left."

Mikal slumped down onto the wagon seat.

Serge broke in. "Look, you two. We're doing Karyn no good standing out here talking. She had a chance if she went down into the canyons. She could have stayed ahead of it."

Mikal choked out the words, "If she had stayed ahead of it, she would be back in Millersburg."

Serge shook his head. "We can't know that. Not until we get some help and search the canyons. Let's head back. When we get to Cay's, I'll ride home and get Papa and Remi. While I'm gone, you and Luc can be packing what we'll need."

Mikal shook his head. "You both need to get home and help fight that fire."

"At the rate that fire was moving, it's already either burned itself out or passed our place. Papa would have burned off the firebreak—maybe the entire yard. Luc and I did that at your place, Mikal. We burned off the whole area inside the firebreak. We wet down the walls, penned up the sow—"

Mikal interrupted him. "Let's get going. You can tell me about all that some other time."

The presence of his friends helped Mikal regain his composure. By the time they rode into Millersburg, he had begun to have hope. He got down from the wagon and reached for his crutch just as Cay came out of the store. Cay had just spoken Mikal's name when Mikal looked across toward the barn and saw Cay's big gelding standing in the corral. Cay said simply, "He came running in about noon, wild-eyed and shaking. The saddlebags are missing, but the rifle's still in the scabbard." Cay paused. "He isn't burned, Mikal. Not one hair singed. That's something. He was able to stay ahead of it."

Mikal sagged against the side of the wagon. Luc and Serge looked at one another and then at Cay. Without a word, they began to unhitch their team.

Mikal spoke up. "Never mind, Luc." His voice cracked. He waited a moment. "There's no need to hurry so much. You boys go on home. See about things." He took a deep breath. "Sophie's probably going mad with worry. Tell her—" He stopped. "Tell her what's happened." He stood up. "I'll stop by Amalia's. I want to get—" He swallowed and let out one desperate sob. "I want to take her trunk home with me." He paused for a moment. Wetting his lips, he looked desperately at Luc. "I don't think I can—I don't think I can ride—"

"It's all right, Mikal," Luc interrupted him. "I understand." Mikal was convinced that they were looking for Karyn's body. And he couldn't face it. Luc said, "We'll take care of it. Go home. Get some rest. We'll start searching first thing in the morning. One of us will come back by nightfall tomorrow and let you know."

Mikal nodded. Then, he started off across the street to ask Amalia for Karyn's trunk.

The fire had burned itself out along Clear Creek just below French Table, leaving the Delhomme homestead and everything east of it untouched. Luc and Serge arrived just as the family was sitting down to supper. They repeated the news Remi had already shared before launching into what they really had to say. They described setting the backfire, and meeting Mikal on his way back from Doane Stoddard's.

Luc paused awkwardly. "When we got back to Cay's," he cleared his throat, "Cay's gelding had come back."

"Thank God," Sophie breathed. "Then Karyn is all right?"

Luc hesitated. "The gelding came back. No rider." He hurried to add, "But he hadn't been in the fire. At least we know he ran clear of it."

"Where is Mikal?" Celest demanded.

"He—uh . . ." Luc swallowed and wet his lips. "He was going to get Karyn's trunk from Amalia's and take it home." Luc looked at his father as he said, "He asked us to let him know."

Emile said softly, "We'll ride to Millersburg tonight so we can start off right away in the morning."

Sophie protested, "But isn't Mikal going to look for her himself?"

"He can't ride into those canyons with a broken ankle," Serge said.

Sophie snorted. "A big, strong man like Mikal? Of course he could. If he wanted to." Sophie looked about her at the Delhommes. They were studying their plates. Her eyes widened. There was no reason why Mikal wouldn't want to look for Karyn. Except one. If Mikal thought Karyn was dead . . . if he thought they were looking for . . . "Oh," Sophie cried out and jumped up. "I've got to go to him. He can't be left alone . . . he needs me . . ."

Celest reached out and grabbed Sophie by the wrist. "No, Sophie. Mikal does not need *you*." Her gray eyes were cold. "He needs his wife. And we are going to find her, if we have to look until snowfall."

Sophie sat back down. "You think she's dead, too, don't you?"

Celest stood up. "What I think is, we need to get these men fed and on their way."

Emile went outside with Remi to saddle up their horses. Celest began to gather supplies. Sophie did her best to help.

When the men had ridden off toward the west, Celest found Sophie sitting in the parlor in the dark, looking out the window. "Are you certain Mikal will be all right alone?" she asked when Celest came in. Then, she hurried to add, "I mean—if you think you should be with him, I can stay here. I would do my best to look after things for you." She laughed sadly. "Although my best is not very satisfactory, sometimes." She began to cry softly. Celest didn't say anything, but she stayed in the room while Sophie cried.

"Could we go to Millersburg tomorrow, Celest? I feel that I should be there for Karyn. For whatever happens."

"Of course."

After a long silence, Sophie murmured, "Something like this makes you stop and consider what is really important in life."

"Yes," Celest answered. "It does."

Sophie rose shakily. "I think I'll be going upstairs now." She paused at the foot of the stairs. "Celest, would you be certain I am awake before you start downstairs in the morning? I know I'm not very good at farmwork, but I will do what I can to help before we leave."

"Thank you, Sophie," Celest said gently. "I appreciate that."

222

CHAPTER 19

Amalia's Biscuit Recipe

And be ye kind one to another, tenderhearted,
forgiving one another, even as God for
Christ's sake hath forgiven you.
Ephesians 4:32

Karyn decided there really was no reason to walk all night just to get back to Millersburg. The sooner she got back, the sooner she would have to face Mikal and Sophie. And she was going to face Mikal and Sophie. She had mulled over the situation while she walked along and came to the conclusion that she would not slink away like a coward. She would be strong enough to face Mikal and say a proper good-bye. She would ride back to the Delhommes', and she would wish Sophie well if it killed her. Then, she could leave and begin a new life somewhere else, with no regrets.

No regrets. Karen sighed. But there would be so many, many regrets. Walking through the canyons toward Millersburg, Karyn thought back over her time in Custer County. The girl who had stood in a church in Grand Island looking forward to a little frame cottage in Nebraska had grown a lot over the past few months. She had taken on a sod house and almost made it a home. And she had fallen in love.

Karyn walked for hours. When the sun began to set she had come to the steep incline she had planned to lead the gelding up on the return to Millersburg. She wondered where the horse was.

Had he found his way home? Looking about her, Karyn gave a little cry of delight as she saw the saddlebags lying at the side of the trail. Obviously the gelding had run this way, and when he scrambled up the trail, the saddlebags had fallen off. Choosing a flat rock against the canyon wall, Karyn settled down to a cold supper that tasted better than anything she had eaten in a long time. She pulled off her boots and rubbed her tired, aching feet. The saddlebags served as her pillow that night.

Early the next morning, Karyn scrambled up the steep trail onto the tableland. Halfway across the table she came to the last blackened strip of prairie. Someone had set a backfire. *Good. That means Millersburg was saved.* She looked off toward the northeast. As far as she could see, the strip of black extended, but didn't cross where the backfire had been set. Maybe the homestead was saved, too.

Karyn was about to descend into the valley that would lead her to Millersburg when she saw four riders in the distance. She took off her hat and jumped up and down and yelled at the top of her lungs. The distant riders spurred their horses, and in a few moments Karyn was surrounded by exuberant Delhomme men fighting to hug her.

After taking a long drink from Luc's canteen, Karyn stammered, "But how did you know to come after me? I didn't tell anyone but Cay—"

"My dear," Emile said with emotion. "Don't you know that Mikal followed you to the homestead? And when he realized you had left, he set out after you."

Luc nodded. "That's right. He followed you to Millersburg, and then to the Stoddards'. But with a team and wagon he couldn't go down into the canyons."

"Is he all right?" Karyn asked, her hand at her throat. "The fire—"

"Yes, the fire caught him, too. He set a backfire—with the very last match and a good amount of prayer he burned off a place big enough for the team. They're all right. He found part of your bedroll at the Stoddards' . . . and then he knew you'd been there. He spent hours riding along the rim of the canyon calling for you."

Serge broke in. "How did you survive? The gelding arrived back at Cay's yesterday morning. Did he run off?"

Karyn nodded her head. "He threw me right at the edge of the canyon . . . right into a thicket of bushes—and just in front of the advancing fire."

"Then how did you escape?"

Karyn described the cave. "It was a miracle I found it again, but God was with me."

"Be grateful it was empty. And don't tell anyone else that you know where that cave is," Emile warned. "It's been rumored for years that Doc Templeton and his gang of horse thieves have a hideout somewhere in those canyons. I doubt they'd be happy knowing someone had discovered their lair."

Karyn laughed wearily. "Well, I guess I can thank God for the horse thieves. If God hadn't led me to that cave . . ." She looked over her shoulder and shivered.

"Yes," Emile said soberly. "Thank God. And now we have to get you home. Mikal picked up your trunk from Amalia. He's waiting at home to hear from us."

At Karyn's look of surprise, Luc explained, "When we got back to Cay's and saw the gelding we all feared the worst."

The reality of what Luc was saying sunk in. Mikal thought she had died in the fire. Mikal had taken her trunk and gone home. The Delhommes were looking for her. But they were looking for a body.

Serge broke in. "You're a smart girl, Karyn, but you've been wrong about a lot of things. The most important of which is Mikal's opinion of you."

Remi took Karyn by the arm. "Come on, Karyn. Ride with me." Karyn settled behind Remi, who said gently, "Just put your arms around me and lean your head on my back. I know you're exhausted. Maybe you can get some rest on the way back." Karyn was half asleep before they had gone a mile.

Cay Miller had just ushered Celest and Sophie inside his store when Amalia tap-tapped with her cane across the dusty street and joined them. "They've gone to find Karyn, I see."

Sophie began to cry.

225

Celest nodded.

Amalia cleared her throat. "May I wait with you?"

"Of course," Celest answered.

The three women made their way to the back corner of the store. Amalia plopped a basket of biscuits on the table. She sat down and sighed heavily. "No one wants to eat at a time like this. I don't know why I always think biscuits are the answer to everything."

Celest smiled. "It's kind of you to think of us, Amalia." She took a biscuit.

"Oh, I was not thinking of you," Amalia said bluntly. "I always bake when I am upset. But my daughter-in-law does not want me heating up her kitchen any more this morning. She saw you both arrive and suggested I come over here." She sighed. "I will get coffee."

"You'll need more firewood," Cay said, excusing himself.

Amalia stirred up the fire in Cay's stove. Celest opened a small French testament and began reading. Sophie sniffed and blew her nose.

When the coffee was ready, Amalia poured each woman a cup before sitting down at the table. Finally, she spoke to Celest. "If what you are reading brings you comfort, Celest, could you perhaps translate a little into German for Sophie and me?"

Celest looked up in surprise. Amalia shrugged and smiled. "I have been reading a little myself. Karyn said she found it helpful. I thought I would try it and see if it could change even a sour old woman like me."

"I was really just reading the same thing over and over again," Celest explained. She began to translate the passage aloud, " 'Be careful for nothing; but in everything by prayer and supplication with thanksgiving let your requests be made known unto God. And the peace of God, which passeth all understanding, shall keep your hearts and minds through Christ Jesus.' " She paused to say, "I don't know if my German is good enough to translate it perfectly. Does it sound right?"

Amalia nodded. "Your German is very good." She asked, "So tell me, Celest. At times like this, does the peace of God keep your heart? Do you think the peace of God will keep Mikal's

226

mind? Or will he go half mad with grief again if another wife is found dead on the prairie?"

Sophie began to cry louder. Celest patted her hand and whispered, "Right now I can only cling to the promise and pray that Mikal will do the same."

When Karyn slid off Remi's horse and landed on the boardwalk in front of Cay Miller's store, she was inundated with questions, overwhelmed with kisses and hugs, and almost smothered with attention. Everyone went inside to hear her account of her escape from the fire. When she finished, she pulled the gold coin out of her pocket. "My souvenir of the ordeal," she said. "Don't tell Doc Templeton I have some of his money. I certainly don't want him to come looking for me."

There was an awkward silence. Celest whispered something to Cay, who nodded his head, motioned to Remi and Serge, and left the room. Luc and Emile took one look at Celest and headed out the front door. When the men were gone, Celest said, "Amalia, I think Sophie has something she needs to say to Karyn in private." With a little shove, she pushed Sophie toward Karyn. "Tell her now, Sophie. You must, or you will never be happy. And neither will she." Celest and Amalia disappeared into Cay's private quarters.

Sophie trembled. Tears began to slide down her cheeks. "Oh, Karyn. Will you ever forgive me? I was so jealous of you. Jealous of everything you had. And I almost—I almost destroyed you." She slumped down into a chair and began to sob.

"Jealous? You were jealous of *me*? Of what? Of my ability to plow and hoe? Of my sunburned skin?" Karyn asked, "Of what is there to be jealous?"

Sophie glanced up at her, her blue eyes brimming with tears. "Mikal."

"Mikal?" The sound of the name sent a pang of regret through her so strong that Karyn had to sit down. The Delhommes had given her reason to hope that Mikal was waiting for her . . . but now the specter of Mikal and Sophie had once again reared its head.

"Oh, Karyn. Can you ever forgive me? I did so many wrong

things." Sophie took a deep breath. "I have been such a flirt. Even when I knew Mikal did not care for me . . . I kept on with my flirting. And that day with the shirt-fitting. He was so embarrassed. But I just kept on . . . pretending . . ." She stopped and whispered hoarsely, "And even when I knew it was hurting you terribly, still I did not stop. Yesterday, when Mikal went after you, he told me I had caused so much trouble for him. He said he had tolerated it because I was your sister. But he warned me. I knew I had to apologize to you. I knew I had to stop. I was going to tell you. And then, the fire . . . and I thought you were dead and I would never have a chance. Oh, Karyn, can you ever forgive me?"

Karyn leaned forward in her chair. She reached across the table and clasped Sophie's hands tightly. Giving them a little shake she said, "Tell me what Mikal said, Sophie. Tell me. He was coming for *me*? I mean, because he wanted *me*?"

Sophie nodded her head and murmured, "Of course, Karyn. Mikal never cared for me. He only tolerated me because I was your sister. And—" Sophie ducked her head and confessed, "I kept talking about Hans. About how very different he is from Hans."

Karyn released Sophie's hands and sat back without making any comment. Sophie blurted out, "I won't be in your way anymore, Karyn. I can go home with Celest tonight, and send Luc for my trunk and my things tomorrow. Cay has encouraged me to open my dressmaking shop. He says I can rent the rooms upstairs, and I think the time is right for me to do it. He is going to give my customers a discount when they buy their fabric from him. And Luc has promised to write to me often from Philadelphia."

Celest and Amalia appeared at the doorway leading into Cay's quarters. "Your bath is ready, Karyn. Are you finished here?"

Karyn looked up, surprised. Standing up, she reached out to pat Sophie on the shoulder. "It's all right, Sophie. Thank you for telling me. Even if I had stayed with Mikal, I would always have wondered . . . unless I heard it from you."

Celest called out, "Sophie, Cay said that Karyn was to take

whatever she needs. He said he just got three women's dresses in. They are in boxes along the north wall. See what you think."

Amalia put her hand on Karyn's arm and said quietly, "And I will bake fresh biscuits for your wedding breakfast." She leaned over to whisper, "I will even send the recipe home with you." She hurried to make her way to the front of the store and out the door.

CHAPTER 20

A Lace Collar

There be three things which are too wonderful
for me, yea, four which I know not: The way of an
eagle in the air; the way of a serpent upon a rock;
the way of a ship in the midst of the sea;
and the way of a man with a maid.
Proverbs 30:18–19

The afternoon of her rescue, Karyn Ensinger Ritter (in name only) emerged from Cay's store trembling with excitement. She had enjoyed the exquisite opulence of a bath followed by a long nap. Her thick brown hair was done up in an elaborate braid wrapped about her head, and she was dressed in a new, wine-colored calico dress with an ivory lace collar.

Sophie was waiting to hand her Sugar's reins. "I'll ride to the Delhommes' with Luc. You will need Sugar for visiting, and Luc has promised to drive me back to Millersburg as soon as I am ready to move into my new rooms."

Amalia came hurrying across the street and handed up a sack. "Biscuits," she said. "For your wedding breakfast. And I included the recipe." She blew Karyn a kiss.

The Delhommes and Sophie headed out of Millersburg toward the northeast. Remi hung back. "I am to be the escort to ensure that you have an uneventful ride home to Mikal."

The moment the soddy came into view, Remi said, "See you soon, Karyn," and rode off toward home. Karyn watched him ride away before turning to survey her homestead. The earth around the house was black, but she knew that in a short while green shoots would appear, and the grass would be more lush than ever. Tomorrow they would ride to the Delhommes' and get Ella and the calf and bring them home. By the end of the week, they would have the sow slaughtered, and Karyn would make a feast of sausage and ham and invite Sophie and the Delhommes and Cay Miller over. She would embrace Sophie and let her know that all was forgiven.

But that was tomorrow and the days after. Before tomorrow came tonight. She felt a surge of joy at the thought of Mikal waiting for her inside the little house made of dirt. On the footsteps of joy came nervousness. Karyn slid to the ground, aware of a new sensation in her midsection. The sun was setting. A pinprick of golden light shining from the direction of the soddy told her that Mikal had lit the lantern and set it in the window. She walked quietly toward the homestead, her heart beating more and more rapidly as she approached the door. She knocked softly, but there was no answer. Opening the door, she noticed that Mikal had put her trunk back by the bed. But Mikal was not there.

Sugar nudged her from behind. She tied Sugar's reins to a porch post and, taking the bag of Amalia's biscuits, went inside and opened her trunk. She spread her lace tablecloth on the table and arranged the biscuits on a plate. With every addition to the table, she listened for Mikal's footsteps outside. But he didn't come. When she had finished setting the table with her grandmother's tea set, she went back outside and untied Sugar.

"All right, girl, I'll take you down to the barn." Somewhat disappointed that her dramatic entrance had been ruined, Karyn led Sugar down the hill. And then, she saw Mikal. Golden light from a lantern spilled out of the opening to the dugout. He was inside sitting on the bed, his head in his hands.

Karyn turned Sugar into the corral and tiptoed inside to where Mikal sat. Reaching out with a trembling hand, she touched his shoulder. "Mikal."

Mikal looked up at her, blinking in disbelief. His eyes filled with tears. He grabbed her hands, squeezing them so tightly they hurt. "I thought you were Luc coming to tell me—" Finally, he fell to his knees and wrapped his arms around her. Choking back his tears, he said again, "I thought it was Luc—"

Karyn caressed the mane of black hair. "I know. You thought I perished in the fire. But you see, I am here." She put her hands on his shoulders and pushed herself away from him so that she could see his blue eyes when he looked up at her.

He sat back up on the bed. Karyn sat down beside him. Gently he brushed one of her cheeks with his fingertips. Then his fingers traced along her jawline and down her throat to the lace collar of her new dress. He sighed and pulled his hand away. He didn't look at Karyn as he said, "Have I really been so cold and unfeeling that I have driven you away, Karyn?"

Karyn bit her lip. She said as matter-of-factly as possible, "Why would you want me when you could have Sophie?"

Mikal sputtered, "Sophie? What would I want with Sophie?"

"She's so tiny—so ladylike—with soft hands . . ." Karyn looked down at her own work-worn hands. "And I—"

Mikal sounded almost angry. "Was it Sophie who plastered the walls of my house? Was it Sophie who tended a garden all summer, fighting off insects and heat? Was it Sophie who had the courage to kill a rattlesnake? Did Sophie ever cook over a hot fire to make certain I had a good supper after a day in the fields? Did Sophie wear herself out collecting my lost fence posts? Did Sophie know what to do to survive a prairie fire?" He made a sound of derision. "What would I want with a tiny woman who faints at everything and pleads sickness to avoid hard work?"

Mikal grasped her by both shoulders. "Stop talking about Sophie, Karyn. I have loved you since the day you wore that rose-colored silk gown and sang at the Delhommes'."

"But why didn't you ever tell me?"

He dropped his hands to his sides as he answered. "I didn't want to force myself on you. I am loud and rough—not at all like your Hans Gilhoff, with his refined manners. And I will never be rich enough to give you a great house like his. Comparing my little soddy to an estate in Germany, I began to see I was crazy to think you could ever really care for a hulk of a boy with a few acres planted in corn and a house made of dirt."

"Mikal," Karyn said tenderly, "you think you understand so many things. How is it that you do not understand how very much I love you?" She looked up to see doubt in his blue eyes. Finally, she cried out, "Oh, Mikal. What woman on earth would not want to be held in these arms of yours? How could I not love you?" Karyn reached up to touch his hair. She put a hand on each of his cheeks. Staring intently into his eyes she said, "You listen to me, Mikal Ritter. Hans Gilhoff was a lifetime ago. I was a girl, and he was a boy going off to war. It was all very romantic, and for a while I reveled in the tragedy. But, Mikal, I could never have married Hans Gilhoff." She ran her fingers through his long hair. "I was meant to come to America and to live in a house made of dirt with a raven-haired giant." Impulsively, she kissed him on the cheek.

Mikal turned and engulfed her in his arms, murmuring, "I love you, *mein Schatz.*"

Snuggling against his shoulder, Karyn sighed. "I can hardly believe it yet."

Mikal took a deep breath. Karyn felt his heart begin to beat more quickly. Finally, he leaned down towards her and whispered, "Something tells me that it's time I did more than simply *tell* you that I love you, Mrs.-Ritter-in-name-only. I think it is time that I *show* you."

And he did.

The Diary
August 29, 1880
Song of Solomon 2:16

Epilogue

1998

The moment she finished reading the translation of Karyn Ritter's diary, Reagan scrambled for her father's Bible to look up Song of Solomon 2:16. "My beloved is mine, and I am his . . ." She sighed and sat back. It was two o'clock in the morning. She had spent the entire night reading the diary, hoping for a fairy-tale ending to the story of two people she had grown to care about. And while the Bible verse that Karyn had referenced hinted at "happily ever after," Reagan was not satisfied. *It wasn't an ending at all. It was only the beginning.*

Karyn and Mikal Ritter had been married for over sixty years. They had raised a family and endured the Dust Bowl. Reagan Bishop did not want to leave them in a one-room soddy at the beginning of their lives together. Indeed, having read the diary, Reagan had more questions than ever. Where had all the beautiful quilts come from? Karyn hadn't mentioned quilting once in her diary. What happened to Sophie? And what about the other sisters? Did they ever come to America? Sighing, Reagan snuggled down into the nest of pillows on her bed. She finally fell asleep to dream of sod houses and prairie fires, buried treasure and a tall, black-haired man with beautiful blue eyes.

When Reagan's phone rang early the next morning, she woke slowly and stretched. Intending to let the answering machine pick up a message, she came instantly awake when she heard Irene's voice say, "I just couldn't wait to ask you—"

"You must be psychic," Reagan said as soon as she snatched up the phone. "I couldn't put it down. I read until 2:00 A.M."

"That means I woke you. I'm sorry."

"No, it's all right." Reagan sat up in bed. "Hold on a minute. Let me switch to the cordless." Reagan pushed the "wait" button on her bedside phone and hurried out to the living room. Once she had her cordless phone she said, "Okay, I'm back. I just want to make coffee while we talk."

"Well, did you enjoy Oma's story?" Irene wanted to know.

"You know I did. Except for one thing," Reagan said. "The end of the diary is really only the beginning. I still have a million questions."

Irene chuckled. "I thought you might. That's why I'm calling so early. Do you have plans for the weekend?"

"Not if you need something."

"Oh, I don't need anything. But I'm driving up to the homestead, and I thought you might want to go along. We can talk about the diary. Who knows? Maybe we'll even drive around a bit. If you're interested."

"I'll be there in half an hour," Reagan said.

Irene cautioned, "Be prepared to 'rough it.' The house is almost empty. I have some neighbors helping with burning off the prairie. I won't want to leave until late tomorrow night."

"Okay, so give me forty-five minutes. I'll locate a sleeping bag and my work boots. Anything else I need?"

Irene laughed. "We can stop at the store on the way up and get food and bottled water. I'll bring an empty cooler. Do you mind driving?"

Less than an hour after Irene called, Reagan pulled up her driveway. In no time they had stowed Irene's camping gear in the back of Reagan's pickup and were cruising down Interstate 80 toward Grand Island.

"What on earth . . . ?" Irene exclaimed.

Reagan's truck had just topped the last rise on the road to the Ritter homestead. Someone had pitched a tent beneath one of the cottonwoods in the front yard. A bright red Dodge Ram pickup was parked next to the barn. Behind the pickup sat a four-wheeler, its tires caked with mud.

Irene was fuming. "How dare they just move in like this, just because the house needs paint, and there's no one around. If they drove that infernal four-wheeler through Opa Mikal's prairie . . ."

Reagan pulled up to the house and hopped out of the truck. "Settle down, Irene," she said. "It's probably just some kids having fun. I'll see if I can find them."

"Having fun?!" Irene was indignant. "Having fun, indeed! Opa Mikal never planted that sixty acres, and he protected it for decades. He knew the prairie would disappear some day. He wanted a piece of it preserved. And if they've put tire tracks through one of the few remaining pieces of virgin prairie in the state . . ." Irene fumbled for the car phone. "I'm going to call the sheriff."

Just as Irene put the phone to her ear Reagan saw someone appear at the top of the ridge behind the house. "Someone's coming. I'll go talk—"

"Get in and lock the door, Reagan," Irene said, locking her own door.

"Don't be ridiculous," Reagan said, laughing. "I'll just go talk to him." She headed up toward the house, calling and waving. The man had seen her and was striding purposefully down the hill. Reagan called out, "You're on private proper—" As the man came closer, the words died in her mouth. He was very tall. With long black hair. And large hands. As he came nearer, Reagan saw the blue eyes and gulped.

The stranger smiled. "Excuse me—I couldn't hear you. Are you lost? This is private property."

"Yes. I know. I just—" Reagan fumbled and turned around and pointed toward her truck. She didn't have to say anything else, because they had finally come around the corner of the house where Irene was watching out the back window of the

236

pickup. The moment the stranger came into view Irene's face lit up. She dropped the phone, pushed open her door, and scrambled out of the truck, exclaiming, "Noah? Noah! It really is you!" She laughed happily and hurried across the lawn.

Noah held out his arms, engulfed Irene in a hug, and then picked her up and swung her around as if she were a child.

Irene patted him on the shoulders. "When did you come? Why didn't you call? How long have you been here?" She was breathless. "How are things in California?"

Noah answered her last question. "As crowded and crime-ridden as ever. I needed to get away for a while."

Irene pulled Reagan over. "This is Reagan Bishop, a friend of mine from Lincoln." Irene turned to Reagan. "Reagan, this is my nephew, Noah. Noah Ritter." Irene took one look at Reagan and laughed. "Yes, I know. It's quite a shock, isn't it? As if Mikal Ritter just came back to life."

Reagan looked up at Noah and smiled, secretly wishing with all her might that she had dark coloring that would possibly hide the crimson she could feel creeping up the back of her neck and onto her cheeks. She couldn't think of anything to say.

Irene saved her further embarrassment. "Since when do you drive a pickup, Noah?" She turned toward Reagan and winked. "The last time he was here he tore the muffler off his little red sports car speeding along one of the back roads."

Noah laughed. "Well, you can see that I came much better prepared this time."

"You look like you're moving in," Irene commented.

"Fact is, I'd like to stay a while, if you don't mind." Noah was suddenly very serious. He looked up toward the roofline of the house. "I thought I might paint the place. Fix a few things."

Irene looked concerned. "Is everything all right with you?"

Reagan cleared her throat. "Look, you two. You probably have a million things to discuss. Irene, if you'll give me the keys, I'll take our things inside."

"Let me help," Noah offered.

Reagan shook her head. "No, thanks. I can manage." She already had the cooler hoisted out of the back of her truck and was headed for the door. She set it down and called, "Just toss the house keys in the bed of the truck, Irene. I'll enjoy looking around inside."

Reagan made several trips back and forth from the pickup to the front door of the house, piling things on the concrete slab that served as a porch. When she finally unlocked the door and went inside, she was disappointed. It was just a half-empty farmhouse. But then, she began to really look about her, and soon she was lost in imagining. She wandered through the rooms on the first floor.

Saddened by the run-down state of the house, Reagan pushed back the musty curtains at the parlor window. Sun streamed into the room. She looked out. Noah was sitting on the tailgate of his truck. Irene was standing at his side, her hand on his knee. Whatever they were talking about, Noah didn't look very happy.

Reagan marveled once again at how closely Noah Ritter resembled his great-grandfather. *Replace the pickup with a farm wagon, and take that ponytail out of his hair* . . . Reagan rubbed the goose bumps from her forearms and stepped away from the window, unaware that God was about to use the legacy of Mikal and Karyn Ritter to mold a future for Reagan Bishop. For the run-down homestead and the fallen-in dugout weren't really an ending at all. They were only the beginning . . .

Behold, I make all things new.
Revelation 21:5

Noras' Ribbon of Memories

OTHER BOOKS BY
STEPHANIE GRACE WHITSON:

The Prairie Winds Series
Walks the Fire
Soaring Eagle
Red Bird

The Keepsake Legacies Series
Sarah's Patchwork
Karyn's Memory Box

Noras' Ribbon of Memories

Stephanie Grace Whitson

THOMAS NELSON PUBLISHERS
Nashville

Copyright © 1999 by Stephanie Grace Whitson

All rights reserved. Written permission must be secured from the publisher to use or reproduce any part of this book, except for brief quotations in critical reviews or articles.

Published in Nashville, Tennessee, by Thomas Nelson, Inc.

Scripture quotations are from the KING JAMES VERSION of the Bible.

2 in 1 ISBN: 0-7394-0698-1

Printed in the United States of America

In loving memory of
Mother
1913–1996

In about 1929, a motherless teenaged girl was dropped off on a street corner, suitcase in hand, and wished a good life by her father, who then drove away, leaving her to make her own way in life. The girl went door-to-door, asking if anyone needed a housekeeper. One woman gave the girl a chance, ordering her to clean a room. When the girl had finished, the woman inspected her work. There were a few pennies lying on the bed. The girl had found them under the bed. The woman scooped the pennies up, congratulated the girl on her honesty, and gave her a job and a home.

The girl eventually married a truck driver with little education and not much to offer other than a strong work ethic and an incredible capacity for commitment that was to last through nearly fifty-five years of marriage. Together, the couple built a life. It wasn't a fairy tale, and they did not always live happily-ever-after. But they raised four children and endured and now they are enjoying an eternity where there is no abandonment, no unhappiness, and no fear.

One of the couple's four children was me.

This book is my way of celebrating my Mother's tenacity. I once read an epitaph that said, "She done what she could." That was my mother. She done what she could. For me, it was enough.

Prologue

1998

*I*t's a stroke."

Reagan's stomach tightened with dread. Memories assaulted her: a hallway lined with wheelchairs; aged hands reaching for her; meaningless babble escaping from toothless mouths. She had always tried to touch each one encountered on her way to her own parents' room, even if it was only a hand on a slumped shoulder or a gentle squeeze of a wrinkled hand. Always, the thought that her touch might be the only personal kindness they might know for that day brought her near tears.

Reagan forced herself out of the past and back into the moment. Cupping her half-empty coffee cup in her hands, she bowed her head and murmured, "I was afraid of that."

Mason Ritter slumped down into the chair opposite hers. The waiting room was empty except for the two of them. Reagan looked up at the clock. She had been there only about two hours before Irene's brother arrived, rushing through the doors to the intensive care unit to check on his sister before conferencing with various doctors.

"What's the prognosis?" Reagan asked.

"They don't know. Thank God you were there when it happened. They gave her that new wonder drug—what do they call it?"

"t-PA," Reagan offered.

"Yes, that's it. She might not be severely impaired. That's all they can say." The elderly gentleman's hands shook as he raised them to smooth his rumpled white hair.

Reagan tried to remember what Irene had said about her brother. Was he older or younger than Irene? Younger, Reagan thought. In his late sixties, if she remembered correctly.

"Who can I call for you? What can I do?" Reagan offered.

Mason shook his head. "I don't know. Lila called everyone as soon as we heard." Lila was Mason's second wife. Irene hadn't said much about her, only that Mason had re-married not long after the death of his wife of forty years. Reagan remembered a faint tone of dislike in her friend's voice every time she mentioned Lila's name.

Reagan gathered that Lila had been the one who instigated the previous year's auction on the Ritter homestead northwest of Lincoln. Mason had sold the farmland nearly ten years earlier than that. Except for his grandfather's forty acres of virgin prairie and an additional ten acres around the nearly-empty house, there wasn't much left to remind the Ritter family how closely they had once been tied to Nebraska soil.

Irene had been adamantly opposed to the auction. She begged her brother to delay it, insisting she could find room for things in her own mansion in Lincoln. But then the farmhouse was broken into and Lila finally had the upper hand in family discussions. No one wanted to see the place go to ruin, Lila argued. It was poor stewardship to leave the house filled with family treasures with no one there to check on things. Lila made room for a few of the family treasures in her own home. Irene rescued a few things, but not much.

As a sometimes-antique-dealer, Reagan had attended the Ritter auction and purchased a cracked water cooler full of dusty grain bags. Weeks later, intending to plant geraniums in the cooler, she had pulled the bags out and discovered a memory box and a diary. When Irene Peale was notified of the find through the auctioneer and came to reclaim her family treasures, she and Reagan had immediately connected on a level that transcended the generations between them.

Reagan willed herself to listen more carefully to what Mason was saying. "Of course you know that Irene and Henry didn't have children. So there are only a few distant relatives. We've managed to reach everyone who would want to know. Everyone, that is, but Noah. We'll keep trying. Lila has said," Mason said, then hastened to add, "and I agree—that there's no reason for everyone to flock in here. It would make Irene mad, having everyone flutter around. And heaven forbid that she misunderstand and think we were keeping some sort of deathwatch."

In the past months, Reagan had become familiar with Irene's fierce battle for independence. The "seventy-something" widow still lived alone in a historic Lincoln mansion filled with several generations of her husband's family memories. She swam nearly a mile three times a week. On the days she didn't swim, she walked, her brisk gait belying her age. *Mason is right,* Reagan thought. *Irene would despise having anyone fluttering about. Except Noah.* Reagan said aloud, "She won't feel that way about Noah, though."

Mason nodded. "I agree. Noah always spent his summers with Irene and Henry. They have been close since he was eight years old. I hope we can find him soon." He shook his head. "I thought he was staying in Nebraska for a while. But I'm only the boy's father. I never know what he's going to do next." Mason pressed his lips together as if he had just revealed a family secret and regretted it. He continued in a more even tone. "He doesn't have service installed at the farm yet. I've left a dozen messages on his voice mail, at both his condo in Tiburon and the office in Sausalito. It doesn't make sense that he would just turn off his cell phone. Even if he did, he always checks in with his office at least twice a day." Mason shrugged his shoulders. "Maybe all his high-tech machines just aren't working right. Or maybe he's off on a fishing trip. As I said, I never know what Noah is going to do next."

Reagan stood up, talking as she pulled on her denim jacket. "I'll drive up to the farm and see if he's there. If I leave right now, I can be there early in the morning."

"You don't have to do that."

"I know." Reagan reached behind her to lift her long dark hair outside her jacket collar. "I want to. Irene would want Noah here."

Mason nodded and stood up. "Thank you." He patted her arm.

Reagan stopped at the ATM in the hospital lobby and withdrew cash for gas and meals for the next two days. It would be a long drive to the Ritter homestead in Custer County, and she hadn't had much sleep. Once she had found Noah and headed him toward Lincoln and his aunt's bedside, she might need to check into a motel and get some sleep before driving back.

As she drove by the university football stadium and headed north for the interstate, Reagan clicked on a CD. The soothing first notes of John Tesh at the piano helped her settle back and relax.

She reached for her coffee. *It's amazing, Lord, how quickly life can change. One minute we were laughing at Cary Grant, the next Irene's coffee cup dropped to the floor and she slumped over.*

The thought that she and Irene might have enjoyed their last Cary Grant movie together brought tears to Reagan's eyes. She blinked them away and focused on the road. *Help me find Noah, Lord. Use Noah and me to show Irene how much You love her. And the nurses, Lord—help them to see more than just a wrinkled old woman. She has so much life in her . . . give her back to me, God.* Reagan stopped praying. She corrected herself. *No . . . that's not what I should be asking for, is it? I should be asking for Your will. And help me to adjust to whatever it is.*

Reagan put her coffee cup back in the drink holder and gripped the steering wheel with both hands. *You know I want Irene back, Lord. I want things the way they were. But if that's not in Your plan, then help me accept it. Help me to help Irene. Thank You for the joy she has added to my life.*

As Reagan's pickup truck headed west on Interstate 80, she smiled to herself. Reading Karyn Ritter's diary had made her feel almost a part of the Ritter family. In recent months, Irene had often invited Reagan to come along when she drove out to inspect some new project of her nephew's. Reagan was almost as thrilled as Irene to see Noah's love for the past bear fruit at the old homestead.

Noah's interest in Nebraska made Reagan curious. She wondered just what it was that would motivate a man to leave a lucrative position with a computer firm for a broken-down homestead in a remote corner of Nebraska. She assumed Noah had shared his reasons with Irene. Reagan sighed. *Don't be nosy. That's family business—and you're not family.*

Reagan had to admit that Noah Ritter made her self-conscious and nervous. He refused to fit neatly into any of the slots she mentally prepared for him. He was a computer expert, but he defied every stereotype ever given the technologically gifted. No thick-framed glasses camouflaged his brilliant blue eyes. His posture never hinted of the hours he must have spent hunched over a keyboard. He might have a job that exercised only his brain, but he lifted weights. The effects showed through his cotton work shirts.

Reagan thought that hours in a computer lab appealed only to the kind of men who were ill at ease in social settings, but Noah quickly disproved that stereotype when he and Reagan went to the local diner for coffee one morning while running an errand for Irene. The moment the two strangers entered the diner, conversation at the tables halted. After a brief moment, an early morning card game among ranchers at a table in the corner resumed, and everyone took that as a cue to restart their conversations. Noah walked up to the table and asked in a friendly voice, "What's a guy got to do to get into this game?" A grizzled old man squinted up at him, noticeably inspecting the long black ponytail pulled through the back of Noah's seed cap. "About thirty years on three sections," was the curt reply.

Noah had laughed easily. "Then I don't qualify, but my dad does." He had introduced himself, and at the mention of Mason Ritter the table erupted.

"He sold out—how many years ago was it? Sure miss seeing 'Mace.' How's he doing these days?"

"I remember you when you were only this tall. You fell off your dad's tractor and scared us half to death. Thought you got run over . . . but you just had the wind knocked out of you."

Noah chuckled and pulled up a chair. You would have thought he had never been away from Custer County.

Reagan's thoughts drifted from Noah back to Irene. She drove nonstop to Grand Island, then northwest to Millersburg, and finally down the narrow gravel road that led to the deserted Ritter homestead.

There was no sign of Noah Ritter's red pickup. The farmhouse door was locked and it appeared as if no one had been there in days. Reagan made her way back into Millersburg and inquired at the diner. One of the card players at the corner table answered her question. "Noah's headed back to California. Didn't say when he'd be back."

"Irene, please," Reagan begged. "You have to try." She held up a spoonful of tapioca, but the tiny white-haired woman in the hospital bed just stared defiantly back at her.

"N-n-n-NO!" the woman squeezed out the words. "Doooo-nn wann." She turned her head away.

"All right then, here," Reagan said. Taking Irene's right hand in hers, she pried open the resistant fingers. "You can feed yourself, you know. Your therapist said so. Just don't put so much on the spoon."

Irene gripped the spoon. With excruciating slowness, she managed to put a small amount of tapioca on the spoon. It spilled on her pale blue bib before it ever reached her mouth. She let go of the spoon and turned away from Reagan. A tear trickled down her cheek.

Reagan took her hand. "It's all right, Irene. Try again in a minute. I need to run down the hall to the rest room. I'll be back." Reagan hurried out of the room. She was leaning against the wall sobbing when a nurse came down the hall.

"I can't do it," she said through her tears. "I can't get Irene to eat. What's going to happen to her if we can't get her to eat?"

"We'll think of something," the nurse assured Reagan, patting her arm. "She's made wonderful strides in every other way. And in a remarkably short time."

"But her speech just isn't coming back. She's so frustrated. And it's so hard for her to swallow. I'm afraid she's going to give up." Reagan's voice lowered. "Her family is talking about selling her house. They don't think she'll ever go back home." She bit her lip and shook her head. "If they sell her house, it will kill her." Reagan straightened up and took a deep breath. "I'm only a friend. I can't do anything to stop it but try to get her to prove them all wrong. To show them that she is going to get better. She *will* go home." She sighed. "Sorry. I didn't mean to dump all that on you."

The nurse smiled in response. "I only wish all of my patients had such devoted friends. You're doing more good than you know for Mrs. Peale. Just be patient . . . and don't give up."

Reagan didn't want to give up, but as the days passed she saw Irene growing smaller, not just physically, but in spirit. And then there was the day that Lila Ritter broached the topic of selling Irene's house. Reagan saw the effect it had on her friend. Something died in the old woman's eyes. She closed her eyes, nodded, and said, "Yessssss. I unnner-stan." Then she pretended to fall asleep.

Reagan wanted to slap the smug look off Lila's face. As Lila and Mason headed off down the corridor of the rehabilitation center, Reagan heard her say, "We won't move in right away. But we'll go ahead and have the carriage house taken down. That will make room for the new garage."

Later that night, Reagan sat in the worn recliner in her own little living room trying to concentrate on an editorial from the morning paper. She finally gave up, rolling up the paper and adding it to the others that rested in the broken water cooler that had belonged to Irene's grandmother. Looking at the crack that meandered down one side of it, Reagan smiled to herself. Who would have thought that a broken old cooler dragged out of a fallen-in dugout could change someone's life?

Leaning back in her recliner, Reagan thought about Karyn Ritter. What she knew of Irene's grandmother included a devout Christian faith. Mrs. Ritter's faith had apparently helped her through some incredibly hard times. Unfortunately, Irene seemed too depressed to respond when Reagan mentioned things like "God's will" and "trust and obey."

"What can I do for her if she can't even pray, Lord?" Reagan spoke the words aloud. The answer seemed to come: *You pray for her.* Reagan answered, *I believe, Lord, but You're going to have to help my unbelief. Things are looking pretty bleak. Mason and Lila are selling the house, and right now Irene won't even try to get better. It looks to me like we need a miracle, Lord. But I don't know if I have enough faith to ask You for that.*

The next morning Reagan's phone rang. A familiar voice said, "Reagan? Dad finally got hold of me. He said you drove all the way out to the place looking for me. Sorry to be so much trouble. I've been out of touch. I guess I should have told someone I was leaving. Tell me about Aunt Rini." Noah pronounced the nickname with long e's.

Reagan told him. As soon as they hung up, she set out for Mahoney Manor to be with Irene.

Two days later, Reagan was reading aloud to her friend when a tall young man with long black hair burst through the door pushing a wheelchair. Irene had been listening quietly, her hands at her side, her eyes closed. At the sound of Noah's voice, her eyes flitted open. But the joy in her face changed to dismay when Noah said, "Aunt Rini, I've come to take you for a ride. I have your doctor's permission, and I won't take 'no' for an answer." Gently pulling aside Irene's lap robe, he lifted her out of the hospital bed and into the wheelchair.

The old woman stiffened with protest.

"I don't want to hear it," Noah said crisply. "You need some fresh air." He turned to Reagan. "Can you come with us?" His blue eyes pleaded.

"Of course," Reagan said, closing the book and standing up. "But—where?"

Noah leaned down and whispered, "I'm taking her to the one place I think I can get through to her to stop this deathwatch nonsense. We're stopping on our way out of Lincoln to pick up a nurse to make the trip with us. But I'd like you to come if you can. It shouldn't take more than a day or two."

Noah was taking Irene to Custer County. He had rented a full-size van, and as he gently settled Irene into the plush captain's chair at his side, he said, "Don't worry about a thing, Aunt Rini. We've a nurse, and Reagan's boss said she could have a couple of days off. So relax and enjoy the drive."

From her seat behind Noah, Reagan noticed that Irene watched the familiar landscape with something approaching interest. More than once Reagan caught Noah's eye in the rearview mirror. She smiled and nodded encouragement.

Irene fell asleep long before they arrived at her grandparents' homestead. Noah carried her into the old farmhouse and upstairs to bed. As Reagan covered the frail form with a quilt, Irene sighed almost happily. The nurse was to share Irene's room, and Reagan would be across the hall.

Irene slept until mid-morning the next day. The nurse called for Noah and Reagan. At the sound of Noah's voice saying good morning, Irene opened her eyes wide and looked around her. She let out a cry of delight.

Noah asked gently, "Did I get the color right, Aunt Rini?"

Tears of joy slid down Irene's cheeks. She nodded. Then, very carefully, she formed the word "Yes." With great effort she added, "Jus—T righ-T."

After the nurse had helped Irene eat breakfast and get dressed, Noah carried her downstairs and outside. Reagan followed, but the moment she was certain Irene was secure and comfortable in her wheelchair, she headed back inside.

Irene called her back. "Ray—ray."

Reagan turned. Irene was motioning feebly. "Ray. Come."

Reagan looked doubtfully at Noah, but he nodded *yes*. "We're just going for a walk. Please come." Without another word, Noah wheeled the chair around and headed for the ridge that ran along the back of the house. He stopped at the top of the ridge where a small wrought iron fence guarded two small graves. Noah sat down beside the chair. Reagan knelt down on the opposite side of Irene's wheelchair, smiling to herself as

Irene moved her crippled hand as if to stroke Noah's long black hair.

Abruptly, Noah moved to where he could kneel directly in front of his aunt. He reached up to grip the armrests of the wheelchair and peered into Irene's face, his blue eyes brilliant with emotion. "I did what you said, Aunt Rini. I broke it off with Angela. Quit my job. Packed up." He paused, looking away briefly before adding, "And I think I've started to make things right with God, too." He cleared his throat. "It took a while to get things straight in my head . . . to know what I want. That's why I took so long to get back here. I disconnected from everything for a few days."

Noah looked soberly up at his aunt. "But I'm not disconnected anymore. I'm back to stay. And now I want you to take your own advice. You said doing what is right isn't easy. You said I shouldn't be afraid of hard work. That building a good life is always worth the work."

Noah took his aunt's aged hands in his. "Listen to yourself, Aunt Rini. You've never been afraid of hard work." He squeezed her hands, gently shaking them, "Listen to me. You can build your life again. I'll help you." He glanced at Reagan. "And from what I've seen of her, so will Reagan."

Irene took in a sharp breath. It was punctuated by something that almost sounded like sobs. Reagan put her hand on her friend's shoulder. At her touch, Irene shook her head.

Noah interrupted her thoughts. "Aunt Rini, no one—do you hear me?—no one is going to sell your home. Not now. Not ever. I don't care whether you live in it or not. If you want it to just stand there and rot, then it will stand there and rot." He raised a hand to stroke his aunt's cheek and half-whispered, "I promise."

Irene sucked in a breath. She pulled her hands from Noah's grasp, laid one palm on each of Noah's cheeks, and with great effort leaned down and kissed him on his forehead. Then, she turned to look at Reagan, her face filled with joy.

Reagan would one day look back on that moment and realize that she had witnessed the rebirth of Irene Peale's spirit. And it was all thanks to a six-foot-five-inch angel with long black hair and startlingly pale blue eyes.

"No, Reagan, no," Irene said, laughing. "Not that box."

Reagan had extracted a ridiculously large, ancient hat from the box, plopped it on her head, and posed in dramatic profile to see if she could get Irene to laugh again. It was so wonderful to hear her friend laugh.

From the overstuffed chair where she sat, Irene gestured. "The other one—the one back there—on top of that old sewing machine."

Reagan picked her way through various piles of boxes in the room and finally came to the old sewing machine, which was half hidden from view. She lifted the box Irene wanted, sneezing as a cloud of dust filled the air. Rubbing her nose, Reagan made her way back to where Irene sat and plopped the box in her lap. "Honestly, Irene," Reagan teased, "life was easier before you rehabilitated."

Irene chuckled. "Well, dearie, too bad for you. I'm back home now, and I realize that no one but me can get all of these things sorted properly. I won't have happen to my things what happened to Oma Karyn's." She paused before adding, "Someone as thoughtful about returning family heirlooms as you might not be at the next Ritter auction. There's no one much to care about these things, but the Historical Society might be interested in some of it"—Irene touched Reagan's nose lightly—"and there is a certain dark-haired friend of mine with a nose for history who might enjoy sleuthing out some of the more unusual items." Irene rattled the box, then lifted the lid and held it out for Reagan's inspection. "Like this."

Reagan looked in the box. It was nearly filled with hundreds of buttons in every imaginable size and shape. Atop the pile of loose buttons was a long strand of individual buttons threaded onto a narrow piece of frayed yellow ribbon.

"Be careful," Irene warned as Reagan reached it. "The ribbon may be rotted, and if it breaks, the mystery of the charm string will be more difficult to solve."

"Mystery?" Reagan asked. "Charm string?"

Irene nodded. "Charm strings were a passion of Victorian ladies. They traded buttons, and young men of the day gave their special friends buttons as gifts." Irene smiled. "One bit of folklore says that the goal was to get 999 buttons on a string. Then the giver of the thousandth button would be the young lady's husband." Irene ran her finger along the string of buttons. "But another story said that if the thousandth button was ever added to the string, its owner was destined to be an old maid."

"I like the first story better," Reagan said.

"Yes, I thought you might," Irene teased. "Shall I call Noah and ask him to stop at Prairie Pieceworks and buy a special button the next time he's in town? With what's in here it shouldn't take you long at all to get the other 999."

Reagan pretended to study the button string. "I don't know anything about buttons." She fingered the first one on the string, a large round button with initials engraved on its shiny gold surface.

Irene offered. "Interesting isn't it? It's from President Washington's inauguration."

Reagan looked up in amazement. "You're kidding!"

Irene shook her head from side to side. "Nope. Not kidding. I found the exact button in a book."

Reagan laid the button string back in the box. "This has to be valuable."

Irene shrugged. "It doesn't matter. I wouldn't sell it. I think the Historical Society might be interested. I've heard that complete strings are becoming more and more rare. This one belonged to a milliner who lived up in Millersburg. That's even a stronger reason for the Nebraska society to have it." Irene paused before adding, "Of course, I'm certain they would be especially delighted if the donation could be accompanied by a history of the woman who collected all these buttons."

Reagan took the bait. "I could see what I could find out."

Irene smiled. "Yes. I know." Then she added slyly, "You'll want to visit the county museum in Broken Bow. Noah might even help with some of the research. He's been trying to learn more about county history. He has some project in mind, although he won't tell me about it yet." Irene smiled slyly. "Who knows? You two might discover something else along the way."

Reagan felt herself blushing again.

Irene said, "Why don't you take it all home? All I know is that her name was Nora O'Dell. She gave the buttons and some quilts to my grandmother. Oma Karyn gave the buttons to me a few weeks before she had her stroke. She promised that the next time I came out she would tell me about Miss O'Dell. But there was no 'next time.' Oma died before I got a chance to go back."

That evening at home, Reagan set the box on her kitchen table. She brewed a fresh pot of coffee and settled into a chair. Laying the charm string aside, she began to filter through the buttons in the tin. It wasn't long before she began to sort them by color and size. She moved a desk light to the kitchen table and got a magnifying glass. The intricate designs atop some of the buttons were fascinating. There were buttons of every imaginable color. Some had scenes embossed in metals. Others seemed to be made of porcelain. There was even one that had a detailed drawing of a human eye under glass.

Reagan finally spilled all the buttons out on the tabletop. As she leveled the colorful mound with her hand, a piece of paper fluttered to the kitchen floor. Bending to retrieve it, Reagan let out a little "oh." The paper was a business card, beautifully engraved with a line drawing of women trying on hats. The card was imprinted with Nora O'Dell's name. Reagan frowned as she read the imprint. Irene had said that Nora O'Dell was a milliner in Millersburg, but the card bore a Lincoln address.

Reagan went to get her planner. Opening it to Saturday, she added to her list, *Library-buttons* and *Hist. Soc.-Nora O'Dell, milliner, 123 N. 11th St—18??*. Beside each item, Nora printed the letter A. She would do them first. Mowing the grass had just become a C.

When Irene had mentioned Noah Ritter helping to research buttons, Reagan had smiled inwardly. Noah might be unusually interested in history, but she couldn't quite picture him bent over button books or researching a nineteenth-century hatmaker. Once again, Noah surprised her. And, while he never gave Reagan the thousandth button, which would have assured

her he would be her husband, he did help her discover clues to
the story of Nora O'Dell. And while they researched the story of
Nora O'Dell, they began another of their own.

When I was just a little girl, my granny said to me,
"Come here, my child and sit a while upon your granny's
*   knee.*
I'll bet you didn't know that I was once a child like you.
I laughed and sang, and jumped and ran, and sometimes
*   felt sad, too."*
And then my granny opened up her magic button box,
It held more fun than dolls or tops, or wooden building
*   blocks.*
For Granny had a story for the buttons, red and blue,
Some came from dresses, some from coats, and some
*   from baby shoes.*
The black one was her wedding dress, the gold one was
*   Grandpa's,*
He wore it when he went to war, to fight for freedom's
*   cause.*
I've stored up all the stories, and I've written them for
*   you,*
Some I made up, some Granny told, and some of them
*   are true.*

CHAPTER 1

Remembering Mama

When my father and my mother forsake me,
then the LORD will take me up.
Psalm 27:10

Elnora Calhoun didn't know why Pap didn't love her. Oh, it was true that Pap didn't seem to love anyone, for he snarled and snapped at her brother Will, too. Still, when he yelled at her that the biscuits were too hard or the pie tasted sour, it hurt. Elnora took the hurt deep inside herself and hid it. But it stayed there, forming a cold, hard lump that seemed to grow heavier with time. There were days when the weight of it made Elnora want to curl up around the tight ball of hurt and stay hidden in bed. But fear of Pap's buggy whip always made her get up.

Tall, fair-haired Will saw what Pap's anger was doing to his sister. He tried to comfort her, telling her that Pap hadn't always been that way. Will could remember when Pap's dark eyes still knew how to smile. He thought that maybe, if they were patient, Pap would remember the good times when Mama was still alive, would remember smiling and try it again.

Elnora couldn't remember Mama. It was Elnora's birthday that had become what the girl thought of as her mother's "death-day." And thus, Elnora reasoned, it was her coming that had taken the smile from Pap's eyes. Will said it wasn't her fault that Mama had died. He said to just forget it and ignore Pap. But Elnora couldn't forget. She couldn't ignore Pap, either.

On a clear spring morning when Elnora was nearly sixteen years old, Pap threw an entire batch of biscuits against the wall and stormed out of the kitchen, swearing. Will was in the barn milking the cow when it happened. He didn't see how Elnora's hands shook as she picked up the biscuits. He didn't see her position them carefully on the painted drop-leaf table, first making a small circle and then piling them up in layers, just like a cake.

Will knew his father was angry, but he didn't dare ask questions. He finished the milking. Uncurling his lanky body from the milking stool, he crossed the farmyard to set the pail on the back porch by the door and called good-bye to Elnora through the screen before loping back to the barn to help harness the team. He would go without breakfast, hoping that Elnora had packed unusually large portions in the lunch basket.

Elnora half-whispered her good-bye to Will. Trembling, she retrieved the broom from the corner behind the stove and swept up the pieces of the crockery bowl that had held the biscuits. She bit her lower lip, forcing back the words she wanted to shout at the walls of the kitchen. *How am I supposed to bake good biscuits without a receipt?* It was hard to know just how much saleratus to put in. And try as she might, sometimes she got confused about whether to put saleratus or soda in. You used one with sweet milk, and the other with sour . . . but Elnora couldn't always remember which went with which. *Mrs. Johnson up the road offered to teach me, but you wouldn't let me go up there. You said the Johnsons should mind their business and we'd mind ours.*

Elnora sighed and shook her head. She stopped sweeping and looked through the back door toward the barn where Will and Pap were harnessing the team. They were going to plow what Pap called the "north forty" today. At supper last night Pap had warned her to pack an extra-big lunch for the next day. He had said that he and Will would "Likely be gone till sundown tomorrow, Elnora. Pack us plenty of grub. And don't you be letting our supper get cold, no matter how late we come in."

2

Gone till sundown . . . the words rang in Elnora's ears. She stepped out on the back porch, taking care to avoid a loose board. Pap didn't seem to think it important to fix that board. It never got in anybody's way but hers.

To the south, Elnora could see the smoke rising from the Johnsons' chimney. Mrs. Johnson was likely cleaning off the breakfast table, sending her men out to the fields, too. But Elnora knew that at the Johnsons' breakfast table there had been no harsh words. Mrs. Johnson's biscuits had probably been perfect. *And even if they weren't,* Elnora thought bitterly, *Olli Johnson wouldn't say a word.* Everyone in the section knew that Olli Johnson worshiped his wife, loved his sons, and doted on his only daughter, Ida. Sometimes Elnora was tempted to think that the stork had dropped her at the wrong house.

Elnora shook her head. She knew storks didn't bring babies. Anyone living on a farm knew that. She just liked to pretend about it.

She passed the flat palm of her thin hand across her forehead as if to erase the beautiful specter of life at the Johnsons from her mind. Her hand dropped to her mid-section, and she pushed against her stomach as if to tame the churning, hard lump that never seemed to go away these days.

Gone till sundown. Elnora went back inside. Crossing the small room that served as both parlor and kitchen, she pushed aside a frayed red gingham curtain and entered the pantry that had been her room for as long as she could remember. A narrow cot tucked beneath one window and an inverted produce box that served as a combination desk and dressing table were all the furniture she had ever known. Three hooks had been pounded into the wall at the foot of her cot to accommodate her wardrobe. Elnora pulled off her stained apron. Shivering with nervousness, she pulled her clothes down off the hooks. Then, she sat down abruptly on the edge of the cot, breathless with wondering if she had the courage to carry out what she had begun.

Finally, she stood up. On the opposite side of the kitchen was Pap's room. As Elnora crossed the kitchen she almost clung to the wall opposite the door to her father's room. Even when he was gone he left something behind that threatened to hold her back.

Elnora hurried across the kitchen, out onto the porch with the broken board, across the farmyard, and into the barn. She paused just inside the barn door, waiting for her eyes to adjust to the dusky light before climbing the ladder to the loft. In the far corner of the loft, behind a dank-smelling pile of half-rotten hay, stood a small painted trunk bearing the name *Kathleen O'Dell* and the date 1852. Elnora raised the lid and pulled out an empty sack of heavy striped fabric that had once been filled with goose down. It was one of two such pillows Kathleen had made for her marriage bed.

There wasn't much left of Kathleen O'Dell. Will had told her how Pap had built a huge bonfire in the farmyard and burned nearly everything that reminded him of Kathleen. The pillow cases and the few other things in the trunk had survived only because they were tucked in a dark corner of the barn loft. Since Will did all the chores that required ascending into the loft, the trunk had been left alone.

Will had told Elnora how Pap had refused anyone's help with his squalling, premature, infant daughter. Lining a shoe box with a fat quilt batt and setting it on the oven door to keep her warm, he had persistently fed her with an eyedropper. When he knew she was going to live he handed Elnora to nine-year-old Will. "This is your sister. Take good care of her. Anything you need to know, hightail it up to the Johnsons' and ask. She'll make us a good cook someday." Pap had left the naming of the child to Will, who pondered for days before finally deciding to call his sister Elnora after the heroine in a story his mother once told.

Will had managed to save a picture of Mama. It was hidden in the trunk. As Elnora grew, he told her everything he could remember. Mama was from a far-off place called Ireland, where the hills were green and there were crumbling castles just on the hill above her village. She called her town a village. She had a different way of talking that sounded almost like music. In the evenings, Will said, she would finish her chores and sit down by

4

the stove and tell stories about knights and battles and someone called Saint Christopher.

Will said in those days, when Pap came in from the fields with a scowl on his face, Mama could tease him into smiling. Will said that the very air in the kitchen used to relax, just because Mama was there. It made Elnora feel terrible, knowing that if she had never been born, the magic would still be there. Somehow she knew that if it were not for her, the paint on the house would never have been allowed to peel. And the loose board on the porch would have been fixed right away.

Now, kneeling before the open trunk, Elnora held her mother's photo tenderly, trying to memorize the gentle expression, the pale eyes. Self-consciously, Elnora reached up to touch her hair. Her mother had dark hair, but Elnora's was the color of the straw in the fields. Will had told her that sometimes her hair glowed, just like the bales of hay against a dark sky when the sun made them shine brighter than ever. Peering at Kathleen's photograph, Elnora reassured herself that while her hair might be a different color from her mama's, nearly everything else about her was an exact replica of the photograph before her.

Pap had once called Elnora's eyes "watery gray," but they were not really gray. Elnora knew that Pap's comment had just been his way of trying not to say anything nice at all. That was his way. Will had told her that Mama's eyes had flecks of blue and green so that they could be different colors, depending on the weather and the season and her mood. Will had said Elnora's eyes were exactly the same way, and that most of the time they tended toward green. If Pap thought his daughter's eyes were "watery gray," that was because Pap had never really looked at her. Elnora had always held herself away from Pap. Respectful but aloof. Gray eyes, no emotion. That seemed to work the best with Pap.

Elnora put the photo back in the trunk. As much as she wanted it, she could not bring herself to take it away from Will. She pulled a second pillow tick from the bottom of the trunk and stuffed it inside the first. Something fell out of the tick. The sound of it hitting the bottom of the trunk made Elnora jump.

Laughing at herself for being so nervous, Elnora picked up the small cloth bag. Mama's mending kit. The soft bag held a useless thimble so old that it had holes worn through the top, two rusty needles . . . and one brass button.

The button was something special. Will didn't know why, but he had told Elnora that Mama had always made certain that that button was in her mending kit. He said that once, when she had dropped it and it went under the porch, she had made Pap rip up a board to retrieve it. Elnora couldn't imagine Pap taking time to do such a thing just to retrieve a button. Will shrugged. "That's the way he was with Mama. Whatever she asked, he did it. Didn't mind it, either. Just did it and smiled."

Elnora looked down at the metal button that bore the letters *GW* in the center, encircled with the words *Long Live the President*. Interlocking ovals around the edge of the button had other initials, including *RI, NC,* and *SC.* Elnora didn't know what the letters meant, but it didn't matter. The button had meant something to her mother. Will wouldn't care about the button. Elnora held it tightly in her left hand as she descended the ladder from the loft.

Back in her room, Elnora used a safety pin to affix the *GW* button to the inside of the bag. She stuffed her clothes inside the bag and headed toward the door, where she paused momentarily to take one last look at the room that had been her universe for all of her fifteen years. She would miss Will. Swallowing hard, Elnora opened the screen door and stepped outside. She took a deep breath to reassure herself and headed up the rocky path toward the road.

Driving up the road toward Falls City, Olli Johnson couldn't resist looking up toward the Calhoun place. Thinking of Elnora and Will, Olli sighed. He shook the reins, urging his team up the incline that stretched ahead. "Get along there, Bess. Go on, there, Bones."

Bess and Bones picked up the pace, unaware that as they jerked the wagon ahead, Elnora nearly fell off the back. She clung to the edge, finally managing to pull herself up and slip beneath the tarp Olli Johnson had drawn across the load to protect his wife's eggs and butter from the sun.

Elnora remained hidden beneath the tarp for what seemed like hours. Finally, she heard the hollow sound of the horses' feet clomping across the bridge just outside of town. When the wagon cleared the boards of the bridge, Elnora squeezed between the tarp and the back of the wagon, lowered herself to the road, and skittered into the underbrush growing alongside the creek.

She waited until Mr. Johnson was well out of sight before standing up and heading across the fields toward the northwest. She doubted that Pap would look very hard for her, but he would make some effort just so the neighbors wouldn't talk. And Will—Elnora knew that Pap might try to beat something out of Will. She hoped not. She had never hinted of her plan to run off. And with her gone, he would need Will more than ever. She doubted he would use the buggy whip. Even if he did, he wouldn't hit hard.

She had biscuits to last four days, if she was careful. She would follow the creek toward the northwest, hoping to come across the old freighter's trail she had heard Pap talk about. That would take her to a better road.

Somewhere to the north and west there was a big city. If she wore the black and tan calico dress stuffed in the pillowcase and tied her hair back, she could pass for at least sixteen. Maybe older. She would hide near the train station and wait for a passenger train to arrive. Then she could mix in with the crowd. She would pretend she had just gotten off the train, head for a hotel, and ask for work. She could pretend she had left her bags at the station. Just thinking about it made Elnora shiver. Elnora told herself it was excitement.

When Will and Pap came in from the "north forty" that evening, they were greeted by the frantic bawling of the unmilked cow. Pap frowned towards the house. No lamp shown in 'the window. No smoke rose from the chimney. Swearing violently, Pap left Will to milk the cow and stormed toward the house.

Will cringed inwardly. While he milked the cow, he strained to hear what might be happening up at the house.

The sound of the back door slamming preceded Pap's return to the barn. He grabbed an old bridle down from where it hung beside the harness. "Breakfast dishes still soaking in the washpan. Fire gone out in the stove." Pap's voice wavered a little. He thrust one dirty hand through his tangled hair, adding, "She's taken her clothes. Run off, I guess." He thrust the bridle at Will. "She's probably up at the Johnsons telling all kind of tales. Go get her. She's had the day to think it over. Likely she's ready to come back. Olli Johnson knows better than to interfere in my affairs. He won't be keeping her against my will."

Will thought it odd that Pap didn't seem to want to face the Johnsons himself. He put the bridle on old Winny and plodded across the dark fields toward where a pinprick of light shone from the Johnsons' farmhouse. Mrs. Johnson came to the door, clucking in sympathy even as she shook her head. "Why, no, Will. I haven't seen Elnora. Why?"

From his chair beside the stove, Olli Johnson listened as Will explained. He lowered his newspaper and spoke across the top of the editorial column toward the door. "You tell Eli I drove into town this morning. Couldn't have been long after you two headed for the fields. Didn't see a thing."

Olli paused and took a puff from the pipe he was smoking. His eyes narrowed as he remembered something. Something that had made him turn around just as the team pulled across the bridge and into town. Olli pondered and took another puff on his pipe. Finally, he shook his head. "Nope, can't say as I know a thing. But I'll tell you this, Will, if that girl's run off I wish her Godspeed. And I'd say the same if you was to follow." Olli looked meaningfully at Will. When the boy didn't respond, Olli raised the paper back up so that his bifocals would adjust to the tiny print on the editorial page.

Just as Will turned to go, he heard Olli Johnson's voice from behind the paper. "If you *was* to follow, Will, I'd say heading for the old freighter's trail and then northwest toward Lincoln might be the way to go."

The morning after Elnora disappeared, Pap took the road

southeast to a nearby town. He returned with a wizened, stringy-haired woman in tow.

"This here's Selma," he announced curtly to Will. "She'll be cooking for us now."

Pap never said Elnora's name again. He ordered Will to "stay out of your sister's room," and made up a cot for Selma in the lean-to next to the kitchen.

CHAPTER 2

Defending Lily

Fools because of their transgression, and because
of their iniquities, are afflicted.
Psalm 107:17

Three days of walking across a succession of freshly plowed fields and virgin prairie dampened Elnora's enthusiasm about her new life. One morning she had to traverse several acres that had been burned off to promote more lush spring growth. The trek left her bare feet tender from contact with blackened stubble and exposed rocks. More than once she climbed up creek banks still covered with late-melting spring snow.

Her diet of increasingly stale biscuits washed down with whatever creek water she could find left her ravenously hungry. She slept fitfully at night, terrified by the sounds of yelping coyotes. She shivered at the thought that perhaps all the Pawnee and Otoe Indians were not on the reservation, after all.

When Elnora finally came within sight of the city, it was after dark on the fourth night of her trek. She had walked nearly eighty miles. The hem of her dress was torn, her hair was tangled and dirty, and she felt shaky and weak. She dared not go into town until she could put on her clean dress. And she must try to do something with her hair. Perhaps she could simply tuck it all up under a bonnet.

In the moonlight she saw the outline of what appeared to be a barn. It proved to be more of a shed than a barn, but inside there were two stalls, one vacant. Other than to momentarily stop nibbling the top of the board that divided his stall from his former partner's, the broken-down old nag in one stall made no protest when Elnora crept in the door. She sank into the hay and fell asleep almost instantly.

"Stop that, Frank! I said I'd meet you, but I don't want any rough stuff. Hey, you heard what I—"

The sound of someone being slapped brought Elnora instantly, completely awake.

A female voice tinged with fear pleaded, "What's the matter, honey? Settle down. We're going to have plenty of fun. Just don't be so—"

This time, there was the sound of a struggle, then ripping fabric. A muffled voice was protesting, but it sounded odd. Elnora peered over the edge of the stall where she had slept. A man with his back to her was forcing a woman against the wall. Her dress was ripped, and there was a wad of cloth stuffed in her mouth.

Elnora sank back into the hay, her heart pounding, her mind racing. She had been afraid that she had been discovered. But now fear gave way to rage. There was a shovel leaning against the opposite corner of the stall. She grabbed it, peeking over the side of the stall again to get her bearings. There was no door on the stall where she had spent the night, and she reasoned that if she moved quickly enough, she could land a blow to the man's head before he had a chance to whirl around and defend himself.

Taking a deep breath, Elnora stood up. She grasped the shovel near the base and raised it over her head. It felt as if she were moving in slow motion as she lunged across the space between herself and the couple. The man barely had time to turn his head before she landed a blow on his right shoulder. He reached out to grab the shovel, but he had been caught off guard and off balance. He missed, and Elnora raised the shovel again and slammed him hard against the side of his head. He toppled over like a felled tree and lay silent in the dust. The woman pulled the wad of cloth from her mouth and scooted herself away. She sat in the dirt, trying to catch her breath, staring up at Elnora in disbelief.

Elnora was trembling all over. She gulped for air before croaking, "Do you think he's dead?" She dropped the shovel and slid down the side of the stall opposite the woman.

"Frank? Dead?" came the reply. The woman clutched at her torn dress and laughed bitterly. "Nah. Frank's too mean to die." She leaned forward and watched him for a moment. "See? He's breathing. But he's gonna have a whopper of a headache when he comes to." The woman brushed a lock of white-blonde hair back from her forehead. She raised one knee, revealing ornately ruffled and trimmed petticoats. Resting her arm on her knee she looked back at Elnora and said, "Thanks."

Elnora nodded.

"Where'd you come from?"

"I was asleep in the empty stall."

A tall black rooster strutted its way across the doorway of the shed. It paused and crowed, heartily flapping gigantic wings. Frank stirred momentarily. Elnora started to jump up, but then he moaned and sank back into unconsciousness.

Elnora remembered the outline of a small house not far from the shack. "What if the owners find us?"

The woman nodded toward Frank. "This is his place—miserable as it is." She started to stand up. When she did, the entire bodice of her dress fell down around her waist, exposing more elegant "unmentionables."

At sight of how bad the damage was to the bodice of her dress the woman moaned, "Oh, I'm in for it now. Goldie will tan my hide good when she sees this. It's brand new." She sank back to the earth in dismay.

"Goldie?" Elnora asked.

The woman looked up. With a sardonic grin she said, "Yeah, Goldie. My—uh—employer."

Elnora just stared.

The woman's expression changed. She stopped teasing. "How old are you, honey?" she asked.

"Fif—sixteen," Elnora lied.

12

"Where you from?"

"From somewhere I'm not going back to. Ever."

Understanding filled the woman's eyes. "Me, too." She held out her hand. "My name's Lily. Lily Langley. I was about 'fif-sixteen' myself when I decided I didn't like where I was from and I was going somewhere else. That's when I met Goldie. All her girls have flower names. There's Rose, and Pansy, and Vio-let, and Iris. I always liked lilies, so that's my name." Lily gath-ered the bodice of her dress up. "You looking for work?"

Elnora shook her head. "No—I mean, yes, but—"

Lily interrupted her. "Not my kind of work, honey. I can tell you're not ready for that. Goldie needs a cook."

"I been cleaning and cooking most all my life."

Lily smiled. "Bet you never got paid for it."

Elnora shook her head.

"Goldie pays her girls well. Even the cook. Come on. You'll like her." Lily got up and headed for the door. "What'd you say your name was?"

"Nora. Nora O'Dell." Elnora hoped it sounded natural.

"Well, Nora, pleased to make your acquaintance. I'm going to get a blanket out of Frank's house to cover myself up. Goldie won't be up yet. Maybe I can sneak in and get this mended before she finds out."

"I've got an extra dress," Nora offered. She went back to the empty stall and retrieved her pillowcase. "We're about the same size. If you've got a needle and thread, I can mend your dress for you. I've done lots of mending." As she talked, Nora pulled her black calico dress from the bag, apologizing. "It's not much, but—"

Lily reached out and grabbed the dress. "It's perfect." Lily was already pulling her torn dress down over her petticoats. She stepped out of it and then tried to pull Nora's black calico on. "Just a minute—" She wriggled out of two petticoats and handed them to Nora. Smoothing the skirt of Nora's good dress down over her petticoats, she said, "There. That's better. How do I look?"

"Plain," Nora said.

"Plain is good. I shouldn't have snuck out on Goldie like that.

This way, if she catches me before we get upstairs, at least I'm not dressed for work."

Together, Lily and Nora managed to stuff the yards and yards of satin and lace that made up Lily's "work dress" into the two old pillowcases Nora had brought with her. Nora picked up two buttons that had popped off the dress and added them to the pillowcase. Finally, they stepped across Frank's motionless body and out into the sunshine.

Nora hesitated. "Do you think he'll be all right? Shouldn't we—"

Lily swore softly. "No, we shouldn't. He's a varmint. He deserves what he got." As the girls walked toward the road, Lily added, "I deserve what I got, too. I was cheating on Goldie. Trying to make some money on my own. Guess I learned my lesson." Lily shivered slightly. "I hate to think what would have happened if you hadn't been in that stall—" Lily grabbed Nora by the elbow and pulled her toward the road. "Guess you're my guardian angel, honey."

The two women headed into town. As they walked, Lily told Nora about Goldie's Garden. "Violet is Goldie's favorite. We all know that, but we don't mind. Violet's a sweetie. The professor is teaching her to sing. Ivy and Rose are best friends. They both have black, curly hair. Some people think they're sisters, but they're not. Iris is real smart. She kind of mothers us all. Then there's Fern. Stay clear of her. She's been here the longest, and the longer she's here the meaner she seems to get. Just don't get in Fern's way and you'll be all right."

They had reached the edge of Lincoln. The streets were quiet. One- and two-story buildings, some brick, some frame, stretched to the north and east. Imagining the broad, dusty streets filled with wagons and people made Nora's stomach lurch with a combination of excitement and fear.

Lily continued with her lecture on the finer points of operating Goldie's Garden. "As long as we keep things quiet, the sheriff is happy to look the other way. Goldie doesn't allow any rough stuff, and she isn't afraid to run a man off. She packs a pistol in her pocket and she gets mean real fast when anybody tries anything out of line. She pays a lady doctor to take care of us."

The girls had been making their way up an alley between two long rows of buildings. Lily paused to catch her breath. "Be straight with Goldie, and she'll make you glad you work for her. Cross her, and she'll kick you out on your ear faster than you can pack your pillowcase. Which is why I'm grateful you were there with a shovel and a dress to help me out. And why I'd appreciate your not saying anything about Frank. I learned my lesson."

"What if Frank tells?" Nora wanted to know.

Lily smiled smugly. "Frank won't say a word. If Goldie finds out he tried to rough me up he'll be banned for life. Men like Frank don't want to have to deal with women like Goldie. I don't have to worry about Frank."

CHAPTER 3

Goldie's Garden

I was envious at the foolish,
when I saw the prosperity of the wicked.
Psalm 73:3

Never in her fifteen years had Nora imagined the existence of a place as beautiful as Goldie's. When Lily led her through the back door of the two-story brick building, down a long hall paneled with dark mahogany wood and to the parlor doorway at the front of the house, Nora let out an amazed "ohhhh." Three immense cut-glass chandeliers hung from the ceiling of the parlor, which was one vast, sparkling, light-filled room with walls completely covered by floor-to-ceiling mirrors. At the east end of the parlor, an ornately carved bar was set into the wall, partitioned off from the room with heavy purple velvet draperies trimmed with wide gold fringe.

"Goldie calls this her Hall of Mirrors," Lily said proudly. "It's where we entertain." The Hall of Mirrors was furnished with several lounges upholstered in thick, deep-red velvet. Each sofa was adorned with several silk pillows, most of which had been embroidered with homey mottoes. Nora reached out to touch one that said *Remember Me* in bright yellow satin stitches made on blue silk.

"I made that one," Lily said. "I can teach you. We do a lot of handwork in our spare time. Sometimes Goldie or the professor

16

reads to us while we sew." Lily sighed. "Goldie looks out for all of the boarders. That's a nice word, don't you think? *Boarders.* Helps us feel more respectable."

Nora bent down to run her hands over the surface of the carpet that covered the polished wood floor. It was so thick that it sunk beneath the pressure of her hand. Its surface was covered with a maze of elaborate designs in rich dark reds, blues, and golds.

"The carpets are from the Orient," Lily said. "We waited nearly a year for them to come."

Nora had no idea where the Orient was, but if the people there could create such gorgeous things as this carpet, she wanted to go there someday.

"I'll show you the dining room and the rest of the house later. We'd better scoot if we're going to get this dress fixed before Goldie gets up."

Nora followed Lily up the wide stairway, tripping as she looked about her. The same wonderful designs from the parlor carpet were repeated in a runner on the stairs. The intricately carved railing and the spindles shone with polish. Nora was loathe to touch the railing for fear of marring its shine with her handprints.

At the top of the stairs, Lily held a finger up to her lips. The two girls tiptoed down the hallway and past two heavy closed doors. Lily opened the third door and Nora followed her in.

"This—this room—this whole big room is yours?" Nora asked in wonder.

Lily shrugged. "This? Sure." She was already struggling to pull her torn dress from Nora's pillowcase. "You should see Violet's room. It's much bigger than mine."

Nora looked about her at Lily's room. A motto hanging on the wall said, *All the Comforts of Home.* There was a soft blue coverlet on the brass bed, and while no Oriental carpet covered Lily's floor, there was a small rug right where her feet would hit it when she got out of bed.

Looking at the rug, Nora remembered trying to dress under the covers at home, pulling on three pairs of stockings before reaching down for the heavy leather boots Pap gave her when

Will outgrew them. The boots never fit, but of course Pap was never concerned about that. Nora thought it the supreme height of luxury to be able to actually get out of bed barefoot on a cold morning and have one's feet land on a rug.

The walls in the room were papered. Huge clusters of open pink roses danced across a background of fancy designs. A panel of exquisite lace hung from a rod at the top of the long, narrow window. The lace was gathered up the middle to give it a soft fullness. Everything in Lily's room was covered with a beautiful cloth of some kind, and the edge of each cloth was decorated with silk fringe in a rainbow of colors.

Lily said, "Goldie has the most elegant room you'll ever see. Her curtains are velvet. And she has an Oriental carpet that goes almost wall to wall. And a four-poster bed, and a lamp with beaded fringe. One of her best customers is a hunter. Goldie has bearskins and even a tiger skin high up on the walls." Lily sighed. "Wait until you see it."

Lily opened a trunk that stood in the corner of her room and pulled out a small sewing kit. She sat down on the floor next to the window to examine her torn dress and shook her head. "This is a mess. I don't know what I'm going to do. If Goldie finds out I was trying to go it on my own—"

Nora sat down beside her. "Here, let me have a look." She held the dress up, admiring the soft sheen of the fabric. Frank had popped several buttons off the front, and there was a jagged tear at the neckline near the shoulder.

"I only found these two buttons in the dirt," Nora said.

Lily knelt before the trunk and fumbled in the tray that formed the uppermost storage layer. She pulled out a small, clear jar, unscrewed the top, and spilled a pile of buttons on the floor. "They aren't very fancy. Maybe there are some that will match."

Nora found a match for the small white pearl buttons. "I don't know about this tear," she said. Then she had an idea. "Do you have any ribbon this color?"

Lily shook her head. "Why?"

"Well," Nora reasoned, "if you had ribbon, we could just sew the rip up and not worry how it looks. Then I could add the

18

ribbon as a trim here at the neck. We could ruffle it up some and it would cover the rip. No one would ever see it." She smiled. "If I do it just right, it will look like the dress came that way. Goldie might not even notice."

Lily removed the top tray from the trunk. Reaching into the depths of the bottom section, she pulled out a pair of elaborately trimmed drawers. She pointed to the rows of peach-colored trim along the bottom edges. "Is there enough of this?"

Nora examined the undergarment. It would take only a few moments to take the trim off. She nodded. Turning the garment wrong side out, she began to snip away at the threads holding the ribbon in place.

"Here," Lily said, reaching for the drawers, "let me do that. You start mending the rip."

The two girls worked for nearly an hour, during which Lily learned that Nora was quite innocent regarding the ways of the world and took it upon herself to initiate her protégé. "Goldie doesn't usually entertain the gentlemen. But she does just about everything else, from ordering the groceries to buying our clothes to arranging the doctor's visits. She lets us keep half of what we make and she pays the bills with the rest. There are six of us. I already told you we're called boarders." She jumped up. "Some of us even have our own business cards."

Lily went to the nightstand beside her bed where a few small cards were stacked next to a vase of flowers. She held out a card to Nora, who took it and read, "Miss Lily Langley, Gent's Furnishings, 134 South Ninth Street—All the Comforts of Home."

She sat down next to Nora again and took up the mending. "I get lots of business because of the name Lily." At Nora's noncommittal nod, Lily sighed. "My, my, dearie . . . you really do come from the back forty, don't you? Miss Lilie Langtry is an actress. She's very famous, and everyone loves her." Lily reached up and twined a finger through a long curl just in front of one ear. "That's why I did the peroxide job on my hair. I'm not a natural blonde like *the* Miss Langtry, but it helps the image."

Nora had just secured the last ruffle to the neckline of Lily's dress when footsteps sounded in the hall. Someone knocked at the door, and a mellow voice said, "Lily, darlin', breakfas' is suhved."

Lily grabbed the sewing kit and the untrimmed lingerie and tossed them into the trunk. Quickly closing the lid, she hung the dress on a hook behind the door just as the woman knocked again. "Lily. Is ev-uh-ry-thin' all right?"

Lily ran to the door and opened it. "Everything's fine. I've been out for a walk already and—and—I've brought you a surprise." She stepped back to allow the tallest woman Nora had ever seen into the room.

Nora jumped up quickly, managing to cover the pile of buttons on Lily's floor with her skirt as she reached down to grab her nearly empty pillowcase.

"This is Nora O'Dell," Lily said. "She needs a job. I told her you've been looking for a cook, and she thought she'd come talk to you about it."

"Aftuh breakfas', honey," Goldie said. Her voice was mellow, calm, gentle. She looked at Nora and laughed. "Y'all bringin' that bag to thuh table with yuh?"

Nora looked down at the pillowcase and blushed. "No, ma'am." She set the bag down on the floor. Goldie winked at her and left the room, continuing on down the hallway knocking at doors.

"Thanks for remembering the buttons," Lily whispered as she led Nora down the back stairs to the kitchen. Nora marveled at the reality of a house that actually had two stairways, but her wonder at the food piled on the breakfast table was even greater. Her stomach growled and her mouth began to water as she anticipated the feast. Lily poured them each a cup of coffee. "I know you're near starved, but we should wait for the others. It won't be long." She sat down and pulled Nora down beside her. "Goldie was born in the South. Way South. She doesn't usually talk with that accent, but sometimes it comes back. Especially early in the morning and if she's tired. Most of the time she tries not to talk like a southerner."

Nora just nodded. She was longing to grab the platter of sausage—or potatoes—or eggs—or gravy . . .

Lily continued. "Her voice is mellow, but whooo-*eee*—she's

got a temper. Cross her and she turns cold as ice." Lily shivered. "Trust me, honey, you do *not* want to see that side of Goldie."

To keep herself from stuffing an entire biscuit into her mouth, Nora grasped her coffee cup with both hands and took a huge gulp. It was too strong and too hot. Coughing and sputtering, Nora set the cup down. She reached for the milk and sugar and doctored the coffee liberally with both, good-naturedly enduring Lily's comments about her being a babe-in-the-woods.

Nora drank coffee while Lily talked and talked. The liquid helped her stomach stop churning so violently. When were the others going to come down, anyway? Nora looked hopefully toward the stairs.

"Violet told me Goldie's family was real wealthy. She learned to sing and dance. She's smart, too. But they wanted her to marry someone she hated, so she ran off. She worked in New Orleans and learned the ropes from one of the best madames. Then she quit for a while. She moved north and set up a dress-making business, but it wasn't two years before she moved again and opened this parlor. Nothing but the best of everything. The prettiest girls, the best professors, the finest wines—"

The concept of a professor in a brothel confused Nora, but she had no time to ask Lily to explain. At last, footsteps sounded on the stairs. Goldie was scolding someone, but when she came into the kitchen Nora saw that her arm was about the waist of the girl she was scolding. She gave the girl a friendly shake and then shoved her into a chair.

"Well, girls," Goldie said. "If we're lucky, Lily has brought us a cook." While the other girls pulled their chairs up to the table, Goldie seated herself opposite Nora. Finally, the platters of food were passed. She tried, but Nora could not concentrate on what Goldie was saying. All Nora was to remember of that meal was the food—that, and the sudden realization that she had found a place where Pap's anger could not reach her, and that she would do whatever it took to make certain that she could stay.

CHAPTER 4

Firing the Cook

For the love of money is the root of all evil.
1 Timothy 6:10

"Face it, honey," Goldie said. "You can't cook." As she spoke, the older woman was inserting a knife into what was supposed to be gravy and spreading it on a piece of bread. It was early evening. A gray sky had forced Nora to light the gas lamps in the kitchen. She had set the table for supper between bursts of activity at the kitchen counter, but as Goldie inspected the gravy, Nora realized her first day in the city was about to end in disaster.

Nora had spent the afternoon in the back parlor, listening while Lily and the other girls bantered back and forth about past conquests and future plans. It was Sunday, and Goldie dared not risk ignoring the social taboo of doing business on the Sabbath. Rose, Fern, and Ivy had dressed modestly and gone out for a carriage ride, accompanied by a fully bearded pencil-thin man Goldie introduced as "Shep, the Professor."

Lily said, "I don't know why they call themselves professors . . . unless it's because they have to know so much about everything. But every parlor house has a professor. They usually travel around quite a bit, but Shep's been here ever since I can remember. Goldie depends on him a lot. He knows how to fix just about anything. Wherever we go, Shep goes. That way we have an escort, just like all the respectable ladies in town.

"Shep comes from back east somewhere. He plays the piano and the violin. He even acted on the stage for a while. We're lucky to have someone like Shep around. Violet says the professor before Shep was a low-life drunk, plain and simple. Shep never gets drunk. Except maybe on Sunday once in a while. Even then, he's never mean. When Shep gets drunk he just crashes to the floor wherever he is." Lily giggled. "We all drag him off to bed to sleep it off."

While Lily talked Nora was sewing beautiful flower-shaped buttons on one of Iris's new dresses. Lily, Violet, and Pansy boasted freely about their earnings from the past week. Nora was flabbergasted to hear Iris complain she would get only about ninety dollars when Goldie "settled up" after supper.

Lily and the other girls had introduced Nora to many new realities of life in the city before Goldie interrupted them. "It's time for Nora to really earn her keep." Goldie had hustled Nora down the hall and into the kitchen, pulled an apron off a hook by the back door, and then presented her with three freshly plucked chickens and a myriad of instructions regarding supper. Nora's head was swimming when Goldie finally departed to spend the next few hours in her room "settling up with the girls."

Nora had done her best, but, remembering the luncheon earlier in the day, she knew the results of her hours in the kitchen fell woefully short of Goldie's expectations. When she heard Goldie's steps coming down the back stairs, Nora was filled with dread. Visions of Pap throwing her last batch of biscuits against the kitchen wall resurfaced. Remembering Lily's warning, "Whooo—she's got a temper," Nora was tempted to pull off the apron and run out the back door. But the four-day trek from home had worn her out. Unwilling to face the thought of running away again, she prepared to endure Goldie's temper.

Nora watched Goldie spread the congealed gravy on the piece of white bread and hand it to the small black poodle that sat waiting expectantly at her feet. The little black dog took the bread in its mouth and carried it to a rag rug next to the kitchen door, where it lay down and began daintily licking the gravy from the bread with its pink tongue.

Lifting the lid of another pan on the stove, Goldie wrinkled up her nose.

Nora twisted her apron nervously. "I—I—*can* cook," she said firmly. "I just don't know how to make fancy dishes, that's all. My Pap and my brother ate plain. Fried eggs and corn bread and stew, mostly. We never in our life roasted a whole bird. And Pap never wanted gravy." She turned the heat down under the gravy and tried to stir it. It had congealed into something resembling a light brown mass of glue. " 'Ceptin' maybe milk gravy from the bacon grease in the mornings."

Goldie shuddered and held up her hand. "I get the general idea." She sat down at the kitchen table. Nora was still standing by the stove, alternately rolling and smoothing the edge of her apron. Her hands shook as she reached up to tuck a few strands of blonde hair behind her ears.

Goldie pulled another chair out from the table. "Sit down, Nora. We need to talk." She leaned back in her chair. Reaching into the pocket of her silk robe, she withdrew a small black cigar and lit it.

Nora perched on the edge of the chair opposite Goldie, fidgeting with the hem of her apron and trying not to appear surprised at the sight of a woman smoking.

After taking a few long drags on the cigar, Goldie said, "Two days ago my cook ran off with a boy from across town. I really was hoping you were the answer to that problem." Goldie sighed and looked sadly toward the stove. "But I just don't think this is going to work out."

"I didn't mean to lie." It was all Nora could do to hold back the tears. Already she was wondering which of the dozen city streets she should walk up first, which doors she should knock on looking for a place to stay. She wondered if Goldie would let her sleep in the kitchen until she found another job.

"Why, honey," Goldie was saying. "You didn't lie." She chuckled. "You just didn't know what I meant when I said I needed a cook." She patted Nora's hand. "I'm a good judge of people, and I knew from the minute I saw you that we'd get on.

I can hire another cook." She laughed. "But what I can't do is ask my girls to eat *that*." She nodded toward the stove. "So, what we have to do is decide what we're going to do with you."

Nora studied the floor of the kitchen intensely. The poodle had finished its bread and gravy. It padded across the floor to where the women sat and shoved its head under Nora's hand, demanding to be petted.

Finally, Goldie broke the silence. "Lily told me how the two of you really met." When Nora looked up, startled, Goldie was smiling. "The girls can't keep secrets from me. Sooner or later I find out." She puffed on the cigar a few more times before adding, "I admire your gumption, girl. I don't know many girls who'd take Frank Albers on like that."

"I didn't really take him on," Nora said. "I snuck up from behind. He never knew what hit him."

Goldie threw back her head and laughed. "So you did, so you did. And it's a good thing, too." Suddenly, she grew very serious. "Frank's a mean so-and-so when he's drunk. When you get a little older, you'll understand men better. And you'll stay away from the ones like Frank."

Goldie took another drag on her cigar, blowing little circles of smoke toward the ceiling. She shook her head. "That Lily. Someday she's going to get herself into real trouble. It's lucky for her you were in that barn. Lucky for her you found that shovel in the hay."

Goldie smoked quietly for a few more moments while Nora concentrated on petting the poodle, who had succeeded in begging its way into her lap.

"But we were talking about you," Goldie said quietly. She tilted her head while she smoked, inspecting Nora. "You're going to be what we call a 'real looker' before long, Nora." She took another drag on her cigar, then put it out on a saucer before asking, "Can you keep house any better than you cook?"

Nora nodded.

Goldie warned, "You have no idea what a mess this place can be after a busy evening."

"I don't care about that. I'll work hard." Nora gulped. "I've never been around fancy carpet and things like that. You might have to show me how you want it."

"Lily showed me what you did to cover up that tear on her gown," Goldie said. "Some of the girls aren't as careful about their clothes as they should be. If you can sew, that'll help me out, too."

Nora nodded. "I did all the sewing at home. Pap didn't like my cooking, but he never complained about my sewing or keeping house. I made his shirts and everything."

Goldie laughed again, reaching up to touch Nora's golden hair. "You wouldn't believe it now, but my hair used to be just this color. I got my name because of my hair." She reminisced. "There was a gambler used to call on me in New Orleans. 'Goldie,' he'd say, 'your hair would assay as nearly pure gold ore, the way it shines in the lamplight.' "

Goldie reached out and patted Nora on the head. "You have potential, and I'd like to keep you around. What do you say to five dollars a week, room and board included?"

"You mean,"—Nora took in a deep breath—"you mean I don't have to leave?"

"Why on earth would you think I wanted you to leave? I just don't want you to cook anymore, that's all!" Goldie laughed. "Now get upstairs. Iris still needs help with some sewing. She's got some new idea for a costume."

She turned towards the stove. "Send Violet down to me. Maybe we can resurrect something edible from this mess." She said it with mock anger, snapping a kitchen towel at Nora's posterior as the young girl bent to set the poodle down.

The setting sun was just beginning to peek through gray clouds and light the back alley with an uncanny brightness when Nora, up to her elbows in dishwater, saw a woman driving a carriage pulled by a rangy white gelding arrive at Goldie's back door. The woman didn't come right in. Instead, she sat, her head bowed, almost as if she were half asleep. With her head bowed, her entire face and shoulder were obscured from view by the brim of the largest, most elaborate hat Nora had ever seen.

Nora smiled to herself when the gelding cranked its thin neck around and eyed the driver. She could see the horse's muzzle vibrate gently, and although she could not hear the soft whicker, she knew the sound.

The woman dozing in the carriage seat started awake. Nora saw her arch her back and rub her neck wearily before climbing down from the carriage. Not wanting to be seen spying on the visitor, Nora bent her head and gave renewed energy to scraping the last bit of burned chicken from the bottom of the roasting pot before her.

The visitor clomped up the back steps. Nora waited for her to knock, but instead of knocking the woman came in.

"Where's Olga?" she asked abruptly.

"If Olga was the cook, Goldie said she ran off with a boy from across town."

Nora's announcement regarding Olga's defection had an odd effect on the visitor. Closing her eyes, she pressed her lips together and said quietly, "Hallelujah."

Suddenly infused with a burst of energy, the woman set a large black bag on the table and removed her hat. Her hair had once been black. Now it was graying, white streaks sweeping up from her temples and back from the left side of her forehead.

As the visitor looked her over, Nora began to feel self-conscious. "I'll get Goldie," she said.

"There's no hurry about that," the woman said crisply. She removed her wrapper and tossed it on a chair. "I'm Maude Allbright. Dr. Maude Allbright."

The doctor held out her hand. Nora hastened to dry her hands on her apron before returning the woman's firm handshake, all the while wondering why meeting a doctor should make her blush. "I'm Nora," she said.

Maude Allbright did not beat about any bushes getting to her point. "Well, Nora, you are probably thinking that I am going to pull a long face and ask a million questions and then read you a tract and preach a little to try to talk you out of the error of your ways." Dr. Allbright snapped open her medical bag as she talked. "But the truth is I am going to do nothing of the sort. I don't pull long faces and I hate tracts and lectures. And I don't ask questions because I already know the answers. Every one of you girls probably makes more in a week than I do." The doctor removed a stethoscope from her bag and put it around her neck.

Dr. Allbright's voice was sad. "You don't know me and I don't know you, young lady, but I know who you will be in a few years. You'll be Fern, knowing you don't have much longer before Goldie will pass you over for a younger girl, mixing potions and pots to try to cover the wrinkles and bring a youthful blush back to your faded cheeks, desperate because you squandered all that money you made instead of saving up for a good retirement."

Dr. Allbright snapped the medical bag shut and headed for the back steps. She stopped abruptly and turned around. "What did you say your name was?"

Nora answered, "Nora O'Dell." She lifted her chin before adding, "And I'm not one of Goldie's girls. Not the way you think. I'm the new housekeeper."

Dr. Allbright smiled. "How long have you been in Lincoln?"

"Just since this morning."

"And your family?" Dr. Allbright raised her hand. "Never mind. I know better than to ask that." She looked Nora over, taking in the golden blonde hair, the wide-set green eyes set off by beautifully arched eyebrows, the tiny dark brown mole just above one corner of the girl's full mouth. "You may be the housekeeper today, dear, but I can assure you Goldie has other plans for you in the very near future."

The older woman pointed upstairs. "Goldie would try to laugh it off if she heard me say this, Miss O'Dell, but I want you to know something. This is not the place to realize your dreams. You're very young and you'll get on quite well for a while. But when you've scratched through the veneer of beautiful furnishings and fancy dresses, you're not going to like what you see."

Nora heard Goldie call from the upstairs hall. Dr. Allbright leaned over and whispered to her, "We'll talk again." Then she tripped up the stairs, calling out to Goldie in a cheery voice that belied the weariness Nora could see in every line of her face.

Nora returned her attention to the kitchen. She might not know how to cook, and she might be ignorant of caring for fine things, but she was going to clean the kitchen until it shone. She dismissed the doctor's harangue as the tired blatherings of an eccentric old woman. It seemed to Nora that a lot of dreams could be realized with ninety dollars a week.

CHAPTER 5

Thornhill Dressers

To him that is afflicted pity should be shewed
from his friend.
Job 6:14

A week after her arrival in the big city of Lincoln, Nebraska, Nora still had not ventured beyond the back stoop of the two-story brick building on the edge of town. Goldie and the girls kept her busy cleaning, dusting, sewing, mending, combing hair, ironing ruffles, sweeping stairs. Chores were as endless as they had been at home, with one all-important difference: No one yelled or threw things at her. She actually felt welcome. For Nora, Goldie's was a haven. If she did not feel loved, she did feel liked, and that was enough.

Nora's happiness went undisturbed for two weeks, until one Monday morning when Goldie rose from the breakfast table and headed upstairs to change. "I'm going to do some market-ing, Nora," she said. "It would save me a lot of time if you learned how. Why don't you come along. Meet me at the front door in an hour."

Goldie retreated upstairs to dress, unaware that her simple invitation had wreaked havoc with Nora's newfound peace of mind.

Lily and Iris exchanged knowing glances. The effect of Goldie's invitation on Nora had not been lost on them.

"You can borrow my blue calico," Lily offered.

"Come on, honey," Iris said, taking Nora's hand. "I'll help you with your hair."

An hour later Nora, primly dressed in indigo calico, her hair completely hidden beneath a huge bonnet, met Goldie as ordered by the front door. Goldie wore a simple dark blue morning dress with linen collar and cuffs and matching hat. Nora thought that together they looked like a mother and daughter going out to do the marketing.

Once in the carriage, Nora shifted nervously in her seat. Lily and Iris appeared at an upstairs window, laughing and making faces at her as she did her best to pretend that a carriage ride to town was nothing out of the ordinary. She watched Goldie, trying to imitate the older woman's proud carriage, hoping no one could see how terrified she was.

On the handful of times Pap had allowed her to ride with him to town, they had encountered only a few other wagons. This morning, dozens of carriages filled the wide streets of Lincoln. Streams of farm wagons flowed down the street toward what Shep called Haymarket Square.

Just as they rounded the corner of Ninth and O Streets, a runaway came charging down the road. The horse nearly grazed the side of the carriage where Nora sat. While Shep did his best to control his own terrified horse, the runaway reared, flailing the air with its hooves. Nora squeezed her eyes shut against a shower of foam from the runaway's bit. She ducked toward Goldie, who laid a protective hand on her shoulder. In a moment, the runaway was off in the opposite direction from them, finally disappearing to the north where Nora could see the tower of a building Goldie said was the university.

People were everywhere—on the boardwalks, entering stores, exiting stores, riding in carriages, climbing into wagons, perched on the rafters of buildings under construction. A throng of people exited the train station, flocking about carriages waiting to take them home or to local hotels. From her vantage point in Goldie's carriage, Nora could see more people than she had seen in fifteen years of living in Hickory Grove.

She pointed out a strange sort of iron wheeled wagon being

pulled along a metal track by a team of mules. Nora thought it looked like a cheese box with windows cut out. Shep explained that the Lincoln Cable Car Company operated a line of horse- and mule-drawn taxis that, for the reasonable fare of only five cents, could transport more than a dozen people to various destinations throughout the growing city.

"You should ride out to Wyuka some afternoon," Shep said. "It's a cemetery, but it's in a kind of garden setting. Nice place to walk."

"Sounds like fun," Nora lied, already wondering when Goldie would be finished with her shopping so that they could return to the familiar quiet of the house.

Finally, Shep pulled the carriage up to the doorway of a store. Gazing down the half-block-long row of display windows, Nora thought of the little general store in Hickory Grove, one corner dedicated to checkers by the stove, and another corner serving as the post office. She could have spent the remainder of the day simply gazing at the array of merchandise in the windows of the gargantuan store.

The entrance to the store was a double-wide wonder with leaded glass transoms and fancy woodwork. Above the street level, a rounded turret soared upward from the entrance for two full stories. Nora thought Herpolsheimer's must look like one of the castles in her mother's stories about knights and fair ladies.

While Goldie swept through the door without a glance at the dozens of display cases they passed, Nora gawked openly, her head turning from side to side. There were linen collars, and silver spoons, and kid gloves in every hue of the rainbow. Nora wondered how anyone could turn a calf's skin to such glorious shades of lavender and red, yellow and blue. Her eye sockets ached with the effort of taking everything in.

Goldie finally paused at a counter near the back of the store to inspect a newly arrived assortment of ribbons and laces. Initially she was assisted by a sallow-complexioned girl with a space between her front teeth and a slight lisp when she spoke.

"You'll like these." The girl laid an assortment of black laces on a tray.

Goldie picked up a piece of lace and fingered it. Frowning

slightly, she laid the first sample aside and examined another. Finally, she put it down and looked sharply at the girl. "You are new here, I believe?" she asked with the tone of a queen requesting the history of a servant. When the girl nodded, Goldie said abruptly, "I believe I made it clear that I was interested in authentic Egyptian lace, young lady. I have no interest in these cheap imitations."

The sallow-faced girl looked surprised. She opened her mouth to reply just as another shop girl strode up. "Thank you, Liza, I'll take over. I believe Mr. Herbert was looking for you."

The girl with the space between her front teeth disappeared into the nether regions of the store. Her replacement looked down at the tray of lace with distaste and pushed it away. "I'm sorry, Miss Meyer," she apologized. "Liza is new, and she doesn't know the merchandise very well." Pulling a second tray of lace from a huge drawer behind her, the girl said, "I believe this is more what you want."

Nora found herself wondering how this girl had managed to arrange her hair in the elaborate updo that made her appear even taller and more elegant than she was. Then she remembered a trick with hair that Fern had shown her. *Rats.* Fern had called the extra pieces of human hair that she used to expand her coiffure "rats." Nora decided that this girl probably had several "rats" tucked beneath the layers of her own hair. No one could have that much hair.

The girl lowered her voice and asked, "Do you have any openings yet, Miss Meyer?"

Goldie shook her head. "I'll take fifteen yards of this." She pointed to a roll of wide black lace. Then, pointing out three other rolls, she said quickly, "Twenty of that, thirty of that, fifteen of that. Have it sent to Elise Thornhill, and put it on my tab." Goldie turned briskly away from the counter, ignoring the disappointed expression on the young girl's face.

It did not take many more stops before Nora began to notice that while gentlemen who walked alone surreptitiously nodded and tipped their hats to Goldie, those who walked with ladies on their arm pretended not to see her. All women looked away half-frowning as if an invisible string holding the corners of their mouths upturned had suddenly broken. Goldie made eye contact with only a few of the men and pretended to ignore everyone else.

The noise and bustle so foreign to her soon began to grate on Nora's already frazzled nerves. While Goldie explained her preferences in everything from flour to feathers and wine to cigars, Nora listened with growing dismay, wondering how she would ever manage to remember any of it. She realized that she had lost track of where they were in the city. With her sense of direction confused, she grew even more uneasy. Everything in her yearned for the familiar interior of the establishment on Ninth Street.

Just when Nora thought they might actually be headed back, Goldie shouldered her way through a group of women clustered around a sale table and Nora lost sight of her. Trying not to show her sense of panic, she made her way to the front of the store and out onto the boardwalk. The carriage was nowhere in sight. Her heart pounding, she stepped toward the street, craning her neck to look for Shep. Someone shoved her from behind, and she stumbled into the street, mortified when one foot landed in a steaming pile left by one of the city's four-legged citizens.

Someone laughed derisively. Nora looked up and into the eyes of an ill-kempt man with an equally-disheveled woman on his arm. The couple clung to one another, weaving back and forth as they howled with laughter. "Looks like Goldie's new filly just made a little mess."

Passersby hurried away, almost pressing themselves against the building to create a wide berth between themselves and Nora. The expressions of disgust on their faces filled her with dismay.

Suddenly, Shep appeared. He grabbed the drunken man by the shoulder with one huge hand and spun him around. "Be on your way, Frank."

The drunken man stumbled backward. He would have fallen, save for being propped up by the equally inebriated but more balanced woman clinging to his arm. Hearing his name helped

Nora remember. This was the man she had slugged with a shovel. What if he somehow recognized her?

Shep helped Nora back up on the boardwalk. He led her around the corner of the store and into the back alley, where he had taken the team to rest in the shade. He directed her to sit down and remove her shoes. While he wiped them clean with an old newspaper he found in a trash barrel he said quietly, "Frank Albers is a bad 'un. Stay clear of him."

Nora bit her lip and nodded obediently.

He squinted up at the sky, then back at Nora. "Guess now is as good a time as any to tell you how it is. The storeowners are glad to take Goldie's money, but they have to maintain their respectability. Which means they won't be overly friendly and they expect you to conduct your business and get out."

Nora nodded again. "Are we finished shopping yet?"

"Not yet," Shep shook his head. "One more stop." He helped Nora into the carriage and headed the team toward the front of the store just as Goldie came outside.

Thornhill Dressers Established 1880. The sign was painted with gold letters on a black background, one word centered above each of the four display windows that fronted the store. Bonnets and trims, dresses and capes, and other related merchandise, filled the windows.

Shep helped Nora and Goldie down. "I'll get the horses a drink," he said, "then I'll drive around back and wait." Climbing back aboard, he headed the team in the direction of a huge square fountain and watering trough in the center of the intersection at the end of the street.

Nora followed Goldie inside.

While other establishments they had been in that day were so full of merchandise it was hard to navigate the aisles, this shop exuded order and calm. Directly opposite the door was a massive table. At the moment it was bare, but Nora was soon to see that it was used for spreading out lengths of fabric for inspection. Beyond the table on the far wall was a beautiful oil painting and below it, a narrow piece of furniture consisting of several dozen small drawers, each with a glass front. Each drawer held a different ribbon or trim. A doorway to the right led to what Nora assumed must be a workroom at the back of the shop.

A fireplace surrounded with ceramic blue- and white-painted tiles was centered on the wall to the left. It boasted a massive oak mantle with another oil painting above it. Before the fireplace a large overstuffed chair had been positioned on an Oriental carpet to face the back corner and three huge dressing mirrors. A woman standing before the mirrors could get a full view of the front, sides, and back of a dress. To the right of the mirrors, standing away from the wall, were floor-to-ceiling shelves filled with every imaginable kind of cloth.

Just as Nora's eye was drawn to a deep green bolt of fabric on the top shelf, a middle-aged woman stepped out from behind the shelves and stood before the dressing mirrors, eyeing her profile critically. Nora realized that the shelving must have been built away from the back wall to create space for a dressing room. Another woman she assumed was the dressmaker stepped out from behind the shelves and joined her customer in front of the mirrors. She nodded at Goldie before turning her attention to her customer.

"Elise is busy," Goldie whispered. "Follow me into the back room. We'll help ourselves to coffee until she's free."

Goldie led Nora past the beautifully carved table toward the doorway to the workroom. The wall to the right boasted more small drawers and a long, narrow table displaying several different styles of hats on stands of varying heights. Behind the display table was a broader worktable where two partially finished hats sat on forms clamped to the edge of the table.

Going through the door, Nora and Goldie entered the workroom. It was just as long, but narrower than Miss Thornhill's studio. Where the studio exuded order and peace, the workroom was a jumble of activity. Boxes were stacked nearly to the ceiling, their contents scribbled in pencil on the flaps. At the far end of the room, a narrow stairway leading up to a second floor was also cluttered with boxes, some so full their contents spilled onto the stairs.

A row of tall windows on the rear wall of the building bathed the workroom in natural light. Beneath these windows sat two young women, each one pedaling furiously as they maneuvered yards of fabric beneath the racing needle of a treadle sewing machine.

Both girls glanced up when Goldie and Nora appeared. They smiled and nodded a greeting, but didn't stop working. Above the noise of the machines, Goldie explained, "The redhead is Hannah. The fat one is Lucy. Nice girls."

Goldie made herself at home in Elise Thornhill's workshop. A small stove in the corner was still warm. Opening a cupboard on the wall to the right of the stove, she withdrew two coffee cups. Motioning for Nora to sit down at the small table opposite the back door, she poured them each a cup of coffee and sat down opposite Nora.

Lucy finished and stood up. "Hello, Miss Meyer. Sorry we couldn't stop, but Miss Thornhill is about to have our hide today. These dresses are supposed to be packed in a trunk at the rail station even as we speak." Lucy leaned forward and whispered, "That's Mrs. Judge Cranston out there right now, and she expected to try both these on yesterday." Lucy rolled her eyes. "Of course Mrs. Judge doesn't care that the lace came late and the buttons—" Lucy reached behind her. She showed them a huge black button painted with a grotesque white face. "Can you believe she insisted we put *these* on *this*?" She laid one of the buttons against the soft yellow plaid and shuddered. "Of course she wouldn't believe us that they weren't quite right . . . until we had thirty-five of them sewn on!"

Elise appeared at the doorway to the studio. She called in a stage whisper, "Lucy! We're ready for the next gown."

Lucy draped the gown over her arm and headed for the studio. As she did, Hannah lifted her head. "Just one last hem, Miss Thornhill."

Elise gave Goldie an apologetic look.

Goldie shooed her toward the studio. "Go. We can wait."

With a sigh, Elise headed back into the studio.

Goldie said, "I keep telling her she needs more help, but Elise is too tight with a dollar to want to hire anyone else." She got up and walked to where the boxes were piled haphazardly along the far wall. "She probably had the exact lace she needed in one of these boxes . . . but how could she know with everything in such a mess."

Hannah finally stopped pedaling her machine. "Whew," she breathed. Jumping up, she spread the skirt of the dress along the length of the pressing table behind her. Then, she crossed the room to where two flatirons waited on the stove. Hannah wielded one flatiron expertly, then plopped it back onto the stove, grabbed up the dress, and hurried into the studio.

Finally, Nora heard someone she assumed was Elise bidding Mrs. Judge Cranston good-bye. Goldie got up and Nora followed her into the studio where Miss Thornhill was leaning against the door. At the sight of Goldie she exclaimed, "Honestly, that woman!" Then she held out her hand to Nora. "Goldie didn't tell me she had a new boarder."

"Nora's not a boarder," Goldie said. "She's my housekeeper. As it turns out, she's also quite good with a needle and thread."

"Really?" Elise asked, eyeing Nora with curiosity.

"I can read your mind, Elise Thornhill, and forget it. You're not taking any more of my girls out from under my nose." Goldie walked across the studio to the shelves filled with bolts of cloth. She pointed to a soft yellow and blue plaid silk. "This is new."

"I thought you'd like that," Elise said. "Let me get the sample book the salesman left. It comes in several different colorways."

The two women were soon lost in sample books and fashion magazines. Lucy peeked in from the storeroom. Catching Nora's eye, she motioned for the newcomer to join her. Once back in the storeroom, Lucy and Hannah introduced themselves while they unrolled several yards of a fabric they called foulard on the workroom table.

"Sit down and relax," Hannah urged Nora. "They'll be a while. They always are."

Just then someone knocked at the back door. Lucy hurried to open the door to a young man with a thin auburn mustache. He smiled shyly. "Hey, Luce," he pronounced it "loose." "Want to go for a walk?"

Lucy grinned at him before looking doubtfully over her shoulder at Hannah. "We didn't get lunch yet. Do you think Miss Thornhill would mind?"

Hannah smiled. "Just don't be gone too long. We have to get this gown cut out today, and it's that new pattern."

Lucy grabbed her bonnet from its hook by the door and the two left. Nora saw the young man slip his arm around Lucy's broad waist as they walked off. Lucy pushed him away, but it was a playful refusal.

Nora turned toward Hannah, "Can I help?"

"Sure," Hannah said. She pointed to a wrinkle in the foulard. "Smooth that out. Then lay this—" she handed Nora an oddly shaped piece of paper—"along the folded edge and pin it down." Hannah opened a notebook and ran her finger down a row of penciled notes. "Oh, wait a minute," she said, taking the pattern piece back. "We have to lengthen the sleeve at least an inch. Here—" She cut the pattern piece in two. "Now when you lay it along the fold, put this bottom piece one inch away from the top piece. Like this." She demonstrated what Nora should do before handing her a measuring tape. "Measure exactly. Miss Thornhill is very, very exacting. Which, I suppose," Hannah said, sighing, "is why she is so successful, although it can be a trial at times."

While Nora laid the pattern piece in place on the fabric, Hannah referred again to her notes. "You one of Goldie's boarders?" Hannah asked.

Nora bristled. "No. I'm the housekeeper."

"You from Lincoln?" Hannah wanted to know.

"No." Nora didn't offer any more information.

"Hey," Hannah said. "I'm just trying to be friendly. You don't have to talk if you don't want to. I just wondered how you knew Goldie, that's all. If you're not a boarder I thought you might be family. Goldie's Miss Thornhill's sister, you know."

Nora had never imagined that women like Goldie had families. She was clearly surprised. Hannah smiled and nodded. "Yup. Sisters. Funny, ain't it? Word is, they were both dressmakers at first. Then Miss Thornhill fell in love and ran off. All

39

the way to Paris, France. She learned a lot about dressmaking from the high-fashion people over there. I don't know what happened. When she came back, she had a different last name but no husband. By then, Goldie was already set up in the house over on Ninth Street. Miss Thornhill threw a fit. She told me that herself. But Goldie didn't want to come back to the old life."

"Thank you for the history lesson, Hannah." Goldie was standing in the doorway.

"Oh, Miss Meyer—I didn't mean to—" Hannah's freckled face flushed crimson. She swallowed hard and took a deep breath. "I'm sorry, ma'am. Guess I can't resist gossip."

"It wasn't really gossip. Every word I heard was the truth. And there wasn't a drop of ill will in it, either. Thank you for that."

Hannah was flustered. She had obviously expected a full "dressing-down." But Goldie didn't seem bothered. Instead, Goldie said, "I suppose I should add that since then Elise and I agreed to disagree about our career choices and declared a truce, it's worked out very well. My girls enjoy having their own dressmaker, and my business has helped Elise make ends meet through some lean times. We get along very well, as long as Elise doesn't steal my girls."

"Where's Lucy?" Miss Thornhill peeked into the workroom just as the front bell rang.

"I told her to go ahead and get some lunch," Hannah said.

"I don't suppose lunch included a Mr. Fielding?" Elise asked.

Hannah blushed again. "I told her not to be gone too long. I didn't think you'd mind after she worked so late last night."

Elise sighed. "No, of course I don't mind." She retreated back into the studio.

Nora heard her say, "Good afternoon, Mrs. Gilbert. What can I do for you?"

"We'll be going," Goldie said. "Elise is coming to do a fitting later this evening after she closes the shop."

Shep pulled up to the back door. Nora followed Goldie outside and climbed into the carriage. As they pulled away from the shop, Lucy and Mr. Fielding came around the corner of the building, arm in arm. Lucy waved happily to Nora, who waved back. It was an odd sensation, having someone in the crowded city recognize her. Nora liked it.

CHAPTER 6

Hopes and Dreams

Wine is a mocker, strong drink is raging: and whosoever is deceived thereby is not wise.
Proverbs 20:1

Nora had been a housekeeper for only a few weeks when Goldie suggested she help serve "the guests." Taking Nora behind the ornately carved bar that stretched nearly the full length of one end of the front parlor, Goldie explained, "If Shep hits a sour note on the piano when a customer steps up to the bar, pour the drink out of these bottles." Goldie reached for some beautiful wine bottles under the counter. "Be certain you use the good crystal glasses and pour it like you're measuring every drop carefully. If Shep just plays on, you'll know to give the customer the really good stuff from here—" Goldie indicated another rack of wine bottles. She explained, "I buy the best, but I'd be stupid to waste it on men who don't know the difference." She patted Nora's shoulder. "If you're not sure what to do, ask Iris—but be discreet. She'll be working with you tonight."

When Nora only nodded, Goldie asked, "Something wrong, honey?"

Nora shook her head. "I'm just nervous."

"Nothing to be nervous about. A big city's just like a small town—full of both varmints and nice folks. There's just a few more of each, that's the only difference. Working the bar is easy. Just smile and be polite and the nice folks will love you. Shep and I take care of the varmints." Goldie paused before adding, "I never rush anyone to the next level before they're ready, honey. Now, get on upstairs and help the girls get dressed."

Nora hustled upstairs. The door to Iris's room was open. Nora peeked in. "You need any help?"

Iris was sitting at her dressing table, trying to decide exactly how to place a comb in her curly black hair. Watching her, Nora marveled at the absolute perfection of her coffee-colored skin. Iris smiled at her in the mirror and nodded. "Come on in. Help me decide how to wear this comb." Iris positioned the comb in various ways before deciding to secure it behind one ear.

Nora rubbed one forearm nervously. "Goldie said I should help you at the bar tonight."

Iris turned around. "Don't let that scare you. You'll do fine. Just smile and be friendly." She picked up another comb from her dressing table. "Maybe we can wear our hair the same way. Let's see if my other comb will stay in your hair."

Nora sat down at Iris's dressing table. Just as Iris took the last pin out of her blonde hair, Nora blurted out, "I don't know if I want to be a boarder."

Iris looked at her in the mirror. She began to brush Nora's hair. "You happy making five dollars a week?"

"I didn't get anything for doing the same work—and more— not so long ago," Nora said.

Iris sat down on the bed next to the dressing table. "I read an ad in the paper today," she said. "There's a man hiring strawberry pickers out east of the statehouse. Pays three dollars a week." She snorted. "That same man thinks nothing of handing Goldie twenty-five dollars for an hour of my time on Saturday night. Now which pay would you rather collect?"

Nora shook her head and bit her lip.

"Don't you have any plans, Nora? Any dreams?"

The girl shrugged. "Sure. To get away from being yelled at and hit when Pap didn't like my cooking or the way I walked or the way I sat at the table or—"

"—I get the picture." Iris stood up and began to brush Nora's hair again. In a maternal tone of voice, she said, "Listen, honey. No woman plans this career. But life has a way of crushing dreams. That's how Goldie stays in business." She waved her brush in the air as she added, "That, and the fact that most men are low-life good-for-nothings who talk out of both sides of their mouths and are totally dominated by one thing."

She was quiet for a moment, then said abruptly, "I was a teacher before I came to Goldie's." At Nora's look of amazement she smiled. "Surprised you, didn't I? Of course I could only teach black children. But I loved it." She sighed. "Then I made a big, big mistake. I trusted someone I shouldn't have. When I found myself *enceinte,* that was the end of teaching. And the end of the relationship." Iris swallowed before continuing. "It was almost the end of me." Her eyes filled with tears. "My little darling died when she was only three days old. I buried her under a big oak tree in the woods, and said a prayer over her. And then I headed for New Orleans. I was a mess when Goldie took me in. I've been with her ever since."

Iris opened the trunk against the far wall and pulled out a pale green silk dress. She held it out to Nora. "Put this on. It will bring out the color of your eyes." Nora stepped behind the folding screen in the corner of the room and began to unbutton the bodice of her work dress while Iris talked.

"I'm not like the other girls, wasting every dollar that comes my way on baubles and candy. I've been saving up for a long time. One day very soon I'm heading out west to Denver. I'm going to buy a little house and take in every unloved black child that comes my way. I'll teach them to read. Give them a dream." Iris sighed. "The day I die, I'm going to be able to look back and know I did something with my life."

Nora stepped out from behind the screen.

"I knew that green would make your eyes shine. Come see." Iris directed Nora to the full-length mirror in the corner of the room.

"Well now, ain't that just touchin'?" Fern was standing in the doorway, her thin arms folded across her flat chest. Fern's abundant hair had probably once been beautiful, but time was not being kind to the color, which was fading to a mousy light brown. Fortunately, it was not thinning. Fern spent hours doing it up. She was knowledgeable about fashion and meticulous about having the latest styles in the finest fabrics. Her hazel eyes were streaked with gold.

She peered at Nora, her voice dripping with sarcasm as she said, "So Iris is gonna teach all the little 'chillen' to read. I thought I heard Goldie send you upstairs to help us all. You gonna' help anybody besides her?"

"Of course," Nora answered quickly.

"Come on, then."

Nora followed Fern to her room at the far end of the hall. It was the smallest room on the floor, and when Nora followed her in she wrinkled her nose with distaste. The stale air smelled of powders, heavy perfume, and a chamber pot.

Every surface in Fern's room assaulted the eye with a different garish pattern. Fringed runners and cloths adorned every piece of furniture. Even the top of Fern's mirror and folding screen were laden with fringe and tassels. Her dressing table was cluttered with an array of bottles and powder puffs.

Fern shed her duster. Grasping the edge of the bed with both hands, she braced herself and ordered, "Lace me up. Tight."

Nora pulled and tugged on the laces of Fern's elaborate corset in vain. She could not pull the waist in far enough to please. Fern sucked in air, thrusting her bosom forward and holding her breath. Nora tugged harder, and suddenly Fern lunged across the room and gave lunch to her chamber pot. She paused to rinse her mouth and then returned to grab the bed. "Again."

Nora protested, "You'll hurt yourself."

"Don't you tell me what to do, little miss," Fern snapped angrily. "I've been at this long enough to know what I'm doing. Now lace it tighter."

Finally, Fern nodded at Nora, gasping, "Okay. That's good." She nearly collapsed on the bed struggling to catch her breath. When she finally recovered, she directed Nora to help her position her bustle, a spring-loaded affair designed to ride low over the hips until the wearer needed to sit down. Then, the bustle lifted to allow its wearer's posterior to come in contact with a chair. The moment the wearer stood up, the bustle sprang back into position. Nora nearly shook with laughter at the ridiculous contraption. But she had to admit that when Fern was completely dressed, the bustle gave a pleasing line to her elaborate gown.

Nora was turning to go when Fern said abruptly, "You and Iris had a nice talk, did you?" When Nora didn't speak, Fern answered for her. "She told you about her little plan for a house in Denver, and all that. Well, let me tell you something, Nora. Hopes like that are what destroy women like you and me. Take my advice. Forget hope. Just take today. That's all you have. It's when hopes are disappointed that life gets dreary. So don't hope. I once read a description of a house like Goldie's that stuck with me. 'Bounded on the north by stumbling virtue, on the south by wrecked hopes, on the east by a miserably gray dawn of shame, and on the west by the sunset of dissipation'." Fern laughed sadly. "Once I realized how true that description was, I gave up hoping for anything different. This life is as regular as sunrise, and that's what gets me through the day. It ain't much, but lying about the future is worse. Don't think for a moment that some strong, classy rich man is going to come along and whisk you away from Goldie's. There's no grand mansion or vine-covered cottage with big roses growing all over it for Goldie's girls."

"I don't want any cottage with roses," Nora blurted out.

Fern nodded approvingly. "You remember what I said. Don't get false hopes. They'll kill you in the end. And don't bother with religion, either."

"My family didn't have any religion," Nora said.

"Good. Religion kills more good livin' than anything." Fern adjusted her bosom. While she talked, she leaned over to inspect her teeth in the mirror. She rubbed across them with her finger, then reapplied color to her lips. "I went to a meetin' once. Man got up and starts to tell us all that there's only one faith, and his is it. Next time I went to a meetin' there was another man telling me the same thing. Only his faith was different from the first. Now, tell me, what good is that?"

Fern turned around to face Nora. "Worst of it was, both

those preachers who claimed theirs was 'the only way' checked in at Goldie's the night after their meetin's was over. That was it for me. I say forget religion. Pay your way and don't be a hypocrite."

Nora nodded. "Yes, ma'am."

"Has Dr. Allbright given you her speech yet?"

"What speech?"

"Oh, the one about how this is no way for a woman to live and how she'll help you get out whenever you want."

Something kept Nora from confiding in Fern.

Seeing Nora's hesitation, Fern said, "That's all right, girlie. You don't have to say anything. If she hasn't gotten to you yet, she will. She says the same to all the girls. *Humph.* Self-righteous old bag. Ought to mind her own business."

Fern turned to examine herself in the mirror again. She reached for another pot on the dressing table and dabbed herself with powder. "Well, that's it for me I guess. You can see if the other girls need anything. Check with Pansy first. She's practically a half-wit, you know. I don't understand why Goldie keeps her around." Fern shoved past Nora and headed downstairs.

Nora could hear the tinkling of the piano as Shep warmed up his fingers. There was no particular melody to what he was playing, he simply progressed up and down the keyboard, going faster and faster. Nora moved on to Pansy's room.

"Oh, Nora," the girl panted. "I'll never be ready in time. And Lars said he would come tonight. I must look my best for Lars." Pansy stared into her dressing mirror. She had a dress in each hand and kept holding one up and then the other. "I can't decide. I can't decide." She seemed on the verge of tears.

Nora walked up behind Pansy and looked in the mirror. "Wear the red one. It makes your dark hair glow with red highlights."

"Really? Will Lars think I look beautiful in the red dress?"

Fern was right. Pansy was slow-witted. But she had maintained a sweetness that amazed Nora, considering her surroundings. Nora smiled at Pansy and patted her on the shoulder. "Here, Pansy, I'll put a red ribbon in your hair, too. And maybe this flower." Nora reached into the lid of Pansy's trunk for a ribbon rose. She held it up to Pansy's hair. "See? Won't that look nice?"

Pansy giggled. "Lars is going to propose to me tonight. He told me last week that the next time he came, he would ask me to be his wife. He's going up to Dakota Territory to homestead, and he's going to take me with him." Pansy whirled happily. "No more Goldie's for Pansy. Just a home and a husband." Her voice softened. "And maybe a baby. Dr. Allbright said it could happen. She said I'm healthy." Pansy's cheeks colored. "Lars said he wants lots of sons."

Nora's heart ached for the plump, simple-minded girl, who trusted a man's word and believed his promises for the future. *Maybe I'm more like Fern than I thought.*

By eleven o'clock, Goldie's girls had all descended to the Hall of Mirrors and another evening was in full swing. Nora worked behind the bar, grateful for the physical barrier between herself and Goldie's clientele. She did her best to smile and be nice, but she never stopped longing for the quiet of her little room off the kitchen.

Near midnight, Nora noticed Pansy casting nervous glances toward the front door. As it grew later and later, Pansy drooped visibly. By midnight, she was sitting in a corner by herself, her chin trembling with the effort of keeping back a flood of tears.

Goldie finally went to her, and laid a hand on her shoulder, and whispered something. Pansy shook her head and protested, but whatever Goldie had said finally resulted in the baby-faced girl rising and heading up the stairs.

Just as Pansy reached the landing, the doorbell rang. When Goldie opened the door, there was a shout of joy as Pansy rushed down the stairs and into the arms of a gigantic, blonde-haired man. He put his arm about Pansy's shoulder and held her close while he whispered something to Goldie. The trio disappeared down the back hall in the direction of the kitchen. When they emerged, Pansy's face was shining with joy. The man leaned over and kissed her on the cheek, then left. Pansy fairly bounced up the stairs.

It was nearly dawn when Nora was awakened by the sound of footsteps in the front hall. Her heart pounding, she tiptoed through the kitchen and peeked into the parlor. Fern stood at the bar, guzzling down whiskey. Nora cleared her throat. "Fern, is something wrong?"

Fern sneered at her. "What are you looking at?"

"I just heard something and came to check."

"Well, you've checked. Now get back to your little room. Or would you rather just move on in to my room right now? That's where you're headed, you know. Right up the ladder into my room. And out I go."

"Fern." Goldie stood on the front stairs. She spoke calmly, but the coldness in her voice frightened Nora. "I warned you before about your drinking. I won't have any boarders who can't hold their liquor. Get back to bed."

Fern grasped the whiskey bottle by the neck and waved it at Goldie. "Get yourself back to bed, Madame Meyer. I know what the score is around here. I know."

"You don't know anything. I don't have any plans to ditch you. Unless you start drinking again. Then you've done it to yourself. You know I won't have a drunk in my establishment."

Goldie came all the way down the stairs and stood, her arms folded. There was no hint of the warm southern accent that usually surfaced when Goldie was tired. Her eyes were cold, her face expressionless as she said, "Make up your mind, Fern. Put down the bottle or get out."

Fern wavered. "Oh, all right. Have it your way." She set the bottle down on the bar, threw back her shoulders, and started across the room. She stumbled and Nora went to help her, but Fern shoved her away. "I don't want your help, thank you very much." She drew herself up and said with drunken dignity, "I can take care of myself."

She made her way past Goldie and slowly up the stairs.

"Should I check on her?" Nora asked Goldie.

Goldie shook her head. "No. Let her take care of herself. If she can." Goldie turned to go back upstairs, then stopped and called to Nora, "Pansy is leaving this morning. Believe it or not, that big lummox Lars really does want to marry her. Would you set the table with the good dishes? I'm making a special farewell meal for her."

Nora hesitated before asking, "Do you think Pansy and Lars will—I mean, does Lars know—"

"—that she's simpleminded?" Goldie finished Nora's sentence. "Yes. And he seems to love her anyway." Goldie chuckled.

"I hope she's happy," Nora said.

Goldie smiled. "Yes. So do I. It happens rarely enough. It would be nice to see one of the girls truly happy." She hastened to add, "If one can call living in a shack on the prairie having babies happiness." She laughed nervously. "That certainly wouldn't be my definition of happiness. But it seems to suit poor, simpleminded Pansy."

Nora nodded and headed back to her room. Lying in bed, she was suddenly overwhelmed by a great feeling of sadness. The veneer Dr. Allbright had spoken of had been scratched, and Nora did not like what lurked beneath the surface.

CHAPTER 7

Life Goes On

There is no hope: no; for I have loved strangers,
and after them will I go.
Jeremiah 2:25

Nora had never had difficulty sleeping—until the night Goldie ordered Fern to "sober up or leave." That night, Nora tossed and turned through dreams where she alternately played the roles of Dr. Allbright, a madame, and a boarder. Frank Albers was there, too, fighting with Shep. There was no logical sequence of events. Instead, short bursts of bizarre activity played themselves out and then melded into other scenes. Even though she was asleep, Nora felt she were watching rather than participating in the events. *This is really stupid, I wish I'd wake up.* The thought would occur, and then another sequence of dreams would begin.

Nothing was frightening until the last dream, which seemed very real. Someone was shrieking so loudly that Nora jerked awake, terrified, only to realize the shrieks were filling the house, echoing from the upstairs hall down both stairways.

Nora stumbled out of bed and lunged up the back stairs. At the end of the hallway she stopped abruptly, panting. Near the front of the house, Goldie's girls were clustered in a little knot of humanity. They clung to one another, whispering just outside Fern's door.

Nora padded barefoot down the hallway. She intended to walk by them and go into Fern's room, but Iris reached out and tugged on the sleeve of her nightgown. "Don't, honey. There's no need for you to see what's in there."

Just then Goldie came out of the room, practically supporting a shaking, deathly white Lily. Nora reached out, wrapping her arm around Lily's waist.

Goldie turned to the clutch of girls and said, "You can all go downstairs and make some coffee. Shep's gone for the sheriff and Dr. Allbright. You can't do Fern any good standing up here in the hall shivering."

When no one moved, Goldie repeated herself. "Go on, now. Downstairs."

Iris pulled Ivy after her, holding the trembling girl's hand. The others followed, filing down the front stairs.

Lily began to sob violently. In spite of the support of Goldie and Nora, she sank to the floor. Goldie sat down next to her. Lily laid her head on Goldie's shoulder and reached for Nora, who took her hand.

"We had a fight," Lily sobbed. "An awful fight. I shouldn't have said those things." She moaned softly, pulling her hand away from Nora's covering her face. "I shouldn't have said those things." Lily dissolved in tears.

Nora patted Lily's shoulder while Goldie gathered the girl into her arms. "Don't do this to yourself, Lily. You didn't know Fern was over the edge." Goldie's voice mellowed, and her southern accent crept in. "We all know that Fern had seen bet-tuh days. She knew it was jus' a matter o' time. It wasn't your fault she hadn' saved up an' prepared. Fern made thousands o' dolluhs in her day. She could o' retired comfortably. But she let drinkin' get the best o' her. None o' that's yo' fault."

Lily shook her head. "But I made it worse. I just wanted to borrow that pink chiffon gown of hers for one night. She was so nasty about it. She called me terrible names, raged on and on about how we were all just counting the days, hoping she'd kick the bucket so we could divide all her things. I got so mad." Lily shuddered. In a hoarse half-whisper she said, "I told her if she was going to be so mean all the time, I hoped she did kick the bucket. I told her she was getting old and it wouldn't be long before you'd tell her to go anyway." Lily looked up at Goldie, tears streaming down her face. "I said I'd be glad when she was gone. That maybe we'd get someone nice in her place."

Goldie's expression hardened. "You didn' say anythin' Fern didn' already know. Fact is, I prob'ly woulda made Fern leave before too much longuh."

Goldie gently shook Lily by the shoulders. "And she was mean to y'all. She had no call to treat you bad. Fern was havin' hard times. So what? Ever'body has hard times."

Goldie nodded toward Nora, who noticed that the accent was fading as Goldie reasoned, "Look at Nora, here. She's had hard times. But she didn' get mean. She got out. She's making somethin' of herself. Fern had the chance to do the same thing. It's a shame she hung herself, but *she* did it. Not you. It's not your fault. People make all kinds of sloppy excuses for what they do. It just shows their weakness. I've never stood for excuses, and I won't make any excuses for Fern. I'm just glad she didn't shoot herself. That's an ugly way to die. And it sticks somebody else with a mess."

Goldie's final remark shocked Nora. She had never felt any particular affection for Fern, but it seemed incredibly sad for them to be sitting in the hallway just outside her room talking this way.

Goldie began to talk about who might be taking Fern's room. "Of course, I'll have it redone first."

Lily stopped crying and said that the least she could do was take care of Fern's things.

As Lily and Goldie talked, Nora looked over her shoulder toward Fern's little room. Morning light spilled through the doorway, leaving a small dapple of gold on the hallway floor. The aroma of coffee floated up the stairs. Nora thought about how all across town, people were climbing out of bed, getting dressed, and beginning a new day. Their lives would go on unaffected by the fact that at Goldie's Garden, Fern was dead.

Nora shivered thinking of the body that was still in that room. Was it still hanging there? Murmuring an excuse, she got up and went downstairs. The other girls were sitting around the table sipping coffee. Nora walked past them and into her little room off the kitchen. She closed the door and sat down on her bed. Burying her face in her pillow, she cried.

"You don't belong here."

Nora was standing in the alley behind Goldie's patting the neck of Dr. Allbright's horse when she heard the doctor's voice. She leaned her head against Casey's thin neck.

Dr. Allbright repeated. "I said, you don't belong here."

"I heard you." Nora patted the horse's neck again before turning around. Picking up her skirts, she climbed up on the stoop and sat down. She leaned over, putting her chin on her knees as she scratched meaninglessly in the dirt with a stick.

Dr. Allbright sat down beside her. "The undertaker's on his way," she said matter-of-factly. "He'll be coming through the back."

"I can handle that," Nora said.

"That's not what I meant when I said you don't belong here."

Nora twisted her neck and looked up at Dr. Allbright. "I know." She sighed and straightened up, arching her back and moving her feet back and forth in the gravel. "Is Lily all right?"

"She will be. Iris made her some tea. I gave her something to help her sleep."

"The others?" Nora asked.

"They're all in shock, like you. I think Goldie has them all gathered in the parlor, trying to come up with a service of some kind." The doctor shook her head sadly. "Shep will serve as the minister, I suppose. I think the sheriff has finally found a place for the burial."

Seeing Nora's puzzled expression, Dr. Allbright said quietly, "You don't think all the good Christians in Lincoln are going to want someone like Fern buried in their cemetery, do you?"

"Oh," Nora said. "I hadn't thought."

"Yes," Dr. Allbright said crisply. "I believe that's a good summary of your life in this city to date." She barely paused before saying, "May I suggest that you do some very thorough thinking now?"

Nora protested. "I'll never end up like Fern."

Dr. Allbright sighed deeply. "I pray to God not. And I'm not a praying woman." She reached over and patted the back of Nora's hand. "Do you think Fern expected her life to end this way when she was fifteen or sixteen?"

A wagon rounded the corner at the end of the block and headed up the alley. Dr. Allbright stood up. She went down the two back porch steps and led her horse up the alley a few feet, making room for the undertaker to pull his wagon up to the back door.

Nora stood up just as the sheriff stepped out the door. "Sam," he said, nodding to the driver of the wagon.

"Henry." The undertaker nodded back.

Goldie came out on the porch and handed Sam an envelope. "This should be enough for a respectable coffin," she said. "Red velvet for the lining. If you don't have red, send to Thornhill Dressers for a bolt. Elise will take care of it." Goldie motioned to Nora. "Come inside. The other girls are in the parlor. Stay there until I come for you."

The rest of the day was a blur of activity. The girls gathered for a melancholy farewell breakfast for Pansy. The minute the undertaker's wagon pulled away from the back door, they were all sent to get dressed. Lars arrived to claim his bride just as Shep pulled up at the back door driving Goldie's carriage. Behind him was a rented phaeton driven by a stranger. Goldie insisted that Pansy go with her fiancé, while the rest of the girls all piled into the two other vehicles. They drove off toward the south, waving good-bye to Pansy and Lars who headed north.

At the edge of town, the mourners were met by the undertaker, who now drove a team of four black horses pulling a hearse. A dark wooden coffin could be seen through the windows of the hearse. The three vehicles made their way south of Lincoln, to a small cemetery on the side of a hill. Someone had already dug a grave. While the girls stood by, Fern's casket was lowered into the grave. There were no flowers, and there was no minister. Shep read two verses of a song he knew Fern liked. That was all. The girls filed by the open grave, each one taking a handful of earth to sprinkle on the casket. They rode back to town in silence.

The girls ate an early supper. After the meal, Goldie stood up at the end of the table and said, "We all feel bad that Fern had to go out the way she did. But we did right by her. She had a respectable funeral. I've sent Shep to the florist for a mourning wreath, and he's going to hang it on the front door in Fern's memory. We won't be open tonight." Goldie paused for a moment, clearing her throat before she continued. "I'll not have you all tiptoeing past the door to Fern's room like it was some sort of shrine. I've been thinking how I can help you all get past this, and I've decided it would be fitting if you girls were the ones to take care of Fern's things. I'm putting Lily in charge and I want you all to go up there together and get the job done. It's not meant to disrespect Fern, but life goes on. So, go on up there and get started."

Violet asked, "You want us to go do it *now*?"

Even Lily protested. "But, Goldie—she's just in her grave. Don't you think we ought to wait at least a couple of days?"

Goldie shook her head. "No. I want it done right now. You girls just need to trust me that I know what's best. I don't want you haunted by this. We need to close the books on Fern and let her rest in peace."

Nora simply could not just "close the books on Fern." And she didn't think Fern could rest in peace, either. The way Goldie had handled things wasn't right. Nora had no particular creed from which to draw that conclusion, and yet something deep inside her knew that even Fern deserved something better than a hastily dug, unmarked grave.

A week after Fern's death, Nora decided that she was going to do something more. When she ran errands for Goldie on Saturday, she stopped at the undertaker's and made certain she knew the way to the cemetery where Fern was buried. At Herpolsheimer's she bought a length of the most beautiful red ribbon she could find. On Sunday, Nora went to the livery and rented a farm wagon. Climbing up onto the wagon seat, she couldn't help smiling to herself. Being raised on a farm was finally doing her some good. She could drive a wagon.

When Nora finally reached the little country cemetery, it was late afternoon. She spent nearly an hour walking along the field that joined the cemetery, collecting stones, each one about the size of a potato. When she had a pile of stones by Fern's grave, she collected a huge bouquet of wildflowers, tying it with the red ribbon.

To complete her task, Nora knelt beside the fresh grave and used stones to spell the name F-E-R-N. Once the name was spelled, Nora laid the bouquet above it. She stood up, brushing the dirt off her skirt, wishing she knew something appropriate to say.

Swallowing hard, she finally spoke aloud. "I hope you're in a better place, Fern. I know it was hard for you down here. I'm sorry for the way things ended up." Looking up, Nora said, "God, you and I don't know each other much. But I thought you'd want to know about Fern. I marked her resting place. So now I guess she's all yours." Nora paused uncertainly. Something was missing. She remembered hearing her neighbor Mrs. Johnson pray at a church picnic once. What had she said when she was finished? "Oh," Nora said. "And hay-men."

She lingered for a little while in the cemetery, reading headstones, wishing she could have done better for Fern. Finally, she climbed back up into the wagon seat and headed for Lincoln. The setting sun shed a rosy glow on everything in sight. Nora wondered if the sunset meant that God thought that she had done a good thing.

It was dark when Nora finally returned the horse and wagon to the livery. She hurried up the block and ducked into the alley that ran just east of the row of buildings where Goldie's was located. She was humming to herself when someone stumbled out of the shadows and grabbed her. A gritty hand clamped over her mouth as a man threw his weight at her and pinned her against a brick wall.

In spite of the dark, Nora recognized Frank Albers. His breath testified to the fact that he had spent far too much time in a saloon, but he sounded frighteningly sober as he leaned close to Nora and said, "Thought you got away with it, didn't you?"

"What?" Nora gasped. "What are you talking about?"

"You know what I'm talking about," he sneered. "I heard

Lily laughing about it. She was uptown today. Telling some friend of hers the whole story about how she and a friend of hers made a fool of Frank Albers." He belched before continuing, "As long as she kept quiet, I was ready to forget it. But I won't have anyone spreading garbage about me to anyone." He slammed Nora's head against the wall. "Anyone. You hear?"

"I wouldn't," Nora gasped. "I didn't. Please. I won't ever say—"

"You got that right," Frank said. There was the glint of steel as Frank laid the blade of a huge knife against Nora's throat.

At the touch of the cold steel against her neck, Nora gathered all her strength and brought up one knee as hard as she could. She didn't quite hit her target, but Frank was caught off guard enough that he let go of her momentarily. In an instant, Nora pulled away from him and was running up the alley. She let out one desperate cry for help before Frank caught her from behind, dragging her down to the ground by her skirt.

Nora heard tearing fabric and felt him kick her before a voice called out of the darkness. "Let her go." Frank refused to relent. The voice in the darkness spat out the order. "I said, let her go. I have a gun and I know how to use it."

Rage and intent to do evil deafened Frank to the warning in the voice. He slapped Nora across the face. She felt searing pain across her left side as he punched her midsection. She nearly fainted, but not before she heard the other voice shout again. There was a loud sound and then, suddenly, Frank was no longer sitting on her legs. Dr. Allbright was kneeling by her, laying two fingers on her neck, asking, "Nora, can you hear me?"

"Yes," Nora gasped. She tried to sit up, but excruciating pain prevented it.

Dr. Allbright pushed her gently back to the earth. "Lay still. I can't tell a thing in the dark. Wait until I get some help to get you inside."

"Frank? What—"

Dr. Allbright stood up. "Henry," she said firmly, "I've killed Frank Albers. I'm not sorry and I'd do it again in similar circumstances. Here's my gun. Can you wait to arrest me until I tend to this poor girl? Help me carry her up to Goldie's, will you?"

Nora closed her eyes and tried to keep from fainting. She pulled air into her lungs in short bursts, struggling against the pain that accompanied each tiny gasp. She realized the sheriff must be examining Frank's body.

"Well, well, Maude," he said, clucking his tongue. "See that? It's loaded. Appears to me this is a case of self-defense, pure and simple. I don't think I'll be hauling you off to jail."

The sheriff crouched down next to Nora. "Now, miss, I've got to carry you up to Goldie's where Dr. Allbright can tend to you. I'm sorry to have to hurt you."

It really didn't hurt much. In fact, it was the next morning before Nora knew it hurt at all, because she passed out the minute the sheriff bent to help her up.

CHAPTER 8

Bombazine and Black Jet

Hath God forgotten to be gracious?
hath he in anger shut up his tender mercies?
Psalm 77:9

"I'm sorry this has to be so painful," Dr. Allbright was saying, "but I don't want to run the risk of your becoming dependent on morphine."

"It's all right," Nora mumbled through her swollen lips. She wondered how long she had been drifting in and out of sleep. Was it just hours, or days? She didn't have the energy to ask.

Dr. Allbright seemed to sense the question. "It's Tuesday morning. You got hurt Sunday night. Don't be frightened if you don't remember. That's normal. You're going to feel awful for quite a few days to come. Don't fight it. Let your body rest and heal. You endured quite a beating, but you're going to be fine."

Nora had already drifted off to sleep before Dr. Allbright finished her reassurance. The next time she opened her eyes, Lily and Iris were standing over her, concern etched into their faces. Nora tried to smile, wondering if both sides of her mouth were even moving.

Iris pulled up a chair and sat down next to the bed. "Where'd you go so late, Nora?"

Closing her eyes and frowning she thought back. "Fern. Took Fern some flowers."

"Oh, honey, that was nice. Real nice."

Lily spoke up. "Guess you wonder what really happened. It was Frank. He must have been laying for us both. We don't have to worry about him anymore."

Nora raised her hand to her face, laying her open palm against her swollen cheek. Iris nodded. "Several shades of purple. And your eye's swollen shut. Dr. Allbright had to take a few stitches, but they're right along your hairline and I don't think the scar will show much at all." Iris barely touched Nora's hair along her left temple. "She left it open to the air. Said it would heal better that way."

Nora reached up and carefully felt for the stitches. It was numb along the line her finger traced. She hoped Iris was being truthful, that it wasn't a very long row of thread.

"Dr. Allbright said none of the bones in your face are broken," Lily offered. "But you're going to be a walking rainbow for a while." Lily paused awkwardly. "I'm going to get you some tea, Nora. You want some?"

Nora shook her head, but Lily was already gone. Iris sat holding her hand, and Nora could not bear the compassion on her face. It made her cry again. What was wrong with her anyway? It seemed like everything made her cry. She hated being a crybaby. And besides, the broken ribs made it hurt.

As Nora's tears slid out the corners of her eyes and into the hair at her temples, Iris took up one of her hands, squeezing it affectionately. "It's all right. Go ahead and cry. It must have been awful."

Nora winced against the pain in her midsection as she tried to control her sobs. Through swollen lips she managed to whisper, "Hurts terrible."

"I know it does. I had broken ribs once."

Nora opened her eyes, blinking to clear her vision. Iris nodded her head. "You know how it is. The men are the masters. We do what they say. Period. Well, one time—and only one—I made the mistake of refusing." She called the man a name. "He broke two of my ribs."

The thought of Iris being hurt made Nora start to cry again. Lily came back in with tea, but Nora only shook her head.

"Why don't you leave the two of us alone for a few minutes?" Iris said to Lily. "I want to have a little talk with Nora."

Lily left, visibly relieved to have an excuse to escape.

Iris got up and closed Nora's door. Sitting down again, she began, "This thing with Fern, and now you, has got me thinking. I don't have quite as much saved up as I would like, but there's enough for a start out in Denver. I can take in laundry or do whatever else I have to do to make ends meet. I'm finished with this life."

She put her hand on Nora's shoulder. "Don't answer right now. But think on it. If you decide you want to come with me, I'll wait until you're better."

Iris stroked Nora's forehead tenderly. Nora took a breath and let it out slowly. She wanted to whisper her thanks, but she didn't have the energy. Iris kissed her on the cheek and left the room.

Dr. Allbright came daily for the first week, urging Nora to get up and move around as soon as she could bear it. "The longer you stay in bed, the weaker you'll become and the longer it will take you to fight your way back."

At each visit, Nora struggled to keep from crying. She felt as if she had done nothing since that dreadful night but cry and wince from pain. The girls took turns helping her drink soup and tea. Every kindness brought more tears. Unexpected noises made her jump with fright. She braced a broom handle in the window sashing, but it wasn't enough. She could not sleep at night until she had braced a chair beneath the doorknob on her side of the door.

When Nora made her first efforts to shuffle out of her room, Goldie saw it as a triumph. She sent Shep to the store for a luxurious treat. "You ever had fresh orange juice, honey? No? Well, just wait until you taste it. It's a little bit of heaven."

Nora nodded. She had bitten her tongue in the struggle with Frank, and the orange juice made it sting. Still, she had to agree with Goldie that orange juice tasted good.

Days passed. Nora wanted to sleep late, but found that she couldn't. She developed the routine of making herself breakfast while the house was quiet. By the time the girls awoke, Nora was ready for a nap. In the afternoon, she took a walk. At first, the walk was simply to the back porch and then to the kitchen table where, trembling with weakness, she would manage to gulp a cup of coffee before creeping back to bed.

The evenings were the worst. When the girls were busy at work, the house echoed with noise. Shep played the piano by the hour; there was laughter and the sound of footsteps clomping up and down the stairs. One day, Goldie asked Nora what her favorite color was. Having heard that Fern's room was being redone, Nora wondered if Goldie was going to invite her to move upstairs. The thought made her ill.

Nora floated from day to day, making progress physically, but in suspended animation emotionally. Every time she saw Goldie coming her way, a sense of dread loomed up. She began to feel the same way about Iris. Some days, she thought she would simply resign herself to life as a boarder and get it over with. Then, she would think about Denver. Sometimes she even wished she was back on the farm with Pap and Will.

Goldie assured Nora she would "cheer up directly." Dr. Allbright said that healing would take time. But as the days passed, and her sense of confusion and despair grew, Nora began to doubt that she would ever feel better.

When Nora finally felt well enough to get dressed and take a carriage ride, Goldie had Shep drive her to Thornhill Dressers. "Pick out something for a new dress, Nora. Something that'll cheer you up."

Nora nodded and mumbled a thank-you. Although she was no longer frightened by Lincoln's busy streets, Nora still spent the ride to the dressmaker's fighting back tears. Goldie's idea that a new dress could fix what was wrong inside of her only made her sadness worse.

When Shep lifted her down from the carriage and deposited her on the boardwalk, Nora stumbled against him, gasping for breath. She reached for him and put a hand on his shoulder to steady herself.

"Hey," Shep said tenderly. "If this is too much for you—"

"No," Nora said. "I'm all right. It just hurt a little more than

I expected. I'll be fine. I'm not going to miss a chance to get a new dress."

Shep chuckled. "That's my girl."

Nora looked up at him sharply. Was Shep actually blushing? He was looking down at her with an odd expression on his face. Nora realized that beneath his beard, Shep wasn't all that old. She had never noticed.

Shep cleared his throat nervously. "You've been through some bad business, Nora. I guess I know that getting a new dress isn't going to fix things." He put his hand on the side of the carriage and, removing his hat, took a deep breath. "What I wanted to say was, Goldie expects me to keep an eye on things. I wish I would have been there when that happened. I wish I could have stopped it."

Nora felt herself blushing. She blinked back the tears that were welling up in her eyes and managed to croak, "Thank you." Then, she headed inside Thornhill Dressers.

Miss Thornhill directed Nora to the corner of the studio where the three-way mirrors stood. It was the first time Nora had looked in a mirror since that awful night. Dr. Allbright had taken the stitches out, but turning her head Nora saw that an angry red line ran nearly the entire length of the left side of her hairline and then to her cheekbone. Iris had been wrong. There would be a scar, and it would show. She reached up to touch the welt. Her eye was no longer swollen shut, but the skin on the left side of her face was still a sickly greenish-yellow color with some rings of darker red still apparent around her eye.

Miss Thornhill cleared her throat. "My sister said you were to have anything you wanted, Miss O'Dell. From what I can see, you should spend her money liberally."

Nora cupped her hand over the injured side of her face. "It wasn't her fault," she said loyally.

"I didn't say it was," Miss Thornhill snapped back. "But I know my sister's affairs pretty well, and I also know she isn't given to fits of generosity often. So let's get you something really wonderful while Goldie's in a spending mood. She can afford it and you deserve it. What's your favorite color?"

"I don't—know," Nora said. After a moment's hesitation, she replied, "Green, I guess."

Elise pulled down three bolts of green fabric, each one a different shade. Holding the fabric up to Nora's face, she shook her head. "I'm afraid green isn't the right color. At least not right now. It makes your face look like death."

Nora looked in the mirror. Miss Thornhill was right. One of the bolts of fabric matched her bruised skin almost perfectly. "I look like a pickle—bumps and lumps included," she said.

Miss Thornhill chuckled. "A good analogy. However," she said, grabbing another bolt of cloth, "if we ignore your pickled skin and concentrate on your eyes, I can see why you like green."

"I guess I hadn't really thought about that," Nora said. "I just like green." She was beginning to feel weak. "Would you mind if I sit down for just a minute?" She apologized. "I haven't been out much, and—"

Miss Thornhill's voice was warm with kindness. "I'm sorry. I should have thought about that. I'm going to get you some tea. You sit right there." She directed Nora to the plush chair beside the fireplace and disappeared into the workroom.

Once again, Nora fought against the tears that seemed to flow so freely.

Nora was wiping her eyes when Miss Thornhill returned with tea. True concern sounded in her voice as she asked, "Is there anything I can do for you, Miss O'Dell?"

Nora took the tea and shrugged, embarrassed. "Not unless you can come up with a cure for being a crybaby. I can't seem to do anything lately but cry. I don't know what's wrong with me. It isn't like me. I'm usually pretty tough. But not lately. I cry when I hurt. I cry when I go to sleep. Now, it seems, I cry when someone is nice to me, too." She set the cup of tea down and bent her head, rubbing her forehead with the tips of her fingers.

Miss Thornhill said gently, "Don't be so demanding of yourself." She hesitated before saying, "There's a promise that I return to often that says, 'Wait on the LORD: be of good courage, and he shall strengthen thine heart.' Have you tried asking the Lord for strength? It always helps me."

Nora frowned slightly. "You mean, like he was a real person or something?"

"Of course," Miss Thornhill said with a smile. "He *is* a real person. Maybe not flesh and blood like you and me, but He certainly cares about our problems. And He listens when we talk to Him."

Nora shook her head doubtfully. "Maybe he cares about you, but he sure doesn't spend much time worrying about the likes of me."

Miss Thornhill replied, "I understand why you would feel that way. I don't know why you've had such a hard time, but I know God does love you." She guided the conversation back to Nora's new dress. "You know, I think I have something you'll like in the back. If you'll just relax and enjoy your tea, I'll bring it out." She went back to the workroom.

Just as Miss Thornhill disappeared through the doorway the bell on the back door rang. Nora heard Lucy and Hannah chattering and laughing. They came into the studio together and greeted Nora.

Lucy spoke first. "Heard about what happened. I'm awful sorry."

"Me, too," Hannah agreed. Then she said quickly, "You don't look half as bad as I expected."

Nora smiled weakly. "Thank you. I think."

Miss Thornhill came out of the workroom with a bolt of cloth in her arms. "Hannah. Lucy. Pull out my box of special buttons."

Nora's eyes grew wide as Miss Thornhill spread out a length of fabric. "Oh," she said softly. She reached out to touch it. "It's so soft." She gathered some of it up in her hands. Looking at Elise, she said, "It makes a real pretty bustle, I bet."

"Yes," Miss Thornhill agreed. "You're quite right. This manufacturer has a special way with the weaving process. This is called bombazine. Most are cotton and worsted, and have a dull surface. But this manufacturer combines silk and wool. That's what gives it the twilled surface. And it does drape more gracefully."

Nora shook her head. "It's far too nice for me. Where would I ever wear it?"

" 'Get the gown and the occasion will present itself,' " Miss Thornhill said. She winked. "Don't you think that's a good motto for a dressmaker?"

Nora smiled. "Yes, I suppose it is. But I don't think—"

"I'll tell you what," Miss Thornhill said. "Let's go ahead and get you measured. You can be thinking about it while I do your fitting."

In the end, Nora could not resist the bombazine. She selected black corded silk trim. When Miss Thornhill insisted that Nora sort through her personal "stash," of buttons, she selected a set of tiny jet buttons.

"Those will be just perfect," Miss Thornhill said. "I insist you take them. As a gift from me." She smiled. "I won't even charge Goldie for them."

. "What about a hat?" Lucy wanted to know.

"Oh, no," Nora protested. "Goldie didn't say anything about a hat."

"There'll be enough left from cutting out the dress to make something nice," Lucy said convincingly. "It really won't cost that much more."

"I'm certain Goldie expected we'd make a hat," Miss Thornhill agreed, pulling out a lightweight buckram frame. "I think this base would be perfect. It really does compliment an oval face. Here, try it."

"How do you turn this little thing into a hat?" Nora wanted to know. She put the frame on her head, wincing a little as she stretched her arms upward. The hat frame featured a short, squarish crown. The brim was narrower at the back to allow for an abundance of curls in the wearer's coiffure, then the brim curved around the side of the head and grew wider over the forehead.

"Here, I'll show you," Lucy said. "We cover the frame with fabric—in your case the bombazine. With a black velvet bow on this side, and a black ostrich feather curving up across the top, it'll be stunning." She indicated the underside of the front brim. "I'll gather some dark purple moiré here."

Nora shook her head. "It's too much."

"Perhaps you're right," Miss Thornhill interrupted. "Simpler is sometimes better." She handed the hat frame to Lucy and returned her attention to the dress fabric. "You know, Miss O'Dell, you have a good fashion sense. You were right about that one trim I pulled out. What you selected is much more in keeping with the feel of the bombazine. And you knew the moment you saw them that those jet buttons were right."

The bell on the shop door rang. Nora started and turned away from the door, hoping to hide the bruised side of her face.

"Oh," the gentleman said. "I see you're busy. I can come back."

"No, no, Mr. Chandler. It's quite all right. Please. Come in," Miss Thornhill insisted.

Nora had learned a great deal about judging men from behind the bar at Goldie's. Viewing Mr. Chandler in the dressing mirrors, she thought that here was one who was very well aware of the effect he had on women. He was clean shaven except for a thick, blonde mustache. Almost a goatee, the mustache drooped down both sides of his mouth, framing a well-formed chin. Nora took note of brilliant blue eyes and an aristocratic nose. And, when he removed his hat, thick, curly blonde hair.

The man glanced her way. Quickly, Nora lifted a gloved hand to hide her cheek. Hoping her demeanor was realistic, she said, "Miss Thornhill, if you don't mind, I'll have a cup of tea with Lucy and Hannah before we proceed with my fitting." She kept her face turned away from the stranger as she got up. Brushing her hand across the bombazine, she said, "This will be lovely."

Miss Thornhill rose to the occasion. "Thank you, Miss O'Dell. I appreciate your patience. Mr. Chandler did have an appointment. Are you certain you can wait?"

"Of course," Nora said. Making her way across the shop, she nodded at Mr. Chandler. Back in the workroom, she sank gratefully into a chair.

Hannah and Lucy were beside themselves. "Is it really Mr. Chandler? Did you see him?"

"Miss Thornhill called him Mr. Chandler. Why?"

"Oh," Lucy said, "I wish I had some excuse to go out there. To see for myself."

"Well," Nora said, "I suppose you could make a case for getting the cloth for my dress."

Lucy smiled in triumph. "Of course!" She patted Nora on the shoulder. "Perfect." Lucy took a deep breath. She looked at herself in the mirror, smoothing her hair, pinching her cheeks. She clasped her hands before her, closed her eyes, and took a few deep breaths. Then, she went into the studio.

She was back in a moment, flushed with excitement. Clutching Nora's bolt of cloth in her arms, she whirled happily about the room. "It *is* him! It is! He's talking to Miss Thornhill about making a special costume for the theatrical troupe. That means he'll have to come back. Oh, wait until the girls at meeting hear about this. They'll just die from envy. They'll just die."

"And wait until Mr. Fielding hears about it," Hannah teased.

"Oh, Hannah, you wouldn't!" Lucy exclaimed.

Hannah shook her head. "Of course not. Unless I need to blackmail you sometime."

"Oh, you!" Lucy shot back. "You know I like Adam Fielding better than anything. But, Hannah," she sighed. "Greyson *Chandler,* for heaven's sake! And in the *next room!*"

Nora was beginning to feel shaky. When was Shep coming for her? Listening to Lucy and Hannah chatter taught her more about Greyson Chandler than she ever wanted to know. Apparently this was an important person who came to Lincoln infrequently. He was an actor. A famous one. Everyone knew that he and Mamie Patterson were lovers. That's how they could play their love scenes so convincingly.

Nora's back was beginning to hurt, she was hungry, and she needed a nap. Neither Lucy nor Hannah showed much inclination to get on with her dress fitting. She wanted to leave, but she didn't want to go through the studio to look for Shep. She might not be a fan of Greyson Chandler, but she didn't want any stranger staring at her green and yellow face.

Finally, she heard the bell on the front door ring. Shep. She practically sighed with relief. Making her way to the studio, she was dismayed to see a stranger closing the shop door and heading across the street. Nora's knees were wobbly. She began shaking. She was too afraid of fainting now to worry about hiding her face. It took all her concentration to keep her head erect and take another step toward the workroom. *Oh, Lord, am I going to faint?* Suddenly, someone was at her side, taking her arm, helping her to a chair. Nora closed her eyes and took a deep breath. When she opened them, a very handsome man with incredibly blue eyes was offering her a glass of water.

"Thank you." She closed her eyes as she drank the water, feeling her cheeks go crimson. Had she believed in the power of prayer at that moment, she would have prayed fervently for Miss Thornhill's floor to open up and swallow her.

Miss Thornhill was there, too, patting her shoulder. "I've sent Hannah for Mr. Roberts, Miss O'Dell. We can do the fitting another day. I'll reserve that bolt of cloth for you."

"Please accept my apologies for making you wait so long," Chandler said. "I feel responsible for the delay. You've obviously been convalescing. I should have waited."

Nora wasn't certain what "convalescing" meant, but she knew that Chandler had seen her bruised face. Unconsciously she lifted her gloved hand to her cheek. "I'm better now."

Shep drove up. Nora pushed herself up from the chair, only to find her head swimming again. Greyson Chandler took the opportunity to live up to his reputation as a dashing rescuer of distressed damsels. With a quick apology for "taking the liberty," he swept Nora up in his arms just as Shep was opening the door. The two men's eyes met. Shep laughed. "Still up to your old tricks, I see," he said.

"This one's yours?" Chandler asked. In spite of Nora's weak protests, Chandler carried her out the door and deposited her in the carriage.

Then he turned toward Shep, slapping him on the back and shaking his hand. "Well, you old scalawag. What are you doing all the way up here? I thought you were never leaving New Orleans."

"And I thought you were going to be a famous symphony conductor," Shep retorted, shoving his hat back on his head.

"Just goes to show," Chandler said, laughing, "what fools we both were a few years back."

The two men arranged to have a drink together later that evening. Chandler turned toward Nora. "Are you all right, Miss O'Dell?" When Nora nodded, he directed one last jab at Shep. "I'd say she's a 'keeper.' "

He turned quickly back to Nora. "No disrespect intended, ma'am."

Nora couldn't be certain, but she thought Chandler winked at her.

71

CHAPTER 9

A Lost Lamb

A man's heart deviseth his way: but the LORD
directeth his steps.
Proverbs 16:9

When Dr. Maude Allbright pulled her white gelding up to the back door of Thornhill Dressers and knocked at the workroom door, Lucy and Hannah were still in a state of profound excitement over Greyson Chandler's visit. Lucy blurted out the story of Nora O'Dell's encounter with the famous actor. "Can you believe it? He actually picked her up and carried her. Oh," Lucy sighed, "isn't that *romantic?*"

Dr. Allbright removed her hat and plunked it down on the workroom table. "I suppose so. If you like blond-haired fops who masquerade as talented actors and think they can have the world because they can spout a few lines of Shakespeare."

Dr. Allbright marched into Miss Thornhill's studio.

"The girls said that Nora O'Dell was here. How is she doing? I mean to call on her later."

Miss Thornhill shook her head. "She had a little fainting spell."

Dr. Allbright asked, "Did she seem melancholy to you? I know she's going to be fine physically. But I'm concerned about her in other ways."

"I know what you mean. There is something—something that

72

a new dress isn't going to heal," Miss Thornhill said. She sighed. "She does *not* belong at Goldie's. I wish my sister would admit that. If ever I saw a little lost lamb, that girl is one. She makes you just want to put your arms around her and mother her."

"*Humph,*" Dr. Allbright replied. "That's where you and I are different. You want to mother everyone and introduce them to the Almighty. I want to give them a shake and tell them to get on with life."

"But I don't think Nora is pretending so we'll feel sorry for her."

Dr. Allbright grimaced. "I didn't mean Nora." She sighed. "But it is getting so I see so many pampered, hysterical women, I hardly know what to do when I encounter one who is honestly traumatized."

Miss Thornhill said, "I know you won't approve, Dr. Allbright, but I'm thinking of inviting Nora to go to church with me. She needs to know that God loves her."

Maude replied testily, "And if God loves her so much, where was He that night Frank Albers was beating the tar out of her?"

Miss Thornhill smiled. "I've wondered about that. Didn't you tell me there was something odd about that night?"

Maude frowned slightly. "Yes. There was. It wasn't my usual night to call at Goldie's. Something—" She stopped and held up her hand. "Don't start."

Miss Thornhill nodded. "Yes. That's what you said. Something just seemed to head you over that way. And you'd taken Casey to be shod, and had to walk, so you tucked the gun in your bag—at the last minute—almost as an afterthought."

"Are you trying to tell me that my being in that alley with a gun was an act of God?"

Miss Thornhill smiled.

"That's drivel," Maude said. "It was just a fortunate coincidence. If there *were* a God involved in people's affairs, surely he would have intervened before that poor girl got hurt."

Elise said quietly, "Perhaps Nora needed something shocking to happen to move her in a different direction." She looked at Dr. Allbright. "Some people are uniquely stubborn, you know—present company excluded, of course."

While they talked, Miss Thornhill had been pulling bolts of cloth down from the shelf.

"Well," Dr. Allbright interjected, "I'll agree with you that it was fortunate for Nora that I was in that alley. But as to it being God who put me there, don't you think he would have used one of his own instead of an old infidel like me?"

Miss Thornhill turned to the fabric on the table. "See anything you like?"

Dr. Allbright thumped three bolts. "Brown. Gray. Black. One of each."

"Do you want me to use the same pattern?" Miss Thornhill asked. "*Peterson's* is showing a return of the high bustle for next year."

"I doubt a single fashion editor of *Peterson's* has ever had to drive a rig twenty miles at breakneck speed in the dead of Nebraska winter," Dr. Allbright said. "If they had, they wouldn't be trying to resurrect anything so ridiculous as that. I declare, I saw a bustle yesterday a person could set a tea tray on." She shook her head. "I'm not objecting to a little feminine fullness at the back, you understand, but let's do be sensible."

"What about the sleeves?" Miss Thornhill wanted to know. "They're more puffed this season . . . and the cuffs can be quite exaggerated."

"Oh, good," Dr. Allbright said dryly. "Bigger cuffs. Just the thing for facilitating an appendectomy." She chuckled. "No. Just cut three of the same old thing, and never mind *The Delineator,* or *Peterson's.*" Dr. Allbright headed for the opposite corner of the shop. "Now," she said, briskly rubbing her hands together, "let's talk hats."

She may not have been a slave to fashion, but Dr. Maude Allbright was definitely a slave to hats. She could order three new suits in less than ten minutes, but she spent the next two hours looking over sketches and selecting fabric and trims for three new hats.

"Every red-tailed hawk in the county will be dive-bombing me if I wear that," she scoffed, pointing to a French creation sporting three gray birds perched on the crown. "I like the shape, though. Can you make a tower of posies or something at the front instead of the dead birds?"

"What color?"

"How about something salmony-pink—with brown trim to go with the brown suit?" Turning the pages of Miss Thornhill's *Fashion Guide,* Dr. Allbright pointed to a large-brimmed hat entirely camouflaged in felt-gray plumes and curled blue and yellow striped ribbon. "Make this one to go with the gray suit. And that"—Dr. Allbright pointed to another gigantic hat— "that to go with the black."

She finished her order and said abruptly, "Now. What do you think might be done to help Miss Nora O'Dell?"

An hour later, Elise Thornhill walked Dr. Allbright to her carriage behind the shop. As Dr. Allbright took up the reins, she nodded. "Thank you, Elise, talking with you always renews my hope in humanity. Now, if the humanity in question will only do what we say, I think we'll have done some good."

"Let's pray that she listens," Miss Thornhill said, stepping away from the carriage.

"I'll leave the praying to you," Dr. Allbright said. "I think God hung up on me long, long ago." She slapped the reins across her gelding's flanks and set off up the alley.

Nora was attempting to sweep the kitchen floor at Goldie's when Miss Thornhill came to the back door.

"Goldie's not here right now," Nora said. "But if you want to wait, I can make you some coffee."

Miss Thornhill replied, "Thank you, but I just had lunch. I don't need any coffee. Actually, I came to see you." She reached into her bag and withdrew a measuring tape, notebook, and pencil. "I'm glad to see you're feeling better. If I can take a few measurements, Hannah and Lucy can get started cutting out your new gown."

"I've been thinking about that," Nora said doubtfully. "I really shouldn't be getting anything so fancy."

"Are we back to that again?" Miss Thornhill asked. While she talked, she draped the measuring tape about her shoulders. "Well, I'll tell you what. I need the same measurements whether

I'm making a dress from a potato sack or bombazine, so let's get started anyway."

Smiling softly, Nora set the broom aside. "All right."

"I don't use ready-made patterns, and with today's styles, the measurements have to be very exact. Shall we remove to your room?"

In her room, Nora stripped down to only three petticoats and her chemise. Miss Thornhill began to take measurements. "With all those numbers you'll be able to build an entire new me."

Finally, Miss Thornhill wrote the last measurement in her notebook. Snapping it shut, she headed for the kitchen. "I'll make coffee. I believe I would like some now."

Nora winced as she pulled her dress over her head. She was buttoning the last button at her neckline when Miss Thornhill called from the stove, "It's good to see you feeling so much better. We've been worried about you."

"Worried? About me?"

"Lucy and Hannah both took a liking to you," Miss Thornhill said matter-of-factly.

"They were nice to me, even if I was out of sorts." Nora tied her apron about her waist and joined Elise in the kitchen. "I bet they have some good times together."

Elise thought Nora sounded like a child standing outside a store window wishing for a piece of candy she knew she could not have. She poured two cups of coffee and settled into a chair at the kitchen table. "Yes, they do. They share a room at a boardinghouse a few blocks from the shop. Most of the time, they are inseparable. They attend the same church, too. Perhaps you'd like to go with them sometime." Elise didn't wait for Nora to react to the mention of church. "They can be a bit much at times—especially when Greyson Chandler *himself* comes into the shop!" Miss Thornhill imitated Lucy, clasping her hands before her and sighing.

Nora said, "I wanted to roll up into a ball and die from embarrassment." She smiled faintly. "It helped a little that Shep knows him." She set down her coffee and said abruptly. "I'm feeling better. At least I'm not such a crybaby."

Elise asked, "Is that because you really *are* better? Or because you're getting better at hiding your true feelings?"

Nora shrugged. "Nobody wants to be around a crybaby all the time."

"Are you happy here at Goldie's?"

Nora looked away. "It's all right."

Miss Thornhill cleared her throat. She lifted her eyebrows toward the second floor. "Do you see yourself up there?"

"Lily and Iris have done all right."

"What about Fern?"

"Fern was stupid. She didn't plan ahead."

"Are you planning ahead? Is this where you want to be when you get old?"

Nora sounded defensive. "Up 'til now, I never planned anything—except getting away from my pap. But I'm learning fast." She reached up to touch her bruised face.

Miss Thornhill set down her coffee cup. "Perhaps you could make some plans of your own before Goldie does it for you." She paused, pointing a finger to the ceiling and asked again, "Is that where you want to end up?"

Goldie's steps sounded in the front hall. Miss Thornhill called out a greeting, and Goldie joined them in the kitchen, pouring herself a cup of coffee, and joining Nora and Elise at the table.

Nora was amazed when Miss Thornhill said, "Goldie knows that I love her. She also knows I hate what she does. And I hate what becomes of most of the girls who stay with her."

Goldie interrupted. "And Elise knows that I see no particular value in becoming a poor drudge just to gain the respect of people I don't give a hoot for."

Miss Thornhill didn't seem to mind Goldie's comparing dressmaking to drudgery. She continued talking to Nora, "Not a day goes by that I don't pray that God will reach out and grab Goldie—by the throat, if necessary—and turn her life back around."

Goldie interrupted dryly, "I'll be certain to tell Reverend you-know-who that you shared the faith with me when he stops in next time."

"Oh, Goldie," Miss Thornhill sighed. "You keep making the

same mistake over and over again. You know there are snake oil salesmen, but you still trust Dr. Allbright to care for the girls. So why does Reverend Cooper's hypocrisy make you deny Christ? The existence of men like him doesn't mean that what Christ said and what He did have no meaning, any more than quacks negate the good of true medicine."

Goldie waved her hand in the air. "All right, Elise. All right. Point taken. But, let's finish up here. I know you're trying to talk Nora into leaving behind this dreaded life of sin and woe." Goldie mocked her sister without bitterness or anger.

Miss Thornhill removed the measuring tape that was still draped about her neck and began to fold it up. She waited until the tape was tucked back into her bag before looking at Nora. "Do you remember what I said the other day about your having a knack for fashion?" She pulled the drawstring on her bag tight as she said, "Would you be interested in coming to work for me?"

"At the Dressers?"

Miss Thornhill nodded. "After you left, Mr. Chandler presented me with the opportunity to do some regular work for his theatrical troupe. When I realized how large the troupe is, I also realized that I will need more help if I accept his proposal. Even before that, I was considering expanding the millinery part of my business."

"But I don't know very much about sewing."

"Goldie told me you've been helping the girls with their mending."

Nora shrugged. "That's just poke in the needle and take a few stitches. What you do is—art—compared to that."

"Everyone has to start some place," Miss Thornhill said. "All it takes is enthusiasm and interest. I can teach you the rest. My old apartment over the shop is empty. It was too small for both Lucy and Hannah. But I'd like knowing there was someone on the premises. It's not fancy, but it's available."

"You'd trust me to live upstairs? You barely know me."

Goldie interrupted. "We know you well enough."

"Yes." Miss Thornhill nodded. "You didn't take the pennies."

"What?"

Goldie explained. "Do you remember when I told you I'm a good judge of character? Well, I don't just trust my instincts with new girls. Sometimes I give them a little test to find out if I'm going to have to worry about them stealing me blind behind my back. Remember that day when we talked about you being a housekeeper instead of a cook?"

Nora nodded.

"Do you remember your first assignment?"

"You had me clean Ivy's room to see if I could clean better than I cooked." Nora smiled.

Goldie nodded. "Right. And when you did, what did you find under Ivy's bed?"

"Some pennies."

"And what did you do with them?" Goldie asked.

"Put them on top of Ivy's bed."

"Why didn't you take them?" Goldie asked. "Most girls would have. It was only four pennies."

"It wouldn't have been right," Nora said. "They weren't mine. My pap might not have taught me much, but he taught me to be honest. Tanned my hide good once for hiding an apple under my pillow and then lying about it."

Miss Thornhill spoke up. "So there you have it, Nora. Most girls would have thought, 'No one's going to miss four pennies.' But you did the right thing."

Goldie cut the final threads tying Nora to her. "Go, Nora. The truth is, you don't have the temperament for this kind of work. And while I was tempted to make an exception on account of those green eyes and that blonde hair, I usually don't hire girls without experience. I think I've known for a while it wasn't going to work out for you to stay here. Elise's proposal solves it for everyone. And no hard feelings."

Goldie turned to Elise. "I'll send Shep by later today to help get Nora's apartment ready. Dr. Allbright is stopping by to check her over. I suspect she'll agree that Nora is about ready to get back to work."

Goldie stood up. Laying a hand on Nora's shoulder, she said,

"As for you, Miss O'Dell, I know what you're thinking. You'll accept the bombazine, and I'll not hear another word about it." She winked. "You *could* clean better than you cook, dearie. You earned your way. Now it's time you moved on."

CHAPTER 10

More Than Cloth and Cutting

Whatsoever thy hand findeth to do,
do it with thy might.
Ecclesiastes 9:10

The first day Nora came to Thornhill Dressers for training, she worked with Lucy and Hannah. "You'll grow to love Miss Thornhill," Hannah said. "She's truly an angel. You wouldn't believe how some of the dressmakers treat their back room girls. We used to work for Madame Hart over on N Street."

"You mean Madame Heartless," Lucy corrected her. She had been rummaging through some boxes along one wall. She finally found what she needed and turned around, a length of lace in one hand. "You won't catch *her* customers confiding in *her*." She looked at Nora. "Miss Thornhill's patrons tell her everything. Sometimes I think she knows more about what really goes on in Lincoln than anyone."

"But she never gossips," Hannah said. "She just listens."

Lucy giggled. "I heard Dr. Allbright tell her once that she was tempted to start prescribing a visit to Thornhill Dressers for all her hysterical and melancholy patients."

The day after Lucy and Hannah's comments, Mrs. Sadie Hawks came in the shop to order a new walking dress and Nora had the opportunity to see what Lucy and Hannah had been talking about. As Nora jotted down measurements for Miss

Thornhill, the portly older woman launched into a discussion of family events that ended in her mentioning several recent financial setbacks in her husband's business. She sighed. "I told Phillip I didn't need to order this dress, but he insists I can't be seen walking about town with a frayed hem. He says it gives the wrong impression."

"Well," Miss Thornhill offered, "perhaps we can come up with an alternative." She reached for a bolt of cloth. "I could insert a panel of this as a contrast near the bottom of the skirt. Then we could salvage a good piece and lower it to the hemline. We could also make new cuffs and a new collar to match the insert."

When Mrs. Hawks hesitated, Nora retrieved a copy of *The Delineator* from the workroom. Opening it to a page of illustrations, she pointed out a dress with a contrasting fabric set into the skirt.

Mrs. Hawks was thrilled. "Phillip is always so concerned about appearances. Now if he says I look like I've been trying to 'make-do', I can tell him I saw the idea in the latest fashion magazine. That should hush him up." She went on, "And that provides the solution to another difficulty. Phillip is taking our Martha to visit a girl's school in St. Louis next week. I simply cannot send her in last year's dress, but our clothing budget is only forty dollars a month." She smiled with satisfaction, "Now I can do everything without having to bother Phillip about money."

Nora could barely hide her amazement. Here was a woman who could spend the equivalent of two *months* of Nora's salary on clothing every month, and yet she was not happy. Nora thought back to Iris's complaint that she made "only" ninety dollars a week at Goldie's. It made one wonder about the notion that money and happiness were connected.

After Mrs. Hawks left, Miss Thornhill took Nora aside, "Now you see that there is more to dressmaking than cloth and cutting. A dressmaker's most valuable asset is often the ability to lend a sympathetic ear." She explained. "A woman can purchase a hat or a new dress any number of places in Lincoln. But God seems to have made me a good listener. They know that they can pour out their troubles to me, and I will never breathe a word of it to anyone but the Lord. It seems to mean something to them." She sighed. "You'd never guess that Mrs. Hawks has money troubles, would you? And hers is not a unique position. The finest gown in the city is sometimes only a thin disguise, hiding heart-breaking circumstances. You'd be surprised how many of my patrons are wrestling with very real problems, and all they have at home is an uncaring man who pats them on the shoulder and says, 'there, there, it will be all right' over his newspaper."

Nora shared what Lucy had said about Dr. Allbright's prescribing Thornhill Dressers as a cure for hysteria.

Elise smiled and shook her head. "I don't think I'm all *that* important. It is good, though, to end the day knowing that I've made someone else feel better."

When Mrs. Hawks brought "our Martha" in to order her new travelling ensemble, Nora learned that tact and patience were not always easily practiced. The girl bore absolutely no resemblance to her kind-hearted, well-intentioned mother. She simpered over every decision and grew positively hostile when her mother hesitated regarding a high-priced trim. Nora wondered if the girl didn't know about her father's precarious finances, or if she simply didn't care.

Trying her best to learn from Miss Thornhill's example, Nora said, "Well of course, Miss Hawks. Whatever you think. Just this morning I saw this very trim on a bonnet in the most recent issue of *Peterson's*. But if you don't care that the more expensive one is a bit outdated—"

Miss Hawks quickly changed her mind. Nora appreciated the grateful nod of Mrs. Hawks' head as the two left the shop. Miss Thornhill's praise made her blush with pleasure. "Very good, Miss O'Dell. Very good indeed."

Nora was thankful to know that her handling of Martha Hawks pleased Miss Thornhill. She was less certain of her ability to please when it came to the technical aspects of the trade. At times she felt that she was wallowing in an endless sea of new words and terms. Miss Thornhill spoke of morning dresses for street and home, for welcoming visitors, or for housekeeping. There were carriage dresses and riding dresses, dinner dresses and ordinary evening dresses. Church, theater, and the opera, each had its own etiquette. Miss Thornhill sometimes made a "yachting dress" or a "bathing dress" for wealthy clients' outings to Capitol Beach just west of the city.

Bustles and silks, which had been "out," were coming back "in." Satins were going "out," but Scotch plaids were all the furor. The homeless girl who owned only two garments of her own struggled to learn the advantages of bombazine over broadcloth and cambric over chintz. A dress with a natural waistline had a "bodice," but if it extended below the waistline, it was called a "basque." Miss Thornhill called trims "garniture," and a glove a "gauntlet." Nora's head swam with so much to learn.

And then there were the nearly endless rules connected to mourning. "We don't observe strict time periods," Miss Thornhill said. "The change from full- to half-mourning garments is dictated more by the wearer's feelings. Toward the end of mourning, ladies add white, purple, and gray to their black ensembles. Children under twelve wear white in summer and gray in winter, with black trims."

"How do you remember it all?" Nora wanted to know. "Do things change quickly? How do you know what's fashionable and what isn't?"

Miss Thornhill smiled. "I'm constantly perusing the fashion magazines—as should you. It helps that my average customer really only has a simple calico wrapper for housekeeping, one or two silk dresses for making and receiving calls, and a silk gown for special occasions. Some of my more thrifty patrons even like to make their own clothing. They have me do the fitting and the cutting, then they take the project home to finish."

When it came time to make Nora's work clothes, Miss Thornhill cautioned, "Businesswomen must take care not to overdress. Superfluous trim must be avoided, although a watch and chain are certainly acceptable. I would suggest gray and brown as the best colors to wear."

Nora knew without asking which buttons to choose for her work dresses. Dull. Boring. Boring. Dull. She made a mental note to begin saving for a watch and chain, thinking longingly of the green bombazine that hung inside a dustcover on a hook upstairs.

Miss Thornhill seemed to read her mind. She patted Nora's hand. "Don't worry, Miss O'Dell. We can make an exception for the green bombazine. It is, after all, a more conservative shade of green."

It was not long before Nora met someone who paid no heed to the "rule" that dictated dull colors and understated styles for businesswomen. Mrs. Augusta Hathaway, a local hotel owner known for her philanthropy, entered the shop one day dressed in a bright purple walking dress with wide lace cuffs and a shamelessly huge opal brooch. She was a large woman who sported stylish clothing and a broad smile. It was not long before Nora realized that Mrs. Hathaway knew the "rules." She simply didn't care to obey them. Nora liked her.

"Well, Elise," Mrs. Hathaway inquired. "Who's this?"

"My new associate, Miss O'Dell," was the answer. "She's just learning the trade, and if you have no objection, I'd like yours to be the first fitting she conducts—with my supervision, of course."

Mrs. Hathaway nodded. "Mind? Of course not. Why would I mind?" She headed for the dressing room. Pausing in front of the mirror, she shook her finger at Nora as a mock threat. "However, young lady, if you ever breathe a word of my relentlessly increasing measurements, I shall have you summarily dispatched!"

From the dressing room, Mrs. Hathaway kept up a running monologue that required little response from either Nora or Miss Thornhill. When she was finally ready for her fitting, she flung open the door. "All right then, let's get this disagreeable business over with."

Miss Thornhill talked to Nora as she worked. "I used to follow S. T. Taylor's system for cutting, but that requires ten measurements for the basque alone. Now I use a system developed by Elizabeth Gartland—"

"Leave it to a woman to improve upon things," Mrs. Hathaway interjected. Nora decided she liked Augusta Hathaway very much.

Miss Thornhill continued, "With the Gartland System we only need thirteen measurements for the entire garment. It's much more efficient."

"Of course it is," Mrs. Hathaway added. "A woman developed it with women in mind."

Miss Thornhill showed Nora how to take the final measurement and then sent Nora to the workroom. "Give your figures to Lucy and Hannah. They will demonstrate the rest of the process for you. You'll be doing it yourself in no time."

Taking her leave of Mrs. Hathaway, Nora made her way back to the workroom where she gave Lucy the measurements and prepared to watch while Lucy and Hannah created a pattern for Mrs. Hathaway's new wrapper.

Hannah spread out a huge piece of plain brown paper on the worktable. Referring to a chart on the wall labeled *The Gartland System for Cutting Women's Clothing,* she began to draw as Lucy read step-by-step instructions.

" 'Draw line 1 ten inches above the bottom of the paper, the entire length of the square, for waistline.' "

Wielding a ruler and a freshly sharpened pencil, Hannah drew.

"All right," Lucy said, " 'Step two: Draw line 2 from center of line 1, according to length of back. Step three: On line 2 make a dot above the waistline for the underarm measure. Draw a line parallel to line 1, for line 3.' "

Nora gave up trying to follow exactly what the girls were doing. Lucy and Hannah finally completed step number 40 and held up the completed pattern. "There," Hannah said. "That's all there is to it. Simple, huh?" She started to laugh. "Don't worry. It won't seem like Greek to you for long."

Nora spent her evenings restoring order to Miss Thornhill's workroom. She eliminated the clutter on the stairs to her apartment and devised an inventory method so that there would be no last-minute telegrams to suppliers for items that lay forgotten in the bottom of a box in the workroom. In less than a month, Miss Thornhill grew to depend on Nora's organizational skills.

Nora began to learn proper grammar by imitating Miss Thornhill and Dr. Allbright. She became more at ease with patrons, although she doubted she would ever have the patience Miss Thornhill exhibited with her more difficult ones.

"I know," Miss Thornhill said one day. "Mrs. Judge Cranston has never really considered the possibility that a mere dressmaker might be intelligent. But I'm not too proud to adopt a servile stance when it's good business. I have enough Augusta Hathaways that I don't mind the few Mrs. Judge Cranstons. If she needs to treat me like a servant to assure her superior place in society, I don't mind. Especially when it brings me business."

"If you pay attention," Miss Thornhill said, "you can learn nearly all you need to know to get along in society by observing and imitating our patrons. You have already improved your grammar tenfold. The next time Mrs. Judge Bryan stops in, observe her ease of manner and the way she carries herself. The mannerisms of a lady are easily learned. Just look around you."

Lucy interrupted, giggling. "Just remember that if you take to imitating Mrs. Judge Cranston, we'll kick you out the back door."

During the day, Nora concentrated on the craft of dressmaking and the art of being a lady. In the evenings, Dr. Allbright stopped by and helped Nora develop her mind. She began to move toward answering the questions she had been asked about her dreams and plans for the future.

Her days settled into a routine. Every evening, she said good night to Lucy and Hannah and locked up. She ate a cold supper while poring over the newspaper or some book supplied by Dr. Allbright. Shortly after dark, she mounted the stairs to her apartment, where she quickly fell asleep. On the evenings when she was tempted to wish for more, she reminded herself of the half-starved, shabbily dressed girl who had stood in the kitchen of a run-down farmhouse less than six months ago and determined to make a change.

Perhaps she did not have a family or a home, but no one was yelling at her, and the fear of moving upstairs at Goldie's was gone. She had a regular income, two new friends, and a kind employer. She began to think that millinery might be her niche at the Thornhill Dressers.

For now, it was enough.

CHAPTER 11

Nature's Limit

----

*For what hath man of all his labour, and of the
vexation of his heart, wherein he hath labored
under the sun? For all his days are sorrows, and
his travail grief; yea, his heart taketh not rest in
the night. This is also vanity.*
Ecclesiastes 2:22–23

"This simply will not do, Miss O'Dell." Mrs. Judge Cranston
clicked her tongue against the roof of her mouth as she inspected herself in the mirror. "It doesn't look a bit like the
drawing I brought you." As she turned her head from side to
side, her small dark eyes flickered angrily. Finally, she jerked the
hat off her head and nearly slammed it down on Nora's work
counter.

Nora drew a deep breath and tried to calm herself. She had
remade the hat in question three times in as many days. "If
you'll excuse me for a moment," Nora said, "I'll just get the
drawing and you can point out the deficiencies."

"I'd prefer to take the matter up with Miss Thornhill," Mrs.
Cranston said. She reached up to smooth her auburn hair. From
where she stood by Nora's work counter she screeched toward
the workroom, "Miss Thornhill, are you *there*?"

Nora went into the workroom where a page from *Demorest's*
was tacked up on the wall. It pictured several beautiful models
wearing elegant hats, one of which was circled. Mrs. Cranston
had selected the hat and then spoken the fateful words, "Of
course, I'll want a few changes. I don't want to simply copy the

picture." *No woman wants a hat like any other hat that has ever been made.* Nora had read that warning in the *Milliner's Guide,* and now she was about to enter millinery hell with a customer who expected her to realize that dream.

Mrs. Cranston had selected a hat that featured huge ridges of embroidered yellow taffeta anchored on a high-crowned base covered with folded black satin and a towering black ostrich feather. Nora had contacted several wholesalers before finding just the right shade of taffeta for the project, when Mrs. Cranston announced that she thought perhaps a pale aquamarine would be better with the tone of her skin.

When Lucy and Hannah overheard the request, Lucy mumbled under her breath, "Tone? What tone? Is *sallow* a tone?"

For one moment, Nora had wished it was seven months earlier when she was still a "back room girl," so that she could say what she was thinking. But she couldn't. She had worked through the fall and winter learning dressmaking and millinery, and begun to think she wanted her own shop someday. Miss Thornhill was gone on her annual spring buying trip, and it was time she, Nora, learned to deal with irascible customers on her own.

Snatching the drawing that inspired Mrs. Cranston's hat down from the wall in the workroom, Nora went back into the studio. "I'm sorry, Mrs. Cranston, but Miss Thornhill isn't here. She's in St. Louis, combining a holiday with visits to some of the more important designer showrooms in the city." Nora picked up the hat and set it on a stand. Spreading the illustration out before her, she asked, "Now then, perhaps you could show me where I've gone wrong."

Mrs. Cranston wore reading glasses about her neck on a long gold chain. She unfolded them and put them on the bridge of her nose. Her eyes went from the drawing to the hat and back again. "This—" She waggled her index finger at the taffeta. "It just isn't right. It makes my head look—well—pointed."

"I believe, if you'll recall, madame," Nora said quietly, "we discussed the possibility that that might happen. Your face is much narrower than the model's. But we tried to accommodate that with a little more fullness along the sides."

"Well, I don't like it. I want it to look like the picture."

No, Nora thought, *you want to look like the picture.* "I have honestly done my best, Mrs. Cranston. I don't know what else to do. There are limitations. I can't make you look like the model."

"Well." Mrs. Cranston drew herself up and crossed her scarecrow-thin arms. "I guess I know that. There's no need to be impertinent."

"I don't mean to be impertinent," Nora said as evenly as possible.

"I've been a good customer of Elise Thornhill's for more years than you've been alive, young lady," Mrs. Cranston said imperiously, "and I won't be spoken to in that tone by the hired help. There are plenty of other hat shops in Lincoln, you know. I don't have to tolerate impertinence from some little snippet who, less than a year ago, was residing over on South Ninth Street."

It took a moment for Nora to understand exactly what Mrs. Judge Cranston was saying. At first, she wanted to cry. But she wouldn't give Mrs. Cranston the satisfaction of seeing the hurt. Instead of crying, she got angry. Grabbing the edge of her work counter, she retorted, "Yes ma'am, I *do* know there are many other millinery establishments in the city. And not a single one of *them* can make you look like the model in the magazine, either."

Mrs. Judge Cranston removed her glasses from her nose and folded them so they would lie flat on her flat chest. Pressing her lips together, she wheeled about and made for the door.

Nora controlled her tears until the door closed. Trembling all over, she crossed the studio and put the "Closed" sign in the window. She drew the blinds before walking to the back of the studio where Lucy and Hannah were working, pretending they had not heard the exchange.

It began to rain. *At least I know why my side has been aching all day,* Nora thought. Frank Albers had given her an internal weather-minder when he broke her ribs.

"Lucy, Hannah," Nora said. "Why don't you two take the

afternoon off. I'm going upstairs to lie down." Nora headed for
the stairs.

"Nora," Lucy said softly, "don't let it bother you. Miss
Thornhill never even *liked* Mrs. Cranston."

"Thank you, Lucy. It's kind of you to say that." Wearily,
Nora climbed the stairs. She heard the door to the workroom
close as Lucy and Hannah left. The rain beat steadily down on
the roof over her bed.

What's wrong *with me? I made the break with Goldie's. I
have my own corner at Thornhill Dressers. Only last week,
Elise said I should begin to order in and keep my own stock of
supplies instead of sending customers shopping for their own.
She's even having business cards printed for me. I'm making ten
dollars a week. More than I ever expected.*

Nora found herself wondering if anyone had ever gone back
to Fern's grave. Perhaps she would go out there on Decoration
Day. She wondered if Will was all right. If Pap had changed. She
thought that if Lucy and Hannah asked her one more time to go
to church with them, she just might go. Nora began to cry tears
that had nothing to do with Mrs. Judge Cranston's hat.

Silence woke Nora early in the evening. It had stopped raining. She sat up and looked out the small window on the wall
opposite her bed. The sky was clear. The sun was beginning to
go down. Her stomach rumbled. Sighing, Nora got up and went
downstairs. Her favorite time of day was approaching, the brief
moment when the sun had barely dipped behind the horizon,
and the world was bathed in a light that was at once bright and
mellow. Nora stepped outside on the back stoop, leaning back
against the wall of the building. Closing her eyes, she inhaled
deeply. The air smelled of damp earth and wet brick. A ray of
sunshine dappled the brick of the building across the alley with
spots of gold. Someone had set a blooming geranium on a windowsill up on the second level. It glowed scarlet in the dusky
light.

Just as Nora bent to retrieve a small bundle of firewood from
the stack by the back door, she heard a now-familiar cadence,
and she looked up just in time to see Casey, Dr. Allbright's

rangy white gelding, come into view around the corner at the end of the block.

Nora waved and headed inside, leaving the door open for Dr. Allbright. Maude came in just as Nora bent to stoke the fire in the little woodstove in the workroom corner.

"I'm just making some supper. Have you eaten?"

Dr. Allbright climbed down from her carriage and grabbed her medical bag. "I haven't had a minute since early this morning. That seems a long, long time ago." She followed Nora inside, set the medical bag on a table, and pulled an apron off its hook. "Why don't you go over there and read the newspaper and let me çook something?"

"You?" Nora made no attempt to hide her surprise.

"Yes, *me*. I can tell you aren't feeling well." She shook her finger at Nora. "Now listen, you. I *can* cook. I just don't generally *choose* to." She teased, "As I recall, you're not known for your cuisine, either." She opened her medical bag and withdrew a quart-size canning jar filled with white liquid. "Cream of potato soup. I stopped at the hotel and ordered some." She headed for the stove. "I'll heat this up. There are rolls and butter in there, too."

Nora looked inside Maude's bag, smiling at the sight of four huge dinner rolls wrapped in a linen napkin.

Maude wasted no time getting to the point. "I was surprised to see Lucy and Hannah downtown this afternoon." She slathered a roll with butter and handed it to Nora. "Don't let Mrs. Judge Cranston get your goat, Nora. She's a difficult old broad. If it's any comfort to you, she doesn't treat her physician"—she pointed to herself—"any better than she treats her milliner."

"Well," Nora said, "I don't think I'm her milliner anymore."

"I guarantee you she will be back in less than a week with some excuse as to why she behaved so badly. She'll want the hat and she'll probably pay you more than you initially agreed upon. She never, *ever* apologizes with words, but she always apologizes."

Nora swallowed a tablespoonful of soup. "The business with the hat didn't bother me so much. It's part of being a milliner.

They expect us to remake them in spite of nature." She hesitated. "It was her reference to Goldie's that hurt. The way she said it made me feel—" Nora thought for a moment. "Oh, I don't know. I probably made more of it than it was. I've been out of sorts all week. I overreacted."

"Perhaps it's the weather," Dr. Allbright said. "I haven't had the best week, either." She went on. "But I'm old and allowed to be cranky. You have your life ahead of you, my dear, hopes and dreams, dreams and hopes . . ."

Nora replied, "I do appreciate your taking time for me this way. I told Lucy and Hannah that our talks take the place of all the education I missed. You always make me feel better. Like I'm—important."

Dr. Allbright leaned forward. "You *are* important. It's very gratifying for a sour old bird like me to have a lovely young lady like you interested in spending time with her." She smiled gently. "I've never regretted not being married, but at times I do regret not having had children. I could have a daughter about your age, you know."

Nora's face flushed with pleasure as she got up and cleared the table. "I want to show you something," she said. Opening a large brown envelope that lay on the table, she handed Dr. Allbright a sheet of paper, before sitting down. "Miss Thornhill said I should write it myself. It goes in the paper next week."

Dr. Allbright read, *Miss Elise Thornhill announces that Thornhill Dressers has employed a first-rate milliner and invites those who desire the finest in hats, flowers, hair, and fancy goods to stop by and make the acquaintance of Miss Nora O'Dell.*

"Good work. I like the way you've worded it."

Smiling shyly, Nora held out a small card for Dr. Allbright's inspection. "She had these printed up for me. Surprised me with them before she left for St. Louis." The card featured a black-and-white engraving of a millinery shop. A table took up the left lower corner, and the side of the table provided space for printing. *Miss Nora O'Dell, Fashionable Millinery, Thornhill Dressers, 123 N. 11th Street, Lincoln. Mode de Paris Straws, Ribbons, Feathers, Flowers &c.* Atop the table on the card was an array of hats on ornate stands of various heights. Behind the table stood a fashionably dressed milliner, handing a hat to a female customer while her two young daughters looked on. The scene suggested wealthy patrons and a thriving business.

"Congratulations," Dr. Allbright said. "I know that Elise is very, very happy to have you as a part of her business. You've enabled her to expand, and your talent with hats has brought her new business."

"I felt a little odd about getting my own card, so soon," Nora said. "But Lucy and Hannah don't seem to mind. They seem happy just being the 'back room girls.' "

Dr. Allbright nodded. "Lucy and Hannah are good girls, but they have neither your drive nor your potential. Both are content being barely literate, and they'll probably work for Elise the rest of their lives—unless Lucy marries young Fielding, which is highly likely from what I can tell. And you know what I think of that."

Nora knew. Dr. Allbright made no secret of her opinions about women and marriage, which she tended to call legalized slavery.

"Hannah will, I dare say, be a common seamstress for the rest of her days," Dr. Allbright continued. "Not that that's anything to be ashamed of, mind you. She's content and that's more than you or I can say." She held out her hand. "May I take a few cards with me? I'll send some home with the other physicians after our next Medical Society meeting."

Nora handed Dr. Allbright a half-dozen cards, then turned to the newspaper. "Have you seen this?" She pointed to an article titled "The Color of the Eyes. Shades of Character Indicated by the Shades of Color."

Dr. Allbright scanned the article. "Well, it isn't very complimentary to me, is it? 'In women, brown eyes mean jealousy and cruelty.' " Dr. Allbright sipped her tea. "What does it say about you?" She handed the paper to Nora.

Nora read aloud, " 'Self-satisfaction and conceit are commonly the characteristic traits represented by the green eye.' " She frowned. "What is *conceit*?"

"It means you think you're absolutely wonderful just the way you are. A little better than everyone else, in fact."

"Well," Nora said, grinning, "I do think I know more than Mrs. Judge Cranston about fashion."

"That's not conceit, my dear. That's a fact," Dr. Allbright shot back.

"Listen to this," Nora said, turning back to the paper. " 'The main characteristic of the violet eye, which is called the woman's eye, is affection and purity'—now get this," she said, " 'affection and purity . . . and limited or deficient intellectuality.' "

Dr. Allbright snorted. "Let me see that." She grabbed the paper.

Nora baited her. "It's written by one of your colleagues."

Maude read through the article. "Humph. Dr. John Gannon. I should have known." She rattled the paper.

"Well, what do you think? Can you tell what someone is like by the color of their eyes?"

"I think," Dr. Allbright said, "this makes just about as much sense as shaving your head so some idiot can inspect the bumps on your head and tell you what career you should follow."

"What?"

"It's called phrenology," Dr. Allbright explained. "When I went to Chicago a few years ago, Dr. Gannon was espousing some new version of a practice that was popular earlier in this century. It seems he has expanded his repertoire. Interesting, don't you think, that he says it's the *woman's* eye that's connected with *limited* intellectuality . . ."

"He's lecturing at the GAR hall this Friday evening at eight o'clock." Nora said quietly. "Want to go with me to hear what he has to say?"

"Absolutely," Dr. Allbright said. "I'll pick you up at seven-thirty."

CHAPTER 12

Shades of Character

I am not alone, because the Father is with me.
John 16:32

Nora's interest in Dr. Gannon's theories had resulted in her overlooking another announcement in the *Daily State Journal*. Funke's Opera House had engaged the Daniel Frost Theatrical Troupe, and from the moment they arrived at work the next morning, Lucy and Hannah talked of little else. They spoke of Greyson Chandler as Hamlet, Greyson Chandler as the lead in a comedic farce, Greyson Chandler at Thornhill Dressers. They planned to join the crowd expected to greet the troupe at the railroad station Friday afternoon and invited Nora to go along.

Nora shook her head. "I promised Mrs. Cranston I'd have her hat ready on Friday, and I don't want to risk missing the lecture that evening with Dr. Allbright." (Just as the doctor had predicted, the "old bat" had come in the day after Miss Thornhill returned from St. Louis. She had explained that she and Nora had had a "slight disagreement," but she hoped that the hat could be salvaged, and she would be willing to pay an additional three dollars if it could be ready in time for the opening of the next production at Funke's Opera House.)

Lucy and Hannah exchanged glances. They were not quite certain it was good for Nora to be spending so much time with

Dr. Allbright. Nora said it was her way of getting an education instead of going to school, and that she was very grateful that Dr. Allbright considered her worth the trouble. Miss Thornhill said she feared Nora's spending so much time with an atheist would put an obstacle between Nora and God, and that she wished Dr. Allbright would get called away on more emergencies.

Nora finished Mrs. Judge Cranston's hat early on Friday and proceeded to her next project—adjusting the trim on a mourning hat to signify the next "stage of mourning." Miss Thornhill had explained, "Mrs. Hogsdon is from the old school. She is new to Lincoln and she doesn't care much for our relaxed ways. The more rigorous law requires the veil be worn for three months. Mr. Hogsdon passed away just over three months ago, so now we can remove the crape in the front and replace it with Brussels net. Shorten the knee-length crape at the back so that it merely covers the shoulders. The hem should remain quite deep. In three months we will replace the crape entirely."

Nora smiled to herself, realizing that "city folks" mourning could result in a good income for a skilled milliner. She was just removing the crape from the front of the bonnet when the studio door rattled.

The gentleman did not just come through the door of Thornhill's. He made an entrance, pausing momentarily before giving the door a good shake to make certain the bell rang loudly. After he stepped across the threshold and closed the door behind him, he removed his fedora with a flourish, and waited. From their brief encounter the previous fall, Nora had a vague memory of blue eyes and blonde hair. She had been feeling too ill to notice much else. But she still recognized Greyson Chandler. He was tall, with a wavy lock of blond hair that spilled over his high forehead and softened his classic profile. A thick mustache drooped around the corners of his mouth. He wore an impeccably tailored suit fashioned to make the most of his broad shoulders and small waist.

Nora stood up. Just as she opened her mouth to greet Chandler, Elise appeared at the workroom door. Behind Elise, Nora could see Lucy's and Hannah's eyes grow wide. They nudged one another and quickly disappeared into the workroom.

Nora bit her lower lip, trying to squelch a smile. She pretended to work while Chandler spoke with Elise. At Goldie's Nora had met men with an intangible something that caught women's attention and pulled the unwary in. Chandler had it. Nora reminded herself that Lily and Iris had both warned her about men like that. Drawing her brows together in a scowl, Nora forced herself to concentrate on Widow Hogsdon's hat.

Miss Thornhill was spreading an impressive number of fabric samples out for Chandler's inspection. Nora turned to the pressing board behind her. She reached for a box of black scraps, selecting a few large pieces to press. She hummed softly to herself to close out the sound of Chandler's voice, trying her best not to eavesdrop while he concluded his business with Miss Thornhill. But as Chandler made his way to the door, Nora could not resist the temptation to look up. When she did, Chandler smiled and tipped his hat. "Glad to see you feeling better, Miss O'Dell. May I greet Shep for you? We're having a drink together this evening."

He didn't wait for her to reply. If she hadn't known better, Nora would have thought Greyson Chandler was flirting with her.

Chandler had requested that Miss Thornhill construct an elaborate robe for one of Mamie Patterson's costumes. It was needed for the following Wednesday's performance of *Hamlet,* and it presented one of the greater challenges of Miss Thornhill's designing career.

She personally supervised as Lucy and Hannah cut and stitched, filling the hours with talk of the famous actor. As soon as the basic cape was constructed, Miss Thornhill took over the intricate finish work, which included beading and quillwork.

"Mr. Chandler remembered Nora," Lucy said for what seemed like the tenth time.

"And he knew her given name. Did you tell him, Miss Thornhill?" Hannah asked.

"No," Elise replied. "He didn't speak of Nora to me."

"That means he asked someone else," Lucy teased, casting a glance toward where Nora stood by the stove sipping tea.

"Honestly, girls," Nora exclaimed. "You've been over and over this. Did life as we know it suddenly stop with Greyson Chandler's arrival in Lincoln? Can't you find something else to talk about?"

Lucy and Hannah found something else to talk about—when Nora was within earshot.

Nora finished Widow Hogsdon's bonnet and began working on a ready-made sample to put in the shop window. Even without Lucy and Hannah's constant chatter, she remained short-tempered. She winced inwardly at the mental image of Shep sharing stories with Greyson Chandler. Was her association with Goldie's to haunt her forever?

On Friday evening, Dr. Allbright was called out on an emergency, forcing her to cancel the planned attendance at Dr. Gannon's lecture on "The Color of the Eyes. Shades of Character Indicated by the Shades of Color." Lucy and Hannah already had plans involving a Mr. Fielding and Friend, and Elise had developed a raging headache after hours of eyestrain bent over the intricate beading on Mamie Patterson's costume.

Nora had a flickering thought of attending Dr. Gannon's lecture alone, but she knew that being seen without an escort would only invite raised eyebrows and perhaps a whisper or two about Goldie's, especially if one or two certain gentlemen happened to be present. When intermittent showers became a downpour, Nora determined to spend another Friday evening alone.

After Elise and the girls left, Nora made herself a cup of tea and sat down at the downstairs worktable with a cold supper before her. She got up and retrieved the newspaper from where she had laid it on the stairway that led up to her apartment and prepared to reread Dr. Gannon's proposal about eye color and character. What was it he had said about blue eyes in a man? *In a man it denotes a phlegmatic disposition.* She would have to look the word *phlegmatic* up in the dictionary. She leaned back in her chair. Goodness, but she was weary of encountering words she did not understand.

Darkness came prematurely as the storm outside continued unabated. Sitting alone in the darkened workroom, Nora sighed. Rain always seemed to make her feel out of sorts, and this evening was no exception. She really had been looking forward to attending the lecture with Dr. Allbright. She wondered how young women her age managed to make friends in the city. Miss Thornhill had suggested church several times. She had been tempted to try it, but then reconsidered, thinking she probably wouldn't fit in. What if most of the churchgoing women were like Mrs. Judge Cranston?

She longed for the camaraderie of Goldie's, without the attached reputation. Goldie herself had told Nora that since she had chosen "another life," it would be best if she didn't come back to the house. "It's kind of a black-and-white thing," Goldie had explained. "Either you're one of the girls or you're not. You can't walk a line between both worlds."

Nora missed Iris the most. She wanted to know why Iris was still at Goldie's, after all her talk of leaving. And Lily. She worried about Lily's lack of common sense.

A huge clap of thunder brought Nora back to reality. Looking about her, she sighed again. Leaving her dinner on the table, she climbed the stairs to her tiny apartment and lit a gas light. Another evening alone, reading. Ah, well. At least her education was progressing. Nora reached for the dictionary. What was that word . . . phleg-something. She couldn't remember how to spell it. She would have to go downstairs and get the newspaper. Funny how you had to know how to spell something before you could look it up to see how to spell it.

Nora was halfway down the stairs when someone pounded on the back door yelling, "Hello, hello, is anyone there?" The voice sounded vaguely familiar. She hurried down the stairs and flung the door open.

Greyson Chandler was standing in the rain, his felt hat wilted into a shapeless mess, the ends of his mustache dripping. Mud had totally obliterated any view of what Nora knew to be fine kid boots. Mud was splattered halfway to his knees. In his left hand he held a crushed hatbox.

"Miss Thornhill isn't here," Nora said.

"Yes, I know. She pleaded a headache and went home. And Lucy and Hannah are out with two young gentlemen. I saw them earlier. They mentioned that you were attending a lecture with Dr. Allbright." The blue eyes looked steadily at Nora. "But I happen to know that Dr. Allbright is tending a case. Miss Patterson has a toothache. And I have an emergency that requires a skilled milliner." Chandler held up the crushed hatbox. "At least in theatrical circles, it's an emergency."

Just then, a cloudburst sent torrents of rain, completely drenching Chandler's hat and sending a gush of water down the back of his neck. Nora stepped back from the door. "Come in out of the rain."

Chandler stepped across the threshold and set the hatbox on the table. As he did, Nora grabbed up the newspaper, which she had folded around Dr. Gannon's article. Wondering why her cheeks were growing hot, she hugged the newspaper to herself so that Chandler could not see it.

Chandler removed his dripping coat, hanging it on the hook by the door. He tried to reshape his drenched hat.

"Here," Nora said. "Let me see to that." Plunking the newspaper down on the seat of the chair and shoving it quickly beneath the table, she retrieved a soft cloth from a bin by the worktable and began to dab moisture out of the felt.

Chandler reached up to push a lock of blond hair off his forehead. Then, taking up the crumpled hatbox, he said, "I hope you can do something with this. Some of our more ornate costumes just arrived this morning. Unfortunately this box fell off the carriage on the way from the station. The costume matron didn't miss it right away. By the time she realized it was missing and we found it, it had been run over by a wagon and drenched in the rain."

He opened the box and extracted something that used to be some sort of crown. The metal was intact, but the supporting structure was nearly destroyed.

"Oh, my," Nora said, setting Chandler's hat down on the worktable and taking the headpiece in her hands.

"Yes," Chandler agreed. "Exactly." He sighed. "I've just escaped from a tantrum performed by my leading lady over this fiasco." He grinned at Nora. "And believe me, she throws a magnificent tantrum." He looked at the headdress, shaking his head. "While I admit to being able to handle just about anything that comes my way from the fair sex, I really do *not* want to face Miss Patterson again unless I can tell her that this monstrosity will be complete for the opening."

"What's it supposed to look like?" Nora asked.

"We're doing *Hamlet*," Chandler said.

"Yes?" Nora asked, with the tone of, is that supposed to mean something to me?

"I apologize," Chandler said quickly. "I know it isn't really correct for the time period, but Miss Patterson firmly refused a Queen Gertrude with a head rail and a veil. This was the compromise." He cupped both his hands and covered the back of his head. "That finer brocade fabric is supposed to form a sort of cup here. It completely covers the hair—and Miss Patterson has a *lot* of hair, so it had to be quite full. Obviously the part that looks like a crown sits atop the head, but there was something underneath that"—he pointed to a completely ruined band of fabric—"to frame her face. Sort of like a nun would wear. Have you seen a nun's habit?" He apologized, "I know this is completely outside your area of expertise, but would you try?"

"Let's go into the studio where I can get a better look at it," Nora said. Chandler followed her into the darkened room and waited while she fumbled with the gas lights. When her work area was finally illuminated, Nora placed the headpiece on one of her stands and sat down on a stool to inspect it.

"This is wonderfully made," she murmured almost to herself.

Chandler was standing so close she could feel his breath on the back of her neck. She got up. "Excuse me," she said, indicating one of the drawers built into the wall behind him. He stepped aside so that Nora could open a drawer. She pretended to look through the contents before saying, "I don't have anything like this." She ran her finger along the edge of the head-piece. "This piece that you said frames Miss Patterson's face has to be completely replaced. I can't match it."

Chandler seemed to be watching her instead of looking at the subject of their discussion.

Nora felt herself blushing again and took a step backward. "Don't you have anyone in the troupe who does this sort of thing? Lucy and Hannah said they counted twenty people getting off the train when the troupe arrived."

Chandler smiled. "You didn't come to the station to meet the famous actors?"

Nora felt herself blushing again. "I had work to do. Actually," she said, "I had planned to attend a lecture, but then Dr. Allbright had to cancel." Nora thought, *Why on earth am I telling him this?* Nora asked again, "Doesn't a troupe your size have someone who oversees the costumes?"

"Of course," Chandler said. "The costume matron. She's the one who finally discovered this was missing. She's superb at the day-to-day mending and minor, last-minute changes, but she doesn't have the skill to re-create something like this."

Nora said, "It needs to be completely rebuilt. The bracing that supports the coronet has been broken. I may need to construct an entirely new frame." She bent over to inspect the piece more closely. "If I can let it dry naturally, most of this fabric can be cleaned and reused—except for that piece around the face."

Chandler said, "Miss Patterson was personally involved in its design. Any change would have to be just exactly right. She'd need to see it."

"You said there was a matching cloak. What if I add a border along the cloak to match the new border on this?"

"How long would it take?" Chandler wanted to know.

"I can probably get the framework rebuilt over the weekend," Nora said. "I don't stock anything appropriate, but Herpolsheimer's just got in a new shipment of trims. Would Miss Patterson want to meet me there? If she could bring the cloak, it would make things easier. They open at nine o'clock."

Chandler asked, "Can your schedule accommodate this?"

Nora smiled. "I think I can manage to rearrange my hectic social calendar."

"Were you planning to attend the opening?"

She shook her head. "No. I don't usually go to the theater."

He was amazed. "Why on earth not?"

Nora shrugged. "I want to open my own shop someday. I can't waste money on the theater." She put her hand to her mouth. "Oops. Sorry. I didn't mean—"

Chandler didn't take offense. He simply said, "Well then, you must be my guest. I insist." He headed to the workroom, where he flung his damp coat over his shoulders and clapped the half-ruined fedora on his head. "Nine o'clock tomorrow morning?"

"Right," Nora said from the doorway to the studio. "It's right on the corner of Tenth and O Streets. You can't miss it."

Not long after Greyson Chandler left, Nora went upstairs and retrieved the dictionary. Settling at the workroom table, she searched until she found and read, *Phlegmatic: Not easily aroused. Composed. Apathetic.* Nora closed the dictionary. Crossing the workroom, she lifted the lid of the little woodstove and fed Dr. Gannon's article to the flames.

CHAPTER 13

A Good Friend

Therefore all things whatsoever ye would that
men should do to you, do ye even so to them.
Matthew 7:12

"Well, if it isn't Nora O'Dell. Hey, Nora!"

Nora was on her way to meet Mr. Chandler and Miss Patterson and had just crossed O Street on Saturday morning when a drunken female voice called her name. Nora turned around, horrified to see Lily stumbling across the street toward her, obviously at the end of a long, long night. She was dressed in an electric purple satin gown, and she had dyed her hair an unbelievable shade of red.

Nora shrank inwardly from the expressions on the faces of several passersby. Her first instinct was to turn away, hurry into Herpolsheimer's, and hope that Lily was sober enough to know she shouldn't follow, and drunk enough to forget the snub. But her second instinct to be a loyal friend won out. Just as Lily arrived at the boardwalk, Nora held out one arm to steady the girl and asked, "Lily, what's happened? What's the matter?"

"Nothin's the matter, Nora. Nothin' a-tall," Lily said, weaving uncertainly and looking up at the sky. "Everthin's jus' fine." A little "Uh-oh," was followed by a gigantic hiccup. Lily giggled then squinted, as if the bright morning sun hurt her eyes. "Nothin' 'cept I did a little business on the side and Goldie kicked me out. Tha's all." She puckered up her face and began to cry. "Oh, Nora, what'm I gonna do *now*?"

People walking by were glowering at the drunken girl sobbing loudly into a none-too-clean handkerchief. Just as Lily said, "Oh, Nora, what'm I gonna do *now*?" Greyson Chandler walked up with Mamie Patterson on his arm.

She took one look at Lily and sniffed audibly.

"Good morning, Miss O'Dell," Chandler said. "Is there some trouble?"

Lily looked up at him. "Hey! I know you. Yer that actor Shep was drinkin' with las' night." She nodded and patted Chandler on the chest. "How are ya?"

Chandler smiled. "I'm fine, miss. But I think you may need some assistance. Can I be of help?"

"Not unless you need a live-in, sweetie," Lily said. She looked at Miss Patterson and covered her mouth with her hand in an exaggerated pose. "Oops. Sorry. Now I've gotten you in trouble."

The long feathers on Miss Patterson's hat waved furiously as she hissed, "Greyson. People are beginning to stare."

"It's all right, Mr. Chandler," Nora said quickly. She linked her arm through Lily's. "I'll take care of Lily."

"Good ol' Nora," Lily sighed, patting Nora's shoulder. "Always takes care of her frens." She turned and looked at Nora. "Don' ya, Nora? Jus' like when you saved my behind that morning when Frank was punchin' on me . . ." She began to tear up again. "You always been a good fren', Nora," she added, drunkenly nodding and beginning to alternately hiccup and sob.

"Nora?" Miss Patterson said in disbelief. She looked at Chandler. "Oh, Grey. What were you thinking? We can't possibly deal with—"

"Miss O'Dell is a first-rate milliner," Chandler said. "She works at Thornhill Dressers. We need her if you want to appear on stage Wednesday evening in that costume. Now behave yourself and go inside. Miss O'Dell and I will be along directly."

"Greyson Chandler," Miss Patterson said firmly. "I am not

about to be ordered about by you or anyone else. And certainly not so you can assist some drunken trollop."

Clasping her gloved hands in front of her, she said to Nora, "I am much too busy to wait while you tend to this *person,* Miss O'Dell."

Nora held fast. "I'm sorry you feel that way, Miss Patterson. Are you certain you cannot meet me later this morning? This really shouldn't take long."

"No," Mamie said firmly.

"It's all right, Nora," Lily said. She pulled away, weaving uncertainly. "You go on. I'll be all right."

"Miss O'Dell." Miss Patterson actually stamped her neatly booted not-so-little foot. "We have an appointment."

"Which, you can see, I cannot keep," Nora said. She reached for Lily and held on to her arm.

Miss Patterson threatened, "We shall take our business elsewhere."

"Do what you must, Miss Patterson." Nora wrapped her arm through Lily's and began to guide her around the corner, thinking to get her to a more inconspicuous spot while she decided what to do.

Miss Patterson thrust her nose high in the air, whirled about, and stormed into Herpolsheimer's.

Greyson Chandler hurried after Nora. "What can I do?"

"You'd better tend to your own troubles," Nora said, nodding toward the store. "Lily can sleep it off in my apartment. Then I'll take her to talk to Goldie."

Lily stirred. "You think if I apologize, she might take me back?"

"Well," Nora said, smiling, "we'll see what we can do." They rounded the corner and were nearing the alley when Lily stumbled.

"Do you think she can walk to Thornhill's?" Chandler asked.

"I doubt it," Nora said truthfully.

"Well then," Chandler said, "wait here and I'll get a carriage."

"You don't have to—"

"I know that. I want to help." He was already hurrying up the street toward the livery stable in the next block.

Nora put her arm around Lily, wrinkling her nose in distaste at the strong smell of whiskey on Lily's breath. She pulled Lily to sit down beside her on the steps of a boarded-up warehouse. "Now, tell me what happened," she said quietly.

"You know me," Lily said, sighing heavily. "Never learn from the first mistake. I told Goldie that Shep was taking me shopping, but I went somewhere else instead." She giggled, then began to cry again.

"Never mind," Nora said quietly. "We'll talk later."

"She'll sleep for hours," Nora said. She was descending the stairs from her apartment over Thornhill Dressers, surprised that Greyson Chandler was still there.

"I imagine so. And have a terrible hangover." He asked abruptly, "Do you think Goldie will take her back?"

"I don't know. Goldie can be—"

"—unbending," Chandler said. At Nora's look of surprise, he smiled. "You can't exactly keep in touch with an old friend like Shep without encountering Goldie." Chandler shook his head. "I wish Shep did something else for a living. He really had a lot of promise."

"What happened?" Nora asked.

"The bottle," Chandler said, shaking his head.

Nora sighed. "I don't know why they can't see it's ruining their lives."

"You're a good friend."

"Well, I owe Lily. She helped me out when I first came to Lincoln."

"I would think broken ribs and not a few stitches had already paid that debt in full," Chandler said. At Nora's look of surprise, he said, "Shep likes to tell stories."

"Yes," Nora said, half whispering. "I imagine he does."

"Don't worry," Chandler said suddenly, "his stories about you haven't damaged your reputation. Quite the contrary."

Nora shook her head. "I can't imagine anything connecting me to Goldie's could help my reputation."

"Actually," Chandler said, "Shep speaks very highly of you. Loyal, true—"

Nora held up her hand, blushing and laughing. "Enough. You make me sound like a prize hunting dog."

Chandler smiled back at her. "Only half right, Miss O'Dell."

"Which half—the head or the tail?" Nora wanted to know.

"The prize." Chandler turned to go. "If you think you can endure another session with Miss Patterson, I'll have her at Herpolsheimer's in an hour."

Nora raised her eyebrows. "Are you certain? She was really angry."

"Haven't you heard about me?" Chandler grinned. "The powers of Svengali. Beware." He closed the door behind him.

Herpolsheimer's "Parade of Parasols" stopped Nora short when she entered the store an hour after putting Lily to bed in her apartment. Every counter sported at least one open parasol, and sunshades and umbrellas had been suspended from the ceiling by thin wire so that it appeared to be raining parasols inside the store. Nora saw samples of the eccentric shapes one of her trade publications had predicted: triangles, pentagons, hexagons, and octagons. Handles ranged from common wood in crooks and loops, to carved pheasants' heads and German porcelain balls. Nora noted that apples, pears, and oranges seemed popular, as did ducks, owls, and swans. She would have to remember those trends for hat trims.

She made one quick trip around the store looking for Chandler and Miss Patterson. When it appeared they had not yet arrived, she indulged herself the opportunity to inspect a few parasols. Her eye was drawn to a white satin one painted in the Japanese style with butterflies. It boasted a chiffon ruffle and a porcelain handle. Nora opened it and looked at herself in the mirror. There was a shade of green in some of the larger butterflies that exactly matched the green bombazine gown hanging in her apartment. Nora glanced at the price. Ah, well. As if she ever had need to dress like a well-to-do lady, anyway.

Apparently Mamie Patterson really had decided to take her business to someone else. Looking at her watch, Nora decided she should check on Lily. She circled round the store once more, enjoying the display overhead, when she was stopped dead in her tracks at the sight of the most elegant parasol she had ever seen. Its ivory handle was carved as a girl in a classical costume picking roses. The entire cover was made of unbelievably intricate, handmade lace over lilac silk. A dark green tassel dangled from the carved ivory tip. Nora dared not touch it, but she stopped, and bent down to look underneath at the lilac silk.

"Something has caught the fair Irish lass's fancy," someone said.

Nora stood up abruptly.

Greyson Chandler was standing on the opposite side of the island of counters, watching her.

Nora blushed. "I—uh—I have to keep up with what's being shown in accessories. It helps me know trends."

"Of course," Chandler said quietly, nodding toward the parasol. "Why don't you pick it up and see how it looks?"

Nora shook her head. "No. That's not necessary." She had seen the price tag. Mrs. Judge Cranston herself would have to save quite a while to afford this treasure. Nora had no intention of touching it.

Chandler made his way around the counter, took the parasol down, closed it, and handed it to Nora. "Really. I insist. Miss Patterson said she'd come, but she's always late. It will give us something to do."

Nora marveled at the intricate workmanship in the parasol's handle.

"There's a mirror over there." Chandler motioned to the back of the store. Then, he touched her arm. Not wanting to appear rude, Nora allowed herself to be led to the mirrors. Mr. Herpolsheimer himself appeared. "May I help you, Mr. Chandler?"

"We're just enjoying your display," Chandler said easily. He turned to Nora. "Go on, Miss O'Dell. See how you like it."

Nora shook her head and held the parasol out to Mr. Herpolsheimer. "No, that's all right. I can't begin to afford it. It is exquisite, though."

The store owner smiled kindly. "Please, Miss O'Dell. One need not be buying to enjoy the Parade of Parasols. Perhaps if you like my things, you will mention me to your millinery customers." He nodded toward the mirror.

Carefully, Nora opened the parasol. She set it over her shoulder.

Mr. Herpolsheimer smiled with approval. "You see, Miss O'Dell, how elegant a lady feels with the right accessories. But that is probably why you enjoy your art so well, eh?"

Mamie Patterson strode up.

Quickly, Nora lowered the parasol and handed it to Mr. Herpolsheimer. "Thank you, sir. It's lovely." She nodded upward. "And that is truly an inspired way to display your wares."

"Well?" Miss Patterson said. "Can we get on with it?"

Greyson Chandler took Nora's arm. "Lead the way, Miss O'Dell. And please rescue Miss Patterson's costume for us." He took Miss Patterson's arm as well, and the three walked to a counter closer to the front of the store.

Miss Patterson was dour and determined not to be pleasant, but in the wake of Greyson Chandler's attentions and Mr. Herpolsheimer's kindness, Nora was just as determined to appear professional.

Several trays of wide ribbon had been laid out and inspected before Chandler saved the day by lifting a piece of ribbon and saying casually, "Look at this one, Mamie. It's very nearly the exact color of your eyes." The ribbon was violet. Mamie had gray eyes.

"Why, Grey," she purred. "How sweet of you to think of that."

"What about this, Miss O'Dell," Grey said. "Will this work?" His eyes pleaded with her.

Nora examined the ribbon. "Well, it could be stiffer. But if I line it—"

"Perfect," Miss Patterson said, snatching up the ribbon and holding it to her face.

Chandler and Miss Patterson left the store after arranging to try on the completed headdress on Monday. Nora waited for the ribbon to be cut. Tucking it in her bag, she went back to take one last admiring look at the lace parasol before returning home to check on Lily.

On Monday morning, a completely restored headpiece stood at Nora's workstation. Miss Thornhill inspected it and nodded with satisfaction. "Let's move the dress frame over here so that when Miss Patterson comes in, she gets the full effect of the cape and the headdress at once."

The morning seemed to drag on, and with every ring of the front doorbell, the knot in Nora's stomach grew larger. But when Greyson Chandler finally escorted his leading lady into the studio, Miss Patterson let out an exclamation of delight. While she primped before the mirror, Chandler spoke with Elise.

"With your permission, Mr. Frost would like to recommend you to the other troupes that come through Lincoln."

Miss Thornhill was delighted, thanking Chandler and asking him to forward a resounding "yes" to Mr. Frost regarding future business.

Miss Patterson finally finished preening before the dressing mirrors. Removing the headdress, she handed it to Miss Thornhill with an imperious, "Have it sent over at once."

As Miss Patterson and Chandler left, the actress pressed two gold coins into Nora's hand. "Thank you so much, dear. You really are an *artiste*." She squeezed Chandler's arm affectionately as they headed out the door.

Nora mumbled her thanks and avoided looking at Chandler, busying herself with packing the headdress in a new bandbox.

The moment the shop door closed, Miss Thornhill crossed the studio to pat Nora on the shoulder. "Congratulations, Miss O'Dell. And thank you. Between your work on the headdress, and my finishing the cape, I think we can call this encounter a resounding success. Mr. Chandler left four tickets to the opening performance so that we can all see our work on stage."

"That will be nice," Nora said noncommittally.

"And," Elise said, "I think you may expect a raise to, shall we say, fifteen dollars a week?"

"Thank you, Miss Thornhill," Nora said sincerely. "It's nice to be appreciated."

113

"I think you might dispense with the 'Miss Thornhill,' Nora." She smiled. "Please call me Elise."

Nora thanked Elise and bent to her work. She wasn't certain she wanted to go to the theater to watch Greyson Chandler and Mamie Patterson together . . . onstage. She was making a braided straw hat to be worn the next week to a meeting at Epworth Park. She wondered if she would ever be invited to Epworth Park . . . or anywhere, for that matter . . . with a nice young man.

Twisting the end of a straw braid, Nora formed a small rosette that she held firmly between thumb and forefinger while she sewed it in place with hidden stitches. Once the rosette was secure, she continued adding rows of braided straw, stopping after each row to sew the inner edge of braid. The coins that Mamie had pressed into her palm lay on the table beside her. She picked them up and tossed them into a drawer. Miss Thornhill might not mind adopting a servile stance with certain customers, but it was something Nora could not seem to manage. She wondered why receiving a tip should bother her so much. She could certainly use the money.

When she had a straw disk the size of the crown of the wire frame she had selected, she affixed it to the wire frame. As she worked, she continued thinking about Mamie Patterson on Greyson Chandler's arm . . . about Lucy and Mr. Fielding . . . about Shep Roberts . . . and Epworth Park. When she finally admitted it, she realized that she would not have minded being tipped, if it had not been Greyson Chandler looking on as Mamie reminded Nora of her place.

Sighing, Nora pondered whether church might be a place to begin after all. Perhaps there, she could meet someone who would be her friend. Dr. Allbright might not approve of the idea, but Nora was beginning to think that for all her bravado, Dr. Allbright was a bit lonely, herself. Certainly she didn't have all of the answers to the questions Nora was beginning to ask.

Nora was in the workroom sipping tea when Elise appeared at the doorway to the studio, her arms filled with a massive bouquet of yellow roses. "Lucy," Nora teased, "is there something about you and Mr. Fielding you need to be telling us?"

Lucy blushed.

Elise held out the card. "These are for you, Nora."

Nora read the card. *For Miss O'Dell, with sincere thanks. G. Chandler.*

CHAPTER 14

Acting the Part

---

*Who whet their tongue like a sword, and bend
their bows to shoot their arrows,
even bitter words.*
Psalm 64:3

On Sunday afternoon Nora was returning from a cable car
ride to Wyuka Cemetery when she encountered Greyson Chandler. He was wearing a pale gray tweed coat with dark gray
trousers and a matching felt hat. Nora tried not to stare at the
huge diamond pin tucked into the fold of his ascot.

He tipped his hat. "I was just going for a walk. Would you
join me for tea?"

Nora said yes and took his arm. They walked several blocks
to the Lindell Hotel. Over tea, Chandler asked, "How did
things turn out for Lily?"

"The way she hoped," Nora said. "Goldie took her back."

"You don't sound pleased."

"Well, I wonder if it would have been better if she would have
had to look for something else."

"But would she have done what you think is best?" Chandler
asked quietly.

Nora shook her head. "No. Probably not."

"It's the same with Shep. I see him once or twice a year when
we come through Lincoln on tour. This time he's more sober. I

guess that's something." He leaned back. "Do you take the cable car out to Wyuka often?"

"Oh, no." Nora laughed. "This was the first time. Shep used to tease me about it. I was terrified of the cable cars when I first came to Lincoln. I guess I just wanted to prove to myself that I wasn't afraid anymore."

"Was your young man busy elsewhere this afternoon?"

Nora look confused. "My—what?" She laughed and shook her head. "I don't have a young man, Mr. Chandler. I'm just me."

He winked at her. "I'm glad to know the roses didn't cause you any trouble."

Nora raised her hand to her mouth. "Oh, how rude of me. I'm so sorry. Thank you. They're beautiful." She put sugar in her tea. "They did cause me a little trouble, though. Lucy and Hannah like to tease me."

Chandler smiled. "Well, if it's any comfort, they caused me a little trouble, too. Mamie found out."

On Tuesday, Chandler ran into Nora when she was on her way to deliver a hat to a patron. He walked with her, waiting at the gate, tipping his hat, and smiling brilliantly while the customer stared and asked Nora if that was really Greyson Chandler waiting for her.

On Wednesday morning, Chandler, came into the shop. He had been just a short distance from Thornhill Dressers when he realized he had a loose vest button. Would Nora mind sewing it on? He accepted a cup of coffee from Hannah and stayed long after the button was reaffixed.

After Chandler left, the hours crawled by. Finally, at five o'clock, Nora rose to lock the door. Just then, a messenger ran up with a package for Miss Nora O'Dell. It contained the lace parasol from Herpolsheimer's. She didn't need to read the card. Who else could have sent it?

Nora told herself it was too expensive, that she couldn't accept it. But when she had donned her green bombazine gown and looked at herself in the mirror with that parasol over her shoulder she couldn't help herself. Besides, she reasoned, any man who could afford a diamond the size of Chandler's tiepin, could afford a parasol.

She might not understand every word of *Hamlet,* but she would be dressed as well as anyone there.

"Who's there?"

"Nay, answer me: Stand, and unfold yourself."

"You come most carefully upon your hour."

" 'Tis now struck twelve; get thee to bed, Francisco."

"For this relief much thanks: 'Tis bitter cold, and I am sick at heart."

Nora had not known what to expect at the opera house. Certainly not this. Listening to the opening lines of the play called *Hamlet* by someone named Shakespeare, she frowned. She reached up with a gloved hand to push at an imaginary out-of-place blonde curl, wondering how she would endure the evening. Her eyes wandered over the theater. Gilt pillars soared up both sides of the stage. Atop each pillar was the imposing bust of a man. Miss Thornhill had told Nora he was the one who had written the play they were to see. Between the busts, heavily carved wooden flowers and clusters of grapes and pears arched over the stage. At the back of the stage was a curtain painted to look like a castle. Nora bent over and looked up, wondering what scenes the other curtains she could see high above the stage displayed.

A ghostly figure appeared onstage, catching Nora's attention. Two men blathered on to one another about it. Apparently they thought the ghost was a king. Nora leaned toward Elise and whispered, "Are they really speaking English?"

Elise whispered encouragement. "Don't try to listen to every individual word. Just let yourself follow the flow of it. Get involved with the actors. Watch and listen with your heart as well as your eyes."

When the two men exited, Nora gathered that the action had moved inside the castle. The same curtain remained in place, but two huge chairs were pushed onto the stage. A dozen people filed in from the wings. Nora recognized Mamie Patterson first.

She was wearing the crown and cape Nora and Elise had worked so hard to realize.

Greyson Chandler stepped from the background, dressed completely in black. His hair shone more golden than Nora remembered it. She had admired his broad shoulders before, but his stage costume revealed much more . . . all of it very, very pleasing. She had always liked the rich tenor of his voice, but his stage voice was remarkable. Nora would read the next day that critics had described Chandler's voice as having "the ring of the trumpet." People would say that his voice enabled him to "exhibit vast power" and "assume unequaled dignity for a man so young." Nora didn't think in such lofty terms. She only knew that with Chandler's first speech as Hamlet, prince of Denmark, Lincoln, Nebraska, ceased to exist. Gone were the gilt pillars and carvings that soared up the sides of the proscenium arch. Gone were the other theatergoers. Nora was swept up in the drama of the events on stage, oblivious to everything around her.

Clasping her hands in her lap, she listened as Elise had advised—with her eyes and her heart. The next two hours were complete magic. She agonized with Hamlet over the death of his father, wept at the madness of Ophelia, and hated Claudius for his duplicity. When at last Horatio said, "Good night, sweet prince, and flights of angels sing thee to thy rest," Nora was embarrassed to realize that tears were stinging her eyes. She hastily brushed them away, relieved that the gaslights along the theater walls were not yet turned up.

Once the actors had taken their bows and the thunderous applause died down, Elise prepared to lead the way toward the exit, but Nora had barely reached the end of the aisle when a dark-haired young man stepped forward. Bowing low, he introduced himself as Ned Gallagher, handed her a card, and waited.

"It's an invitation to join Mr. Chandler backstage."

Lucy's eyes grew wide.

Hannah covered her mouth with a gloved hand.

Nora felt her stomach lurch. She shoved the card toward Elise. "You go, Elise. I don't want to."

"You cannot refuse, Nora. It would be very rude." Elise bent down and said quietly, "We cannot offend these people, Nora. I want their business. It's not all that unexpected. You are, after all, the one who rescued Miss Patterson's costume."

"But you made the cape," Nora protested.

"But *you* are the one invited," Elise said, with a smile.

Lucy nodded. "Go on."

Hannah agreed. "You have to, Nora."

Nora was not anxious to encounter Mamie Patterson again, especially not with the lace parasol in hand.

"Hey," Ned Gallagher interjected. "I don't know what you've heard about actors, but most of us are perfectly nice." He grinned at Nora, raising one hand to his left eyebrow and saluting. "I won't let them boil you in oil or anything. Honest." He offered Nora his arm. "Come on. It won't hurt a bit. I promise."

Reluctantly, Nora took Ned's arm. Bidding Elise, Lucy, and Hannah good evening, she went with Ned. He led her up a narrow stairway and around the proscenium arch where they ducked behind the stage curtain and headed down a long, narrow hallway crowded with trunks and other assorted baggage.

"You ever been backstage before?" Ned asked.

Nora shook her head. "I've never been to a play before tonight."

"What'd you think?"

"It was magical. Even if I didn't understand everything."

Ned laughed, a friendly, easy sound that helped Nora relax. "Don't worry. I don't always understand everything, either, and I can recite the whole thing—every single part. Even Ophelia's."

He led Nora down a narrow hallway where everything was complete bedlam. Rosencrantz and Guildenstern pushed by them, followed by the two clowns who had been grave diggers. The more portly of the clowns was wondering aloud if dinner at the hotel would be beef or pork that evening. He was hoping for both. Claudius, the king of Denmark, disappeared behind one door. Ned finally stopped at the end of the hallway and knocked on a door. Without waiting for a reply, he pushed it ajar and announced, "Miss O'Dell to see Mr. Chandler."

"Thanks, Ned," Chandler answered. He did not come to the door, but Nora heard him call, "Please come in."

Ned opened the door wide, standing aside for Nora to step across the threshold. A woman's touch was evident everywhere in the room, from the painted dressing screen in the corner to the carpet on the floor. Nora realized that what Hannah had said about Chandler and Miss Patterson sharing a dressing room was true.

Greyson Chandler was standing with his back to the doorway, leaning toward a mirror as he wiped makeup off his face. Nora was amazed at the dark lines around his eyes, across his forehead, down his cheeks. He caught her eye in the mirror. "See what they do to me to make me look mad." He winked at her and continued scrubbing the makeup away. Finally, he ran his fingers through his blond hair and turned around.

"Your fine work helped us be a success this evening, Miss O'Dell. Mamie and I wanted to say thank you."

Mamie stepped out from behind the dressing screen in the corner. She wore a flowing silk robe tied about her waist. Instead of echoing Chandler's gratitude, she reached up and removed a wig. Plunking it onto a stand nearby, she began to take down her own hair, which had been plastered against her head to accommodate the wig.

"The roses said thanks enough," Nora said. She did not miss the effect her comment had on Mamie and hurried to add, "And thank you very much for the tickets."

"Did you like our little play?" Mamie interrupted.

Nora nodded. "It was wonderful."

"I thought perhaps you would join us for dinner this evening," Chandler said. "The cast always dines at the Hathaway House after a performance. Would you be my guest?"

Nora saw Mamie pause, hairbrush in midair, and throw an icy stare at Chandler.

Nora shook her head. "I can't. Miss Thornhill expects me at my workstation no later than five-thirty in the morning."

Mamie spoke up. "You'll have to forgive Grey," she said. "He's so accustomed to the actor's schedule, he forgets that most of the world rises with the sun." She tossed the length of hair she had been brushing over her shoulder and put a hand on Chandler's shoulder. "I'm so glad you enjoyed the performance. When Grey said he had invited you, I was worried. Shakespeare can be so difficult for one who hasn't studied."

Nora looked at Chandler. He had noticed that she was carrying the parasol. She blushed and looked away. "Well, at first, I wasn't certain I would like it, but then you—" She corrected herself. "Then Hamlet began to talk, and everything just—" She stopped. "When Hamlet died, it made me cry."

Mamie had begun to pin her hair up while Nora talked. She moved to recapture center stage in the dressing room. "You'll have to come tomorrow. Grey is hilarious in the lead. It's a farce. And the language isn't nearly as difficult as Shakespeare." She finished pinning up her hair and turned around to look at Nora pointedly as she said, "It's much more like what you would have been used to at Goldie's."

"Oh, Mamie," Chandler scolded. He frowned.

"Oh, Mamie, what?" the actress asked as she disappeared behind the dressing screen. "It's the truth, Grey. She'll understand the farce much more easily."

Goldie's. Total surprise was followed by hurt, which quickly melded into anger. Nora opened her mouth to say something. Then, she thought of Elise. Elise had been treated badly by customers before, and she never ever threw mud back in someone's face. This was different from Mrs. Judge Cranston. If Nora alienated these people, the ramifications for Thornhill Dressers could be terrible. Reaching deep inside, Nora found the will to ignore Mamie's barbs. She said quietly, "Thank you, Miss Patterson. Perhaps I will take your advice and attend again tomorrow night. I have a great deal to learn, and I want to take advantage of every opportunity to do so."

She turned to look at Chandler. Swallowing hard to keep her voice from trembling, she said, "Thank you, Mr. Chandler, for the invitation to dinner. You really don't owe me anything more. You paid Miss Thornhill generously, and hopefully Mr. Frost will continue to recommend Thornhill Dressers to your associates. That's quite enough payment for us." Nora wheeled around, brushed past Ned, and started down the hallway, hoping she was headed for an exit.

Chandler went after her. He caught her arm from behind. "Please, Miss O'Dell—Nora. Wait."

Nora stopped and spun around. "I don't recall giving you permission to call me Nora, Mr. Chandler. I'd appreciate it if you wouldn't—even if I am just one of Goldie's girls."

"Let me apologize. Mamie—" He stopped, seeming to search for words. "Mamie depends on me, and when she feels threatened—"

"I'm just an ignorant milliner, Mr. Chandler," Nora interrupted. "But I don't think I need you to translate what just happened. I understood perfectly. I should have gotten the message the day you two were in the shop and she tipped me. I should have known when she called me 'dear.' And I should never have enjoyed your company at the Lindell, or anywhere else, for that matter."

Angry tears threatened to spill down her cheeks, but Nora blinked rapidly and willed them away. Imitating a flirtatious pose she had learned from Lily, she placed one hand on her hip and the other on Chandler's shoulder. "Listen, honey, you tell Miss Patterson that her feelin' threatened by little ol' me is just silly. Land sakes, I'm just one of Goldie's girls. Nobody takes us seriously." She fluttered her eyelashes. Then, drawing herself up as tall as possible and hoping she seemed dignified, Nora said, "Now, if you don't mind, I've been reminded of my place, and I think it's time I returned to it. And I won't be needing this on my side of the tracks." She handed Chandler the parasol and headed for a door marked "Exit."

Ned followed her. "Hey, that was great. You told *him*. And he'll tell *her*. Can I walk you home?"

"Sure you want to be seen with someone who used to work at Goldie's Garden?" Nora said bitterly.

"What do I care about that?" the boy said.

Nora stopped and stared at him. "Listen up, Mr. Gallagher. I was strictly a housekeeper at Goldie's. A *housekeeper*. Got that? So, if you're thinking—"

"Hey," the boy said, almost angrily, "all I was thinking was you're a nice girl with a lot of spunk and I thought we could have a nice walk. Get the chip off your shoulder, will you? We're not all like Chandler and Patterson."

"All right then," Nora said.

"All right then." Ned held out his arm. They walked along in silence for a block or so, when Ned suddenly asked, "Did Mr. Chandler really send you roses?"

"Yes," Nora said. "Why?"

Ned whistled softly under his breath. "I've known him a long time. He never sent a woman roses before."

CHAPTER 15

Cherubs

Behold, thou art fair, my love.
Song of Solomon 1:15

The Frost Players had been scheduled to remain in Lincoln for a short engagement, but when, at the conclusion of the week, Mr. Funke received a telegram informing him that the next act booked into his opera house would be forced to cancel its engagement, Frost's troupe voted to remain in Lincoln for an extended run. Each of the five women in the troupe flocked to Thornhill Dressers to order new gowns. They didn't seem to mind that the finished work would have to be shipped to their next destination and might need further alterations by another dressmaker.

Ned Gallagher asked Nora for "permission to call." Ned had been in the theater since he was a child, crisscrossing the United States several times and even touring in Europe once. He was a superb storyteller with a generous store of anecdotes. Ned didn't flirt, and he seldom mentioned Chandler or Patterson. Nora spent enough time with Ned that Lucy began to tease her about him instead of Greyson Chandler.

Ned Gallagher's assertion that Chandler had never sent roses to a woman didn't seem to mean anything. Nora had heard nothing from either Chandler or Patterson since the performance of *Hamlet*.

Sewing for the theatrical troupe yielded more than just monetary benefits. Imitating them taught Nora flawless grammar. Knowing them taught Nora not to feel inferior to someone just because they were famous. She knew that the Mamie Patterson the "upper class" invited to dinner was no more real than the innocent ingenue Mamie sometimes played onstage. She knew that Felicia Bonaparte's hourglass figure was created with an ingeniously designed corset, and that beneath her puritanical visage, Rosalind Frey hid a propensity for red and lavender petticoats and outlandishly woven stockings.

Nora would have found a measure of contentment, had it not been for those yellow roses. Lucy reported that Chandler and Patterson dined together every evening and always retired at the same time. But Ned had said that Chandler had never given a woman roses. Hannah saw Chandler and Patterson together in Dover's Dry Goods store. Miss Patterson was examining a pair of striped hose and seemed to be asking Mr. Chandler's opinion. But Ned had said—Nora finally tossed the roses out.

When Chandler and Patterson finally returned to Thornhill Dressers, Nora was out with Ned Gallagher. It had been over a week since the opening of *Hamlet*. The troupe would depart for Denver in two days.

Mamie selected an elegant navy blue watered silk for a new gown, with the stipulation that it must be completed before the train left Lincoln.

In the interest of future business, Elise sacrificed twenty-two of her most treasured French enamel buttons to grace the bodice of the exquisite gown. With Elise and Lucy and Hannah rushing madly to complete it, Nora felt compelled to sacrifice an evening to do her part. "If you can get the thing put together," she said reluctantly, "I'll do the handwork tonight."

On Friday evening, Nora carried the gown upstairs to her tiny apartment, with mixed feelings. She was determined to fulfill her promise to Elise, but she couldn't help resenting the fact that Mamie Patterson, who least deserved it, was once again getting preferential treatment. Set in gilded-copper mountings, the buttons glistened against the navy blue watered silk. Nora was having a great deal of difficulty not envying Mamie Patterson those buttons, each one featuring a cherub painted in white on a blue ground. Nora jerked the sewing thread angrily as it knotted and tangled around a button. Finally, she held the garment up. All twenty-two buttons would march in an unwavering line from Miss Patterson's neckline, across her ample bosom and down to the waist, which, Nora reminded herself, was beginning to thicken.

Nora scolded herself for her unkind thoughts. She had spent a great deal of time trying not to be envious of Mamie Patterson over elegant gowns and delicious buttons . . . and her power over Greyson Chandler. Nora sighed. What *did* he see in that woman?

Downstairs in the studio, Elise closed the shop door and locked it. Although it was a full half hour before her usual closing time, she pulled the cords that lowered the curtains behind each of her four display windows. The drapes operated like individual stage curtains, providing a backdrop to the creations that Elise displayed in her shop windows, while at the same time blocking the view of the shop's interior from passersby. The system of drapes enabled Elise to work late into the night in her shop whenever necessary while protecting her privacy and giving her a sense of security.

Tonight, however, Elise had no plans to work late. A secretive smile played across her face as she produced a gigantic basket from behind a counter and positioned it in the middle of the large table in the center of the studio. She lit the gas lamps, moderating their glow until the studio was bathed in soft golden light. Once everything was arranged to her satisfaction, Elise went to the back door to welcome a latecomer into the shop.

Upstairs in her apartment, Nora stood up and stretched. Picking up the newspaper, she skimmed the headlines. A final review of the production at the opera house caught her eye. She sank into a chair and began to read. The reviewer spoke of Mamie Patterson as "first and last, a natural-born actress." *How right they are,* Nora thought unkindly. She read the next paragraph carefully.

It appears that Miss Patterson has invented a new stage kiss. She stands with her back to the audience near the footlights. The husband, played by Greyson Chandler, rushes wildly into her arms. They hold each other at arm's length. Her bosom heaves. He pants. He looks down at her, and she looks up at him. Then he suddenly places his lips to hers. She clasps him about the head and they are, as it were, glued together. Men around town have their watches out timing them. That is the Patterson kiss.

Nora threw the paper aside, happy that she had planned to be away from the studio when Miss Patterson picked up the garment the next morning.

"Nora," Elise called up the stairs. "I'm leaving. Shall I lock up?"

"No," Nora called back. "I can do it. I'll come down and arrange Miss Patterson's gown on the dress form in the studio before I retire."

"Thank you," Elise said. "I appreciate your extra hours, Nora. Have a good evening. And enjoy your breakfast with Mr. Gallagher."

Regretting that she had read the paper at all, Nora draped Miss Patterson's new gown over her arm and descended the stairs. Halfway down, she thought she heard footsteps in the front studio. She hesitated. Elise was gone and Hannah had flitted out the back door more than an hour ago on some mysterious errand. Lucy was with her Mr. Fielding.

When she reached the bottom step, Nora heard a noise again. Her heart thumping, she called out, "Is someone there?"

No one answered, but Nora knew that someone was, indeed, in the studio. As noiselessly as possible, she tiptoed to the cutting table opposite the back door. Trembling with fear, she grasped a pair of sewing scissors in her right hand. She hid the scissors beneath the folds of Miss Patterson's gown and headed toward the studio.

Nora paused just before launching herself through the door. Someone had lowered the gaslights to cast a warm glow throughout the studio. Someone had pulled the curtains behind the display windows. And someone had covered the worktable with a white linen cloth . . . and then set it with elegant tableware. Greyson Chandler was lighting the last of six candles held by a silver candelabra. What the candlelight did to his already handsome face made Nora take a quick breath.

"What's this?" Nora said.

"I believe it's called dinner," Chandler said. He looked up. "It's also my attempt at an apology. If this doesn't work, I plan to fall on my knees and beg your forgiveness." Nora didn't say anything. He smiled. "If you don't agree to dine with me, I'm going to feel like a first-rate fool. But I wouldn't blame you if you kicked me out."

He walked toward Nora and took the gown into his arms. "Here. Let me help you. This *is* the new gown Mamie ordered?"

Nora nodded, pointing at the waiting empty dress form that stood on the opposite side of the studio. "I was going to put it there. She's to come for it in the morning."

Chandler walked to the dress form. "Well then, let's get the thing on display."

Nora hurried to his side, still clutching the scissors in her hand.

Clumsily, Chandler pulled the gown down over the dress form.

He reached for the scissors. "May I take the fact that you haven't stabbed me with these as a sign that you might consider dinner?"

Nora nodded dumbly. "Of course I'll have dinner. I just— need to—" She fumbled with the gown, wishing her hands would stop trembling. When at last it was arranged to, she stood back to admire it.

From behind her, Chandler asked, "What's this?"

He was standing by her workstation at the opposite end of the studio holding up a string of buttons on a yellow ribbon.

"It's called a charm string." Nora blushed. "It's a silly fad. Hannah and Lucy got me started. Kind of a way to keep memories."

"Tell me about it," Chandler said. He walked toward her.

Looking down, he rubbed his thumb across the face of one of the buttons. "What's special about this one?"

"That was my mother's."

He raised his eyes to hers. "I've been 'pumping' Ned for information about you. I didn't think you knew your mother."

Nora stammered a little. "I—I didn't really know· her. But there were a few things in a little trunk."

"What do you know about it?"

"Only that it was important to my mother." She felt awkward and groped for a topic that would draw attention from herself. She asked abruptly, "What about you? Do you keep in touch with your mother? She must be very proud of you."

Chandler shook his head. "No, I haven't heard from her in a very long time. She was stunned when I took up acting. It's rather scandalous to be an actor where I grew up." He frowned slightly. "It wasn't at all what they had in mind for me. Lately I've begun to understand why they felt the way they did."

"But surely they would be proud—if they knew. I mean, what could be wrong with *Shakespeare?*"

Chandler leaned against the worktable, fingering the string of buttons. "It's not the Shakespeare they objected to. It's the off-stage atmosphere. The temptations." He lowered his voice and said softly, "About which, it seems, they were quite right. I was raised in a very conservative, churchgoing household. They wouldn't be very proud about some of my involvements." He added, "But then, neither am I."

"But they should know how successful you've become. You should write. If you have a family, you shouldn't just give them up." When Chandler looked up, Nora apologized. "I'm sorry. It's really none of my business. I just can't imagine having a family and not wanting them."

"It's not a matter of not wanting them," Chandler said quietly. "It's a matter of if they want *me*." He cleared his throat. "Never mind. Tell me about the other buttons."

Nora pointed to a small white one. "This one is from a dress I mended for Lily at Goldie's."

"And this one?" Chandler pointed to a small black jet button. Had he meant to touch her hand? Nora took a tiny step backward. Holding both hands behind her back, she recited, "That's the kind I put on my first really good dress. Goldie had it made for me . . . sort of as a farewell. I thought I'd never have a place to wear it, but then you sent the tickets to *Hamlet.*"

He looked down at her. "The green dress with the frill at the neck. And a matching bonnet that sits like so—" He gestured with his free hand.

"Yes. That's the one."

He grinned. "You could say, then, that this one commemorates our first evening together."

She nodded.

"Although I suppose you'd just as soon not remember that." He laid aside the charm string. "Let's sit down, shall we?"

They sat down at the table, and Chandler began to take their supper from the basket. While he worked, he asked, "Which story do you believe?"

"What?" Nora asked.

"Which button story is popular here in Lincoln? The one about the old maid or the one about marriage? I believe the thousandth button has something to do with one or the other."

Nora exclaimed, "You tricked me! You already know all about charm strings."

Chandler grinned and shrugged. "A couple of the women in the troupe started strings last year in New York. But you didn't answer my question . . . about the end of the charm string."

"I don't believe either story. I just like buttons." She took a sip of water.

Chandler sat down opposite her and took a deep breath. "You've caused me a great deal of trouble, you know. After Mamie found out about those roses I thought I'd never hear the end of it."

Nora took a deep breath. "You know, Mr. Chandler, you've caused me some trouble, too. Asking me to tea. Walking me to deliver a package. Visiting the shop. You ask me backstage, and Miss Patterson lays into me. What did I ever do to *her?*"

"You attracted my attention," Chandler said quietly. "Mamie knows I've never sent roses to a woman before. Not even her."

"Well, I don't like being in the middle of things," Nora said quickly. "Especially when I'm not even certain what I'm in the middle *of*."

Chandler reached out to touch her arm. "I had no intention of putting you in the middle of anything." He looked at her. "The real reason for this is—" He paused, seeming to grope for words. Finally, he sat back, raising one hand to stroke his mustache while he looked at Nora. "Would you do something for me?"

"What?"

"Would you consider having dinner with me this evening?"

Nora looked at him, confused. "What?"

"With me." He touched his hand to his chest. "Greyson Chandler, the person. Not the actor, not Mamie Patterson's partner. Just me. Could we do that?"

Nora nodded slowly. She saw Chandler's shoulders relax. His smile became more genuine. He took a sip of water. "I never, ever, expected to be a successful actor. I thought I might get a few minor parts from time to time . . . but what I really expected was to be the music director for a troupe. Then one evening our leading man was taken ill, and I, the understudy, stepped onstage. I wasn't at all prepared for the consequences . . . and I've never been really comfortable with some of them."

"Yes, poor boy," Nora teased. "One *would* get weary of all the fluttering eyelashes and sighs. It must be a terrible trial to have every woman you meet falling all over herself to impress you. And enduring the famous Patterson kiss would be pure torture."

"As a matter of fact," Chandler said quietly, "it gets downright annoying at times. In some cities I can't eat in a restaurant without women giggling and watching my every move." He looked across the table at Nora. "The illusion of Mamie and I as a couple provided a sort of buffer. It all seemed perfectly harmless." He sat back and shook his head. "Unfortunately, somewhere along the way Mamie seems to have forgotten that we're just playacting. I didn't realize it until I took an interest in a certain blonde-haired milliner."

Nora took a sudden interest in her dinner.

Chandler shrugged. "Sometimes I forget why I'm in the theater at all. Cancelled engagements and destroyed costumes, homesick troupe members and disagreements with theater owners . . . they take their toll. And then there is Mamie." He took a deep breath and let it out very slowly. "Well. Not your problem, obviously. Masculine whining is very unattractive." He changed the subject. "What about you? *Wherefore art thou,* Miss O'Dell?"

Nora smiled. "There's very little to tell about me. I'm from—"

"—Hickory Grove," Chandler said. "Ned told me. What made you leave?"

"Hard biscuits," Nora replied. The expression on Chandler's face made her laugh. "Really. It's the truth." Having begun the story, Nora felt compelled to finish it. Somehow, what Chandler had requested of her happened. She was no longer dining with Greyson Chandler, actor. She told him more than she intended about her childhood, then apologized. "I'm sorry. I didn't mean to sound quite so pathetic. As you said, whining isn't very attractive." She concluded her autobiography. "After the biscuits, I packed a bag and started walking. I stopped when I got to Lincoln."

"Shep told me about Lily bringing you to Goldie's," he said. He pretended to wield a shovel at an imaginary enemy. "Has the Lincoln baseball team heard about you?"

Nora smiled but changed the subject. "I thought your parents were in the theater like Ned's. But from what you said earlier, that's obviously not the case."

Chandler shook his head. "No. I come from plain American farming stock. But even as a child I was much more interested in music than crops. I had other brothers to take on the farm work, so my parents finally let me go. I was studying in Philadelphia when one evening I saw Edwin Booth in *Hamlet.*"

Chandler's eyes glowed as he shared the memory. "I can't really explain it, but the moment Booth strode onto the stage, the entire audience seemed to be charged with electricity. I don't know if anyone even took a breath during his soliloquy. It was nearly a religious experience, the communion between that actor and his audience—"

Chandler sat back abruptly. He seemed almost embarrassed and stabbed a piece of fruit with his fork before saying nonchalantly, "What you saw at the opera house here was mere caricature compared to Edwin Booth. At any rate, that was the moment I knew I wanted to be on the stage. I knew I would never have Booth's power over an audience, but I knew I had to try."

"You *do* have power over an audience," Nora said. "I felt it that night when you first opened here in Lincoln. They were all with you. Even the fops in the balcony quieted when you walked onstage. I can't imagine having such a gift. Your family should know about it."

"Oh, I imagine they're very content not knowing about a lot of it," Greyson said.

Nora protested, "They would be very proud of you."

He pulled on his mustache as he considered what she said. "Maybe. About the acting. But there are other things." He looked up at her and shrugged. "I'm not very proud of myself." He sighed. "This Mamie business. I've known it was getting out of hand, but I let it go on, because it was to my advantage. That's despicable." He frowned. "Tell me, Miss O'Dell, what does one do to reclaim one's honor?"

Nora shook her head. "You're asking the wrong person about that. I've been too busy trying to survive to think about anything that philosophical. Just getting the next hat finished has been about all I could manage."

"You don't ever contemplate the future? Plans? Dreams?"

"I want my own shop, if that's what you mean. I'm good at millinery, and it's one of the few professions where a woman can make an honorable living."

"See, you *have* considered metaphysics," he chided. "You've considered the matter of honor in selecting a career." He leaned forward. "Does Miss Thornhill know you're planning a defection?"

Nora smiled. "It won't come as a surprise. She's encouraged me from the very beginning to keep learning and growing."

"Do learning and growing include marrying Ned Gallagher?"

Nora was so taken aback by the question, she stared open-mouthed at Chandler. Finally, she gathered her thoughts. "That would be none of your business, Mr. Chandler."

He smiled. "That would be right. Humor me. Answer it anyway."

"I don't have plans to marry anyone," Nora said quietly.

"Why not?"

She took a sip of water and set the glass down firmly. "I'll depend on me and pay my own way through life."

"It sounds like a lonely life." He looked at Nora. "Don't you think people need each other?"

Nora was sitting with her hand on the edge of the table. Chandler covered it with his. The two sat quietly for a moment. Nora's heart raced. *Memorize this moment* she told herself. She looked down at the tangled pattern of veins on the back of Grey's hand. He squeezed her hand softly. She didn't pull away.

"You haven't eaten your dessert," Grey said quietly. Still, he didn't release her hand.

"I'm not hungry anymore."

He pushed his chair away from the table and leaned toward her, taking her hand in both of his. "If someone named Grey Chandler wrote to you, do you think you'd write back?" His eyes searched hers.

"Yes."

"And if he disengaged himself from a certain actress, would you think that a good thing?"

Nora swallowed. "Yes, but—I wouldn't want to be the cause of trouble for you."

Chandler let her hand go. He rubbed his forehead briskly. "The only one who's causing me trouble is myself. I've made some very poor choices in the past. I think it's time I righted them. And—" He smiled slowly. "I think perhaps it *is* time I wrote home. You're right about family. One shouldn't give them up so easily." He stood up and began to pack their supper back into the basket.

Nora stood up to help him, feeling very self-conscious as they worked side by side. When their shoulders touched, she pulled away.

Grey looked down at her. "I hope—I hope you won't let Ned Gallagher steal you away before—"

"I told you, Ned and I are just friends."

"You'd better tell Ned that," Chandler said softly. Then, before Nora knew what was happening, he gathered her into his arms and kissed her. Her mind told her that she should push him away. She put her hands on his shoulders to do that. But then she didn't push. Instead, she kissed him back.

Chandler finally let go. Taking their picnic basket by both hands, he said quietly, "There are two things you need to know about me. Ned was right. I've never in my life sent a woman roses." He looked at her. "And I've never left after a kiss like that. I'm ashamed of that, but it's the truth. I have some things to straighten out. When I get it done, I'll be back. And I'm going to ask for a good deal more than a stolen dinner and one kiss."

CHAPTER 16

Everything in Writing

*Train up a child in the way he should go: and
when he is old, he will not depart from it.*
Proverbs 22:6

On Saturday morning, Nora awoke before dawn. Leaping out
of bed, she washed her face and did her hair before pulling on
the green bombazine dress. Her hands were trembling with excitement as she inspected herself in the mirror. *Green with a frill
at the neck, and a hat worn like this.* He had even remembered
what she wore to the theater!

The morning seemed to drag by. Lucy and Hannah finally
arrived.

Nora descended the stairs trembling with excitement. "I've
changed my mind," she said. "I'd like to go with you to the
train station. Is it still all right?"

Lucy and Hannah exchanged glances. "Of course," Lucy
said, nodding. She added, "You sure dressed up for Ned Gallagher. Anything you want to tell us?"

"Ned?" Nora pursed her lips. "Oh, Ned. I'd forgotten—"

Just then, Ned Gallagher knocked on the back door. Once
inside, he looked Nora over approvingly. "Say, you look great. I
didn't expect you to get all dressed up just for breakfast."

"Well," Nora said, "it's your last day, and I thought I'd look
nice for you."

Ned offered her his arm. "I'm taking you to the Hathaway House today."

"We'll meet you at the station later," Lucy called.

Nora nodded vaguely.

As they walked up the street, Ned said, "Say, Nora, we've had some good times, haven't we?"

"Yes we have. Thank you, Ned. I'm going to miss you."

"Do you mean that? I mean, if I write to you or something, would you maybe answer me?"

Nora patted him on the arm affectionately. "Of course I will. I'd love to hear from you. Will you be with the troupe if they come through Lincoln in the fall?"

"If Mr. Frost still wants me, I will be. But it's going to be strange without Chandler in the company. Hard to know what's going to happen."

Nora stopped. "What do you mean?"

"He and Miss Patterson had a huge fight this morning." Ned corrected himself. "Actually, Chandler was calm about the whole thing. It was Miss Patterson who threw the fit. Everyone on the third floor of the Hathaway House must have heard it. Apparently Chandler didn't come home last night. Patterson was furious. He wouldn't say where he was, and that made her even madder. Then Mr. Frost joined the fray, trying to calm them down. Whatever was said, Chandler got canned." Ned shook his head from side to side. "I couldn't believe it, but I saw it with my own eyes. Greyson Chandler walking out of the hotel with a bag in his hand."

"Where do you think he went?" Nora was doing her best to sound only casually interested.

"Darned if I know," Ned said. "All I know is Mr. Frost said we're leaving as scheduled, that he's wired Denver to find a replacement for Chandler."

They walked to the Hathaway House hotel and in to the dining room. Ned ordered breakfast, and the waiter had just poured coffee when Mr. Frost entered with a red-eyed, puffy-faced Mamie Patterson on his arm.

Miss Patterson had taken up a napkin and spread it on her lap before she saw Ned and Nora. Snatching the napkin up and laying it on the table, she got up and marched to their table. "Miss O'Dell," Mamie said.

Nora stood up, suppressing a smile as she looked down upon the actress. It was difficult to feel inferior to someone so much shorter. "Yes, Miss Patterson."

"If you see Mr. Chandler," she said icily, "or should I say *when* you see him?"

Nora didn't say anything, so Mamie continued. "You may inform him that he can claim his things from Mrs. Hathaway." She drew a lace-edged handkerchief from her sleeve and dabbed at her eyes. "Do you know who Mrs. Hathaway is?"

"Yes. We've met," Nora said.

"Oh, of course. You've made hats for her, I suppose."

Nora began to sit down, but Mamie grabbed her sleeve. "Were you able to finish the watered silk gown?"

"Of course," Nora said. "We always do our best to keep our word, Miss Patterson. I sewed the buttons on myself late last evening."

"Oh," Mamie said, her voice trembling with rage. "You were *sewing* last evening?"

"Yes," Nora replied.

"Well, you can inform Miss Thornhill that I have decided not to take the gown, after all."

Nora narrowed her gaze and stared at Miss Patterson. Mamie had selected some of the most expensive material they carried, and now several yards of it were a complete loss. Could she really be so petty as to cause Elise such a loss because of one dinner? The hatred in the woman's eyes almost frightened her. Nora's anger melted. How unhappy she must be.

"I hope we haven't displeased you in some way, Miss Patterson," Nora said quietly. "The gown is lovely. I'm sure you'd like it."

"I'm afraid that doesn't matter now," Mamie said, lifting her nose in the air and sighing deeply. "I simply cannot bear the thought of wearing that dress. It would be a constant reminder of heartache."

"I'm very sorry, Miss Patterson," Nora said. She almost meant it.

Mamie swept back to where Mr. Frost was seated. Nora and Ned returned to their breakfast, after which Nora accompanied him to the train station. She met up with Lucy and Hannah, and the foursome made their way through the crowd and onto the platform.

As the conductor called, "All aboard," Nora stood on tiptoe and kissed Ned on the cheek. "Good-bye, Ned. I hope I'll see you again."

Ned leaned down to return Nora's kiss, planting a clumsy buss on her lips. He blushed furiously and ran for the train car. Climbing aboard, he took off his hat and waved it in the air. Nora raised her hand to say good-bye. The whistle blew and the train began to move out.

Someone shoved Nora from behind and spun her around. As she raised her hand to steady her hat, Greyson Chandler wrapped one arm around her and kissed her. He shoved the lace parasol in her hands. The train picked up steam, and Chandler ran, bag in hand, to catch it. He barely managed to grab the railing on the last car, pulling himself aboard just at the end of the platform. He turned around and raised his hand. Nora returned the gesture, standing on the platform and watching until the train was out of sight.

Grey kept his word. Nearly every Friday a letter arrived. He was in Denver. He had written home and planned to visit soon. He was living off his savings, trying to find answers to what he called "the deeper questions of life."

Summer's heat brought the dress business to a standstill. In spite of her efforts to the contrary, Nora found herself marking the passage of time by the arrival of Grey's letters.

Dr. Allbright escaped the city and headed for a small town to the northwest called Millersburg. "They've been after me to come out and open a practice there for years," she said.

"But isn't it the worst possible time of year to travel?" Nora asked. "It's so hot. You'll be miserable."

"Exactly," Dr. Allbright replied. "If I see any merit at all to the move, I'll know the worst. If I can bear the heat of summer in Custer County, I can bear anything it has to throw at me."

Dr. Allbright was gone for two weeks. When she returned, she had decided to move. She was more animated than she had been in months. She prepared for the move with gusto, and in less than a month, she had closed her office, and arranged for the railroad to ship her furnishings to Millersburg.

The combination of Dr. Allbright's departure and what seemed to be the death of her millinery business sunk Nora into depression.

"Business always slows down this time of year." Miss Thornhill encouraged her. She had propped the door to the shop open in a vain attempt to capture any passing breeze. "Dressmakers only work a few months out of the year. No one wants to think about layers of cloth when the thermometer is approaching one hundred." She went on, "But we don't have to be idle. Now is the time for us to be perusing all the fashion magazines and making up models for the fall. With the first breath of cool air, we'll be busier than you can imagine."

Grey wrote a strange letter that left Nora feeling more distant from him than ever.

I've had a deep change of heart. A return to my roots. In the Book of Proverbs, it says, "Train up a child in the way he should go: and when he is old he will not depart from it." I don't know if my parents ever claimed that Scripture for their son, but regardless, it has come true in my life.

Have you kept your promise to Miss Thornhill about church? I wish you would. I want you to understand what's happened to me. It's a change at the center of my being. I didn't think that God could forgive all I'd done, but He has.

I can tell you the exact moment it all happened. I was walking alone up in the mountains, and I sat down to read. A grasshopper jumped on the page, and then my eye fell to Isaiah 40. Yes, I was reading the Bible. No one will ever be able to convince me that that grasshopper was coincidence. You must read the entire passage, Nora, to understand the impact it had on me . . . the reminder that I am but a grasshopper, and yet God has His eye on me.

Lessons from my childhood came roaring back into my head. I was overcome with a sense of my own sinfulness and I wept. But then followed a sense of God's great love. I looked at the mountains before me and knew, as surely as I know I am writing this, that I was forgiven. I understood that Christ had to die . . . not for the entire world in general, but specifically and personally for me.

I'm going home a new man, and I'm going to get on my knees and ask my dear mother to forgive her erring son. And then, when the time is right, I'll be back in Lincoln, calling on a certain blonde beauty, and as I promised when I left, I'll be expecting much more than dinner and a kiss.

Each time Nora reread the letter, she had new questions. She knew that Miss Thornhill could probably answer them, but then Miss Thornhill would know more about her and Grey. Nora wanted to keep their growing friendship to herself. She had begun to hope it was a romance, but she didn't want to risk it by telling anyone. Grey's letter made her feel uneasy.

She bought a Bible and found the passage that Grey had referred to, but the only impact it had on her was impressing her mind with the less-than-comforting picture of God blowing on things and making them wither.

As for going to church, she remembered Goldie's opinions about preachers. What if Miss Thornhill's pastor was *that* kind? She remembered what Lucy and Hannah had said about Madame Hart, too. She was a "high-muck-a-muck" in her church, and yet Lucy and Hannah knew her for her cruelty as an employer. Nora didn't know what had happened to Grey, but she hoped he hadn't found the kind of religion that would make him a self-righteous hypocrite.

Just when Nora had determined to write to Dr. Allbright and ask her opinion about some of the things Grey mentioned in his letters, she received an invitation.

Dear Nora,
I am writing to encourage you to take a vacation to Custer County. I enclose a copy of the Millersburg Republi-

can *so that you may see for yourself the spirit of our bustling little city. I also extend an invitation from Mrs. Cay
Miller, wife of the proprietor of the largest dry goods store
in town (indeed, wife of the gentleman who owns most of
the town), to meet with her to discuss opening a millinery
shop in connection with Miller's Emporium. She is no Elise
Thornhill, but she is fair and honest, and your business
would be an instant success.*

*If the opportunity appeals to you, please let me know at
once. I can provide lodging and would be happy to meet
your train, if you only forward your travel particulars. You
can buy a ticket straight through to Millersburg, only be
certain you don't change trains at Grand Island and you
can't go wrong.*

Yours—Maude

Nora read the letter with mixed emotions. She smiled at Dr.
Allbright's having signed her name "Maude." It felt good to be
on a first-name basis with a physician.

She opened the newspaper that Dr. Allbright had enclosed.
The ladies of the First Church were hosting a strawberry and ice
cream social. A first-rate cobbler was needed in town. "Italian
Chris" would provide music for a dance at the Delhommes' on
Friday night. Professor E. A. Garlich offered piano and violin
lessons in his home every weekday except Monday, when he
traveled to Merna to instruct the young people there.

Nora chuckled reading a humorous article purporting to be
the membership roster of the "Millersburg Bachelors' Club."
Lonesome Pratt, Askme Thompson, Gotleft Smith, Allgone An-
drews, and Willing Williams begged the ladies of Millersburg to
"hear their cry" and attend the dance at Delhommes' on Friday
night.

Nora liked the friendly tone of the newspaper. She could
write Grey and let him know her new address. He had only
hinted of the future, and if he had gone off on some religious
tangent, she dare not plan her future around his half-promise to
return to Lincoln "for more than dinner."

Nora slept fitfully that night. When Elise came in the back door of the shop the next morning, Nora was waiting. "I'd like your opinion of something," she said, wishing her hand would stop shaking as she held out the letter.

Elise read it.

"It probably wouldn't work out," Nora said. "I haven't saved nearly enough to open my own shop. The timing is a little off, but—"

"You should definitely go and see what it's like," Elise said firmly. She smiled. "If this Mrs. Miller wants you badly enough, she'll be able to help you with setup expenses. It's a dry goods store, and that means they already have a stock of supplies. It might not cost all that much to get started."

Nora shifted her weight from one foot to the other. "I wouldn't want to leave you shorthanded."

"Business is slow right now. It's an excellent time for you to go exploring this new opportunity. And, if you decide to move, I'll have time to find and train your replacement before we get busy." She patted Nora on the shoulder. "I didn't expect to keep you forever, Nora. I knew you'd be wanting your own shop. And I won't hold you back."

She reached for a pad of paper and a pencil. "Sit down. Let's talk about some of the things you'll need to check into." Elise was already making notes. She spent the next hour educating Nora on opening her own business. "Before you leave, I'll write out a list of questions. Dr. Allbright can refine it to fit Millersburg before you ever talk to Mrs. Miller."

She disappeared into the studio and returned with a huge box. Taking off the lid, she pulled out Mamie Patterson's blue silk gown. "What would you say to our cutting this down to fit you for the trip? You can't be seen in green bombazine for the rest of your life, you know. This will make you look like the prosperous businesswoman I know you'll be. Although," she said, grinning, "I would recommend more conservative buttons."

Nora blinked back tears. She stood up and hugged Elise. "Thank you. I was nervous about asking."

"Well, there's no need to be nervous. I'm happy for you. And

I don't envy you Millersburg one bit. Custer County can be an oven this time of year."

Nora wired Dr. Allbright that she would be coming for a visit. Early on Monday morning, Lucy, Hannah, and Elise all accompanied Nora to the train station. As Miss Thornhill had predicted, Nora looked like a very prosperous businesswoman in Mamie Patterson's remade blue watered-silk gown. They had replaced the cherub buttons with pewter.

"I only wish I felt as confident as I look," Nora said on the platform. "My stomach is tied in knots." Elise hugged her and she climbed aboard, finding her seat and opening the window.

Elise reached up from the platform to squeeze her hand. As the train began to move, she said, "Don't forget to get the answers to all the questions we discussed. And don't let Mrs. Miller push too hard." She walked alongside the train, still talking. "Remember that you have something the entire city needs. Don't sign anything until you have a lawyer look it over." The train chugged off. Elise called out, "Get everything in writing!"

CHAPTER 17

Explanations

----

*Execute true judgment, and shew mercy and
compassions every man to his brother.*
Zechariah 7:9

Nora had considered many of the "what-ifs" surrounding her
move to Millersburg. But one thing she had not contemplated
was *What if I get sick on the train?* What she had dismissed as
nervousness the morning of her departure soon proved to be a
full-blown case of the ague. Nora knew what it was, for her
own symptoms were almost an exact copy of those Pap had
once suffered. First, she began to feel weak and feverish. She
barely made it onto the platform at the front of the train car
before her stomach revolted against breakfast. Weak and shaky,
she clung to the railing around the platform as the train moved
west. When the wind blew the smoke from the engine around
her, she moved back inside, choking and gasping for breath.

Once in her seat, Nora felt chilly. Grabbing her shawl, she
burrowed into it. She had barely stopped shivering when a sudden flash of heat made her throw it aside and head outside for
fresh air. No one on the train seemed inclined to help her. She
finally realized they must be afraid of contagion. She longed for
a drink of water and rejoiced when the train pulled in at Grand
Island for a scheduled stop.

Nora stumbled into the station, splashing her face with water, then dampening her handkerchief, and pressing it against the back of her neck. She knew she had a raging fever. Shivering, she stumbled back toward the train. That was when she saw him.

Greyson Chandler was walking away from her. Nora leaned against the station wall, staring after him in disbelief. She squeezed her eyes shut, thinking to clear the mirage away. But when she opened them again, Grey was still there. She opened her mouth to call to him, but he had removed his hat and was waving to someone—a woman—coming toward him, smiling. It was Iris! She ran to him and they hugged. Grey picked up her bag . . . and together they boarded another train.

Nora stumbled on board her train. Leaning back against her seat, she closed her eyes. *I will not cry. I will not.* Hurt and disappointment washed over her. Everything he said about a new start . . . about religion . . . about his family. Nora wondered if any of it had been true.

Iris was beautiful and educated. Nora certainly couldn't blame Grey for being attracted to Iris. She wondered when they had spent time together. Why hadn't he told her in one of his letters? As the rails of the train clicked by, Nora's mind swirled with scenarios and explanations . . . but always, she came back to one reality: Perhaps he had meant the kiss at the station, but he couldn't have meant the letters. Nora wanted to be angry, but she didn't have the energy for anger. It seemed, however, that hurt did not require any effort at all, for it washed over her in waves until she finally fell asleep, slumped over against the window.

At some point in the night, a stabbing pain in her back awoke her. How could it be even hotter when it was dark? Nora threw her shawl off and dozed again, until a voice called through the haze of deep sleep, "Ticket. Ticket, please."

Frowning, Nora croaked, "But you saw my ticket when I boarded. I'm to get off at Millersburg, remember? You told me you'd wake me if I was asleep."

"Millersburg?" the voice grated. "You want to go to Millersburg, you're on the wrong train, lady. This train arrives in Loup City at midnight. And that's a good ways east of Millersburg.

You shouldn't have changed trains in Grand Island if you wanted to go to Millersburg."

Through a fog of sickness, Nora realized that she must have stumbled back onto the wrong train. She squinted at the rack overhead. It was empty. Overtaken by near-panic, she half stood. "Wait, a moment, please. Let me just look—" Grasping the backs of each seat as she made her way up and down the aisle, she searched in vain for the carpetbag that held her ticket and a small amount of cash.

Slouching back into the seat she had thought was hers, Nora looked up at the conductor. "My bag is on the other train. The one that goes to Millersburg."

The conductor peered at her suspiciously. "You sure you had a ticket to Millersburg?"

"Please," Nora begged. "I'm ill. I can send a message to a friend in Lincoln. Or Millersburg. Will they telegraph for me?"

"I don't know what they'll do if you've no money," the conductor said. "Guess you'll have to see when we get into Loup City."

Nora sighed and closed her eyes. The conductor wasn't being much help, but she was too sick to care. If she could just close her eyes and sleep . . .

Some time in the night the train lurched to a halt, throwing a half-conscious Nora onto the floor. Landing with a thud, she was immediately awake and aware that the sleep had done nothing to improve her condition. She curled up in a ball, trying to forget the acute pain in her head and back. She was aware of shapes moving in the darkness, intense whispering, but she could not tell if the sounds were real or simply part of the remarkable dreams she had been having. Pulling her shawl closer to her, she hunkered on the floor and fell back into a sleep so deep it was close to unconsciousness.

Sometime near dawn, Nora awoke again, this time because of an urgent need to find a relief station. Barely remembering where she was, she half walked, half crawled up the aisle of the empty train and out onto the platform. When she crept down from the train, her feet slipped out from under her and she went down, floundering in the dirt for a moment. She pushed herself to a sitting position. She needed to find water . . . and a place to rest. She could not make herself move. Nora lay down for what she intended to be only a moment.

Mikal Ritter started awake. Cocking his head to one side, he listened. Yes, there it was again. Far off in the distance he could hear the shrill whistle of a train. Turning over, Mikal looked at the face of his sleeping wife. When he reached up to gently touch a lock of her thick brown hair, she opened her eyes, smiling.

"I've always loved that," she said sleepily.

"What is that, *mein shatz*?"

"When *you* are the first thing I see in the morning." She reached for him, snuggling close.

Far off in the distance, a train whistle sounded. Karyn Ritter sighed. "The end of the dream." Kissing her husband on the chin, she said, "You had better get going."

Mikal sat up reluctantly. Flinging his long legs over the side of the bed, he quickly pulled on his overalls, fastening only one strap while he poured water from the pitcher on the washstand into a bowl. He plunged his hands into the water, splashing his face and running his hands over his long mane of black hair. As he pulled on his red plaid shirt, he padded across the hotel room to the window and looked out. "Perhaps it will be cooler today."

Karyn sat up in bed, leaning her forehead on her knees. She reminded him. "If you don't like the weather, stay another day—it will probably change." She slid out of bed and pulled her simple cotton dress over her head.

Standing before the small mirror over the washstand, she wrapped her long dark hair about her head.

Mikal reached from behind to lay one giant hand across his wife's abdomen.

Karyn put both of her hands over her husband's. "I think we have a boy this time, Mikal." She arched one eyebrow at him and said playfully, "Perhaps even two, if God answers my prayers."

Mikal nuzzled her ear. "I will get the team."

When Mikal entered the livery next to the hotel, the first thing he saw was the great black head of his Percheron stallion thrust over the edge of the stall. It was as if the horse were looking for him. At the sight of Mikal, he whickered softly, nodding his head up and down.

"Yes, Midnight, yes. I heard it, too. The train arrives. Time to get to the station."

Mikal reached out to pat the velvet-soft nose of the gigantic horse. He fed the team their morning ration of grain before leading them out of their stalls.

As Mikal worked at harnessing the team to his farm wagon, the grizzled owner of the livery stable clomped in.

Patting Midnight on the rump, he asked Mikal, "You going to be hauling from here often? I'll let the word out if you want to offer thisun' at stud from time to time. He's a fine one. Fellers would come a far piece to breed him."

Mikal shook his head. "Thank you, but I am only here to do a favor for an old friend. The railroad sent an important shipment here instead of leaving it on the train for Millersburg. They finally located it, but it had been unloaded and delivered somewhere farther north. My friend's wife thought they could not wait for the railroad to right the problem. I offered to come this far and haul it to help keep the peace in his house."

Jake nodded knowingly. "When the missus ain't happy, a man's got no peace." He spit out a stream of tobacco juice. "That's the reason I'm still single. No woman's gonna keep me from enjoyin' my cigar when the sun goes down."

Jake walked to the front of the stable and slid the two gigantic doors open, creating a wide berth for Mikal to lead his young team through. Mikal climbed up on the wagon seat and headed for the hotel to find Karyn waiting by the front door.

The bright morning sun promised a warm day. Helping his wife up beside him, Mikal turned the team west and headed for the train station to wait for the new arrival. It had been promised that the misplaced load of goods for Cay Miller's store would be on board. The train was pulling in when Mikal rounded the corner from the hotel. Helping Karyn down from the wagon, Mikal encouraged her to wait inside the station while he drove the wagon down the tracks to the train car. "I should not be long," he said.

Karyn found a seat inside the station, glancing over at the half-dozen passengers who were waiting to board the train. As she watched, a young woman came in from the side of the station near the train tracks. She seemed to be headed for the ticket window, but suddenly she stumbled and crashed to the floor.

Some time after Nora had fallen asleep in the dirt the night before, something had awakened her. Through the waves of nausea that flowed over her she had realized that she must not stay where she was. Half crawling, she had managed to get up onto the station platform where she collapsed on a bench that sat just outside the locked doorway to the station. She spent the night there. In the morning, she felt more miserable and sick than ever.

Finally, someone unlocked the door from the inside. After a few moments, Nora willed herself to get up and go inside. She would go to the ticket window and beg them to let her wire Elise or maybe Dr. Allbright. Perhaps she could find out if her bag had been found on the train she had left. She tried to think clearly, but she was so very ill—she felt herself waver and fall.

A woman's voice pierced the fog about her. There was a hand on her shoulder. More hands pulled her upright and then half carried her back to a bench.

Blinking and squinting against the sunlight coming in the station window, Nora stared up into dark brown eyes. She realized that the sweet voice she was hearing must belong to those eyes. The voice was asking her something—something about where she was going.

Nora forced herself to concentrate. Where was she going? "Millersburg," she mumbled.

"Millersburg!" Karyn said.

"She got on the wrong train in Grand Island," someone was saying. "At least that was what she claimed. She didn't have a ticket. Said it must be in her bag on the other train."

Nora's head was clearing. She recognized the same conductor from the night before.

The conductor said defensively, "I figured if she showed up this morning we could wire Millersburg. You know, to see if anyone found her bag—or asked about her."

Karyn's voice had a hard edge to it as she asked, "And where did she spend the night?"

"I don't know. In the hotel, I guess."

Karyn asked, "You left a sick woman alone? Knowing that she had no bag and no money, you left her *alone*?" She was angry. Her dark eyes blazing, she glared at the uncaring young man. "How could she have stayed at the hotel? Do they give rooms without cost? And what if she had been seriously ill. She could have died, all alone, here in the train station!"

"Now see here, lady." The conductor raised his voice angrily. "I'm not paid to be nursemaid to every passenger on the train. I'm just the conductor, and—"

"—and if you wish to continue being the conductor, you will lower your voice and speak with respect when you are talking to my wife."

The conductor wheeled about. The retort in his mind died, as he came face-to-face with the buttons of a red flannel shirt. Looking up into the man's icy blue eyes, the conductor swallowed hard. "I only meant—"

"Yes," Mikal said quietly. "I know what you meant." He tipped his hat to the man. "We will take care of the young lady. Good-bye."

The conductor hurried toward his departing train.

Mikal knelt on one knee next to where Karyn sat. She explained, "She was to go to Millersburg."

Mikal said to Nora, "You must come with us. We are from Millersburg. I am Mikal Ritter." He turned to look at Karyn. "And this is my wife, Karyn. We came to Loup City on an errand for our friends, the Millers. We would be happy if you would come with us."

Nora nodded, blinking back grateful tears. She half whispered to Karyn, "Thank you. I didn't know what I was going to do."

"Sometimes God answers our prayers even before we say

them," Karyn said, patting Nora on the shoulder. "Do you have friends in Millersburg?"

"Dr. Allbright. I was to stay with her and then talk to a Mrs. Miller about—"

Karyn interrupted her. "You are the new milliner! *Ach,* such a way to meet. Mrs. Miller is my sister."

Mikal stood up. "I will ask the ticketmaster to wire Cay so that he knows what has happened. He can tell Dr. Allbright so that she will not be concerned." He strode away.

"You have not had any breakfast," Karyn said. "Can we get you something before we leave? We have plenty of food in the grub box in the wagon, but you should have something now."

"Oh, no. That's all right," Nora said, shaking her head.

Karyn asked, "You said that you have been ill?"

Nora described her symptoms, finishing with, "I'm afraid it's the ague. I feel better now, but if it's like my pap's was when I was little, it could come back."

"I know," Karyn said and nodded. "Mikal suffered terribly last year." She smiled, "And I know just what to do, so you don't have to worry. Wait here."

Karyn followed her husband to the ticket window. Nora watched her go, marveling as Mikal bent low to speak to her. The man was fully eight inches taller than his wife. Nora had never seen such a giant of a man. He bent his ear to his wife, and then, reaching into his pocket, pulled out a leather coin purse. He counted some change out to Karyn, kissing her on the cheek as she turned to go. She left the station while Mikal turned back to the ticket window.

A sharp whistle sounded, announcing the departure of the train. Mikal came back to where Nora sat. "I have sent word that you are with us. They wired back that your bag was found on the train in Millersburg last evening. Dr. Allbright has it. All is well."

Karyn came hurrying back into the train station, bearing a mug of hot tea and a warm biscuit.

"I'll go and make certain the load is packed properly," Mikal said.

When Nora and Karyn exited the train station, Nora saw that

Mikal had rearranged the load in the wagon, to make room for a narrow bed of comforters just behind the wagon seat. He had even created a pillow by tying a quilt into a roll with a length of twine.

Nora sat in the wagon box, leaning against the side where Karyn only had to look down and back over her right shoulder to talk to her. As they rumbled out of Loup City, Karyn said, "We travel until noon. Then we will give the team a brief rest. We will sleep one night on the way, and tomorrow you will be in Millersburg."

CHAPTER 18

Love Never Fails

I have loved thee with an everlasting love:
therefore with lovingkindness have I drawn thee.
Jeremiah 31:3

"Don't be in such a hurry," Dr. Allbright scolded. "You've only been here for a little over a week. The ague can be tricky. Folks think they are well and then have a relapse of more chills and fever."

Karyn was sitting at the foot of Nora's bed. "You listen to the doctor," she said, patting Nora's legs. She pushed herself awkwardly up off the bed with a little "oof." Laying her arm across her belly, she said, "I like having company. Mikal doesn't worry so to take building jobs in town because you are here." Karyn went to the door of Nora's room. "Better to stay a little longer than to just begin and get sick again."

"But what if Mrs. Miller gives up on me? I don't want her renting my shop space to someone else."

Karyn shook her head. "I know Sophie barks and growls, but she only means to show that you are needed. She has waited this long for a milliner. She will wait a little longer."

Dr. Allbright agreed. "Mrs. Miller doesn't care when you open as long as she has enough notice to advertise in the paper."

"But I'll need time to make some samples before she does that."

"If you can tell me what you need, I'll bring it out when I come at the end of the week," Maude said. She looked at Karyn. "I'll need to be checking on you then, Mrs. Ritter."

"Maybe by then you'll be checking on a new baby, as well," Karyn said hopefully. She nodded at Nora. "Mollie and May are making you a surprise. Shall we share it while Dr. Allbright is here?"

Nora sat up. "I'd love it. Tell them we'll be right out."

"No, no," Karyn said, motioning for Nora to stay put. "You wait. They will come for you."

When Karyn disappeared from the doorway, Dr. Allbright said, "Having you here keeps Mrs. Ritter's mind off her own troubles. I see improvement in her mood since you arrived."

At Nora's questioning look, Dr. Allbright nodded. "She's a very strong woman, but she has been unusually concerned for this baby. Sons are important out here."

Nora nodded. "I know. But Mr. Ritter doesn't seem the kind to—"

"No," Dr. Allbright said. "He's a rare thing—a man who truly adores his wife. I don't think Mr. Ritter would care if Karyn gave birth to kittens, as long as she was well. She puts the pressure on herself. She wants to give her husband the one thing only she can give—a way for his name to continue."

Dr. Allbright sighed. "The older I get, the less I understand. So often it seems that it's the people who trust in God the most who receive the least from him." She shook her head. "And yet even when they are denied what they want, they are more determined than ever to serve the God they believe in."

Two pairs of incredibly blue eyes peeked around the doorframe. Two girlish voices called out, "Please join the Misses Ritter for tea, served in the parlor."

May and Mollie had created a parlor in one corner of the room that served as kitchen, dining room, and living area by setting up a serving table and five chairs. A lace tablecloth had been spread, and a fine china tea set awaited the twins' guests for tea.

"Please be seated," May said, holding Nora's chair for her.

Mollie did the same for Dr. Allbright, while Karyn set a basket of steaming muffins on the table.

Mikal appeared at the doorway. "I believe I was commanded by the Princesses May and Mollie to be present at tea," he said. He bent down and held both arms out. "May I escort the ladies to their places?"

"Oh, Papa," the girls said in unison, skipping to the doorway.

May and Mollie served tea as only four-year-olds could. A pat of butter flipped onto the floor when May attempted to butter a muffin. Tea was spilled, and muffins crumbled. Laughter and love reigned, and all in all, the event was a great success.

Thinking of it later, Nora shed bittersweet tears. She was learning something from the Ritters. She was learning that she was lonely.

After Dr. Allbright left, Karyn asked Nora to help her unpack the contents of one of the trunks that served as a night table in May and Mollie's room.

"Mikal has already taken the trunk outside. I don't want things smelling musty. It's time they were aired out."

While May and Mollie swept the floor in the house, Karyn and Nora went out back where Mikal had strung a clothesline from the back corner of the house to the windmill and back again.

Karyn opened the trunk and removed a sheet of tissue paper to reveal a layer of infant's clothes, each item beautifully made, each item unused. There were two identical blue knit caps and two pairs of booties lying atop two sacques trimmed with several rows of wide, handmade lace. Karyn picked them up and handed them to Nora, explaining, "We have two sons. Over there." She nodded toward the ridge. "You can't see it from here, but walking up the ridge you find it. Beneath that tree. A little white fence. That's where my boys are." Karyn's voice trembled with emotion.

She pulled two indigo blue-and-white crib quilts from the trunk. Hugging the quilts to her, she wiped away tears, as she said, "Of course I know the boys are not really there. They are with our blessed Savior." She sighed, handing Nora one small quilt while she put its twin on the line. "I am so thankful their little bodies are nearby, where I can visit them."

Karyn added softly, "I have much to be thankful for. Mikal loves his daughters." She sighed. "But a farmer needs sons. Every day I ask God for sons for Mikal."

Nora marveled at Karyn's sweet acceptance of her circumstances. Pap had allowed the loss of his wife to destroy his life. As far as Nora knew, Pap had never visited his wife's grave. And instead of taking comfort in his children, he had treated them cruelly. Not one day had passed when Nora was not aware that her very existence caused Pap pain. Seeing Karyn's sadness, yet knowing that she had not allowed her grief to block out the light in her life gave Nora an odd feeling. She began to think that perhaps she was not responsible for all of Pap's misery after all. Maybe Pap could have acted differently. If only—if only what? Nora wondered. What was it that enabled Karyn to bury two children and still smile and laugh and sing?

After the trunk's contents were hung out to air, Karyn called to her daughters, who had been playing nearby. "It's time for you to do your stint at sewing, girls."

May pouted, "I don't want to today, Mama. Can't I have just this one day to play? The wind isn't blowing and"—she smiled prettily—"I'll pick you a bouquet of goldenrod. And take some up the hill." She nodded toward where Karyn had said her babies were buried.

Karyn chuckled knowingly. "That's a very clever attempt at getting out of your work, May. You can collect flowers later. Now, we sew."

May sighed deeply, but she headed for the house.

Karyn called after her, "You and Mollie get your little baskets and meet Nora and I at the front. We can sit there in the shade."

Karyn had cut squares of fabric for the girls to stitch together into nine-patch blocks. "I have them sew a little every day," she explained. "Next year they will begin knitting."

"Did your mama make you sew?" Mollie asked Nora, stabbing angrily at the fabric in her lap. Her little-girl fingers struggled clumsily to hold the needle.

"No," Nora answered. "I didn't have a mama. There was only Pap and my brother, Will."

Both girls looked up, their eyes wide. "You didn't have a mama?"

Karyn interrupted. "Girls, it is not polite to ask so many questions of our guest."

"Here, Mollie, let me show you something that might help." Nora reached down and demonstrated how to make a knot at the end of the thread. "It doesn't have to be so big as you think. Try it." Nora snipped the knot she had just made from the end of the thread. Mollie tried Nora's method, succeeded, and smiled triumphantly.

Karyn hauled her mending basket outside and lifted out a girl's pinafore. "I need to take one of the tucks out along the hem of this, but first—" She disappeared back inside the house. Presently she reappeared, with a blue wool dress thrown over her arm. Her right hand held an outdated hat. "I thought perhaps you could make a few suggestions," she began. "Something I could do to update these."

Mattie looked up sharply. "But Papa said you were to have a new dress for winter, Mama," she protested.

"I know what Papa said," Karyn replied. "But I don't need a new dress. This one suits me."

"We're getting a new house, and you're getting a new dress. That's what Papa said." The little voice was stubborn.

"We must be thankful, Mollie, for all the blessings God has already given us. And we must not be greedy for more. The new house will come in time, but not this year." Karyn smiled at Nora and shook her head. She sat down, still holding her dress and hat. "Mikal dreams of a new house instead of the soddy." She sighed. "But the last two years have not been so good. God gives us perfect weather and abundant harvest, but the railroad takes the profits in shipping fees."

While Nora inspected the worn dress, Karyn repeated, as if reminding herself, "Already we have so much more than when I first came." Hat in hand, she turned to look at the soddy. "When Mikal brought me here, there was just the one little window and the parlor. It was our kitchen, our bedroom—

everything. I was nineteen, and I had left Germany with visions of a white cottage in a meadow. Mikal's tiny house made of dirt was quite a shock."

Nora said, "I don't think I would have stayed."

"Almost I did not," was the answer. "But then—" Karyn shrugged, blushing. "I learned to be content. One year Mikal built the first bedroom. When the girls came, we built the trundle." Nora had helped put the girls to bed one night and seen that Mikal had built a special little bed for his girls that rolled out from beneath the high spool bed where their parents slept. She had thought how nice it was for them to be so near their parents where they knew they were safe and loved.

Karyn continued, "When the boys were coming, Mikal added a second bedroom." She said softly, "But then we didn't need it." She smiled at Nora. "So that is how we have a guest room for visitors." Karyn went on, "When Mikal built the little lean-to on the back, it made things so much easier for me. Now I have a place to store my garden tools and the washtub, and I don't have to walk so far to the well."

She absentmindedly ran her finger down the row of buttons on her well-worn dress. "Mikal is always speaking of a new house. But we manage fine just as things are. He needs a new team, a bigger barn. And another corncrib." Karyn sighed. "Life is hard, but God is good."

Nora was inspecting the dress. "The fabric on these buttons is wearing very thin. If we could replace them, and perhaps add a lace inset here—" She indicated the sleeve of the dress. She took up the hat. "Feathers are popular this year."

Karyn was enthusiastic. "Mikal can go hunting. I'll tell him we need something for stew that has beautiful, long tail feathers." She laughed. "It's a blessing to have God send me such a talented friend."

By the time May and Mollie had finished their sewing stint, their mother and Nora were hard at work ripping seams and removing buttons. When Karyn left to prepare their dinner, Nora remained outside, humming as she worked on her friend's dress. *Friend.* She paused with needle in hand while she tasted the word. With a sudden rush of happiness she realized that yes, Karyn Ritter was becoming her friend.

After dinner that evening, May and Mollie showed their father their sewing. Mikal dutifully praised their progress, pulling the girls into his lap for a hug.

Mollie spoke up. "Mama says we're not going to have a new house this year. Does that mean the new baby can sleep with us when he comes?"

Mikal looked at his wife, who busied herself clearing the table as she spoke cheerfully, "A new team and a bigger barn. And the second corncrib. We need those things more than a new house."

Mikal raked his hand through his hair in a gesture that expressed at once frustration and resignation. "You are right, of course. The house will have to wait. Again." His shoulders slumped wearily. "Perhaps some of the railroad barons should descend from their gilded mansions just long enough to visit our little soddy . . . maybe then it would make a difference in their shipping fees."

Karyn looked at her husband. "Not one of those gilded mansions holds more love than our home, Mikal."

The girls scrambled off their father's lap, and Mikal began to help his wife clear the dishes from the table.

Nora spoke up. "Please, Herr Ritter. Let me do this. The fresh air is good for me. Dr. Allbright said so. You two sit and enjoy the sunset together."

"Thank you, Nora." Karyn turned to Mollie and May. "All right, girls. Time for bed."

Mikal hauled the washtub filled with dirty dishes outside and set it on a bench near the well. He pumped cold water into a cooking pot and said, "I will bring this out as soon as it is hot." He ducked beneath the porch overhang and disappeared inside.

While Nora waited for Mikal to bring heated washwater outside, she made her way up the ridge at the back of the house to where a cottonwood tree marked two little graves. A short black-iron fence surrounded the little plot. Set inside were two small stones, atop which rested a stone lamb, curled up as if asleep. Beneath each lamb, the inscription read, *Onser Liebling.* There were no names, only the dates *December 27* and *31, 1885. She lost two babies within a few days of each other. Right after Christmas.* Nora shivered and headed back for the house.

The sun was setting as Nora finished the dishes. She felt tired, but happy. Her strength was returning. In the remaking of Karyn's best dress and hat, she had found a way to repay her new friend for her care. Soon she would be in Millersburg, with her own shop, and a tiny room that was all her own. How wonderful it would be.

When Nora carried her stack of clean dishes back inside the soddy, Mikal had settled his huge frame into a creaking rocker by the window. He had lit the lamp that sat on the broad windowsill and was reading a newspaper, his profile outlined against the backdrop of golden light and the red geraniums blooming in the window.

Nora sat nearby, removing old trim from Karyn's hat, and contemplating how she would redesign it.

From the bedroom, Mollie's voice could be heard begging, "*Please,* Mama. Just one story. One very little story."

"It's too late, girls."

"But, Mama, we always sleep so very, very, much better when we have heard a story."

There was a pause, and then Karyn began, "Once, a long, long time ago, there was a giant."

"Was he a very big giant, Mama?"

"Yes, Mollie. He was very big indeed."

"And did he have dark, flashing eyes, and white hair, and—"

"Mollie, be quiet," May snapped. "It's Mama's story. You always interrupt."

"As it happens," Karyn said quietly, "this giant had black hair. And flashing blue eyes."

"Black hair like Papa?"

"Just like Papa," Karyn answered.

Nora saw Mikal look up from his paper.

Karyn continued the story. "He was very tall, and his black hair was long and scraggly. His eyes flashed in such a way that he frightened anyone who saw him. They did not know that the giant only growled and acted fierce because he was sad, for he was very, very lonely. One day, the giant went on a journey to the mountains. On his journey he captured a young girl and carried her home to be his wife. He brought her to his hut made of dirt.

"The girl was very strong-willed and very high-spirited. She refused to let the giant know that she feared him. But every night, when the giant slept, the girl went to the doorway of the little house where he kept her, and looked at the stars, and away toward the mountains where she had once lived. She longed for her home, because although the giant treated her well and gave her gifts, he never told her that he loved her.

"At last, the girl became so lonely that she ran away. But as she ran, a terrible thing happened. A prairie fire came rushing from where the sun rose each morning. It encircled the girl and rushed off toward the giant's home. Miraculously, the fire passed her by and did not harm her.

"Far, far away, the giant awakened and saw the fire. Immediately, he ran to the house where he kept his girl. But she was gone. He looked toward the east, toward the mountains, and he knew that the girl had run away. Terrified that she had been caught in the fire, he jumped on his best horse and charged swiftly across the blackened earth, in search of his girl.

"When at last he found her, he jumped from his horse, his eyes blazing with light. Thinking that the giant was angry with her, the girl cringed with fear. But then, a great tear slid down the giant's cheek. He clasped her to his breast, hugging her so tightly, she could hardly breathe.

"And then, the girl knew that the giant loved her. She went back to the hut of mud, and together the giant and the girl lived happily.

"When the girl grew older and had children of her own, she would often tell them the story of the giant and his girl, and she always ended the story this way: 'I grew up where there were mountains, and God took me to a country where there were no mountains, but He gave me mountains of blessings and mountains of love, which are better than any mountain made only of earth and grass. I am content.

" 'I grew up where there were clear, sparkling rivers, and cool, clean lakes. God took me to a country where there are only small springs, and narrow ribbons of muddy water criss-crossing the parched earth. But He gave me the knowledge of Jesus, who is the living water and quenches the thirst of men's hearts. I am content.

" 'I grew up where there were many, many, people. God took me to a country where there were few people. For weeks at a time, I saw no one, except a fearsome giant. But the giant has become my best friend, and my dearest love, and I am content.' "

Karyn stopped talking abruptly. There was a brief pause before she spoke again. "And now, my darlings, you must go to sleep, or I will have *our* giant come in here and—"

"And what, Mama," Mollie teased, "*hug* us to death?"

"Just so," Karyn retorted.

Nora bent her head to hide the tears in her eyes.

The girls murmured their good nights, and Karyn came back into the room. Mikal laid his paper aside. He got up and went to her. Placing a hand on each of her shoulders, he stared down at her for a moment. Then, he dropped his hands to his sides and went outside into the moonlight. Karyn followed him.

Nora bent to her needlework, feeling strangely embarrassed. When she finally laid it aside and retired to her room, she lay awake for a long time, trying to reconcile what she thought she knew of men, and what she had seen of Mikal Ritter.

Pap's behavior had convinced Nora that most farmers valued their children only insofar as they provided free labor. But then she met Mikal Ritter, concerned that his wife was working too hard, gentle with his daughters, never failing to give them their nightly "horsey-ride" by crouching on the floor so they could clamor up onto his back.

While Goldie's clientele had varied widely, Nora had come to regard them all as tragic players in a poorly scripted play. By day, many of the "regulars" were admired citizens. One or two enjoyed the power to mold city affairs after their image. But by night, these men succumbed to fluttering eyelashes and rouged lips like any other weakling. Nora had seen them behave so ridiculously she had to bite her lips to keep from laughing at them. She had finally concluded that true manhood was a clever myth created by someone with a tremendous sense of humor. Power and self-assurance, Nora decided, were only a veneer pulled over the truth that all men were equally weak and vulnerable. But then she met Mikal Ritter.

Karyn and Mikal came back from their walk. Through the doorway, Nora saw Karyn turn toward her husband. He put his arms around her, and she leaned against him, nestling her head against his shoulder as they tiptoed into the bedroom.

Nora lay awake for a long time, trying to push the image of Greyson Chandler from her mind. She relived the last day she had seen him. The day Iris was running to meet him in Grand Island . . . throwing her arms about him . . . their boarding a train . . . together. Nora sighed.

Unlike Greyson Chandler, Mikal Ritter didn't make pretty speeches about finding God and living for others. He just did it. The realization that lasting goodness and happy marriages existed left Nora feeling depressed. If true goodness existed, and if it gave the kind of happiness the Ritters had, Nora wanted it. But she had no idea where to get it.

Interlude—1998

Reagan and Irene were baking Christmas cookies at Irene's one frigid Saturday in December when a red Dodge Ram drove up the drive.

Reagan looked out the kitchen window in time to see Noah climb out of the cab and stretch. He leaned back in the truck to retrieve his coffee cup.

"You didn't tell me you were expecting Noah." Reagan hastened to put down a cookie sheet and brush her hair back out of her face.

Irene was sitting at the table giving frosting smiles to row upon row of gingerbread people. "Oh, didn't I?"

"Irene Peale." Reagan's tone was accusing.

"What?" Irene said with mock innocence.

"What are you up to?"

"Me? I don't know what you mean. Goodness, girl, can't a woman's nephew come to visit without causing a stir?" Irene gave the cone of frosting in her hands an expert twist. Her soft blue eyes twinkled as she said, "You might want to freshen your lipstick, dear."

"Right," Reagan said. She pulled her apron off and disappeared up the back stairway just as Noah reached the back door.

"Is that Reagan's 'bug' out front?" she heard him ask. Then, she forced herself to go on up the stairs and into the bathroom. She inspected her "American-girl-no-makeup-today" face in the mirror. *I'm going to kill Irene. She could have at least warned me. I don't even have my makeup bag with me.*

Reagan lingered as long as she could upstairs. Finally, she descended to the kitchen, where Noah was sprawled in a corner chair, his long legs stretched out before him, a pile of cookies on the table. He greeted Reagan while he chewed.

Reagan said hello and then looked at Irene. "Should I make some fresh coffee?"

Irene moved to get up. "No. Come and sit. I'll make the coffee." She pushed herself to a standing position and headed for the stove, dragging one foot a little.

"Aunt Rini," Noah said firmly, "sit back down. In fact, both of the 'cookie queens' should sit and relax. *I'll* make the coffee."

"Listen, sonny-boy," Irene retorted. "I'm showing off, so don't ruin the moment. It wasn't all that long ago I couldn't make coffee—at least not while standing on my own two feet. So just sit there and watch."

Irene moved slowly across the kitchen to the sink, filling the glass coffee carafe with water, pouring the water into the top of her drip-o-lator. She reached to a shelf above her head for a box of filters. "Watch this, Noah," she said. "Do you have any idea how many weeks I spent in therapy learning to reach above my head again?" Inserting a filter in the coffeemaker, she added grounds and then flipped the "on" switch with a flourish and a bow. She made her way back across the kitchen and sat down. "You can pour when it's ready. I know I am truly amazing," she teased, "but I can't be trusted with a tray of cups filled with hot coffee."

While the coffee was brewing, Noah described his latest project at the farm. He had plans to restore an ancient windmill dragged out of a nearby field. "Judd Hayes up at Ansley said he'd come down and help me get it all hooked up in the spring. Right now, it's just lying out back in the weeds." He went on.

"With the cold, I haven't been able to accomplish much else outside. But I'm almost finished getting all the old laths out of the rest of the rooms. Wiring and drywall next. New windows next spring," Noah said. "You wouldn't believe how much cold air blows in around those windows."

"Oh, wouldn't I?" Irene said. "I remember as a little girl, lying in bed at night when I visited Oma and Opa. I swear I saw snow come in around the windows more than once. There were times when ice formed nearly a half-inch thick on the window-panes."

"Aunt Rini said you're trying to do some research connected to Custer County," Noah said to Reagan. He looked over at the coffeepot, got up and poured coffee for them. Before sitting down, he picked a half-dozen more cookies from the cooling rack.

"That's the absolute end, young man. Those are promised to the church for the children's program tomorrow evening," Irene scolded.

"Tell me about your research," Noah asked, settling back in his chair.

Reagan answered, "There was a tin of buttons in one of the rooms we cleaned out last month." Reagan explained the charm string, without the added folklore. "Irene said it came to Karyn Ritter from a milliner in Millersburg. Apparently they were good friends. There isn't much to go on."

Irene added, "When Reagan sorted the buttons, she found a business card. I'm certain Oma told me Nora had a shop in Millersburg. But the business card said she was working here in Lincoln."

"Have you checked the city directory?" Noah asked.

"Yes," Reagan answered. "Thornhill Dressers was in business from 1880 to after the turn of the century. But I never found the name Nora O'Dell. I found an advertisement in the newspaper for the dressers, but again no reference to Nora."

"What about the Sittler's Index? It would tell you if her name ever appeared in the newspaper."

Reagan looked surprised. "You sound like you've done historical research before."

Noah shrugged. "I'm just learning. But I've been to the archives here in Lincoln a few times. They have some terrific pioneer records from Custer County." He took the head off a gingerbread person, chewing while he talked. "I could help you do some research if you want." He swallowed. "I was going down there tomorrow anyway."

"Sure," Reagan said.

Irene nudged her. Imitating Reagan's voice she said, " 'Oh, right, Irene, that's just how all hunks dream of spending their Saturdays, poking around the historical society archives looking for information about dead people.' "

Reagan blushed furiously and jumped up to rinse out her coffee cup. From the sink, she said, "Thanks, Irene. I was really hoping you'd embarrass me at least once today."

Noah got up and crossed to where she was standing. He leaned against the counter while she filled the sink with water and began to scrub cookie sheets. He leaned over and nudged her with his shoulder. "I said the same thing a couple of weeks ago on the phone. 'Oh, right, Aunt Rini, that's just how all babes want to spend their Saturdays, poking around the library looking for information on dead people. What a great idea for a first date.' " He walked to the back door. "I've got to get my backpack out of the truck. Do we have a date or not?"

Reagan didn't turn around. "The archive opens at ten o'clock. I'll meet you there."

She turned toward Irene. "And you're coming, too, right?"

"Wouldn't miss it," Irene said.

"Runza® sandwiches for supper, Aunt Rini?" Noah called from the back porch.

"Only if you earn it by packing all these cookies up and delivering them over to the church for me."

"Deal." The screen door slammed.

Reagan whirled around. "I-am-going-to-kill-you!" she hissed at Irene. "I've never been more embarrassed in my life!"

"Oh, settle down, Ray-ray," Irene said. "I'd have to be deaf and blind not to see the attraction between you two. I'm not getting any younger. I don't have time to wait for young love to blossom freely. If I can give it a jump-start, I'm going to do it."

Reagan finished the last cookie sheet and removed her apron. "I'm going home and try to resurrect my self-respect."

"No you're not," Irene said firmly. "We had a date tonight and you're going to help me make Runza® sandwiches and then we're watching *North By Northwest*. Just because you have a hot date with my nephew tomorrow does not give you permission to stand me up tonight, young lady!"

Noah came back in and lumbered up the back stairs to the bedroom that had been his since he was a child spending his summers with Aunt Rini and Uncle Henry. He returned and began to help Irene pack cookies into wax-paper-lined shoeboxes, then loaded them into the truck and headed out to deliver them to the church.

While he was gone, Reagan browned hamburger in a skillet, adding onion and then leaving Irene to add her "secret spices" while she kneaded bread dough. She rolled out the dough on the kitchen island, cutting it into rectangles. Irene spooned the ground beef filling in a long line down the center of each rectangle of dough. Then, the women rolled the dough into what resembled long hoagie-style buns. After a few minutes in the oven, the buns began to rise, filling the kitchen with the aroma of fresh bread and spices.

Noah returned with a grocery sack in one arm. He pulled six pints of Ben and Jerry's ice cream from the sack, explaining, "I couldn't decide on a flavor."

The three spent the rest of the evening in Irene's "informal parlor." They ate hot Runza® sandwiches off of TV trays while they watched Cary Grant escape from an airplane intent on dive-bombing him. By the time he was climbing the face of Mt. Rushmore, they were sitting side by side on the couch, eating Ben and Jerry's straight from the carton with a spoon.

Noah stole a bite of Reagan's "New York Super Chunk Fudge."

"Watch it, mister," she warned. "I get very hostile when it comes to sharing chocolate."

"I'll remember that," he whispered back.

By the end of the movie, he was sitting so that his shoulder touched hers.

"Got it!" Noah leaned on one elbow so that he could see around the side of his microfilm reader to where Reagan and Irene sat. They got up and came to look over Noah's shoulder. "There," Noah said, pointing at a few tiny lines of type. "Read that."

Miss Nora O'Dell invites the ladies of Millersburg to inspect her new line of millinery goods, just arrived from the East. Fair prices and the latest styles. At Miller's Emporium, corner of Main and First.

Reagan patted him on the shoulder. "Good work, Sherlock. At least we know she was in Millersburg."

"You know," Noah said, "maybe she wasn't in Lincoln long enough to appear in the city directory."

Irene added, "Maybe she trained at Thornhill Dressers. Then she moved to Millersburg to have her own business."

"But why Millersburg?" Reagan asked.

Noah shrugged. "The railroad arrived in 1887. That would have made it a 'boomtown,' at least for a while. Maybe she was a real 'go-getter.' The 'entrepreneurial spirit' and all that."

"I wish they had a city directory for Millersburg! I can't imagine reading every issue of every *Millersburg Republican,* just hoping for some mention of one business!"

One of the research librarians walked by. "Excuse me for butting in, but since you know the address, you could check *Sanborn's* and at least know how long the dry goods store stayed at that location. And if a millinery shop pops up right next door, it would be a good guess that it was Miss O'Dell expanding."

"*Sanborn's?*" Reagan asked.

The librarian explained, "*Sanborn's Fire Maps* have been made since the 1800s. They provided a schematic of cities for the fire departments. They show the location of businesses and details like type of construction, location of windows—all kinds of things." She said, "I have to help someone check a census

171

record, but if you'll meet me at that big table across the room, I'll be over in just a minute."

"Census records," Noah said. "I know how to check those. You go ahead and look at *Sanborn's*. I'll check for Miss O'Dell in the census."

Noah found Miss O'Dell in the census, and Reagan and Irene found Miller's Emporium on the *Sanborn* maps. They wondered aloud what might be available in the Custer County museum.

"You don't dare travel to Custer County in December," Noah warned, "unless you're willing to get snowed in." He teased, "Although that would make for an interesting second date."

That evening Irene called Reagan. "What about it? You want to brave Custer County in winter?"

"I don't think so, Irene. There's still a lot I can do here. I have five books on the history of buttons piled on my desk right now." She started to say something more, but decided against it.

"What aren't you telling me?" Irene said quietly.

Reagan took a deep breath. She shifted the phone from one hand to the other. "Things are going too fast. At least from my end."

"But I thought you wanted to learn all you could," Irene answered.

"I'm not talking about the research."

"I know that."

Reagan heard Irene sigh before she said, "What *is* it about young people these days? So much caution. Henry proposed to me after our second date, and we were married for over fifty years."

"That's what scares me," Reagan said. "If Noah asked me, I might say yes. That's stupid. I don't know him at all."

"You know he likes ice cream, he's crazy about history, he's kind to old women. What's to know?"

Reagan blurted out, "Look, your nephew is the hottest thing to come my way in a long, long time. But he has a history, and so do I. And mine says that I have to know that a man's relationship with God is personal. I know he said something to you about getting things straight with God, but I need to know exactly what that means."

"Ask him."

"I will. But I have to get my head on straight first. It's too much, too soon. I've never had anything like this happen to me before. Frankly, it's scary. I feel like there's this giant magnet pulling me toward him . . . I just want to make certain God is the source of the magnetic field. But before I do that, I have to make certain that if his answers aren't the right ones, I can walk away. Right now, tonight, the way I'm feeling, I'm not certain I could do that."

"All right. I give up. For now. But I reserve the right to meddle in the very near future." Irene wished Reagan good night and hung up.

Fifteen minutes after she had hung up the phone, Noah Ritter arrived at Reagan's door. The moment she opened the door, he said, "Aunt Rini said to tell you that she didn't define 'very near future' when she said she'd be meddling. May I come in?"

Reagan shook her head. "I don't think that's a good idea."

"Then come for a ride with me. We'll drive around and look at Christmas lights or something."

Reagan shook her head again. "Sorry. My Sunday school kids are all in the children's program at church tonight. I need to be there."

He smiled. "Care if I come along?"

"You don't know when to give up, do you? I assume Irene told you every word I said."

"You assume correctly. And, no, I don't give up easily." He pulled on the bill of his ball cap as if it were a cowboy hat. "Haven't met any foxes like you up in Custer County, ma'am."

"What about the one in California?" Reagan blurted out. "I think her name was Angela."

Noah tilted his head and looked away for a moment. He pressed his lips tightly together and shook his head. "Let me take you to the children's program. Have coffee with me afterward. I'll tell you everything you want to know."

He put one hand on the doorframe and leaned against the door. "Look, Reagan. This is all moving pretty fast for me, too. The magnet isn't just pulling in one direction. I feel it, too. But does it have to be so difficult? Can't it be fun?" He raised one

173

eyebrow and looked at her. "I mean, it's not often two such good-looking people strike up a relationship over microfilm and maps. I'd say it was meant to be, if you look at the evidence." He grinned. "And you did, after all, share your New York Super Chunk Fudge with me. That has to count for something."

"Stop being so blasted charming and get in here," Reagan ordered. She opened the door and headed off to the back of the house. "I'll get my coat. The program starts in fifteen minutes."

CHAPTER 19

A Child Is Born

Lo, children are an heritage of the LORD:
and the fruit of the womb is his reward.
Psalm 127:3

"*Push*, Mrs. Ritter, *push!*" Dr. Allbright sat at the foot of Karyn's bed, holding out her hands, urging her patient on. Nora stood beside Karyn, mopping her brow, feeling generally incompetent. She had offered to leave several times, but each time Karyn would gasp, "No, please, it is so much easier with you here."

Karyn had been in labor since early morning, and already it was near dark. She was exhausted. With each increasingly difficult contraction, she reached up to grab the headboard for leverage to push. Finally, with Dr. Allbright's urging, she yelled at the top of her lungs and forced her reluctant infant into the world. The baby cried, and Karyn's entire being lit up with joy.

"You have a son, Mrs. Ritter," Dr. Allbright said, swaddling the infant in a soft white towel before handing him to Nora and returning to stitching and disinfecting.

Karyn's German exclamations needed no translation. She held out both hands to take her newborn son, cuddling him close while tears streamed down her face.

Nora mumbled something about making a supper for them all. She headed for the doorway to call Mikal and the girls, but they were already running up the hill from the pond, where Mikal had taken the girls to look for baby ducklings.

Dr. Allbright came to the bedroom door just as Mikal arrived. "Congratulations, Mr. Ritter. You have a son."

"And my wife?" Mikal asked.

"Fine," Dr. Allbright assured him. She looked at Mollie and May with a smile. "In fact, you can all take one quick peek at him before I check him over. I'll leave you all alone to get acquainted without my intrusion. Bring him with you out to the kitchen later for a bath."

Mikal ducked his head and entered the bedroom, followed by his girls. He knelt by the bed, reaching out to stroke his wife's cheek and admire his son.

"What's his name?" Mollie wanted to know.

"Friedrich Mikal," Karyn said. "But you may call him Freddie."

"Mama," May said, stroking the back of the baby's hand. "Now we can use all the baby boy things from the trunk."

Karyn smiled, her eyes shining with happy tears. "Yes, *liebling,* now we can."

"No, we need *another* boy to use 'em all," Mollie said.

"Girls," Mikal interrupted. "One baby at a time, please. Let us enjoy this one before we ask God for another." He reached for the baby as he said to Karyn, "Go to sleep, little mother. He will want to eat soon enough." He bent to kiss Karyn and left the room with his son held against his chest, one giant hand supporting more than half the baby's body.

Dr. Allbright had prepared a tub of warm water in the kitchen. "Come here, girls," she beckoned. "You watch and then you can help Nora give Freddie his bath tomorrow." She slipped the baby out of his blanket and into the warm water. "See how he kicks and squeals," Dr. Allbright said. "That's good for him. It gives him strong lungs and muscles."

"Look how big his feet are!" Mikal exclaimed. "He will be a big boy."

"This is a child, Mr. Ritter, not a puppy," Dr. Allbright retorted, with mock sternness. "But you're right." She put the palm of her hand against one of Freddie's feet. The baby pushed back against her hand. "He does have good-sized feet. And strong legs."

Freddie quieted abruptly. "He likes it," Mollie said.

"I believe he does," Dr. Allbright said. "Sensible boy." But by the time Freddie had been bathed, diapered and dressed, he was squalling again.

May clamped her hands over her ears. "Does he have to yell so *loud*?" she wanted to know.

Mikal chucked her under the chin. "Little Freddie is not half so loud as you girls were—and think of it, your mama and I had to listen to two of you!"

Dr. Allbright took Freddie to his mother. Mikal emptied the dishpan that had served as a baby bathtub, and Nora set the table. She had cooked fried sausages and potatoes for supper. Watching the family sit down at the table with Dr. Allbright, she could hardly suppress a smile. Goldie would have been amazed at how quickly the family was devouring her cooking.

While Mikal hitched up Dr. Allbright's horse and buggy, Nora and she sat beneath the crude covering that jutted out over the front door of the soddy.

"I want to stay and help Mrs. Ritter with the new baby," Nora said, "but I think that as soon as she has recovered, I need to be on my way. Elise has been very understanding, but I don't want to take advantage of her patience. She needs to know if I'm going to be there for her busy season this fall or not."

"I think you're safely through with the ague," Dr. Allbright said. "I'll tell Mrs. Miller to expect you next week. You'll stay with me, of course."

After Dr. Allbright left for Millersburg, Mikal went to do his evening chores. Mollie and May were clearing the table when Nora went in to check on Karyn. She was asleep, her arm curved around Freddie, who slept with his tiny infant bottom up in the air. For some reason, Nora found herself blinking away tears. She turned away and hurried outside.

Mollie was standing on an overturned barrel by the well, pumping water into the washtub full of dirty dishes. May waited patiently, a dishrag in one hand and a bar of lye soap in the other. Down the hill, Nora could see Mikal forking hay over the corral fence. Everywhere she looked, Nora saw happiness and contentment. She thought ahead to Millersburg and her fledgling business in the corner of Miller's Emporium. She doubted that success as a milliner would ever give her the happiness that existed among the inhabitants of the soddy on Mikal Ritter's homestead.

"What are you saying!" Karyn said hotly. "You will insult me if you do such a thing. I thought we were friends."

"But I only want to repay you for your kindness," Nora was saying. "Heaven knows what would have happened to me if you had not found me that day in Loup City."

"Exactly," Karyn said. "Heaven knows and Heaven knew, and that is why God sent us to you. You cannot pay someone for doing God's will. That is sacrilege! Would you have me pay you for caring for Freddie and me?"

"Of course not," Nora said. "That was—oh, all right. But how can I thank you?"

"Take my sister's offer to open a little shop in her store. Every woman I know needs a new hat! And that is only among my friends out here on homesteads. Millersburg grows every day."

Nora smiled. "If everyone in Millersburg is as kind as you, I will not be able to say anything but yes."

"Remember what I told you about Sophie," Karyn said. "She can be difficult, but she has a good heart. And be certain you call on Celest Delhomme. She will introduce you to everyone. If there is anything you want to know, ask Celest."

"And if there is anything you *don't* want to know, count on Sophie," Mikal said, laughing.

"Mikal!" Karyn said sternly. "Shame on you. Sophie has made great improvements."

"I know," Mikal said. "But seeing you jump to her defense lets me know that you are completely recovered from having our Freddie." He hugged her briefly. Tipping his hat to Nora, he said, "God's best to you, Miss O'Dell, and thank you for all you have done for us. Please greet Celest, and tell her we will be bringing her new godchild to visit her soon."

Nora bent down and held her arms out to Mollie and May.

They hugged her until she was breathless and laughing. Finally, she climbed up beside Dr. Allbright. As Dr. Allbright's carriage pulled away from the Ritter homestead, Nora looked back. She waved one last time and then turned around. She sighed. "I'm going to miss those two."

"Maybe you'll have some of your own someday."

"I never thought I wanted children," Nora admitted. "But if married life could be like that—"

Dr. Allbright tapped her horse's rear with the buggy whip. "Get along, Grady. It's near dark and you still have to pull us a good four miles." The carriage made its way slowly along two well-worn wagon tracks. As far as they could see around them, there was only a vast, waving sea of grass and wildflowers.

They had ridden along in silence for a while when Dr. Allbright said, "If I could bottle the Ritter's secret for happiness, I could be a very rich woman." She chuckled. "Can't you see it right next to the Lydia Pinkham's Remedy on drugstore shelves—Dr. Allbright's Bitters—Marital Bliss Guaranteed."

"I hardly think you'd want to call it 'bitters,' " Nora said.

"Anti-bitters, then," Maude offered.

"Much better." Nora hesitated before saying, "Karyn told me what it was like when she first came. I doubt things turn out so well for most of the mail-order brides. She credits God with everything."

"Yes," Maude nodded "I've noticed that about her. What seemed different to me was that Mikal seemed to share her beliefs. I've met plenty of women out here who seem to cling to religion almost as a refuge from the insanity of loneliness. It isn't often, though, that I come in contact with a man who is so open about his own faith in God."

"It seems genuine."

Maude shrugged. "I think it is. In fact, quite a few of the folk in Millersburg seem to credit God with things." She said thoughtfully, "I called on an elderly woman in town only last week. Poor thing, she's suffering terribly from arthritis. Can barely get out of bed anymore. Unfortunately, there isn't much I can do. But she didn't complain—and she had her Bible handy and spoke about God like He was a personal acquaintance."

179

Dr. Allbright shook her head. "It's curious. Even with the pain she's in, she had baked biscuits for me. Said she knew I lived alone and thought since I usually eat at the hotel I should have some home cooking." Dr. Allbright smiled. "I'm sure you'll hear about Amalia Kruger's biscuits from someone. Personally, I hope she pays me in biscuits for every fee. She lives with Celest Delhomme. You're certain to meet her."

Maude began to tell Nora about Millersburg. "The town is laid out around a public square. Right now the square is just an expanse of grass, but they have plans for a courthouse as soon as they win the county seat. Mrs. Delhomme is heading a drive to plant trees along one section of the square to create a park. There are two hotels. Stay away from the Commercial. The Grand isn't too bad. Lots of open lots as yet. You'd be the first milliner. There's a two-story building next to Miller's for sale. I checked and it rents for $150 a month. I know you're not ready to think about that kind of money, but I might be interested in the building as an investment. If I can get out of my current lease and move my office there, I could give you a better rate."

Maude flicked the buggy whip toward her horse. "Get up there, you!" She muttered, "Oh, how I miss Casey . . . ," then she returned to the subject of Millersburg. "You'll like Mrs. Delhomme. She lost her husband a few years ago. They owned one of the largest farms in the county. When he died, Mrs. Delhomme turned the place over to her children and moved into Millersburg. She's a pillar of the church and at the forefront of civic improvements. Last winter, she organized a series of quilting bees to send quilts to the Indian reservation up near Wounded Knee." Maude paused. "I think she may be the nicest woman I've ever met."

"What about Mrs. Miller?"

"Hmm." Maude hesitated. "I think I should let you decide about Mrs. Miller without my commentary."

"Now you're making me nervous," Nora said. "Even her own sister says she 'can be difficult.' "

Maude nodded. "Yes. That would be accurate."

"I'm not suggesting you violate doctor-patient privacy," Nora said.

"Let me think how to say this," Maude said. She handed Nora the reins while she reached up to adjust her hat. Taking the reins back, she said, "Mrs. Miller is, next to Celest Delhomme, the most prosperous woman in Millersburg. Her husband dotes on her. She has absolutely everything a woman could want—except children."

"And so she isn't happy," Nora said.

Dr. Allbright nodded. "Right. She is very astute in business, as is her husband. They have a good marriage insofar as they seem to be good friends, and their talents make them very compatible. However, I would caution you that Mrs. Miller is not very—ah—flexible. She has definite ideas about how things should be done."

"Well, it is, after all, her business," Nora offered.

"I really don't think you have anything to worry about. Neither she nor her husband would have made the decision to expand their millinery department if they weren't certain it would succeed. And while there are several other general merchandise stores in Millersburg, theirs is definitely the most well-run with the widest selection."

"You sound like an advertisement for the store. For the entire town, for that matter," Nora said.

"I love it," Maude agreed. "Coming here was the best thing I could have done. The city board has bent over backward to make certain I'm happy and well-received. Everyone is interested in growth. It's a lot like Lincoln was when I first arrived. A little backward, but moving steadily forward. I think you'll like it, too."

She looked out of the corner of her eye at Nora. "You'll definitely like the female-to-male ratio. Prepare to be swamped by male suitors. That article you mentioned about the Bachelors' Club was meant as a joke, but it wasn't far from the truth." She chuckled. "Believe it or not, even *I* get asked to dances."

Nora said firmly, "Well, I'm going to be a hard catch. I'm not going to be swept off my feet by some handsome pretender wanting to play 'Mr. Right' to my 'Mrs. Right.' "

"Had your fill of the theater, eh?" Maude said.

Nora sighed. "Yes. Quite."

"Well, beware, Miss O'Dell, because Millersburg just opened an opera house and I've heard rumors that the Millers are doing all they can to attract a first-rate theatrical troupe for the opening. There will be actors about."

"I'm not worried," Nora said stoutly. "Besides, I don't even know that I'll *like* Millersburg."

CHAPTER 20

Millers and Men

With all lowliness and meekness, with
longsuffering, forbearing one another in love.
Ephesians 4:2

"It won't be so late when we get there," Nora remarked, nodding towards the cluster of lights flickering just ahead.

"Don't let the sight of those lights fool you," Dr. Allbright warned. "Distance is very deceptive out here. We're still at least three miles from town."

Nora settled back against the carriage seat. The night breeze was cool. Once, she was lulled almost to sleep. But then a carriage wheel fell into a wagon rut so deep the carriage pitched sideways. Nora nearly fell out.

Dr. Allbright laughed. "Hold on there, girl. I don't want to lose you before you've even seen Millersburg!"

Nora laughed nervously and held on tighter. To keep herself awake, she ran down a mental checklist of the things Elise had said were important for her to remember. Elise had said to "get everything in writing." She should offer to pay rent for a certain square footage of the Miller's store, making certain it was clear that Nora was not an employee of the store, but rather an independent entity. "Show her you are confident in your abilities, that you don't need an overseer, because you don't. Dr. Allbright will be able to guide you to a good business mentor, but it shouldn't be Mrs. Miller. You want to keep your interests and your financial affairs to yourself."

Nora was anxious to see Millersburg. The idea of a town smaller than Lincoln appealed to her. If the Ritters were any indication of the kind of people she would meet, she knew she would be happy. She wondered who the "Mrs. Judge Cranston" of Millersburg was and hoped that Celest Delhomme would prove to be as kind and helpful as both Karyn and Dr. Allbright had said she would be. Nora determined to get involved right away with one of the charity projects Mrs. Delhomme was heading. She longed to become part of a community, and she knew that giving of herself to those less fortunate was a good way to do it. She had seen that even Goldie Meyer received grudging acceptance because of her philanthropy. Nora was glad she wouldn't have to overcome the stigma of Goldie's.

Her mind wandered to Dr. Allbright's comment about the number of eligible bachelors in Millersburg and the surrounding area. She hoped they were more reliable than Greyson Chandler had proved to be. Starting a new business would keep her very busy, but she no longer thought strictly in terms of business.

Thinking back over the past year, she realized that she had been learning bits and pieces of something that had finally fallen into place for her. Respectability and wealth were sometimes just a thin veneer hiding deep-seated faults. People who seemed to be religious were sometimes the worst of all. Nora thought back to the circuit-riding preachers who stopped at Goldie's after their services. She still didn't understand how that could be.

For a while she had thought Greyson Chandler was different. Beneath all the glamour of fame and good looks, there had seemed to be a genuine person she could really like. But he had proved himself to be no better than the rest of Goldie's customers. All the while he was writing to her about his "return to God," he was planning to run off with Iris. Nora's hurt had subsided. When she thought of Chandler now, it made her angry.

By the time Grady plodded into Millersburg, Nora had decided she was going to like the small town. If it grew marriages like the Ritters', she wanted to be part of it. She hoped that Dr. Allbright was right about the number of eligible bachelors, and she hoped that among them there was another Mikal Ritter— although she had to admit she preferred blond hair and a little less height . . . something more like Greyson Chandler, without the hypocrisy. She might even bear with a little religion, if it was the genuine kind. She wondered how one knew if religion was genuine.

"There's Miller's," Dr. Allbright said, nodding as they drove by a two-story general store. "Cay Miller began everything you see around you with a soddy built right next to that site. Mikal Ritter and one of Celest Delhomme's sons built this store."

She pulled Grady up and they sat, looking across an open field toward the opposite side of the square. Light from a full moon bathed the little town in a soft glow. "Over there, just behind that block, is where you should have gotten off the train." She gestured with the buggy whip as she talked. "As you can see, there are still a few vacant lots, but in the morning what is now a deserted square will be bustling with activity. There are piles of lumber everywhere, and there are always a dozen or more wagons coming and going from the train station hauling in new building supplies."

Dr. Allbright urged Grady forward. They passed another two-story building. "This is the one that's for sale. I'll show it to you tomorrow. But you can see it's well placed. Someday there will be a courthouse in the middle of that open field—unless Broken Bow captures the county seat—and these folks are determined to put up a respectable fight about that. Celest Delhomme has a drive started to plant trees along the east end to begin a public park. It's going to be a great little town someday."

They made their way around the square, and then Dr. Allbright turned east on what she called Cedar Street. Pointing to a two-story house, she said, "That's where Mrs. Delhomme lives. It's the nicest house in town." She chuckled. "Something that grates terribly on Sophie Miller."

They pulled into an alley. "This is it. We're home." Nora helped unhitch and tend to Grady while Dr. Allbright pulled the carriage under an overhang next to the small barn. They walked through a patchy yard and onto a small back porch. Inside, Dr. Allbright lit a kerosene lamp. Its glow revealed an immaculate whitewashed kitchen. She led Nora through the kitchen and toward the front of the house, then up a narrow staircase. "You get the bedroom at the front of the house. I'm being selfish," Dr. Allbright said. "When I'm out half the night I want to be able to sleep, and I wanted the room as far from the street as possible. It's quieter, and there's more of a chance I can actually sleep during the day." She went to the door, "I'll let you get settled. Breakfast at dawn." She added, "I hope you decide to move here, Nora. The older I get the less I like rattling around in an empty house."

Seven years of living in Custer County, Nebraska, looked more like fifteen when applied to Sophie Miller. Karyn had told Nora that Sophie had come to Millersburg not long after her sister, and that she had enjoyed a long reign as the "belle" of every "ball" in the area. Nora could tell that the petite woman had once been a beauty, but the years had taken their toll.

"Sophie had so many suitors, it was hard to keep track," Karyn had said. "But persistence won out. Our dear friend Cay would not give up, and finally Sophie had the sense to marry him." Karyn had sighed. "Sophie always wanted a glamorous life, but she finally realized the worth of financial security and the devotion of a dear man."

Nora was not as certain as Karyn that Sophie appreciated her husband's devotion. Cay Miller was slightly built, with a perfectly trimmed mustache and a black eye patch earned over twenty years earlier while he was serving the Grand Army of the Republic. He had given over the running of his store to his wife, and now served on various civic committees and the board of the First Bank of Millersburg. He had a genuine smile and a twinkle in his one good eye. Nora liked him the moment they met.

Mrs. Miller treated her husband with practiced deference. While Nora and Mrs. Miller talked over their agreement, Cay was present. His wife appeared to consult him, but it quickly became clear that Mr. Miller's presence was for effect only. Miller's Emporium could have been renamed "Sophie's."

Talking things over with Dr. Allbright that evening, Nora said doubtfully, "I don't know. As a business, it's a good opportunity. But you were right when you said that Sophie Miller is no Elise Thornhill. She's almost overbearing."

"Don't let her scare you off," Dr. Allbright urged. "She has a hard shell, but underneath it there's a fairly decent woman."

The next day, Nora was back at Miller's. She had agreed to make a few sample hats for display. She settled in to "her" corner of the store, grateful to be near one of the large front windows.

The worktable was huge. Three mirrors, positioned down the middle of the table, divided it into halves, one for work, one for display. Several hat racks of different heights stood around each mirror. Sophie had ordered elegant cane-seated chairs and upholstered wooden footstools to encourage patrons to relax and shop. The entire wall behind the table was a mass of shelves and drawers, replete with a surprisingly good selection of trims and hat frames. Bandboxes and tissue paper were stored beneath the worktable. Nora's work chair was fitted with casters enabling her to move between each of the five hat stands permanently mounted to her side of the worktable and open the drawers behind her without ever getting up.

Removing her hat, Nora asked, "What would be the best style to start with?"

"I'd like two matching girl's bonnets," Mrs. Miller said. "Make them quite frilly. Something for Sundays." She opened a drawer and pulled out a pile of plain infant's bonnets. "And these need to be trimmed," she said. "I bought them sight unseen from my wholesaler. He can usually be trusted, but these are just—"

"—boring," Nora said.

Sophie smiled. "Exactly."

Nora reached into her bag and drew out some fashion magazines. Opening *The Delineator,* she pointed to a drawing of a child's dressy bonnet. "Is something like this what you had in mind?"

"I don't think I have a frame for anything like that," Sophie said doubtfully.

"I can use those plain straw bonnets on the top shelf."

"You can turn straw into that?"

"All it takes is cutting away half the brim at the back of the hat. The straw will be completely covered. No one will ever suspect I didn't use a wire frame."

Sophie nodded. "Wonderful. You've probably already guessed that these are for Mollie and May."

Nora smiled. "And a baby bonnet for Freddie." She was already pulling the ladder over and climbing up on her chair to reach the two straw bonnets. Nora worked for the rest of the day on Mollie's and May's new hats. By late afternoon, the straw forms were completely covered with a layer of fine white linen. Over the linen, Nora gathered white net with an edging of lace that dipped down in the front over the forehead. A huge bow nestled between the brim and the crown at the front of the hat, tied in place with long streamers that twisted along the edge of the crown to the back of the hat where there was another, smaller bow. White linen and lace streamers flowed off the hat and down the back. Two panels of lace ran across the flat top of the crown of each hat.

The minute Nora had finished the bonnets, she met the "Mrs. Judge Cranston" of Millersburg in the person of a woman who was intent on buying one of the bonnets.

"I'm sorry," Nora said. "these are already sold."

"But my daughter's party is this evening. You can't possibly make another in time."

"No, ma'am. I can't," Nora said. "But I'll be happy to take an order."

"I can't see why you can't just sell me this one and make another for—whoever."

Sophie interrupted. "Hello, Mrs. Smith. I'm sorry, but these are for my nieces. Miss O'Dell is correct. They aren't for sale."

"Are the Ritters coming into town tomorrow?" Mrs. Smith asked.

"I can't be certain," Sophie replied. "It all depends on the new baby and his mother."

"Then there's no reason you can't sell me one of these hats."

"Yes, there is," Sophie said calmly. "These are for Mollie and May."

Mrs. Smith ignored Sophie. "I'll pay you twice the price," she said to Nora.

Nora stood up. "Actually, Mrs. Smith, it's not an issue of price. Mollie and May's mother took care of me when I was ill not long ago, and I made these hats as a way to say thank you. So you see, their sentimental value is what's important. There's a lot of affection stitched into them. I really can't sell them."

Mrs. Smith departed. Sophie shook her head. "It does take all kinds." She turned to Nora. "Most of the people you will meet in Millersburg are easier to please."

Nora shrugged. "Don't worry. We had our Mrs. Smiths in Lincoln. Only there we called them all 'Mrs. Judge Cranston'—although I wouldn't want you to let that be known."

Sophie smiled. "Your work is very good, Miss O'Dell. I hope you decide to become a citizen of Millersburg."

Nora worked until closing time fashioning a spray of blue ribbon forget-me-nots for Freddie's bonnet. From her workstation she had a view of the entire interior of Miller's Emporium. Sophie Miller knew all of her customers by name. Nora also noticed that not a single child left the store without at least one piece of penny candy. Sophie Miller might be an astute businesswoman, but Nora suspected that at the heart of the free candy was just that—a heart.

The next day, Mikal and Karyn Ritter came to town. Mollie and May clambered across the boardwalk and into the store calling for "Aunt Sophie," who grabbed the two girls around their waists and swung them about laughing. She gave them candy and insisted they sit and tell her all about their new brother.

When Karyn came into the store with Freddie, Sophie kissed her sister's cheek. She took the baby in her arms. When Nora saw her struggling to control tears, she suddenly understood. Running the store might keep her busy and provide a sense of accomplishment, but in a world where motherhood was the epitome of success, Sophie Miller felt like a failure. Beneath her terse, businesslike exterior, she was a hurting woman desperate for children of her own. Nora wondered if Cay Miller had realized his wife's need for the store. She suspected that should Sophie Miller become pregnant, Cay Miller might suddenly become interested in running his store again.

That evening, Nora asked Dr. Allbright, "I don't mean to ask you to betray any doctor-patient confidence, but is Mrs. Miller unable to have children?"

Maude set her cup of tea down. "I see you broke through the facade."

"I was there when Karyn and Mikal arrived to show off Freddie. An entirely different woman appeared."

"To answer your question, I don't know why they have no children. As far as I can tell, Mrs. Miller is completely healthy in that respect."

Nora got up and went to the window. Across the street someone was building a new home. In what would be the front yard, a carpenter was constructing a picket fence. "I think I'll walk up to the train station in the morning and get a ticket for the next day. There's no need to put it off. I'm coming to Millersburg."

Packing for the move to Millersburg was no great challenge. Between Nora, Lucy, Hannah, and Elise, they had things ready in half a day. Nora sighed, "I don't have much to show for the last year of my life, do I?"

"Nonsense," Elise said. "Don't look at it in terms of *things*. When I think back to the girl I hired away from my sister, I'd say you have a lot to show for the last year of your life. You're self-assured, you know what you want . . . and you're going to get it." Elise hugged her. "I'm going to miss you, but I wouldn't keep you here for anything."

Early in the afternoon, Nora paid a last visit to Goldie's, where she urged Lily to consider joining her in Millersburg and promised to help her friend find a good job.

Lily shook her head. "That's real nice of you, Nora, but I'm better off here with Goldie. I got a regular string of clients now, and I've settled down a lot." She smiled. "I quit the bottle, and I figure in another year or two, I'll have money saved to do whatever I want."

Nora opened her mouth, then closed it.

Lily said, "I know what you are thinking. You're wishing I'd follow Iris's example. Well I'm not smart like Iris, and I don't have a Greyson Chandler ready to help me out."

At the mention of Grey's name, Nora almost flinched. Not wanting to hear any more, she hugged Lily and said, "Well, just remember, you'll always have a friend in Custer County." She gave each of the girls a hair comb adorned with handmade silk flowers. For Goldie, she had a monogrammed silk scarf. After another round of hugs, Nora left.

The next morning, Nora boarded the train for Millersburg. "I'll be sure to stay on the train at Grand Island," she joked as she stepped up onto the train car. Hidden in her bag were several unopened letters from Greyson Chandler.

Nora opened the first letter as the train went from Lincoln to Woodlawn. Grey was in Denver. He sent her greetings from Iris, who was at last settled in a little house near the heart of the city. She had taken in three children. Grey had put her in touch with an influential benefactor he knew from his "days in the theater," and she would be able to grow her charity without worries for the future.

> *Do you remember that I told you I had some things I had to do. Helping Iris was one of them. I know I have not written as I should, but I did not want to boast about what I was going to do . . . until I had done it. And even now, I do not boast, only in that it has been a blessing to be used in this way. I don't know what He has for me next. Please write and tell me your impressions. I wonder if you have tried any of the Lincoln churches yet.*

Nora read and reread the letter, finally laying it open in her lap while she looked out the window. Her inherent mistrust of men may have destroyed her relationship with Greyson. Why was it so easy for her to categorize him among the "good-for-nothing so-and-so's only interested in one thing"?

Feeling guilty, Nora ripped open the second letter. There was another letter to read while she passed through Marengo . . . Round Grove . . . Janesville. The final letter said that Grey had received Miss Thornhill's note about Nora being away and being ill.

> *I wish I knew where you were so that I could come to you. What are you thinking, Nora? I need to hear from you. I keep praying, but no answers seem to come.*

Nora finished Chandler's last letter just as the train pulled into Millersburg. It was little more than a terse note. He was coming to Lincoln to find out why she hadn't answered his letters.

Nora climbed down from the train in Millersburg, clutching the bundle of Greyson Chandler's letters. As Dr. Allbright hurried toward her, she stuffed them into her carpetbag.

"Well," she said. "Here I am."

"You look as white as a ghost. I hope it's not another attack of the ague," Maude said.

Nora shook her head. "No. Just an attack of terror. I've been asking myself all the way here who I think I am and what I have done."

Maude took her arm and guided her inside the small station. She nodded toward the door. "Go over there and take a look at your new town. See if it feels like home yet. I'll see to having your trunk sent to the house."

Nora stepped outside the small train station. Across the street the new opera house gleamed white in the morning sun, wearing a new coat of whitewash. A few wagons were parked in what would one day be the town square, but for now was simply a wide-open field of prairie. Nora tried to envision a park and a courthouse. The streets around the square were unusually wide. Two children ran by chasing iron hoops they had set to rolling with sticks. Somewhere a dog barked. Remembering her introduction to Lincoln, Nebraska, Nora realized how much better this was. It didn't feel like home yet, but Nora thought it could.

Except for the bundle of letters in her carpetbag, she would not have given Lincoln a second thought.

At Dr. Allbright's house, Nora settled into her room. Later in the day, Dr. Allbright joined her for tea. "There was an entire packet of letters from Greyson Chandler waiting for me in Lincoln. The last one said that he was on his way there to find out why I wasn't answering his letters." Nora set her tea cup down and asked, "What do you think I should do?"

"What do you *want* to do?" Maude asked.

Nora took a deep breath. "I don't know."

"You can be downright irritating at times, young lady. Constantly asking questions I have no answer for. First it was questions about God, when you know I'm agnostic. Now questions about love and marriage. I'm divorced." At Nora's look of surprise, the doctor said tersely, "Scandalous, but true."

Dr. Allbright stood up. "You're searching for answers I can't give you, dear. Not because I don't want to. Because I don't *have* the answers. If I did, I'd be happily married and singing in the choir at First Church." She headed for the back door. "I have to get back to my office. I leave you with this: It has been my experience that when we don't know what to do, it's best to do nothing. The same train that takes Mr. Chandler to Lincoln can bring him to Millersburg. Why don't you just let time take care of that. In the meantime, perhaps you should take a drive out to the Ritters and interview Karyn about marriage and metaphysics. Or talk to Mrs. Delhomme."

Nora lay on her bed that evening staring at the ceiling. She thought back over the day. She had reread all of Greyson Chandler's letters and come to one conclusion. She did, at last, know what she wanted. She wanted to be loved the way Mikal Ritter loved his wife. Nora turned over and pounded her pillow. I wonder if Mikal Ritter has a brother. *Maybe it runs in the family.*

CHAPTER 21

Will

A friend loveth at all times,
and a brother is born for adversity.
Proverbs 17:17

Dear Will,

*I am sending this to Mrs. Johnson for her to give you. I
don't know but what Pap would throw away a letter from
me without ever giving it to you. If you've left home, I'm
hoping the Johnsons can find you.*

*It took nearly four days to walk to Lincoln. Did you
know that was where I was headed? It's been a long road
since the day I left. I spent last year in Lincoln, but I'm
settled in Millersburg now, on the Burlington line west of
Grand Island.*

*I'm a milliner, with my own little corner in Miller's Em-
porium. I have a room at a Dr. Allbright's, a woman doctor I met in Lincoln. She's the one who suggested I look
Millersburg over, and I'm glad I came. Folks make you feel
welcome and the town is growing fast. I hope it never gets
as big as Lincoln. Don't imagine it will.*

*I hope you don't hold it against me for not telling you I
was leaving, but I figured if you really didn't know anything, Pap couldn't hold it against you. I've wanted to
write for a long time, but made myself wait until I felt I*

had something to offer. What I'm writing for now, Will, is to say that if you ever want a place to go, and if Millersburg sounds good to you, come on out.

There is a big spread just northeast of here owned by a family named Delhomme, and they always need hired hands. I already talked to Mrs. Delhomme, and if you decide to come, she is sure her sons, who run the farm, would have a job for you. It won't pay much, but it would be a way to start. The Delhommes have a decent bunkhouse for their hired hands, and as hard as you work, you'd be a foreman in no time. They raise sheep and cattle, and grain enough to feed their own herds. Mrs. Delhomme told me their foremen all have their own houses—one on each section the family owns.

Will, I'll never forget all the times you stood between me and Pap. You were more of a father than a brother to me, but you were pretty good at both, and I'm grateful. Don't let Pap ruin your life. He made his own choices and he didn't have to end up so bitter and unhappy. Since I left home I've met people who've been through much worse than Pap, and they are happy and have good lives.

The difference seems to be that a lot of the happy ones have a strong faith in God. I'm not talking about going to church. I mean these people seem to know God like you and I know each other—maybe better. I've been too busy to learn much about that, but as time goes by and I get more settled, I'm thinking I will check into it for myself. Things that have happened make me think maybe Someone has been watching out for me. It's like maybe God took over when you weren't there anymore. Come to think of it, maybe God was the one who put you there in the first place.

Hope it doesn't embarrass you for me to say I love you, Will.

> *Your sister, Elnora*
> *(Forgot to tell you I*
> *call myself Nora*
> *O'Dell now)*

195

A few days after Nora posted her letter to Will, a messenger came into the emporium and called out, "Telegram for Miss O'Dell."

"Telegram?" Nora was terrified. Had something happened to Elise?

Arriving Friday. Have money for second-rate hotel and big hug for little sis.

Will

Nora clutched the telegram to her chest and cried.

"What is it, Nora—what's wrong?" Sophie hurried to Nora's side and put a hand on her shoulder.

Nora shook her head. She held the telegram out. Sophie read it. "A brother! Coming to visit! How wonderful!"

Nora swallowed hard and tried to regain her composure. How would she ever wait until Friday?

"Well, he's certainly not staying in a 'second-rate hotel,'" Sophie said. "If Dr. Allbright doesn't have room, he's welcome to stay with us."

Dr. Allbright stated firmly that Will would most certainly stay with her, and Nora did not get a complete night's rest for the remainder of the week.

He had already climbed down from the train and was headed for the station to claim his bags when there was a flash of blonde hair in the crowd. Something familiar about the way she moved caught his eye. He raised his hand and started to call her name, but just as he did, she threw herself into the arms of a lanky young man in dire need of a haircut and a new suit of clothes.

The stranger bent down to hug her fiercely, brushing her cheek with his mustache as he kissed her. She was crying, almost clinging to him. When the couple turned to head into the station, Greyson ducked in ahead of them. He grabbed an abandoned newspaper and sat down, watching them over the top of the front page.

Well, at least I know what she's been doing . . . and why she hasn't answered my letters.

Nora and the other man left the train station arm in arm. Grey stood up wearily. He grabbed his bag and headed up the street. It would be suppertime soon. He doubted he would be hungry.

Nora hung on her brother's arm as they crossed the street. After her initial joy at his appearing, she felt awkward. She couldn't think what to say next, and from his silence, she thought Will must feel the same way.

They passed the new opera house, and Nora pointed to a posted announcement on the door. "There's a performance tomorrow night. The whole community's been working hard at it. Millersburg is growing so fast they need a new school. This is the beginning of a long list of fund-raisers."

She went on, "Mrs. Delhomme is at the heart of it. I helped with some of the costumes. Mrs. Delhomme wrote away and got scripts for that comedy." The playbill said that *Love's Lottery* would be performed on *Saturday evening, September 22, 1887, one performance only, at eight o'clock.* "It's supposed to be very funny. Even with amateur actors, it should be fun. Mrs. Delhomme won't tell anyone, but there's some kind of big surprise planned. Nearly the entire town should be there. You could meet a lot of people." She looked up at Will. "Want to come?"

Will shrugged. "I guess."

Nora finally asked, "How's Pap?"

"The same."

"Did you tell him?" Nora hesitated. "About me, I mean."

Will nodded. "Sure."

"What'd he have to say?"

Will shook his head. "Nothing you want to hear."

"Oh." Nora took a deep breath. "Well, I guess I shouldn't be surprised."

They had arrived at Dr. Allbright's. A note tacked to the front door read, *Called to set a broken leg north of town. Welcome, Will! Probably back late. Sorry.*

197

"We could have used her horse and buggy to get your trunk."

Just then, Celest Delhomme came up the street. "Nora!" she called, smiling. "And this must be Will."

Nora introduced them before Celest said, "Maude stopped by my place on her way out of town. You two are welcome to use my horse and buggy if there's anything to be brought over from the station."

"Thank you, ma'am," Will said, pulling on the frayed brim of his straw hat. "I travel light."

Celest excused herself. "You two have so much catching up to do," she said. "I'm going to head back home. If there's anything you need, just let me know." She turned toward Will. "We've already talked about the fact that you're a good farmhand, Mr. Calhoun. You must have dinner with me after church on Sunday so we can talk about that. The boys will all be here. You can meet the entire family."

Will and Nora accepted Celest's invitation, and she headed for home, leaving them still feeling awkward with one another.

Nora opened the front door and gave Will a tour of Dr. All-bright's house before leaving him to observe his new surroundings on his own. He plopped his small bag on the bed in his room before heading downstairs to where Nora was rattling pans in the kitchen.

He sniffed the air. "That supper?"

"You bet," Nora said. She gestured with a wooden spoon. "Smells good, doesn't it? Tastes good, too. I've learned a lot since I left home." She smiled wryly. "And you can't skip my biscuits across the water like rocks anymore, either. I finally got a lesson from the champion biscuit-maker in all of Custer County."

"Now, Elnor—Nora," Will said, "I never used your biscuits like that. 'Cept maybe once or twice."

Nora laughed. "It's so good to have you here. Now I know what I've been missing. It's family. Tell me you're going to stay."

"Guess I will," came the answer. "Pap made it real clear I better not plan on coming back once I walked down that road with my bag in hand." He pulled a chair out and sat down. "I got a little surprise waiting for you over at the train station. We can walk over and get it after we eat, if that's okay."

Nora had dished up two bowls of stew and was pulling biscuits from the oven. She exclaimed, "You brought Mama's trunk!"

Will nodded.

After supper they retrieved their mother's little trunk from the station. Opening it finally bridged two years of silence. By the time Nora and Will retired, it was as if they had never been apart.

CHAPTER 22

The Prodigal Son

----

*To every thing there is a season, and a time to
every purpose under the heaven: . . .
a time to embrace, and a time to
refrain from embracing.*
Ecclesiastes 3:1, 5

Compared to Funke's Opera House in Lincoln, Millersburg
Opera House was little more than a large room with a stage at
one end. Instead of theater seats, patrons occupied folding
wooden seats. Set up in rows for performances, the seats could
be moved against the walls for dances, or arranged around tables for meetings. Lighting was provided by reflector kerosene
lamps instead of gas. There was no carved proscenium arch.
Instead of being decorated with scenic views, the walls around
the stage were painted a soft sage green. There was no crystal
chandelier, but urns and cupids formed an elaborate design in
the pressed tin ceiling.

Nora and Will found seats near the front of the room where
Will could sit on the aisle and have more room for his long legs.
After they were settled, Nora looked around. Mr. and Mrs.
Miller were just coming in. Sophie hurried to the front of the
room to reserve seats for Mrs. Delhomme and her sons, who
would be late getting to their seats. Nora introduced Will,
pleased that he remembered his manners and stood up to shake
Mrs. Miller's hand. She wondered if Dr. Allbright would be at

the performance. It seemed that more and more she was working long into the evening.

Looking up at the stage curtain, Nora remembered her first
theater experience in Lincoln when she asked Elise how many
yards of velvet she thought had been used to create the stage
curtain, which was painted with a scene Elise called "The Ra-
jah's Triumphal Entry into Singapore." Remembering the title,
Nora smiled as she looked at the white canvas curtain before
her. There was a simplistic landscape painted in the center, but
all around it an array of painted portrait frames created ad
space. Most were lettered with the names of businesses owned
by Cay Miller. *The Millers' Triumphal Entry into Custer
County,* Nora thought with a smile.

The capacity of the opera house had been said to be "over
one hundred." Nora guessed at least double that had crowded
into the room. She leaned toward Will. "Mrs. Delhomme said
there was a surprise, but I didn't think this many people would
turn out!" Will tugged at his collar. "I sure hope they open the
windows before too long."

Finally, at eight o'clock, Mrs. Delhomme peeked through the
opening in the center of the curtain. A trickle of applause
greeted her, and after ducking back out of sight for a moment,
she finally parted the curtain and stepped in front of it. A second
round of applause died down. Everyone waited. She opened her
mouth to speak, then closed it. Finally, she clasped her hands
before her and began. "This is the beginning, friends. The beginning of our efforts to build a better school for our children and a
better future for all of Custer County."

When the whoops and cheers died down, Celest said, "I
didn't expect so many to come, and I hope my surprise is big
enough to merit this evening's attendance. As many of you
know, my sons now farm the land their father and I home-
steaded when we first came to America. Many of you also
know, that one of our sons has been away from home for many,
many years."

Celest bowed her head for a moment. Her clasped hands were
shaking. Not a person in the large room stirred. "This son left
to become a musician, but the stage became his vocation. His

father and I were not pleased. We were raised in a home where the theater was believed to be a playground for evil." She tried to make a joke. "But then, the same thing was said about America when we told our parents we wanted to emigrate." There was a trickle of laughter.

Celest smiled nervously before continuing. "This evening, I want to share something with all of you. My prodigal son has come home." There was a murmur in the room. "He is with us, this evening, as my gift to Millersburg. I want to thank the good Lord for answering this mother's prayers and for bringing my boy home to me. And I also want to thank Luc for having the grace to forgive his parents their foolishness."

Celest dropped her hands to her sides and smiled. "He is known by another name in theatrical circles. But here, he is Luc Delhomme. He has come home, and his family rejoices. And now, without any more comments from this foolish old woman, I once again thank you all for coming. We hope that you enjoy our performance of *Love's Lottery*."

Celest disappeared behind the curtain. There was a stir in the room. The kerosene lights along the walls of the hall were turned low. The curtain parted, and the play began. When Luc Delhomme stepped on stage, there was rousing applause, hooting and screeching such that Nora could see him fighting back tears. He finally stepped out of his role long enough to bow to the audience. He saw Nora. He looked at Will. And then he stepped away from the edge of the stage and into *Love's Lottery*.

The play was hilarious. The crowd laughed and applauded, and the paper the next day would report that "a good time was had by all." Nora was to remember nothing of the play itself. Her head was swimming from the revelation that apparently Greyson Chandler's real name was Luc Delhomme.

There was a brief intermission added to *Love's Lottery,* to give the citizens of Millersburg time to bid on a mountain of decorated boxes on a table at the back of the room. Each box was supposed to contain dessert for two, and proceeds from the sale provided another way for the citizens of Millersburg to contribute to their new school.

"Do you want to go?" Nora asked Will, when the lights were turned up and the parade of boxes began. A relay line of eligible bachelors had formed along one wall, and they passed boxes to the stage where Cay Miller was acting as auctioneer.

"No, we should stay," Will said.

"It's so hot in here," Nora said. "And it's only going to get hotter. I didn't make a box, and I don't really care about the play. We can go if you'd like."

"Well," Will said doubtfully, "maybe a walk around the square while the auction is going on. We can come back up later. We don't want people to think we're rude."

"We can give our seats to someone else," Nora urged. "No one is going to notice we're gone."

"All right. If you want to." Will looked at his sister quizzically.

Nora stood up and pulled him after her. Someone slid into their seats immediately.

Outside, Will clamped his limp hat on his head and hurried to catch up with Nora. "You gonna tell me what's wrong? You look like you just saw a three-legged hog jump a fence."

"I'm just so mad I could—*ooo!*" Nora clenched her fists and marched away.

"Hey, I thought it was funny. That one scene was a little risqué . . . but, Nora, it wasn't all that bad. Even Mrs. Delhomme laughed." He stepped in front of her, bent over, and looked at her until she made eye contact. "You mad 'cause that Luc fella was ogling you from the stage?"

Nora closed her eyes and shook her head. "No. I'm not mad about that."

"Well, what is it, then?"

Nora shook her head and closed her eyes. She held her hands up and stepped around her brother. "Just let me walk a little while, okay? I need to think."

"Well, okay, Nora. Walk all you want. I'm gonna head back to Dr. Allbright's and get some of that lemonade you made earlier. When you want me, that's where I'll be."

Nora was already striding away from him. She turned around and walked backward three steps as she said, "Fine. Good. I'll be there directly. I just"—she turned around again—"need to think."

"And that's why I was so mad. I feel like an idiot. He never *once* told me Greyson Chandler wasn't his real name. He never once told me he grew up in Nebraska. Every time we talked about it, he was—vague. I've been corresponding with a man I barely know . . . and now I find out I know even less than I thought I did."

Will pulled on his mustache while he considered what his sister was saying. "Uh, Nora—" he began.

"Don't do that!" Nora said, slapping his hand. "Grey does that and I hate it."

Will put his hand down. "I was just wondering, did you ever tell him your real name is Elnora Calhoun?"

Nora blinked. "Why would I do that? It doesn't matter." She glowered at Will. "Don't look at me like that! It's not the same thing."

"Were you ever—uh—vague when you told him about where you grew up?"

"Of course I was vague. I didn't want to sound like a poor oppressed child."

"Gee, Nora," Will said. "Maybe Mr. Chandler didn't want you to think of him as a poor, disinherited child."

"You're just sticking up for him because you're a man." She slammed her teacup down and stood up. "Wait until Dr. Allbright gets here. She'll understand how I feel."

"And how is that, Miss Elnora-Nora-Calhoun-O'Dell?" Greyson Chandler/Luc Delhomme was standing at the back screen door. "Exactly how do you feel?" He nodded toward Will, who got up and opened the door.

He held out his hand. "I'm Luc Delhomme. And I understand you are Nora's"—he nodded toward Nora—"or is it *El*nora's—brother? Glad to meet you." He looked at Nora. "Aren't you going to invite me to sit down?"

Realizing that Grey had apparently been eavesdropping from

the back porch made Nora blush. She folded her arms across her chest. "It's not my house, but it is a free country as far as I know. I guess you can sit down if you want to, Mr. Chandler/ Delhomme."

"Actually, now that I'm home, Delhomme sounds much better to me. And I always liked the name Luc. My brothers have stupid names like Serge and Remi. Thank God Mama and Papa used up Thierry before I came along. Luc's much more sensible, don't you think?" He smiled benignly. "Care to tell me why you changed *your* name? Oh, and while you're at it, I wouldn't mind hearing why you didn't answer my letters." He stroked his mustache. "Let's see, it would be about ten letters by now, I suppose?"

Nora glowered at him. "You are having fun at my expense, Mr. Delhomme. And I don't appreciate it. I cared for you. At least I cared for Greyson Chandler and—"

Luc leaned forward and put both elbows on the table. "Now we're finally getting somewhere."

Nora blushed. "I can't talk to you. This is too confusing."

Luc sat back. Turning toward Will, he said, "I was at the train station the day you arrived. I don't mind telling you how relieved I was when my mother told me you're Nora's brother. Mother says you're thinking of working on the place?"

While Nora simmered, Will and Luc talked. Nora looked from her brother to Grey, practicing the name Luc in her mind. She poured a cup of tea for the two men and finally got up to make coffee.

While she moved about Dr. Allbright's kitchen, she watched Luc. She had forgotten how much he gestured with his hands when he talked. The memory of her two hands being held in his made her blush. When she finally sat back at the table, Will had been given a good idea of the size and layout of the Delhomme farm. He had also been invited to ride out with Luc when he visited on Monday.

"You should come along, Nora," Luc was saying. "My father built probably the most unique sod house in the state. Have you ever seen one?"

Nora nodded. "I stayed with a family for a while when I first came. Do you know the Ritters?"

"*Know* them!" Luc boomed. "Mikal and I could tell you stories . . . but how did you come to stay with them?"

"It's a long story," Nora said.

"Tell him," Will urged. He could see that his sister was calming down. And he had not missed the way she looked at Luc Delhomme.

Nora shrugged. "I got sick on the train coming out. In Grand Island, I got off to get a cool drink of water . . . but I mistakenly got back on the wrong train and ended up in Loup City. Fortunately, Mr. and Mrs. Ritter had gone there to retrieve a lost shipment for the Millers. They rescued me. I stayed with them for about three weeks." She smiled. "I was there when little Freddie was born."

Luc smiled and nodded. "So, Mikal finally got his boy."

"They have two others," Nora said quietly. "Up on the hill behind the house."

Luc ran a hand through his blonde hair. "I didn't know about that."

"And they have twin girls, about four. Mollie and May."

"Has Mikal added on to the house?" Luc wanted to know.

Nora nodded. "There's a kitchen on the back and two bedrooms."

"Still the soddy?"

"Yes. But all plastered and painted white on the inside, with a wood floor. It's very cozy."

"I know all about that plaster," Luc said. "I'm the one who hauled the clay for the main room. We did that right after Karyn came." He laughed and shook his head. "I had my doubts about Mikal's German bride. I didn't think she'd stay. You could tell she was pretty horrified by the conditions she was expected to live in. But she surprised us all. Did she ever tell you about getting caught out in the prairie fire?"

Nora shook her head. "No."

Dr. Allbright's grandfather clock struck midnight. Luc hesitated. "It's getting late. I shouldn't be keeping you."

Impulsively, Nora reached out and touched the back of his

hand. "Please stay." She blushed and looked at her brother. "We'd like to hear about it. Wouldn't we, Will?"

Will leaned back in his chair. "Well, I would, Nora, but I think I'll be turning in." He looked at Luc. "If you won't take offense."

An unspoken message passed between the two men. Luc grinned and nodded. He stood up and offered his hand. "Good night, Will. I'll see you at my mother's in a few hours."

Will left. Nora moved into his chair opposite Luc. Suddenly the air in the kitchen seemed close. Nora reached up to wipe sweat off her forehead.

"It's cooler outside. There's sure to be a breeze. Why don't we sit on the porch?" Luc suggested. They made their way in the dark through Dr. Allbright's parlor and outside. Maude had dug some wild vines in the country and stuck them in the ground on either side of the path that led up to the porch. They had taken hold in spite of her neglect, climbing up the posts and trailing across the overhang.

"Unfortunately," Nora said as she sank into the cushions that covered one of the cozy chairs on the porch, "Maude hardly ever has leisure time to relax out here." She paused. "It looks like she's to be gone the night again. I don't think I'd like being a doctor much."

Luc perched on the railing opposite her and leaned against a post.

"You were going to tell me about Karyn Ritter and the prairie fire," Nora said.

"When Karyn married Mikal, they were complete strangers. Did you know that?"

"She told me," Nora said. "It was a surprise. I assumed they were sweethearts from childhood. They seem so—perfect for one another."

Luc laughed softly. "They are. But it took about six months for them to figure that out." He looked at Nora. "I guess sometimes it can take even longer."

Nora fidgeted in her chair. "Tell me about the fire."

"Karyn came to America with a group of about forty German women. They arrived one day, filed off a train, lined up in a church and picked mates. Then, Mikal took her to his little one-room soddy."

"She said she almost didn't stay."

"Right. Apparently Karyn's family in Germany was fairly well off." He shook his head. "Whatever she expected, it certainly wasn't Custer County. But she liked Mikal."

"And she had her sister with her," Nora said. "That had to help."

"Oh, no. Karyn came alone. Sophie's arrival was a complete surprise."

Nora took note that Luc called Mrs. Miller by her Christian name. She wondered what the significance of that might be.

Luc quickly told the story of Sophie's arrival. "She stayed with Mikal and Karyn, of course. And somehow Karyn got it in her head that Mikal cared for Sophie. After a few months, she decided things would be better if she left. So she rode out one day to check on another homestead. I guess she was thinking she might try to make a go of it alone. While she was gone, a prairie fire came up."

"And Mikal went after her . . . and when he found her they finally knew they loved each other."

"Yes. She did tell you."

Nora said, "I heard her tell it to Mollie and May one night as a bedtime story. I never guessed it was true." She paused and then said thoughtfully, "I thought they had a fairy-tale romance. But they've worked hard to have a good marriage."

"I don't think there are many fairy tales coming true these days," Luc said thoughtfully. "My mother and father were crazy for one another, but there were times when she wanted to throw him all the way back to Belgium."

"My pap was so crazy about my mother he *went* crazy when she died." Nora shivered. "That's an awful way to live."

"Different people respond differently when bad things come their way. Some can handle it, some can't." Luc peered at Nora through the moonlight. "And some just run away and try to ignore it."

"I didn't run away from home because I wanted to ignore my problems."

"I wasn't talking about that. But I have wondered if you ran away from Lincoln because of me." He reached up to stroke his mustache. "Although I suppose that's giving myself too much importance in your life." When Nora said nothing, he asked, "Are you ever going to tell me why you stopped writing? I know you were sick for a while, but—"

Nora interrupted him. "I saw you and Iris in Grand Island."

"What?!"

She nodded. "I got off the train to get a drink of water. I came out of the station to get back on board the train, and there was Iris running toward you. You took your hat off to hug her. You picked her up and twirled her around."

Luc was quiet for a moment. Without saying anything, he knelt before her on the porch, took one of her hands in his, and kissed the back of it. He held her hand next to his cheek for a moment before speaking. "No wonder you didn't write."

Nora pulled her hand away. "I guess I have to admit that Grey had more than 'turned my head.' Being squired through the streets of Lincoln by the heartthrob of the theater was pretty heady stuff for a little country girl. And that dinner the night before you left." She took a deep breath. "Well." She paused again. "When I saw you and Iris, I thought I had just been a pleasant interlude for you. I told myself that was all right, that that was probably the way actors did things. And I had had fun, so I didn't have any right to whine and feel sorry for myself. And I figured it was time to move on." She paused again to keep her voice from trembling. "I didn't even open your last few letters until I was on my way back to settle here. I almost threw them away."

"Did you believe what I wrote about Iris?"

Nora nodded. "Of course. She told me herself about her plans to settle in Denver." She paused. "But then she stayed in Lincoln so long, I thought it was just talk. That she was just like the other girls, after all." She added softly, "It was wonderful of you to make her dream possible."

"But you still didn't write."

Nora shook her head. "I didn't know what to say. Dr. Allbright reminded me that the same train that took you to Lincoln could bring you to Millersburg, if you really cared."

Luc sat back on the porch floor and leaned against the railing. He raised one knee and balanced his arm on his knee. He could just reach Nora's skirt, and he stroked the fabric where her hand had been. "And here I am."

"To do a benefit performance as a favor to your mother," Nora reminded him.

"—and to find you."

Nora took a deep breath. "Grey—Luc. I'm too confused. I didn't really know Greyson Chandler all that well, and I don't know Luc Delhomme at all."

"Karyn and Mikal Ritter married complete strangers. They're happy."

Nora fidgeted in her chair.

"Do you even *like* me?"

"I can't believe Greyson Chandler is asking that question. He never seemed to have any doubts about his power over women."

"Well, Greyson Chandler isn't asking that question. This is me. Luc Delhomme. Are you going to answer me? Because if I'm not mistaken there is still something pulling us toward each other." He knelt before her once again, putting one hand on each arm of the chair she was sitting in. "I'm not moving until you answer me, Nora. Do you even like me?"

In a very small voice, Nora said, "So much it frightens me." He leaned toward her, and she immediately held a hand up, pushing against him. "I built my weeks around those letters you sent. I can't tell you how hurt I was when I saw you with Iris . . . and then how relieved when I finally read your letters. But, Luc—"

She heard a carriage coming up the street. "That's probably Dr. Allbright—"

Suddenly, Luc leaned forward and covered her mouth with his. He kissed her fiercely before pulling away and standing up. He stood and walked to the stairs that led down into the yard. "I'm going to walk around back and help Dr. Allbright unhitch her horse. She must be exhausted. Will you come to church with me this morning?"

"Yes."

"And you're coming to dinner at Mother's, right?"

"Yes."

"And on Monday, I'd like it very much if you'd ride with Will and me to see my home. We could stop at the Ritters' on our way back if it doesn't get too late."

"That would be nice."

Luc stepped down off the porch. He started around the edge of the house, then stopped. "Nora."

"Yes?"

"You *were* kissing me back just now. I didn't just imagine that, did I?"

Nora got up and crossed the porch. She leaned out over the railing and softly kissed him again. "I just need a little time."

He touched her cheek. "Take all the time you need. I'm not going anywhere." He walked down the side of the house, whistling softly.

CHAPTER 23

The Promise

I am he: before me there was no God formed,
neither shall there be after me.
I, even I, am the Lord; and
beside me there is no savior.
Isaiah 43:10–11

"I have a promise to make to you this morning. What I am going to say is guaranteed to help you overcome any past. What I am going to say this morning will fit you for the future. What I am going to say this morning will make today richer and fuller than you thought possible."

The pastor stood back from his pulpit. "How is that possible, you wonder? How can this short, ugly little man make such an outlandish promise?" He paused and looked about the congregation slowly.

Reverend Martin Underwood was balding, and the fringe about the hairless crown of his knobby little head had a propensity to stick out in all directions. He wore spectacles so thick they made his eyes appear much larger than their actual size. His voice was too high, his face too long, his teeth too large. Nothing about him even approached the confidence and authority with which Greyson Chandler had commanded the attention of an audience. And yet, when Reverend Underwood took the pulpit, Nora could not take her eyes from him. She was certain he was looking directly at her.

The service had begun benignly enough. The Delhomme family was recognized. Luc was welcomed home. The choir sang. Someone announced an ice cream social Thursday evening. Someone else got up and invited the women of the church to a quilting bee at Lottie Hanson's house on Tuesday morning. The offering was taken. But then Reverend Underwood got up and made his outlandish promise.

"It is possible, my friends, for me to make this promise, because the promise is based on this book. The only book God ever wrote. The only book that fits us for life." He picked up his Bible and read, " 'Acquaint now thyself with him, and be at peace: thereby good shall come unto thee.' Do you want peace, my friend? Acquaint now thyself with Him."

Reverend Underwood laid his Bible back on the pulpit and, once again, stared at Nora.

He smiled "Let us begin with love. God is love. He is the very essence of the very thing that humankind longs for. He is the source of eternal, infinite, unchanging, gracious love. I propose, dear brethren, that it is not incompatible with God's love that He permits us to suffer. God's promises are not to remove all affliction. His promise is that when the world hates us, He loves us. He causes all things to work for good. Hate cannot triumph, for God is love.

"Our loving God is patient. How long has He been waiting for you, dearly beloved, to acknowledge His rightful place in your life? How long does He wait while you blame Him for your troubles and refuse to accept His loving comfort for the evils of men? How long does He wait while men deny His Son and refuse the forgiveness freely offered?

"Our loving, patient God is holy. He cannot admit sin into His holy presence. And so, His love is demonstrated in that He provides His own Son to cover our sin. He loves His poor creation enough to give His only Son that we might be saved. He waits for us to come to Him. He allows us to rail against Him, to shake our fist in His holy face . . . and all the while He is loving us. But one day His Holiness will say, 'Enough'! Those who refuse His love must feel His wrath."

Reverend Underwood leaned toward his congregation. "Do not tempt His wrath, dearly beloved. Know His love through

His Son, Jesus Christ. Contemplate His wonderful, magnificent person. For in God alone will you find the ability to overcome the past, to ready yourself for the future, to live today fully. He is all, and all in all. I invite you to Him." Reverend Underwood stood back from the pulpit and opened his arms, as if inviting people to come.

The congregation sang a hymn, and then everyone began to file out of the church. Luc was surrounded by old friends welcoming him home. Nora took Will's arm and followed him out of the church. As they left, Reverend Underwood took Nora's hand. His larger-than-normal eyes seemed to look right through her as he said, "I'll be praying for you, my dear." When Nora looked up at him quizzically, he smiled. "I am available at any hour to meet the needs of my flock. And I pray you become one of the flock very, very soon."

Nora shook his hand and said something noncommittal. Will complemented the reverend's "talk" and led Nora down the stairs of the small, white-framed church and out onto the scrubby lawn. They waited in the shade of a tree until the Delhomme family joined them. Mrs. Delhomme introduced her sons Remi, Serge, and Thierry, and their families.

"Mother said that Mrs. Miller had allowed for some time away from the emporium while your brother gets settled," Remy's wife said. "I hope you can come to the quilting on Tuesday morning." She motioned to the other wives. "We're all coming in together. Five of us could command our own quilting frame. It would be fun!"

Celest said, "Luc is taking Nora to visit the Ritters tomorrow. I'll have him ask Karyn to come in that morning, too."

Serge's wife nodded. "Even better. I haven't seen the baby yet."

"Let's get together tomorrow at home and see if we can't whip up a layette," Thierry's wife chimed in. They began discussing who had which fabric and what they would make.

While the wives were planning Karyn Ritter's impromptu baby shower, Nora looked around for Will and Luc. Luc was standing on the steps of the church, surrounded by young people—mostly female. Just as Nora felt a little pang of jealousy, he looked over at her and smiled. He dismissed himself from the group and came across the church lawn to where she stood, boldly taking her hand and tucking it under his arm.

"Mother, I'm starved," he said.

"Well, some things never change, do they?" Celest laughed. The families headed for their carriages.

Thierry called to Will, "Why don't you ride with us, Will? I can describe the place to you."

"Already did that," Luc said.

Thierry frowned at his brother. "And a lot you know, Mr. I-want-to-be-an-actor-don't-bother-me-with-farming."

Luc dodged the imaginary rock. "All right, all right. I see your point."

Thierry laughed. "Good. And don't interfere the next time big brother tries to provide time alone with your best girl." He looked pointedly at Nora.

Will walked off with Thierry.

Luc turned to Celest. "We'll walk, Mother. If that's all right."

Celest nodded and followed Serge and his family to their carriage. The family drove away, creating something of a parade as they made their way around the future town square and up Cedar Street.

"I like your family," Nora said. "The wives invited me to a quilting here at the church on Tuesday morning. We're supposed to invite Karyn to come."

"I don't know if I like that idea," Luc said as they walked along. "Those women can tell far too many stories about my wayward youth . . . you might get the wrong impression."

Nora was not ready to let go of Luc's arm when they reached Mrs. Delhomme's. But she disengaged herself anyway and helped carry heaping bowls of food from the kitchen, out the back door, and to the yard. A huge grape arbor ran the entire length of the west side of Celest's house, and beneath it the men had erected makeshift tables with sawhorses and planks. Every kind of chair imaginable had been hauled from the house, and the Delhomme children had brought chairs with them in the backs of their wagons.

Sophie and Cay Miller, Dr. Allbright and Reverend Underwood had also been invited.

From where she sat, Nora looked about her. The table was at least twenty feet long, lined on both sides with members of one family who loved one another. What it must be like to be part of such a family. She ducked her head, trying to hide the tears that welled up in her eyes.

"What is it?" Luc said softly, reaching over to squeeze her hand.

Nora shook her head. "Nothing," she murmured. She swallowed hard, finally leaning toward him to whisper, "I just never saw a family like this before, that's all. It's—" She stopped herself just in time, blushing with embarrassment, grateful that Reverend Underwood had stood up to say grace.

Nora had heard recited blessings before, but she had never heard anyone talk to God the way Reverend Underwood did. He said what was on his heart and mind, sounding absolutely certain that the Almighty Himself was paying attention.

"Heavenly Father, thank You for every one around this table. Thank You for the love You have given them for one another. Thank You for the gift of healing represented in Dr. Allbright, for the talents and skills you have given the Delhomme family in raising crops and children, for their willingness to help those less fortunate. Thank You for providing for our material needs through the Millers. Thank You for bringing Luc home, and for his talents in making us laugh—something we all need to do more of. Thank You for Miss O'Dell and her brother, Will. We pray that You would guide them in the decisions that await them in the coming week. May they be decisions that will bring them closer to You. I pray that for us all, dear Lord. That whatever happens in the week ahead may be perfectly designed to make us more like Your dear Son, our Savior, Jesus Christ. And now, heavenly Father, we thank You for this food so lovingly prepared. And that the Delhommes have been so unselfish as to include me in their precious family time. In the name of our Lord Jesus. Amen."

Reverend Underwood sat down and chaos erupted. Remy, Serge, Thierry, and Luc seemed to have regressed several years in age. Bowls of food were passed around the table several times. Nora had never seen so much food consumed. The boys were still at it long after their children had begged and received permission to run to the town square to play. Dr. Allbright and the Millers left after the second pot of coffee. Still, the Delhomme boys ate. Finally sated, Remy tossed a biscuit at Luc. The threat of a food fight was abated only by Celest Delhomme's stern admonition.

The women cleared the table and did the dishes in shifts while the men sat beneath the grape arbor talking of crops and cattle, houses and dreams. In the late afternoon, an impromptu baseball game was organized. The women spread blankets and quilts where it was hoped a courthouse would one day stand. Children played and skinned knees, were comforted and sent on their way.

As the sun set, the Delhomme men collected their families into their carriages and rolled out of town. Will sat on the steps of Miller's Emporium, deep in conversation with Cay Miller. Luc walked Nora home to Dr. Allbright's, hoping for a glass of lemonade and a kiss. Both were willingly offered.

CHAPTER 24

Faith and Peace

If any of you lack wisdom, let him ask of God,
that giveth to all men liberally,
and upbraideth not; and it shall be given him.
James 1:5

Nora, Will, and Luc rode out of Millersburg at dawn on Monday morning. Luc's mother had loaned Nora a split skirt and boots. The three headed north and east across open prairie toward what Luc called "French Table." They rode for about two hours along a barely discernible ridge, then down into a valley, across a creek, and up a steep incline.

Once her horse had climbed the hill, Nora could see a house in the distance. As they approached it, Luc said, "Everyone thought Papa was crazy when he said he was going to build a castle made of sod, but he did it." The house was two stories high, with curved turrets at the corners and a peaked wood shingle roof. They rode into the yard and were greeted by Thierry's wife, Jennie.

"Come in. Are you hungry? The girls are helping our cook make bread."

Luc and Will departed with Thierry to look at outbuildings and discuss Will's future.

"Is that where Will would stay?" Nora pointed to a long, low building a few yards from the barn.

Jennie nodded. "Yes. Thierry and Serge built the bunkhouse

not long after Mother Delhomme moved into Millersburg." Jennie shook her head. "I thought she would just curl up and die when Papa Emile died. They were so devoted to one another. But she surprised us all. She's made a whole new life for herself in Millersburg." A black puppy frolicked up, jumping on Nora's skirt, wriggling and demanding attention.

"If Mother Delhomme could see the way I let her misbehave, she would be horrified. This is one of a long line of Newfoundlands. Mother's dog was named Frona. She was the best-behaved dog you've ever seen." She laughed easily. "This one, on the other hand is incorrigible!" She bent down to rumple the puppy's fur. The puppy rolled on the earth, all four paws dangling in the air, begging for a belly rub. Jennie obliged her and then led Nora inside where a slightly built older man was overseeing the making of bread. "This is Lee, our cook," Jennie said. "He works miracles out of this kitchen. Feeds us and the bunkhouse roustabouts." Jennie introduced Nora and directed her two daughters to take lemonade outside for the men.

"We'll take some coffee into the parlor, Lee. And do you have anything sweet?"

Lee whisked a basket down off a shelf. "Cornbread muffins left from breakfast," he said. "I can put some jelly on the tray. Sound good?"

Nora followed Jennie into the sumptuous parlor. It was carpeted and furnished with elaborately carved pieces that brought Goldie's to mind. In place of a piano, the Delhommes had an organ.

Seeing Nora eye the organ, Jennie asked, "Do you play?"

Nora shook her head. "No. I like music, though."

"That's Luc's. If he ever stays in one place long enough to have it moved." Jennie laughed easily. "Tell me about yourself. You learned millinery in Lincoln?"

Nora nodded.

"So your family is in Lincoln?"

"No. Our mama died when I was born, and Pap doesn't want much to do with us. There's only Will and me."

"I'm sorry," Jennie said, quickly changing the subject. "Do you like Millersburg?"

Nora nodded. "I like being in a smaller town than Lincoln but not so little as where I grew up. Thanks to people like you, Will and I feel very welcome."

Luc stuck his head in the door. "We're riding to take a look at the place. Want to come?"

Nora looked doubtfully at Jennie, but she encouraged her. "Please, go ahead. In fact, I'll join you. Just let me run upstairs and change."

Nora went outside where Thierry and Will were waiting with the horses. When Jennie came down, the party headed out. They looked over a vast herd of cattle grazing one section of Delhomme land. They stopped at Serge and Remi's, and met the foreman for each of the sections. Finally, Luc said, "Well, if you've seen enough, Will, I promised Mother and Nora we'd ride to the Ritters' before the day was out."

Will nodded. "You go on. I'm going to ride back into Millersburg and collect my things. No reason not to get moved right in and get to work." He looked at Thierry. "That is, if it's all right with you, Mr. Delhomme."

Thierry nodded. "Glad you've decided to stay on. When you get back, check in with Jack at the house just south of the bunkhouse. He'll get you introduced around and get you a horse out of the herd."

Thierry added, "If he suggests a long-legged bay with a white blaze, turn him down flat out. That horse's name is 'Killer,' and the boys use him as sort of an initiation to the place. Save yourself the aching posterior and take the buckskin mare or the piebald gelding. They're ugly, but they're reliable."

"Thanks." Will rode up next to Nora and laid a hand over hers. "Well, baby sis. See you at church on Sunday."

Nora looked at him, surprised.

Will laughed. "Don't act so surprised. I want a whole new life." He grinned. "I've got Ida Johnson waiting for me to make good. Figure she'll be real impressed if I tell her I go to church regular. And it never hurts to try to impress the parents, either." He turned and rode off toward Millersburg.

Halfway to the Ritters', Luc suggested they walk for a while.

"Thank you," Nora said, climbing down off her horse. "It's been a long time. I'm going to feel this tomorrow."

"I suppose you'll be back at Miller's before long."

Nora nodded. "Mrs. Miller has been very kind about letting me take this time away so soon. I don't want to take advantage of her."

"Are you glad you moved here?"

"Absolutely," Nora said. "The best thing I could have done."

"I don't mean to pressure you or anything," Luc began.

"Something tells me you're about to pressure me."

"I've had a letter from Daniel Froman. It got mixed up in someone else's mail. They brought it over to Mother's last night. It was waiting when I got back from talking to you." He took a deep breath. "I know that name doesn't mean anything to you, but it's quite something that he's after me. At any rate, he's brought over a married couple from England named Kendal. They're long-established favorites in domestic melodrama. Mr. Froman wants to know if I'd join the touring company."

He waited for Nora to react. When she didn't, he said, "They need me in Denver three weeks from today." Still, Nora said nothing. "They could also use a costume mistress. Daniel heard about Thornhill Dressers from Mamie Patterson. He asked if I knew anyone who might be lured away from Lincoln. I don't. But then I thought perhaps there might be someone who could be lured away from Custer County."

Nora said, "I signed a contract with Mrs. Miller that promised I would never give less than six weeks' notice if I decided to leave. And I'm just getting settled—"

"There, Mikal—just a little farther. I think they were there by that big rock."

Luc and Nora had just topped a rise that overlooked the Ritters' homestead. Down below them, Mikal was creeping along the banks of the pond while Karyn directed him. "There were at least six eggs."

Mikal bent over the water, brushing aside some long reeds growing at the edge of the pond. The moment he bent over, Karyn rushed up behind him and pushed him into the pond. He stood up, sputtering and laughing, slinging water everywhere as he shook his head. "Karyn Ritter, you're going to pay for this!" he roared.

Karyn screeched and started to run up the hill, but Mikal caught her and dragged her, kicking and screaming, back to the pond. He swept her up in his arms, stomped into the pond, and dumped her. They laughed and splashed about like two children for a few moments, and then it grew very quiet as suddenly, Mikal reached for Karyn, pulled her into his arms, and kissed her passionately.

Nora put her hand on Luc's shoulder. "*Say* something so they know we're here. This is already embarrassing enough."

Luc shouted, "Hey, you! Mister! Stop trying to drown that woman or you'll have to answer to the Delhommes!"

Nora saw Karyn's hand go up to her mouth. She hastily reached up to brush her hair back out of her face and began to climb out of the water, but Mikal pulled her back. He kissed her again, then put his arm around her, and together they dragged themselves out of the pond and up the hill. By the time they reached Nora and Luc, they were laughing again.

Mikal clapped Luc on the back and then hugged him. "What a welcome we give you, eh?" He smiled down at Nora. "I ask your forgiveness for such behavior, but even yet I sometimes forget I should be acting more like an old married man." He chucked Karyn under the chin. "She had me out looking for duck's eggs." He turned toward Karyn. "Now tell me, *schatz,* are there really duck eggs?"

"Of course," Karyn said. "Mollie and May have them safely nestled beneath one of our hens."

Mikal grinned and shrugged. Then he said, "You must excuse me to get some dry clothes." He nodded at Luc. "Please put your horses in the corral. Make yourselves as if you were at home." He looked once again at Karyn. "I think you deserve to shiver in the cold after the trick you played on me." He made for the house. Karyn excused herself and followed him.

Luc and Nora walked down the ridge toward the corral, where Luc opened the corral gate and led their horses in. He looked around approvingly. "This corral used to have a sod wall." He nodded at all the trees around the homestead. "Karyn dug every single one of those out of the creek bed and planted them." He shook his head. "And that was before there was a windmill up at the house to pump the water for her to water them with. She had to pump it one bucket at a time, one bucket per tree, every day, for weeks and weeks and weeks."

He unsaddled the horses, and perching the saddles and blankets on the corral fence, then took the bridles off and hung one on each saddle horn. The horses trotted around the corral, snorting and tossing their heads.

Luc put one hand on the top board and jumped the fence. Leaning against it, he looked up toward the house. "Those trees by the porch were just this tall—" He held his hands about a foot apart. "None of the outbuildings were here, except for this dugout behind us." He nodded over his shoulder. "Mikal lived there for two years before he married Karyn."

Nora looked over her shoulder and back around her. "He must be a very determined man."

Luc nodded. "It takes a special breed to succeed here. But, it won't be long before the soddy will be gone. They'll have a new house, and by the time the girls are grown, the hard times will be behind them."

Karyn and Mikal came back down the hill. Karyn was holding the baby in her arms, but Mollie and May ran ahead, calling to Nora. She crouched down, and the girls threw their arms around her neck and hugged her.

Luc admired Freddie, and they all walked up the hill to the little house where a table had been set outside the front door. Karyn put Freddie back to bed and promised supper soon. She put her hand on Nora's shoulder and shoved her into a chair. "You sit. The girls can help me. We want it to be special."

Mollie and May followed their mother into the house. While Mikal and Luc reminisced, Nora watched them, thinking she had never seen two such different men enjoy such a close bond. Mikal was a lumbering giant compared to Luc's trim, athletic physique. Mikal's mane of black hair was slightly unkempt. He reminded Nora of a barely tamed bear she had seen once at a circus in Lincoln. Luc was blond and fair although he had begun to tan since he was home. Watching the two, Nora decided she much preferred Luc to Mikal. She stood up and went to the door of the house. "Are you certain I can't help?"

"I'm certain," Karyn said firmly.

Nora sat back down at the table just as Mollie and May brought dishes out. Both kept a wary eye on Luc as they set the table. Supper was served and the table cleared before Mollie finally said, "Are you the one that got knocked out by the hail?"

Luc nodded. "That's me."

"Can I see the scar? Mama says she helped sew your head back together."

Luc laughed. He leaned down and made a part in the back of his head. "Can you see it?"

Mollie pointed to Luc's head. "Look, May. It's a big scar. Mama had to sew a lot."

"Girls, what are you doing?" Karyn had gone inside to make a fresh pot of coffee and came back outside just in time to see her daughters examining the back of Luc's head. "Where are your manners?"

"We wanted to see where the hail split his head open," Mollie said.

Karyn shook her head. She looked apologetically at Luc. "I'm sorry. Our little adventures make good bedtime stories. But sometimes I exaggerate a little."

Luc laughed. "Don't apologize. It's nice to know I have the leading role in one of their favorite bedtime stories."

Karyn asked, "Do you stay home now, Luc?"

He shook his head. "No. I have to be in Denver three weeks from today."

Karyn looked from Mikal to Luc, to Nora and back to Luc again. She set the coffeepot down. "Well, gentlemen," she said abruptly. "I want to ask Nora some advice about a new hat. So, if you will excuse us."

Nora got up and followed Karyn into the house.

The women were barely through the doorway when Karyn said, "I see what is between the two of you. What is he saying about Denver?"

She turned to Mollie and May. "Girls, I want you to get ready for bed now and to listen for your brother. If he wakes, bring him to me out back. Otherwise, you may play quietly. If you want to do tomorrow's sewing stint now, you will have tomorrow free." The girls scrambled for their sewing boxes. Karyn led Nora through the lean-to and out back, where two crudely made benches provided seating in the shade.

"Someone famous wants Luc to join his company."

"And he is going?" Karyn asked.

Nora looked down at the log bench and pulled at a piece of loose bark. "He said they need a costume mistress. He said—" She blushed and looked up the ridge. "Well, he started to say something, but then we came over the top of the ridge and you were getting dunked in the pond."

Karyn blushed. "The girls were napping. All three were napping at once. Truly a miracle. Time alone with my Mikal." She sighed.

"Did you know right away that you loved Mikal?" Nora asked abruptly.

Karyn laughed quietly. "I knew right away . . . but then it took me a few weeks to admit it to myself . . . and a few more before I admitted it to Mikal." She told Nora what Luc had already said about being selected from the group of women at the church, about the shock of living in a house made of dirt . . . and then she began to talk about Mikal. Her face shone with love.

"How is it that after seven years and three children, you still have this—this—feeling between you?"

Karyn shrugged. "Oh, the feeling comes and goes," she said.

"But you're so happy."

"Yes," Karyn said. "Mostly, we are happy. Except for the times when we are not."

Nora asked earnestly. "What is it that gets you through the times when you are not? What makes the feeling come back? Do you ever fear that you'll lose the love? Lose the will to keep trying?"

"Come with me," Karyn said quietly. She held out her hand, leading Nora up the ridge to the two little graves. The two sat down in the tall grass, and Karyn said, "When this happened, I feared losing the love. For a while, I didn't have the will to keep trying." Her voice trembled with emotion. "But Mikal tried for me. He wouldn't let me give up. Every night, I would cry, and every night, he would cover my cheeks with his kisses, and then he would hold me and tell me that if we never had another child, he would be content. He reminded me of all that God had done for us, of the love of the Lord Jesus, of all the blessing that we had together. He read the Psalms to me while I cried. He did these things over, and over, and over again. Until one night I didn't cry anymore."

Karyn was quiet for a while, looking at the two little graves. "Now I can look back and see that God used those little boys to grow my love for Mikal. Our marriage is stronger because of them. And my love for God is deeper. After we have walked with God through the valley, we learn truly that He is the Good Shepherd."

"Where did you get your faith in God?"

"Where?" Karyn looked at Nora in such a way that she knew that no one had ever asked such a question of her. She thought for a moment. "Somewhere in the Scriptures it says that God gives us the faith that we need."

Nora said, "I wish He'd give me some faith."

Karyn put her hand on Nora's shoulder. "Dear Nora, has no one ever told you that you only ask and He gives? If you are longing so to know God, then He is calling you just as the shepherd calls to his sheep."

"I don't know if it's God I want or not," Nora said honestly. She thought for a moment before saying to Karyn, "But I do know I want to be loved the way Mikal loves you."

Karyn looked soberly at Nora. "I think already you are loved very much by a good man. But better than that, even, is God's love for you. Remember your Sunday school lessons?"

Nora shook her head. "My pap didn't let us go to church. Most of what I know about God comes from talking to people like you. I've read the Bible a little, but I never got past that book where they were numbering the children of Israel."

"Well then, let me tell you the best story of all." Karyn told the story of Jesus Christ's birth, His death, and His resurrection, as if she were talking to Mollie and May. By the time Karyn explained that Christ would be coming again, Nora interrupted her. "I want to believe that's all true. I really do. But I can't." She shook her head.

"Of course you can't," Karyn said. " 'For by grace are ye saved through faith; and that not of yourselves: it is the gift of God.' Do you see, Nora? Even the faith is a gift of our loving God."

"Elise Thornhill once said I could talk to God, just like He was a real person."

"Anyone can," Karyn said softly.

"Okay. I will. I'll ask Him to give me the faith I need." Nora was quiet for a moment. "I hope He answers real fast," she said. "Luc has to be in Denver in three weeks."

Karyn laughed and stood up. "Come along, my friend. The men are probably wanting a second piece of pie, and already you will be riding back to Millersburg in the dark."

CHAPTER 25

The Last Letter

Make haste, O God, to deliver me;
make haste to help me, O LORD.
Psalm 70:1

Nora and Luc rode away from the Ritters at sunset. It was Nora's favorite time of day, those few moments when the sun casts an eerie light over the entire landscape. Nora had not yet become accustomed to the vast sky, the seemingly endless prairie that was Custer County. Even as the sky darkened, and dots of light shown around them marking the location of at least a dozen homesteads, the feeling of aloneness did not diminish.

The evening star appeared low on the horizon, twinkling brightly against a sky that was orange-gold, changing to several shades of violet, then dark blue. A full moon glowed warm orange on the horizon before rising to cast a bluish light over the landscape.

Karyn had promised to drive into Millersburg for the quilting. Nora felt strangely content. What Karyn had said about asking God made sense. In fact, she had done it, right there by the little graves. She had asked God to help her. Looking up at the stars as she rode along, she felt a presence . . . almost as if, this time, there would be answers. With Luc riding along beside her, she felt that perhaps she was on the brink of true happiness, after all. If only she could dissuade Luc from leaving.

Luc was strangely quiet as they rode along. Nora had hoped that he would resume the talk of Denver, but he did not. Nora cleared her throat. "In your letters—the ones I didn't read right away—you talked a lot about God. I remember you saying something about returning to things you knew when you were a child. What did you mean by that?"

"My mother and father were devout Christians. By that I mean they really did try to live as Jesus would want. Believe it or not, around here, 'Christians' like you met at Goldies are usually outnumbered by the real ones like my parents. We read the Bible together at home, and we were expected to abide by what it taught—at least on the outside. My parents knew they couldn't change my heart. Only God can do that. They taught us what we needed to know and left the rest in God's hands.

"When I left home, I got away from their teaching. You already know about all of that. As I said in one of my letters, when I met you I was ashamed of what I had to offer. I knew I had to break things off with Mamie, but even when I did that, I still felt terrible. I didn't want to look back on my life and have it be year after year after year of the same kind of thing. I knew all the right answers about how to find God, but I had to make a personal decision—for me. That day I walked up into the mountains, it all came together." He chuckled. "Who would have thought a little thing like a grasshopper could make such a difference in a man's life?"

"Don't you worry about what could happen if you go back to the theater?"

"Of course. I know my weaknesses. But I'm serious about my relationship with God. I know He's forgiven all the things I've done, and I'm going to do my best to live my life in a way that pleases Him."

He went on, "There are many different kinds of theatrical troupes, Nora. Mr. and Mrs. Kendal from England are well-known for their strong family. They travel with their children. They don't participate in anything questionable. Regular hours, no gambling, no drinking, no shared dressing rooms. It's very nearly puritanical from what I've heard. We'll be doing entirely different material. There won't be any 'Patterson kissing' going on, and I'm going to steer clear of single women—present company excluded, of course."

He thought for a moment. "I think my talent is a gift from God, and I can do a lot of good with the money I make. Which, by the way, is quite a lot. I want to continue supporting Iris's school in Denver. And Mother has given me some other ideas about good causes I could get involved in."

"How often does a traveling troupe get to go home?" Nora saw Luc look up at the night sky, thinking.

"That depends. Probably twice a year."

"Twice a year for how long?"

"A month, a week. It depends on how completely the troupe is booked." He added, "Families that travel together create a kind of home wherever they are. The Kendals have a cottage in the mountains somewhere. They always try to spend a month there in the summer. I think they even get back to London once in a while. But there's no denying that it's a different life from what most expect."

"How can you be certain God wants you to do it? I mean, how does a person know when God is talking to them?"

Luc shook his head. "It's not always easy. Asking advice of people who are more mature in the faith than you, reading the Bible, that sort of thing. I've talked hours and hours with Mother. She's very wise in so many ways."

"Does the Bible talk about being in the theater?"

Luc chuckled. "No. I don't think so. I think I'm into a decision where it could be right for me to go and right for me to stay."

"How can both be right?"

"I think it's right for me to go now. But if I were married, once I started a family, I would want to come back home. Teach music. Help with home talent productions at the opera house. Live happily ever after."

They rode into Millersburg, dismounting in front of Dr. Allbright's house, and tying the horses to a fence post. Luc opened the gate, and they walked up the path to the porch.

"Thank you for including me today," Nora said. "My head is

so filled with things to think about, I probably won't sleep for days."

Luc pulled her close. "Tell me something, Nora. Could you see yourself in 'happily ever after' with me?" He was looking down at her with such intensity that Nora felt her face growing hot despite the cool night air.

She looked away from him. "It's so different from what I've planned for my life."

Luc released her. "Not the man of your dreams, is that what you're trying to say?" He stepped away from her, walking back down the pathway and to the gate before saying "good night" over his shoulder.

"Luc, wait," she called softly. "You're not—I didn't mean." She shook her head. "Luc, come back. I love you." He didn't turn around right away. "Did you hear what I said? I love you. But it's such a long way from being a milliner in Nebraska to all those stages in all those big cities. I don't like big cities, Luc. I don't like crowds . . ." Luc was still standing at the gate. She moved toward him, reaching out to touch his sleeve. Then, she put her hand on his arm.

Luc turned around. "Oh, Nora," he whispered intensely, "can't you see—don't you know—" There was a kiss, and then he pushed her away. "I have to get out of here," he said. He was breathing heavily. Quickly, he mounted his horse and gathered up the reins to the horse Nora had ridden. "I've made promises to God, Nora. I hope you can understand, but I have to get out of here." He moved the horse into a trot.

Nora stood trembling at the gate until his form was lost in the darkness, her hand lifted to her lips.

Dearest Nora,

Another letter. Perhaps the last. I will not be back to see you today. I hope you understand. I told you there would be no more flirting, no more candlelit dinners . . . I'm done with those things, Nora, because I've found you. I don't want flirting and stolen kisses in the dark. I want you—all of you. I don't want to escort you to church, and to friends' homes, and to church picnics, and then say good night. I want to live, breathe, eat, love, and die with you. But I want it honorably and before God so that He can bless it. That means marriage.

There is a one-way train ticket in this letter. It will take you to Denver. There is also money to pay for a cab to the Larrimer Square Theatre, where our company will be for the next three weeks. I know that you said that you promised Mrs. Miller that you wouldn't leave without giving her six weeks advance notice. Perhaps she would change that if she knew it would make an old friend very happy.

Marry me, Nora. I know I don't offer the life you planned, but I offer you my entire heart and soul. Mikal told me that you told Karyn that you want to be loved the way Mikal loves her. Well, I'm not Mikal, but I dare to say that the love I feel for you right now is far more than Mikal Ritter felt the day he married Karyn. Greyson Chandler is dead . . . but Luc Delhomme adores you.

I will pray every day for the next three weeks that God gives me the chance to make you happy. After that, I'll begin to pray for the grace to get over you . . . and that, my precious Nora, will take a good deal longer than three weeks. Please come. Let me love you.

Luc

Nora could not face the Delhomme women at quilting on Tuesday. She went to work instead, grateful that Mrs. Miller didn't ask questions. She kept Luc's letter in her reticule, withdrawing it to read every couple of hours. Even after she had memorized it, she still took it out, running her finger along the lines of ink.

Nora worked until it was nearly dark before finally allowing Mrs. Miller to shoo her out the front door. She walked with her head down, distracted, thinking. *Why can't I just throw it all to the winds and follow him?*

When a familiar voice called her name, Nora looked up, startled to see that she was right in front of Mrs. Delhomme's house. Celest stood on the porch. "You look tired, dear. Why don't you come up on the porch and join us for a glass of lemonade?"

Nora dreaded a confrontation, but something drew her to Luc's mother. "Thank you," she said, opening the gate and dragging herself up the path to Mrs. Delhomme's inviting porch. In the corner, sitting in a rocker, was the wizened old woman who stayed with Mrs. Delhomme.

Mrs. Kruger's face was deeply lined with wrinkles. She wore a cap over her nearly bald head and sat with her hands clasped before her. Nora had never seen such hands. Not one finger was straight. The tip of one index finger was twisted so badly it stood at nearly a right angle to the rest of the finger. Where knuckles should have been, Mrs. Kruger had bumps, some so large it looked like marbles had been inserted beneath her skin. She was sitting with a ball of yarn cupped in one hand, making minuscule movements with the hand.

Although she was crippled with arthritis, Amalia's mind and hearing were keen. When she heard Celest call to Nora, she rose up in her chair with a grunt and watched as Nora walked up the pathway to the porch. Nora's foot had just reached the top step when Amalia Kruger said in a thick German accent, "Come close. Let me see the girl who broke Luc's heart."

Nora obeyed, blushing as she moved across the porch to where Amalia sat.

"Why don't you sit there by Amalia, Nora. I'll be right back with some lemonade."

Nora looked after Celest with dismay. Finally, she said politely, "You're the woman who is so famous for her wonderful biscuits. Mrs. Delhomme showed me how to make your recipe."

"*Humph*," Amalia grunted. She held up both hands. "Not much biscuit making anymore." She eyed Nora closely.

Nora stirred nervously. Did everyone in Millersburg know about her and Luc? She thought back to earlier in the day, when two women had come into Miller's. They had stood across the store from Nora's workstation, whispering. Nora had thought that once they both turned and looked at her, but she scolded herself for being so paranoid. *The entire population of Millers-*

burg does not care about what happens between you and Luc Delhomme. Sitting beneath Amalia Kruger's critical gaze, Nora began to wonder.

Celest came back out on the porch with three tall glasses of lemonade. She held Amalia's glass for her while the old woman drank, smacking her lips with satisfaction as she tasted the sweet liquid. Celest seemed to know when Amalia had had enough. She set the glass down and sat down across from Nora.

She took a sip of lemonade before saying, "We missed you at quilting today." She sighed. "I wish there were some way I could help you to feel better. Being young is so difficult sometimes."

"I thought," Nora began, then hesitated. "I thought you would hate me."

"Hate you? Why on earth would you think that?"

Barely holding back her tears, Nora said, "I don't mean to hurt Luc. I love him. I just," she spoke so quietly that Celest had to turn her head sideways and strain to hear. "I'm just so frightened by the thought of leaving this—to go there—when I—I—" She shook her head and was silent. She finally let the tears go and sat, holding the lemonade in her lap, crying quietly.

Celest reached over and took the lemonade from Nora's hands. She set the glass on the tray, sat down next to Nora, and pulled the girl into her arms. "Everything will work out. I told Luc the same thing. You just need time. And, he needs to be patient. You can't live the way Luc has lived and then expect a girl to follow you to the ends of the earth just because you say you've changed."

"I don't doubt he's changed," Nora said. She sat back up in the porch swing and dabbed at her nose with a handkerchief. "It's me." She looked at Mrs. Delhomme. "I think I used up all my courage just leaving home and getting things started here in Millersburg." She took a deep breath. "I wish I knew what to do."

Celest smiled and shook her head. "If you truly love my son as you say you do, you can't be happy here. Security is no substitute for love."

Nora sighed. She looked up at the roof of the porch, then

bent her head, and reached back to rub her neck. "He could have stayed here. He could teach music. We could have a normal life."

Celest reached out to take one of Nora's hands. "The kind of love that builds walls around people eventually stifles everything . . . even itself. You have to be willing to help Luc do what his heart tells him. The more you push him toward that, the more love will flow back to you."

The only sounds for a few moments were the creaking of Amalia's rocker and the soft swish of Nora's and Celest's skirts brushing the floor of the porch as they moved back and forth in the porch swing. Finally, Nora leaned forward to put her elbows on her knees and her chin on her clasped hands. "He just left, and already I miss him. It's like—" She laughed sadly. "This sounds stupid, but it's like the sun isn't shining quite so brightly anymore. I must have thought of him a thousand times today." She nodded toward the fence where Luc had planted a row of rosebushes for his mother. She shook her head. "He sent me yellow roses once."

Amalia stopped rocking. She grunted with the effort of reaching forward to pat Nora with one of her crippled hands. "I followed a man once to where I did not want to be," she said, "and into years of unhappiness. I decided that love was not enough to make a couple happy." She paused. "I was wrong. My unhappiness was because I did not know God's love. I knew only passion. But love from God never fails. It is always enough. Once you know God's love, you can do anything. Go anywhere. His love goes before you, follows you, surrounds you." Amalia reached up to stroke Nora's cheek with a crooked finger. "Such a lovely young girl and so sad. Don't let it be this way, little one. You must have courage. You must fight for what you want."

Amalia grunted and began to get up. Celest helped pull her to her feet. The old woman grimaced in pain as she put one foot in front of the other. She bade Nora good night by saying, "Remember what I have said. You must fight for what you want. And in your case, I think that means you get on a train."

When the door closed behind Amalia, Nora stood up to go. "Thank you. For everything."

"Come back any time, Nora."

"If you hear from Luc would you tell him—" She shook her head. "Never mind." She made her way down the path and through the front gate. Closing it carefully, she waved good night to Mrs. Delhomme.

CHAPTER 26

L. A. C. D.

Bless the LORD, O my soul:
and all that is within me,
bless His holy name . . .
who forgiveth all thine iniquities . . .
who redeemeth thy life from destruction;
who crowneth thee with lovingkindness and
tender mercies . . . so that thy youth
is renewed like the eagle's.
Psalm 103:1, 3–5

When Will sent word that he could not come to town on Sunday, Nora went to church alone. Somehow it seemed right to go. It was something Luc would want her to do. She came in late and sat in the back. Perhaps, she thought, Reverend Underwood would say something profound that would answer all her questions at once and give her the courage to follow Luc.

In the end, God used a hymn. There was a new song leader, a young man who moved energetically and had the congregation stand to sing. He directed them to page 195 in the hymnal. Nora didn't know any hymns. Perhaps that was why she followed along so closely.

How firm a foundation, ye saints of the Lord,
Is laid for your faith in His excellent Word!
What more can He say than to you He hath said,
To you who for refuge to Jesus have fled?

237

Nora mouthed the words, afraid she would get the notes wrong. She liked the strong tempo, the straightforward kind of marching through each line. The woman next to her sang loudly and off-key. It didn't matter. As they progressed through each verse, it seemed that every word they sang applied personally to her.

Nora barely heard what Reverend Underwood said that morning. Instead of listening to his sermon, she sat with the hymnal in her lap, reading the verses over and over again. What more can He say . . . Her answers were waiting . . . if she fled to Jesus.

> *Fear not, I am with thee; O be not dismayed,*
> *For I am thy God, and will still give thee aid;*
> *I'll strengthen thee, help thee, and cause thee to stand,*
> *Upheld by My righteous, omnipotent hand.*

She did not have to be afraid of taking the train to Denver . . . of the big city . . . of traveling with a theatrical troupe. God said He would be with her. He would be her God and give her aid. He would strengthen and uphold her. Nora remembered Karyn Ritter sharing how God had upheld her in the early days of her marriage, in the times when the feelings dimmed.

> *When through the deep waters I call thee to go,*
> *The rivers of woe shall not thee overflow;*
> *For I will be with thee thy troubles to bless,*
> *And sanctify to thee thy deepest distress.*

Sorrow had overflowed Pap's life, because Pap didn't have God. He tried to go it alone. Karyn Ritter had almost drowned in sorrow, but she looked to God, and He helped her see the blessing.

> *E'en down to old age all My people shall prove*
> *My sove'reign, eternal, unchangeable love;*
> *And when silver hair shall their temples adorn,*
> *Like lambs they shall still in My bosom be borne.*

Nora thought of Celest Delhomme and her crown of silver hair. She was a living example of God taking care of His lambs, even when they grew old. Nora wasn't sure she knew what sovereign meant, exactly. But she knew she longed for eternal, unchanging love. Even if Luc couldn't give her that, God could.

> *The soul that on Jesus still leans for repose,*
> *I will not, I will not desert to His foes;*
> *That soul, though all hell should endeavor to shake,*
> *I'll never, no, never, no, never forsake.*

When the new song leader rose to lead the closing hymn, something compelled him to say, "I can think of no better closing hymn today, than the one we have already sung. Please, allow my unorthodox request. Let us stand and sing together once more, 'How Firm a Foundation.' "

Nora sang this time, her face shining with joy. The words to the hymn rang in her heart, because at last, they were the testimony of her own, personal faith. No one could promise her eternal love but God, but if she and Luc both shared God's love, they had a chance for something wonderful. Something better than she had ever dreamed. Something just like the Ritters'.

As Nora left church that morning, she felt reborn. Some things hadn't changed. The thought of the unknown still terrified her. But the conviction that God was already there, in the unknown, gave her hope.

As Nora walked home from church, she hummed to herself . . . "He'll strengthen and help me, and cause me to stand, upheld by His righteous, omnipotent hand."

Thunderous applause and flower-strewn stages had never been so meaningless. Luc Delhomme's pasted-on smile disappeared the instant he stepped back from the floodlights. The curtain came down. The players congratulated one another. Mr. and Mrs. Kendal patted Luc on the back.

"Are you feeling all right, Luc?" Mrs. Kendal asked.

Luc mumbled an excuse and headed down the crowded hallway for his dressing room.

She had not come. He had promised her everything—commitment, faithfulness, and love. It was a crushing blow to realize that all he had to offer wasn't enough. Where had he gone wrong? What else could he have done? Maybe he would give up the theater. Maybe he would go home.

He stopped and leaned against the wall, reaching up to fumble with the buttons on his shirt. Why did it always have to be so blasted hot and stuffy backstage? He wiped his forehead across the back of his sleeve. Mr. and Mrs. Kendal walked by.

Mr. Kendal held out an envelope. "Someone asked us to give this to you."

Luc opened the envelope. Inside was a large mother-of-pearl button. He laid it in the palm of his open hand, running his finger over the letters engraved on its face. L, A, C, D. He remembered. Saying the letters in French sounded just like the sentence "Elle a cédé." His mother had given the button to Nora, explaining that it was a romantic play on words . . . L, A, C, D . . . *She gives up.*

Ned Gallagher tapped him on the shoulder. "Hey, Luc, there's someone here to see you."

Suddenly, there was no crowd backstage. There was only one person, standing at the end of the hall, just outside his dressing room. She was wearing a green bombazine dress, and just as he looked at her, she opened an elegant lace parasol.

Luc closed his eyes for a moment. But when he opened them, she was still there, her eyes shining, her lips parted in a little nervous smile. He walked toward her, and the closer he got, the more she smiled. When he put his arms around her waist, she said, "Where's my button? I want it back."

"Be quiet and come here," he said, pulling her into his arms.

From where he stood at the opposite end of the backstage hall, Ned Gallagher saw the parasol dip. He opened the door behind him. "Uh, Mr. Froman, I think you can stop the search for a new costume mistress. Luc Delhomme has one all tied up."

Epilogue

1998

"And that's it," Noah said, "I certainly would have preferred the coward's way out, but I knew it wasn't right. I had to go back and talk to Angela face-to-face. I hadn't really cared for her in a long, long time, but after she put up with my nonsense for nearly two years, she deserved a good-bye in person. That's where I was when Aunt Rini had her stroke." He sat back and studied Reagan for a moment before concluding, "And I guess I wouldn't blame you if you ordered me to take you home right now."

Earlier in the evening, Noah had accompanied Reagan to a children's Christmas program. Then, the two had driven downtown, where thousands of white lights outlined the historic buildings of the Haymarket district of Lincoln. Parking Noah's pickup, they had walked the district talking quietly about nothing. It was not until they were seated at a small table in a coffeehouse that Reagan asked Noah about Angela. As far as Reagan could tell, he answered her honestly, without trying to paint himself in a sympathetic light.

"What did she say when you shared the faith with her?" Reagan asked quietly.

Noah grimaced. "It made her mad. She said that if I was ever going anywhere but church to give her a call—and she'd set me up with someone she hated." He took a gulp of coffee.

"I'm sorry." Reagan said.

Noah shook his head. "Don't be. I deserved that and worse. I can imagine how she felt. She gives me two years of her life, and then I 'get religion,' dump her and move back to Nebraska." He leaned on one elbow and rubbed the back of his neck. "Anything else you want to know?"

Reagan shook her head.

"Where do we go from here?"

"Home." Reagan said as she stood up. "It's getting late."

"Would you come to dinner with Aunt Rini and me after church tomorrow?" He tossed a five-dollar bill on the table and they left the coffeehouse. Reagan still hadn't answered Noah's question when he gently took her hand. She didn't pull away, and when they arrived at the truck, Noah kissed her softly before unlocking the door. When he drove into Reagan's driveway, she quickly opened the door and jumped to the ground.

"You didn't answer me about dinner tomorrow," Noah said as they walked to the door together.

She fumbled nervously with her keys before answering "yes." She had already opened the door when Noah cupped her chin in his hand and turned her face toward him. He searched her eyes, saying softly, "What are you thinking?"

Reagan pulled away, pushing her front door open and starting to go inside. At the last minute, she turned around, still keeping one hand on the door as she said, "I'm thinking things are happening too fast."

"And I'm thinking I can't wait to see you again," Noah said, smiling down at her.

Over Sunday dinner at a local cafeteria, Noah launched into a lengthy explanation of his plans for the homestead. "Did you know that Nebraska has one of the premier wildlife-viewing events in the world? The cranes draw thousands of people to the area each year. Surely there are some bird-watchers among them who would enjoy an authentic homesteading experience. Once I

242

get the soddy rebuilt and furnished, I could give people a choice of 1880s soddy or 1930s farmhouse."

"But Noah," Irene protested, "you can't just walk out on the prairie and build a soddy. How would you begin? I mean," she laughed softly, "it's not like one of the neighbors can just drive over and show you how."

"There are books that show how it was done. Just because it hasn't been done in a few decades doesn't mean it's impossible. It will only take about an acre of Opa's prairie. I think he would approve." Noah smiled. "No one has complained so far about my fixing things up, but what I really want to do is buy the homestead so I don't have to worry about convincing the entire family about everything."

"You mean you are worried about your father," Irene said.

Noah nodded. "He is not going to be very excited about this idea." He took a sip of coffee. "And I can't say that I blame him. I haven't exactly modeled consistency and dependability over the years. But Aunt Rini," he leaned forward. "This is what I want to do." He laughed and shook his head, "I think I finally know what I want to be when I grow up."

Irene smiled, "I'll help you all I can, dear. But the kind of things you are talking about take a great deal of money. Where are you going to get the funds? Even if the bed and breakfast idea is a success, the cranes come and go in just a few weeks. What would you do for the rest of your income?"

Noah grinned, "It's the age of computers, Aunt Rini. I've checked around, and I think I could get a respectable consulting business going. I have to learn some of the ag software, but that shouldn't take long. My employer is willing to try a long distance arrangement for a while."

He continued, "The town board is considering my proposal about restoring the old opera house. If it really works out, there is talk of some kind of festival built around the history of theater in rural America. It has the potential of bringing much-needed cash into the area. There aren't many of the original opera houses still standing, you know. We can't just let all our history fall into ruins."

Irene finally said, "I'll help you all I can, Noah, but it makes me tired just thinking of all you have to do!"

Noah winked at Reagan, "And that doesn't even take into account researching Nora O'Dell."

"You don't have to bother with that," Reagan protested.

"Of course I do," Noah said, "It is the perfect subterfuge for courting you."

"Courting?" Irene said, "Did I hear the word 'courting?' "

Reagan felt herself blushing. "Stop it you two. You are ganging up on me, and I won't have it." She slid out of her chair and went to the dessert bar in the cafeteria.

Noah followed her. "All right, I'll back off. But only if you promise that you'll answer my letters and come for a visit in the spring—with Aunt Irene as a chaperone, of course. In the meantime, I'll learn what I can about Miss O'Dell from the museum in the town."

He slid a piece of chocolate cake onto Reagan's tray before selecting gooseberry and rhubarb pie for himself and Irene. The three filled the rest of their dinner together with talk of Noah's bed-and-breakfast soddy.

Reagan's computer said the words, "you've got mail" at least twice a day throughout the winter of 1998–1999.

Have you considered the irony of getting e-mail from a computer geek dressed in a flannel shirt who's involved with restoring a turn-of-the century farmhouse and plans to build a soddy in the spring?

Have you considered moving to Custer County?

1892—There's a Nora Delhomme in the census. Could it be her?

Ask Aunt Irene if she remembers anything about a marriage between Oma's friend and a Delhomme.

I know you dreaded the thought of reading all the old newspapers, but I think the only way you are going to learn much is if you take the time to peruse the Millersburg Republican.

You won't believe this. I found a sign from Miller's Emporium in the back room at the county museum. You'll have to see it when you come out. You are coming out?

The opera house is a mess inside. Some of the guys from the lodge are getting interested in the project. One is a carpenter. He's going to inspect the sills and check for termites.

Tell Aunt Irene I'm having the Ritter babies' tombstone cleaned and reset.

Even my truck couldn't get through the snowdrifts today. I had to turn back before I got to the end of the drive, then ended up getting stuck and had to shovel for nearly an hour before I could get back up to the house. The snow is beautiful, though. Imagining Karyn and Mikal Ritter driving a sleigh down the drive to church. Glad I don't have to break ice and water livestock.

The census shows Sophie and Cay Miller as having three children by 1892.

I drove out to the cemetery and found the Delhommes' graves today. I'll take you there when you come.

Reagan answered every message. She began to spend every Saturday afternoon at the State Historical Society, reading the *Millersburg Republican.* For several weeks, she found nothing. Then, amazingly, there was an announcement that Miss Nora O'Dell had opened a millinery business inside Miller's Emporium. Two Saturdays later, Reagan came across the description of a wedding between "the newly arrived Miss O'Dell and favorite son, Luc Delhomme, who has long graced the stage as the well-known dramatic actor, Greyson Chandler. The couple will tour with the Daniel Froman Company and hope to receive guests in the home of Mrs. Celest Delhomme over the Christmas holiday."

Reagan wound the microfilm furiously, looking ahead to the December issues of the *Republican*. Finally, she located the mention of the reception given in honor of Mr. and Mrs. Luc Delhomme. The list of guests included Mr. and Mrs. Cay Miller and Mr. and Mrs. Mikal Ritter.

She made copies of the articles and raced home to e-mail Noah. A message was waiting that said, *The dry-wall is finished. I'm ready to paint. Could you take Aunt Rini to the paint store and ask her to try to remember what color the rooms were? Send me samples.*

After calling Irene, Reagan replied, *Bringing paint with us last weekend in March. Will stay and help if you want us. Have amazing news of the button keeper.*

"And so," Reagan concluded, "Miss O'Dell and Mr. Delhomme lived happily ever after. They were back in Millersburg by 1892, and I found records that indicated they had five children." She was sitting on the sofa in the Ritter's farmhouse living room, enjoying coffee and cookies with Noah and Irene. She and Irene had driven up late that afternoon. Cans of paint, rollers, brushes, and drop cloths were piled in one corner of the room, awaiting the next day, when the three would begin painting the house.

"The frustrating thing is," Reagan said. "There doesn't seem to be any end to all of this. Now I want to follow the bunny trails to the children. And I wonder about Greyson Chandler's acting career."

Irene spoke up. "It would be fun to see if the Daniel Froman troupe ever played in Lincoln. The Historical Society might have playbills."

"Or," Noah offered, "there are always old newspapers."

Reagan groaned. "Please. No more newspapers on microfilm.

At least for a while. I'm going to need glasses if I spend many more hours squinting at scratched microfilm."

"Did you find their marriage license?" Noah wanted to know. Reagan shook her head. "Not yet."

"Well," he said, standing up and stretching, "let's go into the museum tomorrow and see what we find. We don't have to take the entire day . . . but we can at least check." He looked down at Reagan. "In the meantime would you care to join me on a walk?"

Reagan looked at Irene who shooed her toward Noah. "Go along, you two. I'll wash the coffee cups, and then I'm heading to bed."

Reagan followed Noah out the front door. They made their way around the back of the house and up the ridge, past the little burial ground to where they could see the prairie rolling away from them in every direction.

"I try to imagine what it was like when Opa came," said Noah. "No trees, no tilled fields, just miles and miles of nothing for as far as he could see. And where the nothing ended the sky began." He shook his head. "I don't know if I could have done it."

Reagan smiled. "I have a friend who says that if it had been up to her to settle the west, we'd all still be in Boston drinking tea." She paused and nodded toward the horizon. "Looking at that I'm inclined to agree. I don't think I could have done it either."

She looked behind her at the two little graves. "What women they were," she said. "Nora and Karyn, and all the others like them." She shook her head. "Everyone has such romantic notions about the good old days. A lot of the old days were pretty terrible."

They walked the homestead together. When the moon finally rose over the landscape, they were sitting on the front stoop of the house.

"Thank you for all the help with my research," Reagan said quietly. "I'm going to write it up and give it to the Society when Irene donates the charm string." She added, "I still wish I knew what each button meant to Nora. I wish she could come back just long enough to tell me the stories."

Noah nodded. "I know what you mean. I've wished Opa could be here to tell me if I'm doing things right around this place."

"You're doing just fine," Reagan said. "You're doing it with your heart. It's going to be beautiful when you finish."

Noah said softly, "Beautiful maybe, but still empty." He hesitated, "Do you think you could ever see yourself living up here in the wilds of Custer County?" He reached down to turn her face toward his. "I'm thirty years old, Reagan. I don't want to be alone for the rest of my life. If this is going nowhere . . ."

Reagan reached up to take his hand. She turned it over and kissed the palm. "It's going—somewhere—I think."

Noah pulled her into his arms and kissed her. "I'm falling in love with you, Reagan."

She laughed softly.

"Is that funny?"

She nestled her head on his shoulder. "No, I was just thinking though, here we are sitting on the front porch of your great-grandparents' house, two people who courted after they got married. I guess courting via e-mail isn't so strange after all."

They sat together in the moonlight, looking down the gravel road toward town.

Too late . . . God . . . dear God . . . I'm too late.

Flinging herself down from her horse, Mary shoved and pushed her way through the unheeding crowd. From somewhere up ahead she could hear the death song. The men's voices floated across the crowd as Mary clawed at the back of a man who blocked her way. "Please . . . let me pass . . . let me pass."

The man turned around half angrily, but at the sight of the diminutive girl, he smiled. "Want to get a better view miss? Here . . ." He grabbed her by the shoulders and propelled her forward into the teaming crowd of onlookers. She was lost in a sea of sweating bodies and dust, and for a moment, she thought she might faint. Still, she pressed forward, feeling as though she were caught in a dream where every moment took unbelievable effort, every whispered word had to be shouted.

Before she managed to claw her way to the front of the crowd, the order was given, and Mary's screamed protest was drowned out by the strange sound that went up from the crowd. Not a cheer, really . . . but a collective sigh of satisfaction followed by mutterings from the men around her.

No one really noticed Mary. No one saw her face go white as she collapsed in a heap. Someone helped her up. She pulled away and stumbled to the edge of a boardwalk and sat down. It was a long time before she could bear to look up. When she finally did, they were cutting the bodies down. The faces were hidden by sacks that had covered the heads of each one of thirty-five condemned men. Some of the bodies had already been put into a wagon. There was no way to know which one hid his face.

Suddenly, despair melded into an iron determination to find his body. She had failed to save him, but she would at least see that he was buried properly. The need for immediate action smothered the savage wound of grief that gnawed at her midsection. Someone had said that there would probably be a mass

249

grave. Some local physicians had already offered to pay for the right to claim a body for research.

I can't let that happen. I can't. I won't plead. I'll demand. They can think what they want. At least I can see that he is buried . . . that he can safely be put to rest.

But would they listen to her? Already there were rumors that she had been far too friendly with the Dakota during her captivity. For the first time since she and the children had been handed over at Camp Release, Mary realized that she didn't really care what anyone thought. They could think or say whatever they wanted. She would find his body and see that he had a proper burial in some secret location where no one would ever disturb him. It was the least she could do.

About the Author

STEPHANIE GRACE WHITSON lives in southeast Nebraska with her husband of more than twenty-five years, four children, and a very spoiled German shepherd. The Whitsons are active in their local Bible-teaching church. Stephanie is the author of the best-selling Prairie Winds Series, *Walks the Fire, Soaring Eagle,* and *Red Bird,* as well as the Keepsake Legacies series, *Sarah's Patchwork,* and *Karyn's Memory Box.*

Stephanie can be reached at the following address:

Stephanie Grace Whitson
3800 Old Cheney Road #101–178
Lincoln, NE 68516